PROOF

OTHER TITLES BY
C.E. TOBISMAN

Doubt

A CAROLINE AUDEN LEGAL THRILLER

PROOF

C.E. TOBISMAN

Text copyright © 2017 by Cynthia E. Tobisman
All rights reserved.

Published by Thomas & Mercer, Seattle

www.apub.com

Amazon, the Amazon logo, and Thomas & Mercer are trademarks of Amazon.com, Inc., or its affiliates.

ISBN-13: 9781503942028
ISBN-10: 1503942023

Cover design by David Drummond

Printed in the United States of America

For Dad, who proved the generation-skipping transfer tax is interesting.
Sort of.

CHAPTER 1

On some days, Caroline disliked being a lawyer. Today was one of them.

She eyed the front of The Pastures Assisted Living.

The low-slung building had a wide, circular driveway. Good for ambulances. Good for hearses. A cheerful array of topiary hedges shaped like chickens bordered the entryway.

Caroline had visited the home many times, but this would be her last. As the only lawyer in the family, she had the unhappy errand of closing her grandmother's affairs. It wasn't the task she loathed. It was the finality it symbolized.

Taking a deep breath, she stepped through the sliding glass doors.

Morning light streamed through the windows, casting bright squares on the newly laid laminate floors. As always, Nancy Feinstein sat in a wheelchair beside the social lounge, her sharp eyes surveying all the comings and goings of her confined world.

"Oh, honey, let me give you a hug," she said when she saw Caroline. "I'm so devastated about your grandmother. Kate and I were watching movies together just last week. She seemed fine, other than the IV. And the walker. And whatnot."

"She looked okay to me, too," agreed Caroline. The fact that her most recent visit had been over a month ago hung between them, but thankfully Nancy said nothing about it.

"Can I help you with that sock?" Caroline crouched in front of the wheelchair.

"Thank you, honey, but you don't need to do that. The caregivers here are all so solicitous. They're pushy, if you ask me." The elderly woman's eyes narrowed. "I don't trust them."

Caroline smiled as she pulled up the offending sock. Nancy always saw a conspiracy.

Caroline didn't admit it aloud, but she did, too, lately. Where once she'd given strangers the benefit of the doubt—innocent until proven guilty—she now began from a firm presumption of guilt. It wasn't healthy or fair, but she couldn't stop. In the year since she'd left her first job out of law school, she hadn't stopped wrestling with the betrayals that had forced her departure.

"I'm sure the staff is just trying to be friendly," Caroline said, feeling like a hypocrite for trying to talk Nancy out of her paranoia.

"Is that Miss Caroline I hear?" came a man's deep voice from down the hall.

The owner of the voice soon followed. Harold DuBois, the administrator of the nursing home. He held out one arm for a businesslike hug.

"I'm sorry for your loss. Come on down to my office. We'll get you all sorted out."

• • •

While Caroline waited in a guest chair, Harold leaned over his file cabinet. His fingers strolled slowly through the alphabetized names.

"If you're looking for my grandmother's will, I have it here." Caroline pulled a thick ream of papers from her bag. The will had been prepared by an estate planner shortly after Grandma Kate had moved into The Pastures. Anticipating the need for the hard-copy original, Caroline had brought it along with her.

But Harold shook his head. "Our policy requires us to retain copies of our residents' wills and health care directives if signed after they join us. We have to use our own copies."

"Do you have it digitized?" Caroline asked.

Harold chuckled. "I know you love all of that tech stuff, but we're in the Dark Ages here. Don't you worry—this won't take more than another few minutes."

Caroline exhaled. She didn't have "another few minutes." In less than an hour, she was supposed to be at her grandmother's funeral. There, she'd see her mother and uncle for the first time in three months. Her unstable mother and her alcoholic uncle.

Upon further reflection, Caroline decided perhaps being late wouldn't be so bad.

Finally, Harold pulled a folder from the file cabinet.

He held it aloft, victorious, before spreading it open on his desk.

"Our residents assign their assets to The Pastures to pay for their care," he began. "If there's anything left over when they die, they can bequeath it to whomever they wish."

"I understand," said Caroline. "My grandma has about $97,000 in the bank. Other than that, the only thing of value is a watch. It's an heirloom. It's covered in paragraph 25(d) of her will—Personal Effects."

Harold lifted a single sheet of paper from the file on his desk.

"I don't see any paragraph 25(d) here," he said, squinting at the page.

Caroline's brow wrinkled as she compared the large document on her lap to the small one in Harold's hand.

"That's her will?"

"It is," Harold confirmed. "It's handwritten," he added, although Caroline could see that for herself. Blue ink bled in dots through the thin paper.

"When did she write it?"

Harold squinted again at the document. "Five weeks ago."

"My grandma never said anything about wanting to redo her will," Caroline said halfway to herself. "What does it say?"

"Let's see here . . . it looks like your grandma has left her estate to Oasis Care," Harold said.

"What?" Caroline asked. She wasn't sure she'd heard right.

Harold offered the page to Caroline so she could read it for herself.

Caroline quickly scanned the page. The writing was shaky, but the loops and dips were distinct. Kate had definitely written it. There were no signatures by any witnesses, but that didn't matter. So long as a will was written in the maker's handwriting, it was enforceable.

Law school had been full of stories of handwritten—or holographic—wills. A farmer who'd been trapped under his tractor had scratched his will into the fender: "In case I die in this mess, I leave all to the wife." A court had probated the fender, giving it the full effect of the law.

Now, Caroline's gaze settled on the most unexpected part of the document.

"What's Oasis Care?"

"They're a charity," answered Harold. "Some of our residents make gifts to them—and other charities, too."

The explanation did not calm Caroline's concerns. Her grandmother had suffered from progressive dementia. Even if Oasis was a perfectly lovely charity, her grandmother had never mentioned it before.

"Can you tell me how my grandma came to change her mind about her will in the last month of her life?" Caroline asked.

"I don't know." Harold shrugged apologetically. "We discourage our residents from writing their own wills, but there's nothing we can do to stop them."

Caroline tried to consider her grandmother's bequest dispassionately. Throughout her life, Grandma Kate had supported charitable causes—sometimes with volunteer time, sometimes with money. Although it seemed strange that Kate would become enamored with Oasis to the exclusion of her own heirs, it wasn't impossible.

"Okay, so she left her money to a charity," Caroline said, trying to accept the words as she spoke them, since she had no way to prove they weren't true. "But I still need to make sure I'm getting the watch." In a family of few things, the heirloom was special. Her grandmother might've left her bank account to charity. But not the watch. Never the watch.

"I'm sorry, but your grandmother didn't make any separate gifts of personal property," Harold said. "That means everything goes to Oasis."

Heat rose to Caroline's face.

"Perhaps she made a mistake," Harold offered weakly.

Caroline prized restraint. It was an attribute she appreciated after growing up with a mother who sometimes had none. And so she knew her emotions showed only in the tightening of her mouth, the quick flash of pain in her eyes. Subtle things, really. But things that Harold, who was skilled and schooled at helping people with grief, evidently perceived.

"This watch, it matters an awful lot to you, doesn't it, Miss Caroline?" he asked.

"It does," Caroline croaked. Letting go of the money was difficult. Letting go of the watch was impossible.

A thoughtful expression crossed Harold's face. He tapped his lips with an index finger. "As I am sitting here, it occurs to me that I have not yet seen an inventory of your grandmother's room. If you'd like to go see her things one last time, I've got some work I need to do."

He raised his eyebrows meaningfully.

Caroline rose from her chair and hurried to the door.

"Thank you," she said, casting a grateful look at the administrator. "Thank you so much."

"No problem," said Harold, turning his attention to other matters of pressing importance.

• • •

When Caroline arrived at her grandmother's room, she found a certified nursing assistant folding a quilt. The woman's red hair was plaited in a long braid. Around her neck, she wore a leather-corded necklace with a peace symbol that dangled to just above the V collar of her pink scrubs. Even in the typical attire for a CNA, the woman looked like a New Age hippie.

She stopped midmotion, the quilt hanging from her arms.

"I'm Kate Hitchings's granddaughter," Caroline introduced herself.

"Granddaughter?" The woman's eyebrows rose. "I didn't know Kate had any family."

"She did." Caroline looked down, the embers of guilt flaring again in her chest. "I used to come every week, but I started my own law firm a year ago. My cases have been keeping me super busy lately." She wasn't sure why she felt compelled to explain her absence to this stranger. Perhaps because her grandmother wasn't around to explain it to.

"I'm Patricia." The woman extended a hand.

As she shook it, Caroline noted the tattoo circling Patricia's wrist. A string of characters in some other language. Maybe Sanskrit.

"That's my mantra," Patricia said. "The heart of the lotus is within."

"That's nice," Caroline said absently as she examined the room for places where her grandmother might have stashed the watch.

"I was just organizing Kate's stuff," Patricia said. "Harold wants me to put together an inventory." She gestured with her chin toward a tablet sitting atop the bedside table.

"Thanks so much for doing that," Caroline said, trying to keep her tone neutral. Hopefully Patricia would just assume she was inventorying

Kate's belongings for Kate's family. "I'm looking for a watch my grandma wanted me to have. I was going to bring it to the funeral."

"A watch?" Patricia echoed. "I don't remember Kate wearing a watch."

"She never wore it. It's a man's watch, actually," Caroline said. "You'd know it if you saw it. It has a big, square face and a green glass crystal."

"I haven't seen anything like that," Patricia said, turning back to folding the quilt. "But feel free to look around."

Caroline sat down on the bed and opened the drawer of the bedside table.

Inside, she found an assortment of objects. A deck of cards. A zippered pouch fashioned from bright-green Guatemalan fabric. Some holiday cards. But no watch.

She opened the pouch and withdrew a pile of pictures.

The first showed Kate, crouching beside an Irish setter.

"Was that her dog?" Patricia's voice came from behind Caroline.

Caroline nodded. "His name was Winston. He was a great dog. Big as a moose."

"I have a dog, too," Patricia said. "A little one."

Caroline flipped to the next image. A brown-haired boy in long plaid shorts stood with his arm around a skinny boy with large black eyes and sallow skin.

"Who's that?" Patricia asked.

"My uncle Hitch," Caroline said, tapping the boy in plaid shorts. "And this was Nazim." She tilted her head toward the sallow-skinned boy beside Uncle Hitch. "He was my uncle's best friend . . . until he died," she finished softly.

"What happened?" Patricia asked.

"Congenital heart defect. My uncle was devastated, as you can imagine. The whole story's really sad. Nazim fled the Algerian War with his grandfather. They barely got out. Poor kid survived that, only to die a few years later."

Patricia nodded, her green eyes filled with sympathy.

"Actually, the watch I'm looking for came from Nazim's grandfather," Caroline said. "My grandma took in Rayan Hafaz after his grandson died. She gave him a place to live. She took care of him. The watch was his prized possession. He left it to my grandparents when he passed away."

"I could tell your grandma was special," Patricia said, her voice solemn. "In fact, I was thinking just the other day that it kind of makes sense she'd pass away on September 11. I mean, it's already sort of a messed-up day, so of course a lady as nice as your grandmother would leave us on it, right?"

Caroline smiled sadly at the caregiver's sentimental logic.

"I've got to go," Caroline said, rising to her feet. "Can't be late for the funeral."

She tucked the pouch of pictures into her bag.

Then she reached out to close the drawer of the bedside table.

But then she noticed something: a receipt. Yellow and crumpled, the small piece of paper was lodged in the corner of the drawer.

She tugged it loose and read: REGAL WATCH REPAIR.

The write-up showed that a Mrs. Katherine Hitchings had dropped off an "antique watch" for "annual cleaning and servicing" two months earlier.

Caroline's heart began to pound.

The watch wasn't gone. It was at a repair shop, just waiting to be claimed.

The hours of operation at the bottom of the receipt showed the shop was open all day.

That meant she could pay a visit after the funeral.

As she folded the receipt to put it in her bag, Caroline noted Patricia's eyes on it.

But before the caregiver could ask any questions, Caroline hurried out the door.

• • •

The scent of freshly dug earth hung heavy around the gravesite.

The elderly attendees stood in respectful silence. Hands clasped. Heads bowed. Quietly contemplating their own mortality, the ephemeral nature of existence, or what would be served for lunch later at the nursing home.

A rainbow of scrubs-clad helpers shadowed them like a United Nations of underpaid guardian angels. All stood, awaiting the moment when they would climb back into the van bearing the italicized logo of The Pastures Assisted Living, Chatsworth. The only exceptions were a middle-aged man and woman standing twenty feet away, across the grave from Caroline.

Even with her eyes trained safely on the grass, Caroline could tell things were as worrisome as ever with her relatives. Her uncle had tried to clean up for his mother's funeral. His rumpled shirt smelled recently laundered. His hair didn't spring from the sides of his head like weeds. Yet despite his efforts, Uncle Hitch still looked like the homeless man he was.

Next to him, Caroline's mother toyed incessantly with her bracelet, her fingers jerky as they skittered through the links. Mania. Caroline knew the signs. Her mom had taken her meds with enough regularity to move to Portland with her boyfriend, but Caroline knew the cycle. Joanne would cut back on her mood stabilizers and the sine wave of her psyche would become steeper, its peaks and valleys curving into the Danger Zone. And then the rages would come.

None of it was her problem, Caroline reminded herself. She was an adult, with all the trappings of independence that connoted. Bank account. Profession. Apartment. None was large, but all provided separation from her relatives. Caroline knew their illnesses weren't their fault, but the effects were unavoidable: she didn't depend on family.

Except for Grandma Kate, Caroline amended. In a family full of doctor-stumping psychopathologies, Kate had been as reliable as the rising sun.

Caroline forced herself to look again at her mother and uncle. Kindling some spark of connection with them would be a fitting tribute to the great woman who had passed on.

And so, when the priest concluded the service, Caroline gathered her resolve.

"Beautiful service," she said, approaching her relatives.

"Sure was, kiddo," agreed Hitch. His gravelly voice was thick with emotion.

"The whole thing's still so unreal. So strange. I didn't know Mom was so sick," Joanne said, her words coming too fast. Her eyes held both a question and a subtle accusation.

Caroline didn't answer. The fact that she had a court hearing scheduled for the morning after her grandmother's funeral proved how uneven her work-life balance had become.

"Did you get everything settled?" Joanne asked, her fingers still picking at her bracelet.

"I tried," Caroline said, trying to avoid looking at her mother's hands. "But it turns out Grandma left everything to some charity called Oasis."

The news elicited twin exhales of disbelief.

"Did Grandma ever mention anything about Oasis to you?" Caroline asked.

Joanne and Hitch shook their heads in unison, but Caroline knew it didn't mean much. Her mother lived out of town, and her uncle had probably visited The Pastures infrequently in the ten months since he'd started living on the street. That he wouldn't accept Caroline's offers of a phone or a place to stay meant she had no idea when he'd last seen his mother.

"I've never heard of Oasis, either," Caroline said, crossing her arms.

"I didn't say I hadn't heard of them," corrected Hitch, "just that Mom never mentioned them to me. But I've seen them around. They're not so great," he added.

"Well, they're supposed to get everything," Caroline said.

"Even the watch?" Hitch asked. His gaze held a focused urgency that pushed through the grime and bad luck, bright and concerned in a way that Caroline hadn't seen in years.

"They're supposed to, but it's gone missing." Caroline glanced toward the van, where scrubs-clad helpers were escorting elderly people to their seats. "I think I know where it is—a repair shop. I'm going to pick it up."

"You won't give it to Oasis, right?" asked Hitch.

"Of course not," said Caroline. "I'll take care of it."

"Good," said Joanne, letting her fingers drop from her bracelet. "I know that's what Mom would've wanted."

Caroline exhaled. None of them had seen Kate in the last month of her life. They'd all failed her. The changed will was the proof of it. Caroline didn't believe there was any malice in her grandma's decision to leave her estate to charity, but she'd never know for sure. Even so, she knew in her bones that her grandmother hadn't intended to give the watch away.

"I need to get going," said Joanne. "Bob and I have a cruise planned. I've got to get home to pack, then up to Washington to board the boat on Wednesday."

She leaned forward to hug her daughter.

Caroline clung to the familiar touch, finding it welcome despite the hyper energy flowing through it like an electrical current.

Then it was over, and she watched her mother retreat to the parking lot, her high heels click-clicking down the asphalt, a Doppler effect receding into the distance.

When Caroline turned back to her uncle, she found him chewing on his lower lip.

He probably needed a drink, she realized. She'd watched his decline over the last year with alarm. What had once been an extra beer after work had become drinking before noon, losing his job and, later, his home. And still he hadn't stopped.

"I'll see you tomorrow at the soup kitchen," Caroline said. With the guilt of having missed her grandmother's decline still fresh, she could not ignore her uncle's peril any longer.

But Hitch's eyes narrowed.

"Don't you go bringing me any of those pamphlets," he said.

"I just—"

"You need to stop trying to fix things that aren't your damn business."

Caroline winced at the familiar rebuff.

"Can't you at least let me give you a phone?" she asked.

Hitch waved away the suggestion. "You know where to find me."

Caroline knew the spot. It was grim. Sidewalks banked with trash. Threadbare people with matted hair and insanity in their eyes. Anything could happen there. A fight. A seizure. An overdose. The potential for horror hung thick and real over the place. She had no plans to visit.

She resigned herself to the soup kitchen. That would be her tribute to her grandmother. And her attempt at absolution.

"Do you need a ride somewhere?" Caroline asked.

Hitch shook his head. Then he started the dance he always performed when they parted company. Caroline didn't want to hug him, barely washed and smelling of the streets, and he apparently didn't want to force her to. So they stood awkwardly across from each other.

Finally, Caroline held up a hand.

Hitch returned the gesture.

And then he was gone, leaving Caroline standing alone at her grandmother's grave, castigating herself for seeking some sort of meaningful spark of connection with her family.

It didn't matter, she told herself. She needed to go to the watch repair shop. Then she needed to get back to work. One year of solo practice had impressed on her the link between finishing her work and getting paid. Especially since the Southern California business climate lately seemed to take its cues from the endless Western drought.

· · ·

"I do not have this watch," the repairman said in the accent of some Eastern European country. He handed the receipt back to Caroline.

"Are you sure?" Caroline pressed. "Can you check again?"

"I am sure." He nodded with his chin toward an empty corner of the display case. "All watches for picking up are kept there. It is not here."

"Then I guess it's gone," Caroline said, her hopes of finding the watch dissipating.

"Gone?" The repairman frowned. "I am hoping not. This watch is handmade masterpiece by Karl Geitz of Hessischen Watchmaking School. Last time I am seeing Mrs. Hitchings, I am telling her that she could buy a castle if she is wanting to sell it." He stretched out his arms to show how big a castle he meant. "But she is not interested in selling. Only in servicing."

"Lot of good that did," Caroline murmured. "Do you happen to remember when my grandmother picked it up?" Perhaps if she knew when Kate had retrieved the watch, she could figure out where it was. Maybe there was a safe-deposit box somewhere.

"No, no," the repairman waved a hand. "Your grandmother is not the one picking it up. That nice helper lady—she is the one picking it up four weeks ago."

Caroline's brow furrowed.

"The helper lady is telling me Mrs. Hitchings is too sick to come," he continued.

"And you just gave it to this . . . helper lady?" Caroline asked.

"Yes, I recognize her. She is the same helper who is with Mrs. Hitchings when she is dropping it off. She is wearing those clothes like the people in the hospitals." The repairman gestured around his body to show he meant some kind of uniform.

"You mean she wore scrubs?"

"Yes. Pink ones. Also, a very long braid." The repairman put the flat of his hand down near his waist to show how far the braid fell.

A prickle of recognition skittered across the surface of Caroline's skin.

"You know this lady?" the repairman asked.

"I sure do," Caroline replied darkly.

CHAPTER 2

Caroline's feet burned a trail into the concrete as she paced outside the shop. The repairman watched through the window with a worried scowl. He hadn't believed her when she told him that she had no intention of suing him. But she didn't care what he believed. All that mattered was the voice on the other end of the phone she now held to her ear.

"I'm awful sorry to hear all of that, Miss Caroline," Harold said. "But I had no idea that Patricia was doing errands for your grandmother."

"This wasn't an errand. This was theft," Caroline said, her veins pulsing with heat. Patricia Amos had lied to her. Embarrassment mixed with Caroline's fury as she recalled how she'd shared her memories with Patricia. They'd had a moment together.

"Is she there now?" Caroline asked.

Harold paused before answering.

"Patricia quit. She gave notice right after her shift ended. She said she had a family emergency and had to leave town."

Caroline stopped pacing.

Patricia was gone.

"Miss Caroline? You there?" asked Harold.

"I'm here." Caroline pressed her eyelids together tightly to squeeze off tears. The watch should've been with her grandmother's stuff. With the repairman. Somewhere. The one place it shouldn't have been was in the hands of a thief.

"I don't know what happened," Harold said. "Patricia was one of our best CNAs. I'm going to make a police report right away. I'll also post something on a chat board I belong to. Maybe someone else has a lead about Patricia."

At the earnest tones in the administrator's voice, Caroline's anger ebbed, mellowing into a dull ache that lodged itself just behind her breastbone.

Patricia had done more than steal a watch. She'd deprived Caroline of a vital connection. Kate had been one of the few people on the planet who understood the obsessive tendencies and tuning-fork sensitivities that plagued Caroline. She'd tried to fix in her granddaughter what she couldn't fix in her own children. Instead of pressuring the already-intense child to succeed, she'd counseled her to relax. Instead of feeding her compulsions, she'd urged her to find balance.

And now Kate was gone.

And the watch was gone.

And there wasn't a damn thing Caroline could do about any of it.

"Please let me know what you find out," Caroline said before hanging up.

She leaned back against the wall, took a breath, and let it out slowly.

The watch was just an object. A thing. There were far more important matters in life. Like the fact that her uncle lived on the street. Or that her fledgling law firm was struggling. Or that many of her cases involved indigent clients facing life-shattering events. Wrongful eviction. Denial of benefits. Deportation. All were cases with real stakes.

With a jolt, Caroline realized that between the funeral and the watch, she hadn't even started to prepare for the guardianship hearing she was supposed to attend tomorrow morning.

Hurrying toward her car, Caroline reminded herself that guardianships were usually straightforward. Show up at court. Stipulate to a suitable relative to take care of her minor client. Then sit down. It didn't take much thought.

But it did require performing some due diligence. She needed to focus on the task ahead: vetting the man who wanted to take custody of her seven-year-old client. And that meant she needed to push the business of the watch from her mind.

• • •

"You calling me a liar?" The petitioner's eyes scorched Caroline's cheek like a klieg light from across the courtroom.

"Please address your comments to the bench, Mr. Gonzalez," Judge Flores instructed.

In her periphery, Caroline watched Rogelio Gonzalez turn his attention back to the judge.

Her open-and-shut guardianship hearing had turned into a battle. An unexpected one.

"But what she's saying about me isn't true," Gonzalez protested.

"I have not called Mr. Gonzalez a liar," Caroline said. "I have simply asked the court to verify the truth of some of the statements he has made in his guardianship petition." So she was calling him a liar, but politely. Courtroom etiquette permitted it, even encouraged it.

Judge Flores raised a hand to forestall another burst of outrage from Gonzalez.

"Ms. Auden, in every respect this appears to be a suitable placement. Petitioner has known Mateo Hidalgo since birth, having dated Mateo's aunt before her death eleven months ago of cancer. He maintains a household with his current girlfriend, Floriana Perez, and her two minor children. He has the financial means from his apparel business to provide for Mateo's needs until the boy's father is released from prison."

The judge held Caroline's eyes as if daring her to contradict his analysis.

"I've read the guardianship petition, too, Your Honor," said Caroline, "but I've recently discovered some information suggesting this placement might be ill advised."

She glanced down at the boy sitting beside her.

Mateo Hidalgo looked back with long-lashed brown eyes. Despite a father in jail for manslaughter drunk driving, the boy had retained his innocence. With his wide-eyed awe and his barrage of questions about the judge, the metal detector, the jury box, and every other small detail of the courthouse, Mateo enjoyed the curious openness of childhood.

But the man standing on the other side of the courtroom could be a threat to all of that.

"Permission to approach?" she asked Judge Flores.

The judge gave a curt nod.

Caroline came to stand below the judge's raised bench.

She felt Gonzalez's presence as an angry prickle at her shoulder. She was unaccustomed to facing off against someone who'd made the famously foolhardy choice to represent himself, but so far Gonzalez seemed wily enough to pull it off.

"I'll explain my concerns," Caroline said, "but I request that the court remove my client from the courtroom first."

The judge turned to Gonzalez. "Any objections?"

Gonzalez crossed his arms, forcing his shiny silver tie to do a little wheelie at the bottom.

"Fine with me. Just so long as you tell me where to go to find Mateo when it's time for me to take him home," Gonzalez said.

Ignoring the petitioner's presumptuousness, Judge Flores nodded to the bailiff, who approached Mateo.

The boy's eyes found Caroline's, asking their silent question.

"It's okay," Caroline said. "The bailiff's just going to take you to the Children's Room until we finish up. I remember seeing an Xbox in there."

She raised her eyebrows. She knew how Mateo felt about Xbox.

Satisfied, the seven-year-old allowed himself to be led from the courtroom.

Caroline took a calming breath as she returned to counsel's table. She knew Judge Flores had a reputation for impatience. But she also knew he cared about getting things right. She just had to convince him that Gonzalez's petition wasn't as simple as it seemed. And to do that, her argument needed sufficient heft and weight to propel the proceedings in a new direction.

"When I came to court today," she began, "I was ready to stipulate to awarding custody of Mateo Hidalgo to Rogelio Gonzalez, pending the release of Mateo's father from prison. But as I waited for the courtroom doors to open, Mateo told me something disturbing."

"What did your client say?" Judge Flores asked. His eyes moved across the courtroom. Dozens of litigants waited on uncomfortable wooden benches. All seeking justice before lunch.

"He told me something that makes me worry he's being used as a drug mule or lookout."

Gonzalez slammed his palms on the table in front of him and rose to his feet.

"That lady's crazy!" He stabbed a finger in Caroline's direction like a weapon.

Caroline flinched at the fury that rolled over her like a hot wave. She hoped the judge didn't see the flush of heat rising to her face. She also hoped the bailiff would return soon.

"Sit. Down." The judge held out a hand and firmly gestured downward.

"But—"

"You may believe you have the self-confidence to represent yourself in this matter, Mr. Gonzalez," said the judge, "but I'm beginning to doubt you have the self-control. You'll get your turn in a minute. Please, Ms. Auden, continue."

"I asked Mateo if he was looking forward to living with Mr. Gonzalez," Caroline said, keeping her voice even. "Like you, I'd read the petitioner's declaration. It describes the veritable cocoon of love and shelter available if Mateo goes to live with him. Baseball games on Sundays. Trips to the movies. It all sounded good . . . until Mateo answered my question."

"Okay, I'm listening." The judge propped his chin on his hand. "What did the boy say?"

"He said his temporary foster parents aren't nearly as much fun as his Tío Rogelio. 'Why?' I asked. I figured I knew the answer. Baseball games and movies. Right? But that's not what he said." Now that she had the judge's curiosity, Caroline paused to give her argument some room to breathe. "Mateo said his temporary foster parents aren't as much fun because they don't play spot-the-cop like his uncle does."

Caroline let suspicion blossom in the judge's mind, just as it had in hers.

She watched Judge Flores's eyebrows creep several centimeters toward each other.

"When I asked him what game that was," she continued, "he told me about sitting outside a warehouse, looking for police while his uncle 'met with some important friends.'"

"Who were these friends?" Judge Flores asked.

"I don't know," Caroline admitted, "but Mateo was instructed to let his uncle know right away if he saw any police or other 'suspicious cars.'"

A frown tugged at the corner of Judge Flores's mouth.

"Before court began, I did some quick research," Caroline continued. "I pulled up the police reports for the area where Mr. Gonzalez lives and works."

She turned the screen of her laptop to face the judge.

"Drug-related activity has spiked in this neighborhood in the last year. Someone's doing huge business. The *Times* speculates it could be the Eighteenth Street Vatos or some other gang. Someone's definitely bringing in some new product."

The judge waved away Caroline's offer to show him what she'd found on her laptop.

"I'll take your word on the police reports. But I would like to hear from Mr. Gonzalez." The judge exhaled sharply. "Stop looking at Ms. Auden, Mr. Gonzalez," he ordered.

"Whatever," Gonzalez said. "So she gets to talk smack about me?"

"As the minor's guardian ad litem representing Mateo at the court's request, Ms. Auden is just doing her job," the judge said.

"I'm not in a gang," Gonzalez said, his voice as taught as a tripwire. "No one in my family's in a gang. I'm a businessman. I have a clothing business. You know where my money comes from since I gave you my tax return with my petition."

"What's this about these friends at this warehouse?" Judge Flores asked.

"Business associates. Sometimes I conduct business at the warehouse where I keep the inventory for my store. That's not a crime."

"And this 'spot-the-cop' thing?"

"Just a little game I invented. Like I tell my girlfriend's kids all the time, you got to get used to looking for police. Cops always assume the worst about you if you're black or brown. We need to train our kids early to look out for them. Helps them stay out of trouble."

Judge Flores scowled at the specter of police profiling being raised in his courtroom.

"I'm not saying we know anything for certain yet," Caroline interjected. "I'm just saying we need to be careful with this placement. After all, Mateo's doing fine with his foster family—"

"He should be with his *real* family," Gonzalez shot back. "Not some random couple in Santa Clarita."

"Not to disparage Mr. Gonzalez's relationship to my client," Caroline said, "but it is a remote relationship, at best. He is Mateo's aunt's ex-boyfriend. We're not talking about immediate family here."

"Family means whatever family feels like, and Mateo's my family," Gonzalez said.

Though the words weren't directed at Caroline, they landed squarely. She had a semi-dysfunctional mother, an emotionally distant father, and an alcoholic uncle—that was her family. Her life had long ago ceased to include any family gatherings. There were no birthday parties. No weddings. It had taken her grandmother's death to bring them together.

"Look, I felt real bad when Mateo's aunt died," Gonzalez continued. "She was a really great girlfriend. My new girlfriend isn't nothing like as special as she was." He grinned toward the bench in what Caroline surmised was supposed to be a winning manner, but which only underscored the insult to his current girlfriend.

"My house is the best place for Mateo while his papa's in prison," Gonzalez continued. "Mateo's my *sobrino*. That's true no matter what this paranoid white lady says about me."

Gonzalez turned to glower again at Caroline.

This time, Caroline met his gaze. Some nagging instinct told her that he wasn't just giving Mateo lessons in avoiding the police.

"Let me remind you both to direct your attention to the bench," Judge Flores said, his exasperation verging on true annoyance.

Caroline arranged her features into an affable mask and turned back toward the bench. She'd made her point. Now it was time to sound more reasonable than Gonzalez, despite the desperate clawing of her instincts.

"Maybe I'm being paranoid, as Mr. Gonzalez suggests. If so, I will apologize. But we need to be sure before we move forward."

"But Mateo's current placement was always intended to be temporary, Ms. Auden," the judge said. "We need a more permanent solution."

"Mateo's father will be out of jail in six months," Caroline pressed. "The Castillos, Mateo's current guardians, have not objected to caring for him for another six months—"

"Perhaps not, but they didn't sign up for it, either," the judge pointed out. "We need to be realistic. The minor's father has had issues with alcohol. Yes, Mr. Hidalgo is in recovery during the period of his incarceration, but even if he achieves some measure of sobriety, the stress of his release may compel him to drink again. He may require time to get himself together. We need a longer-term placement in the interim."

Caroline resisted the urge to nod. Everything Judge Flores had said made sense, but it didn't matter.

"I understand the court's concerns," Caroline said. "But if Mateo is being used as part of an illegal enterprise, it could send him down a terrible path. If he gets picked up by law enforcement, he could end up in juvenile hall. If he doesn't get picked up, he could end up being initiated into a way of life that this court and his father certainly want him to avoid. Either way, it's a disaster—a disaster this court has the power to avert."

"I appreciate your passion, Ms. Auden, but a case is only as good as the evidence supporting it, and at this point, all you have is speculation based on the word of a child."

"I know," Caroline conceded. "That's why I request time to investigate my client's statements."

With just another few weeks to do her job, she knew she could incriminate or exonerate Gonzalez. She was a tech whiz and a compulsive researcher. Or, as one client had dubbed her, less flatteringly, a "truffle pig for evidence." In the grip of a hunch, she'd stay up all night. She'd look under every available stone for any pebble of useful information if it gave a client a chance at justice. Or, in this case, if it gave a child the life and family he deserved.

"I'm just asking for a few weeks to do some due diligence," she pressed.

"Twelve days," the judge said. "You have twelve days."

"Thank you, Your Honor," Caroline said quickly. "If I don't find proof of gang affiliation or other wrongdoing, I will stipulate to the placement of Mateo Hidalgo with Rogelio Gonzalez."

It was what the court would order anyway if she couldn't provide proof, so it didn't hurt to signal she would agree to it without a fight. Reasonableness was the currency of the courts, and she might yet need to pay for other concessions from Judge Flores.

"Good. We'll reconvene at one on September 26," the judge ordered, hitting his gavel.

Caroline shoved her laptop into her bag. Her mind raced, forming a to-do list. She needed information. Fast. The court had already run a criminal background check on Gonzalez that hadn't turned up any misdemeanors, let alone felonies. That meant she needed to dig elsewhere for answers to her questions: Where did Mr. Gonzalez work? What was his girlfriend's story? Who were those business associates at the warehouse?

Suddenly, a prickling sensation spread across Caroline's forehead.

She lifted her gaze to find Gonzalez glowering at her from across the courtroom.

Without giving him the satisfaction of a reaction, Caroline returned to packing her bag.

She knew she was an asshole if her suspicions were wrong, but she didn't have time for preemptive self-recrimination. She had a bad feeling about Gonzalez. And now she had enough time to see if that feeling was right.

• • •

As soon as she was outside the courthouse, Caroline wrote a text to her assistant, Amy.

Pls set up call w/Wallace Boyd, assistant DA
Google for his
I'm avail to talk w/him any time today

Caroline didn't know whether her law school classmate Wallace Boyd was in the gangs unit of the district attorney's office, but talking to Boyd would be a start. If she threw a large enough net, she might find information about Gonzalez's neighborhood or business associates.

Amy wrote back ten minutes later, as Caroline was climbing into her Mustang GT.

Meet Boyd @ 3:30 @ adjunct DA's office

Caroline dictated a quick response.

I don't have time for f-2-f. Pls just set up a call

Amy's response was just as fast.

Nope. He wants in-person

Caroline exhaled. Damn. Of course he did. She'd gone on exactly two dates with overeager Wallace Boyd during law school. She'd declined a third.

Okay. Pls get an address for me.

As Caroline resigned herself to wasting hours going to the DA's office to meet with Boyd in person, she considered flaking on the soup kitchen. But she quickly quashed the thought. Her uncle needed her help. She'd just need to make up the time somewhere else in her day.

Leapfrogging from stoplight to stoplight, she sent a barrage of texts, telling Amy about the spot-the-cop game at the warehouse where Gonzalez supposedly stored the merchandise for his apparel business. When she finished, she wrote:

Pls see what you can find out about that warehouse.

I'll be in the office after seeing my uncle.

I expect you to have the whole case solved by then.

Caroline smiled and hit "Send." Amy was more of a friend than a legal assistant, and it was nice to have someone to joke around with, especially after a contentious morning.

Seconds later, the phone rang.

The quip on Caroline's lips died as she read the name of the caller: Harold DuBois.

Caroline cocked her head at the screen.

She hadn't expected to hear from The Pastures' administrator. She'd recognized his promises to help look for the watch as what they were—desperate measures, intended to avert a lawsuit from a would-be heir. She didn't believe his inquiries would yield any actual answers.

"I've got good news for you," Harold said when Caroline answered the call. "A convalescent hospital in Burbank just responded to my post on that chat board. The administrator there says he has an employee named Patricia Amos."

Caroline almost cheered out loud at her good fortune.

"Really? Is she there now? Did you tell the police?"

"She's there, but let's wait before calling the police," said Harold. "I know the administrator, and he e-mailed me Patricia Amos's personnel file. I'm a little foggy on this attachment stuff, but I'll forward it to you if you promise to let me handle the police if this is the same woman."

Caroline's arms tingled at the possibility of catching the thief who'd stolen her grandmother's watch. Patricia had gotten too brave. Now she'd pay for her overconfidence.

"I promise," Caroline said. "Send it over."

CHAPTER 3

"It's not her," Caroline said.

She'd just pulled her Mustang GT into a parking space outside the soup kitchen when Harold's e-mail pinged on her phone. Now, as she talked to Harold on speaker, she studied the brown-haired woman with horn-rimmed glasses on page one of the personnel file.

A smidge over five feet tall, this short brunette was not the tattooed, red-haired Patricia Amos who'd stood beside Caroline in her grandmother's room. In fact, this Patricia Amos wasn't even a CNA. She was a nurse. And she wasn't a recent hire. Instead, she'd been working at Meadowlark Convalescent Hospital for eight years. Plus, there was no indication that the Burbank administrator had ever had any problem with his Patricia Amos—the cover e-mail said Patricia had been an exemplary employee during her long tenure at the convalescent hospital.

Harold *hmm*'ed on the phone. "It says I have to download Adobe Acrobat to see it. Where do I go on the Internet?"

"Look, we can chat later if you need to, but I have some things to do. Thank you for sending this to me." Caroline clicked off, leaving Harold behind in his hapless fog of IT confusion.

In the silence of her car, Caroline closed her eyes.

Disappointment drove away the last vestiges of hope from her heart.

Patricia was probably halfway to Las Vegas. Or Mexico. Or Europe. Grandma Kate had never had the watch appraised, but if that repairman was right, it was worth more than enough to pay for a plane ticket. And a house.

Climbing from the Mustang, Caroline strode toward the soup kitchen.

She had no time to lament what was irretrievably lost.

She needed to focus on trying to save her uncle. Thumbing the AA flyer in her back pocket, she prepared to do battle with him.

• • •

When she stepped inside the fluorescent-lit assembly room, Caroline was greeted by a volunteer from one of the charities hosting the soup kitchen. With bushy white eyebrows and sky-blue eyes, he exuded a kind of vitality usually reserved for retired generals.

"Thanks for coming," he said, handing Caroline an apron to protect her business suit.

Donning it, Caroline followed the man to a row of plastic tables piled high with foodstuff and chafing dishes. Steamed peas. Mashed potatoes. Burgers. All smelled barely edible.

"You're in charge of peas," said the man, stopping in front of the first chafing dish. He offered Caroline a ladle, then pointed toward the table at the beginning of the food line, where neat rows of pamphlets and brochures described the charitable services available to the homeless.

"Please encourage folks to grab a pamphlet or two on their way through the line," he said.

Caroline nodded. Although she'd never been stationed at the first chafing dish, she'd volunteered enough times to have noticed the omnipresent table of brochures.

Settling into her spot, Caroline waited for the first patrons to arrive. She thumbed the AA flyer in her back pocket. She gave the peas a stir. Then she looked down at the pile of pamphlets.

Her breath hitched as her eyes fell on a familiar name.

OASIS CARE

The charity that was supposed to get Grandma Kate's estate.

Caroline grabbed the pamphlet. Opening it, she found glossy images of people studying from books, fixing cars, and cooking meals. The banner across the top of the page trumpeted the aggressively cheerful slogan: **HELPING YOU HELP YOURSELF.**

The next page touted Oasis's alcohol treatment program. Lauded as one of the best in the city, it welcomed the homeless and promised free beds for anyone in treatment.

Suddenly, new understanding dawned for Caroline: her grandmother had died knowing that her only son was an alcoholic who lived on the street. In her estate plan, she'd made a final offering. Her dying act to try to help him.

Swallowing past a wave of emotion, Caroline looked up to greet her first patron, a man with hair like a tumbleweed. Despite the midday heat, he wore a heavy denim jacket.

"Peas?" Caroline asked.

The man with tumbleweed hair nodded.

Caroline scooped a helping onto the man's saggy paper tray.

"Pamphlet?" Caroline asked, offered the Oasis one she held in her hand.

"Naw, just the peas straight up without the side of Jesus," said the man, moving along.

When he'd gone, Caroline studied the Oasis pamphlet again.

He was right. Jesus figured rather prominently in Oasis's stated mission to feed the hungry and care for the weak. But the rest of the pamphlet looked nonreligious. Clinics. Food banks. Substance abuse programs. Job training. Stuff anyone and everyone at the soup kitchen needed.

She folded the pamphlet at the sound of her next patron approaching.

It was her uncle. He'd changed out of the rumpled suit. Instead, he sported the same stained jeans and work boots he always wore.

"Peas?" Caroline asked, holding up a ladleful as he approached.

Hitch grimaced in a way that let her know the peas were too gross even for someone who lived in a tent under a freeway overpass.

Releasing the ladle, Caroline watched it sink slowly down into the layer of peas.

"I told you not to come here," Hitch said. "It isn't safe."

Caroline glanced around the soup kitchen. Other than the line of patrons, it was quiet.

She shrugged. "I'm fine."

"Just stay clear of Li'l Ray," Hitch said. "He's at the table behind me at four o'clock."

Following her uncle's directions, she clocked the man with the tumbleweed hair. He sat hunched over his peas, shoveling them quickly into his mouth.

"Li'l Ray's a fixer, and he's packing today," said Hitch. "You can tell from the jacket."

Caroline repressed the urge to compliment her uncle on his powers of observation. Despite being half-drunk, he hadn't lost his police instincts. The echo of his skills made her sad. There'd once been a time when she would've asked him questions about the tricks of the trade. Now, she just made a mental note to avoid the man called Li'l Ray.

"You get the watch?" Hitch asked.

Caroline exhaled. She'd hoped her uncle would've forgotten to ask.

"Grandma's caregiver stole it." She waited for the barrage of recriminations.

But Hitch just shrugged.

"Doesn't really matter," he said, his voice slurring.

Caroline's chest sparked with annoyance. She'd been worried he'd be upset by the theft. But this drunken indifference was even worse.

She withdrew the AA flyer from her back pocket and extended it toward her uncle.

Hitch glowered down at the yellow page.

"I'm doing fine," he said, though his thirdhand clothes and stale, pickled funk belied his words. "I've got nothing in common with any of the people at those meetings anyway."

"Then how about Oasis?" Caroline said, offering the pamphlet she held in her other hand. If her grandmother had made the sacrifice of funding Oasis, Hitch could at least give that gift some respect by taking advantage of the charity's services.

Hitch's eyes narrowed at the offending pamphlet.

"I don't need their bullshit, either. Why can't you just leave me alone?"

"Because you don't have to live like this. Let me help you," Caroline pled.

"You come down here in your suit and you think you know what's right for everyone." As Hitch's voice rose, the other people in the soup kitchen looked over to see the cause of the disturbance. "Go back to your fancy office and try to fix someone else."

"Just . . . try. Please." Caroline thrust the Oasis pamphlet toward him.

With a sloppy right arm, Hitch tried to push it away but missed and stumbled into the table, toppling the neat piles of pamphlets and brochures of a half dozen charities.

The pamphlets fluttered like doomed butterflies before settling across the linoleum.

Hitch dropped his tray on the table beside the chafing dish.

Without a word, he turned and strode out of the soup kitchen.

Anger and worry clawed at Caroline as she watched him disappear out the door.

Hitch was drunk. He was homeless. And lord knew where he was going.

Unsure what else to do, Caroline squatted to pick up the pamphlets.

The soup kitchen coordinator drifted over to join her. His presence was a silent support.

"He wasn't always like this," Caroline said quietly.

"Everyone here has a story," said the coordinator, looking up in the direction Hitch had disappeared. "I'm sure he does, too."

Caroline appreciated the invitation to tell her uncle's tale. To give his identity more contour and nuance than the drunk, homeless man they'd just witnessed throwing a tantrum.

"My uncle used to be a police detective," she began. "A good one, too. He cracked some huge cases back before . . ." Caroline shook her head. "He wasn't the stereotypical detective whose job drove him to drink. He always drank too much."

The coordinator inclined his head in understanding. "I've seen people dig themselves out of very deep holes. You never know, he might even get his old job back someday."

Caroline gave a humorless laugh. "There's no chance of that." Her uncle had failed enough people enough times that there'd be no chance of any return. He'd missed appointments, meetings, and even court hearings until everyone had, like her, stopped relying on him. His last investigation had almost gotten several people killed, including his own partner.

"Then he could retrain. Many of these charities have job-training programs." The coordinator tilted his head toward the rows of newly piled pamphlets. Then he withdrew.

Caroline considered what kind of work her uncle could do if he wasn't a police detective. Security guard? Private investigator? It was nice to dream about a different future for him.

Opening the Oasis pamphlet again, she flipped to the page about job-training programs.

The list of skills the charity taught to the homeless was long.

Automobile repair. Carpentry. Plumbing. Cooking.

But it was the last job on the list that caught Caroline's attention.

Certified nursing assistant.

"Damn," she breathed.

• • •

"Patricia Amos came from Oasis, didn't she?" Caroline asked. It was her second phone call to Harold DuBois in one day, and it promised to be even more unpleasant than the first.

"Yes, but we've gotten many CNAs through the Oasis training program. They've always been very good." Harold's voice held a defensive note.

"Do you always let them proselytize to residents about Oasis?" Caroline asked. When she'd seen the training program listed in the Oasis pamphlet, she'd known how her grandmother had learned about the charity. Her confused, demented, failing grandmother.

"We let them *educate* residents about their programs," Harold said, as if it were a distinction with a difference. "We also let other charities put on presentations to our residents from time to time," he added.

"But other charities don't provide you with caregivers who develop ongoing relationships with your residents." Caroline recalled Nancy Feinstein's annoyance at the overly solicitous CNAs at The Pastures. Maybe her suspicions about their motives had been well founded.

"Oasis isn't doing anything wrong," Harold said. His tone begged for agreement. "So long as no one unduly influences our residents, they can leave their money wherever they want. You know who Duncan Reed is, right?"

Caroline's brow wrinkled at the non sequitur. Of course she knew who Duncan Reed was. For five decades, he'd hosted a children's show. With his twinkling blue eyes and Irish accent, his cable-knit sweater and penny loafers, Duncan Reed had embodied neighborly values to generations of viewers. He'd suffered a stroke, she recalled, that ended his TV career.

"What's he got to do with this?" she asked.

"Oasis is Mr. Reed's charity."

Caroline considered Harold's reasoning. Duncan Reed's television persona exuded kindness. As far as she knew, he was a decent man. But the fact that Oasis was his charity didn't exonerate it of providing caregivers that proselytized to vulnerable elders in the hope of receiving bequests. Nor did it exonerate nursing home administrators of letting it happen.

"What's in it for you?" Caroline asked quietly.

"Nothing," Harold said, "except that sometimes Oasis hosts social programs and clinics for our residents. It's helpful to us." He didn't have to explain why. The new floors told the tale. Oasis's assistance left The Pastures with a little extra money in its budget.

Harold was corrupted, Caroline realized. Soft corruption, to be sure. Not a bribe. Not exactly. He'd simply succumbed to a modest monetary incentive to think favorably of Oasis.

"How many other wills have you seen like my grandmother's?" Caroline asked. Harold had told her that nursing home policy required him to retain signed copies of residents' wills and to read them with the residents' heirs. He'd know if there were others leaving funds to Oasis.

"I've seen a few each year," Harold admitted. "But no one's ever complained. We're talking about people who would've left their money to the SPCA. Not that there's anything wrong with dogs or anything . . ."

Harold left a space in the conversation to laugh, but Caroline didn't.

The opportunities for abuse were simply stunning. If Harold had been corrupted by Oasis's soft incentives to allow caregivers into his facility to *educate* residents, how many other nursing homes had succumbed to similar incentives? There were ten facilities in Southern California operating under The Pastures' banner. Had Oasis placed caregivers at all of them? And what about all the other nursing homes in Los Angeles—was Oasis operating those?

"Are you going to sue us?" Harold asked.

Caroline considered the question. Depending on whether Oasis was pressuring vulnerable elders to give gifts to it, she could imagine pursuing a suit against Oasis. But what about The Pastures? The nursing home might've been tacitly complicit. That was certainly bad. But was she really going to sue The Pastures?

"No, but I'm going to need some information from you," Caroline said.

• • •

As Caroline rode the elevator up to her office, her mind chewed through questions like a hungry termite. Was Oasis's education of nursing home residents really a benign practice, as Harold had suggested, or was it as shady as Caroline's instincts told her it was? And who was that other Patricia Amos—the nurse in Burbank? Was she connected to Oasis?

Stepping into her small office suite, Caroline was so preoccupied she almost tripped over her assistant.

Amy Garber sat cross-legged on the floor, organizing files. In a lavender blouse, yellow headband, and white scarf, she looked like an iris on fairy dust.

"I've got some great stuff for you on Gonzalez," she said, grinning up at her boss.

It took Caroline's brain a few seconds to catch up. The guardianship. Right.

"What did you find?" Caroline asked.

"That place where Gonzalez told Mateo to play spot-the-cop really is a storage facility. Cooperated Storage. The manager's name is Stanton Escovar. He was a font of information once I told him I was thinking of renting space there." Haloed in blonde curls, Amy's face was the picture of innocence. Her eyes, however, glittered with the subterfuge.

Caroline's conscience gave a weak protest. Initiating Amy into the ways of social engineering might have been a sin. But learning how to find information was part of learning about tech, and Amy wanted to learn all she could from Caroline. One of those lessons included the principle that gaining a gatekeeper's trust was the easiest way to obtain access to information.

"Also, Gonzalez has a girlfriend named Floriana Perez," Amy said.

"We already knew about Perez from Gonzalez's guardianship petition."

"True, but what we didn't know is that her family owns a shipping business called Perez Shipping. They handle all of Gonzalez's shipments of lingerie down to Mexico."

"Lingerie?" Caroline raised an amused eyebrow.

"That's what Gonzalez's apparel business sells." Amy smiled. "Gonzalez has a wholesaler downtown. He buys a bunch of panties and teddies and whatnot, sells some at his store, and ships some to Mexico."

"There's nothing illegal about selling underwear." Caroline shrugged, continuing toward the door of the office. She didn't have time to plumb the depths of Gonzalez's panties business. Not now, anyway.

But Amy followed Caroline to the door of her office.

"Are you going to tell your boy Boyd about what I found out?" she asked.

Caroline turned, scowling at her assistant.

"Boyd isn't *my boy*," Caroline protested.

"Yeah, but he wants to be." Amy kept smiling.

Caroline tried to think of a comeback, but her mind was uncharacteristically blank. That Boyd insisted on having her come down to the DA's office in person suggested Amy was right.

"Anyway, I hope you can use some of the stuff I found," Amy said. "I know it isn't exactly on point, but I was hoping the girlfriend angle might help." She paused. "Here's where you pat me on the head and tell me I'm doing great for a nonlawyer."

"You're doing better than great. For a nonlawyer," Caroline dutifully repeated.

And it was true. Despite Amy's indifference toward the law, she'd become a great legal assistant. She'd needed work after her son, Liam, had fallen ill, and she'd left her job at a title company to care for him. By the time Liam had recovered, Caroline had needed help at her firm. That many of Caroline's clients were poor made payment of full wages difficult, but Amy had agreed to take part of her compensation in tutoring. Amy wanted to become a software engineer. Having worked as one herself, Caroline would teach Amy the skills she'd need to enter the field.

And then Caroline would be alone.

She tried not to think too deeply about it.

Stepping into her office, Caroline felt the tension leave her shoulders at the sight of her familiar things. Two large monitors and a state-of-the-art computer sat on a long, industrial desk. Speed. Bandwidth. Functionality. All were worth paying for. All were necessary to her.

Though she was a lawyer, Caroline had a skill set that most lawyers didn't share.

Her eyes traveled across the walls of her office.

There were two framed diplomas. One for undergrad. One for law school.

A third frame held a printed circuit board. Flat and shaped like a skull the size of a pancake, the Def Con 23 badge was one of many that Caroline had hacked at the famous tech conference. This badge had been the hardest. After hours of experimentation, she'd discovered it had a built-in microphone. She'd won the hacking competition by attaching a Secure Digital card reader to the back of the badge and modifying the code so that it would store the microphone input, effectively turning the badge into a listening device.

Of all the diplomas on the wall, the Def Con badge was the one that mattered most to Caroline. It reminded her that she could think her way out of anything.

Now she tried to think her way out of her current problem.

She had an appointment with an assistant DA in a little over an hour. The meeting was more than a chance to figure out whether Gonzalez was a criminal. It was also an irresistible opportunity to bring the prying fingers of the state into her quest to discover whether Oasis was engaging in elder abuse.

Tasked with representing the state in all criminal proceedings, assistant DAs could snoop and prosecute as their suspicions dictated. Caroline knew she could get her old classmate to help her with the Mateo Hidalgo matter. Ensuring a child's safety would be an easy sell. But convincing Boyd to investigate a charity associated with a beloved TV personality was another matter. To attract Boyd's interest, she needed to intrigue him. And to do that, she needed a hook.

Caroline began her research with one of the hotly burning questions in her mind: Who was Patricia Amos?

Social media provided a golden road to the center of a person's identity.

Caroline searched the name "Patricia Amos" in Los Angeles.

She retrieved no hits showing the face of the red-haired caregiver. No Facebook. No Twitter. No Instagram. Not even Tinder.

Caroline cocked her head at the screen.

In the modern world, it was unlikely for someone to have no social media presence.

But what did it mean? Was Patricia Amos using an alias, like her middle name? Or was it a fake identity? And if so, were other CNAs trained by Oasis using fake names, too?

There was no way to know.

What about that other Patricia Amos—the one from Burbank? Who was she?

Caroline pulled up the personnel file of the woman with short brown hair and horn-rimmed glasses.

This Patricia Amos had graduated from nursing school fifteen years earlier and had started working as a licensed vocational nurse at Meadowlark Convalescent Hospital eight years ago. Nothing in the file described her employment history during the first seven years of her career. But nothing suggested any connection to Oasis, either. Or to the other Patricia Amos.

Another dead end.

Caroline tried another angle. Oasis's CNA-training program.

She found nothing illuminating when the program had started or who had started it.

But she did find that Oasis's job-training programs were a favorite of city government, which regularly gave it grants to help fund projects designed to put Oasis's job trainees to work.

The city's press releases touting the grants invoked Duncan Reed, who had apparently worked side by side with Oasis volunteers to feed the poor and the destitute. Prior to suffering the stroke that had robbed him of his mobility and ended his television career, Duncan Reed had championed Oasis's good works. Although Caroline didn't recall ever having heard about Reed's charitable endeavors, they were certainly consistent with the values he'd espoused on TV.

Still, the information provided no clues about whether anyone had ever complained about Oasis's CNA trainees convincing nursing home residents to leave money to the charity. She needed a way to find those complaints.

Caroline knew that the government kept track of all entities that were registered as charities and thus eligible for tax-preferred status. And all of the information was online.

Navigating to the Internal Revenue Service's website, Caroline found the portal for the Cumulative List of Organizations.

She typed "Oasis Care" into the search pane.

The screen changed, and Caroline's search results appeared:

There are no tax-exempt organizations matching those search values.

Caroline checked the spelling and tried again.

Same response.

Leaning back in her chair, Caroline let the unavoidable conclusion permeate her mind: Oasis was not a registered charity.

Charities were subject to strict rules and government oversight. Oasis's for-profit status meant that its operations were shielded from scrutiny. From oversight.

Caroline stared at the framed circuit board and its painted skull.

Something about Oasis wasn't right.

• • •

When Caroline emerged from her office, she found Amy chewing on the end of a pen, laboring over a coding exercise.

"Hey," Caroline said.

Amy looked up in surprise.

"Sorry to startle you. I need your help," Caroline said.

While Amy put the coding aside, Caroline told her about Oasis.

When she finished, she extended the document that Harold had just sent to her.

"What's that?" Amy asked.

"It's a list of all of the residents who've died at all of The Pastures' facilities in the last five years," Caroline said. To placate her anger, Harold had apparently figured out how to attach and e-mail the list.

Unfortunately, the PDF format of the document wasn't useful to Caroline.

"I need you to run that list through our optical character recognition software," she said. "We need to turn the printed text on the list into machine-encoded text so that I can check the names of the dead residents against the courts' probate records database."

Amy's brow crinkled as she tried to follow.

"When a person dies, the superior court opens a probate so that it can supervise the administration of the estate," Caroline said. "Basically, the judge makes sure the dead person's stuff goes to the right people."

"Okay." Amy's voice rose in question at the end.

"Probate records are public. You can access them online. That means I can take the names of all the people who died at The Pastures' ten facilities in the last five years, and I can cross-check those names against the court's probate records. That'll let me see how many people left their estates to Oasis."

"You're assuming it's a scam," Amy said.

"I'm not assuming anything. I'm just investigating," Caroline said. "If the numbers are large enough, I'm hoping the DA will look into it."

Amy searched Caroline's face, as if trying to decide if her boss was brilliant or crazy.

"Just humor me," Caroline said.

Shrugging, Amy took the page.

• • •

Caroline eyed the list of names that Amy had prepared for her. It would take hours to sort them by county, then laboriously run searches of them against each court's probate records.

Or she could use a quick Python-based bot to do her work for her.

A simple task like filling in templates to search a court's records was perfectly suited to a bot. The bot would employ a script that would run through each search step for each resident at each court's website, and then catalog the information that the search found. If all went well, she'd have a list of people who'd left bequests to Oasis—a list she could give to Wallace Boyd.

The first results for Los Angeles Superior Court were ready in just ten minutes.

Your search has retrieved no hits.

"What?" Caroline asked her empty office. The search results could not be right. Harold had admitted that Oasis had received some bequests from The Pastures' Chatsworth facility in the last year. Those probates should have shown up on the court's website.

There had to be something wrong with the scripts she'd written.

She checked the bots.

No, everything looked right.

Maybe the court's website had glitched?

She tried deploying the bot again.

Your search has retrieved no hits.

This time, Caroline tried inserting the names manually. One after another, she sent the name of a dead resident into the court's database.

But one after another, her searches retrieved nothing.

The bot wasn't bad. The websites weren't glitching. There just weren't any probates showing anyone leaving money to Oasis.

Suddenly, another potential source of the problem occurred to Caroline.

She scanned the practice guides on her bookshelf until she found the one she wanted.

Probate Procedures under the California Probate Code.

• • •

Caroline waited while her ex-classmate took a sip from a chipped coffee cup emblazoned with the district attorney's emblem. Although she'd chafed when Boyd had asked her to waste time coming down to his office, her research had made her glad for the face-to-face meeting.

"Rogelio Gonzalez isn't in a gang," Boyd said, addressing the ostensible reason for her visit. "But I've got a friend over in the gangs unit who told me that Rogelio has a brother named Fernando serving time at Wasco State Prison. He got sent up for drug dealing."

"What's Fernando's sentence?" Caroline asked.

"Five years. Could've been shorter, but he wouldn't roll on his coconspirators."

"That means Fernando is very loyal, very scared, or very related to his cohorts."

"Well put," Boyd said. He graced Caroline with a wide smile. "I'll get Fernando's file for you. Hopefully it'll contain something that'll let you help that little boy who loves Xbox *Madden* as much as I do."

Boyd's charisma was just as Caroline remembered it from law school. So was his ability to remember the small details of people's lives. He'd asked after her mom, her uncle, and even her grandmother. Ambitious and calculating, he was a natural politician. He was going places, though the chipped mug and stained vertical blinds in his office said he hadn't arrived quite yet.

Boyd noted the subject of Caroline's gaze.

"The main office is way nicer." He held up his cup. "Coffee's just as terrible, though. Why don't we go across the street to a great little café I know? They make terrific scones."

"I can't," Caroline said. She'd expected his invitation, and she'd expected to refuse it. Boyd's relentless concern with joining the right societies, working for the right professors, and figuring out how to clerk for the right judges had grown tiresome in law school. She hadn't cared about his climbing then, and she didn't want to pretend she cared now.

"Solo practice too busy?" The bemused glint in Boyd's eyes told Caroline the question was more sarcasm than curiosity.

"Yes, actually," Caroline answered, feeling her face flush with annoyance.

"How do you get clients as a solo only one year out of law school?" Boyd asked.

"I get referrals from the dependency and family courts. Also, there are some lawyers on my floor who give me their overflow work." The explanation sounded weak even to Caroline's own ears. She was scraping for work.

"Everyone was so surprised when you left Hale Stern," Boyd said.

Caroline's stomach sank at the confirmation she'd been the subject of alumni gossip. She'd aced law school. She'd landed a job at the most prestigious firm in the city. Then she'd left after only one month. In her classmates' eyes, it was in inconceivable career move.

"I just feel so bad that things didn't work out better for you," Boyd said.

Caroline forced herself not to respond. She knew that Boyd had chafed when she'd received Hale Stern's offer of employment—the only offer the firm had made to her graduating class. He probably saw her failure at Hale Stern as her comeuppance.

But the frustrating part was that she hadn't failed at all. Before leaving Hale Stern, she'd helped thousands of people—including Amy's son. She'd ended the destructive career of a deadly fixer. The problem was that her means of prevailing weren't entirely legal, so she couldn't tell anyone what she'd done. Or why she'd left Hale Stern.

"What do you need to do to get moved over to the main office?" Caroline asked. That Boyd was stuck in the DA's adjunct office over a year after graduation probably struck him as a flop. Better to put the focus on his failure to launch rather than on her own.

"Good question." Boyd's eyes settled on his chipped mug. "We've got only one DIC—deputy in charge—over here, and he doesn't care about mentoring anyone. He just wants to get through his day. If I'm going to get noticed, I need to get onto one of the bigger cases. All the big guns are across the street. Chief Deputy McFadden and, of course, the DA herself."

Caroline nodded. Like almost everyone else in the city, she'd voted for Donita Johnson. The new DA had branded herself the People's Prosecutor. She'd promised a return to community-based policing and a clampdown on government waste. If Boyd aspired to have a political career, DA Johnson already had one. She was rumored to be on the short list for a cabinet position. Caroline knew Boyd would want to ride her coattails—if he could reach them.

"I think I may have something that could get you where you want to go," Caroline said.

Boyd looked up from his mug. His gray eyes held a question.

Caroline took a breath. It was time for her to make the face-to-face meeting worthwhile.

"I've got a case involving possible fraud on the elderly by an entity posing as a charity. It's a potentially large scam affecting lots of people."

Caroline waited while Boyd did the calculus.

Helping old people was good. Entities posing as charities were bad.

He lifted a curious eyebrow.

In what she hoped were intriguing tones, Caroline told him what she'd discovered: The theft of the watch. The training program for CNAs. The nursing home administrators' incentives to ignore the potential for abuse. The fact that Oasis was not a registered charity.

When she finished, she waited for her ex-classmate's reaction. If he shared her suspicions, he could throw the weight of the state behind an investigation. He could file criminal charges. He could subpoena witnesses and get search warrants.

But Boyd just took another sip of cold coffee.

"Oasis is Duncan Reed," he said. "Why would he steal from old ladies?"

"It isn't clear that Duncan Reed is actually running Oasis anymore," Caroline countered. The beloved television star had stayed out of the public eye since suffering his stroke. "And anyway, just because someone looks good doesn't mean they aren't capable of evil conduct."

"Fine, but I've got to be honest with you, Caro, this all seems really unlikely," Boyd said. "I think you should keep your focus on what's real—some woman stole your family's watch." This time the sympathy in his eyes was real.

Caroline exhaled. The case was about more than the theft of a watch. There was one woman, maybe two, maybe a whole fake charity taking advantage of vulnerable old people. She had to make Boyd see that.

"There's something going on here. I didn't find a single probate showing anyone leaving a gift to Oasis," Caroline said. "The administrator at The Pastures facility in Chatsworth admitted that some of his residents left their estates to Oasis. At the very least, there should've been probates opened for those. There should've been court records."

"Why weren't there?" Boyd asked.

"It turns out there's a loophole in the Probate Code. The courts don't supervise the administration of small estates. If you die with less than $150,000, your estate can be disposed of without a court proceeding—there's no probate opened."

"But then how does your heir get your money?" Boyd asked.

"It's dangerously simple," Caroline said, holding his gaze. "He just shows up at your bank with a certified copy of your death certificate, the will, an affidavit swearing that he's entitled to the money in your account, and an ID. He gives those materials to the bank, and the teller cuts him a cashier's check. Right there. Right then. No judicial oversight. No public records."

"No public records?" Boyd raised an eyebrow.

"None. Only the banks have records of these transactions—presumably, they keep track of every time someone shows up with proper documentation and walks away with a cashier's check. But other than those bank records, these affidavit-withdrawal transactions leave no tracks. As a result, they're completely invisible to law enforcement."

Caroline paused to give Boyd a chance to catch up.

"So, your theory is that these Oasis caregivers manipulate elderly people into writing wills naming Oasis as the beneficiary. Then, when one of these people dies, Oasis is entitled to a certified death certificate since they're named in the will as an heir. After that, it's as simple as going down to the dead person's bank, presenting the documents, and cleaning out the account?"

"Exactly," Caroline said. "It's the perfect scam. There are no witnesses for the wills. There are no probate court records. And to the banks, it's just a small, routine bank transaction closing a dead person's account. There's no way Oasis can get caught."

Boyd leaned back, the springs in his ancient desk chair groaning in agony. "Let's not forget there's another possibility here: no one's doing anything wrong. The absence of probates doesn't have to be proof of a scam. It could just be proof that no one's left any serious money to Oasis. Maybe they just get small estates left to them from time to time."

"Fine, let's agree that two possibilities exist here: extreme innocence or extreme guilt," Caroline allowed. "Wouldn't it be irresponsible for the DA not to at least look into the possibility that it's a case of extreme guilt?"

Boyd frowned, his gray eyes narrowing.

Caroline knew he was considering the possibility that she might be paranoid and weighing it against the possibility that she wasn't. He might believe she'd bombed at a big firm, but he also knew she'd bested him in every class they'd shared. Plus, he needed a way to get out of the DA's adjunct office with its secondhand furniture and second-tier cases. Bringing in a new case involving widespread elder abuse would make that happen.

"If this is a scam, Oasis and these caregivers could be making a fortune," Caroline pressed. "If they get $100,000 from ten estates, that's a quick $1 million. All they need to do is hang around nursing homes long enough to convince or coerce the residents to write new wills. They could fly under the radar forever so long as they kept moving around."

Boyd tapped his fingers together as he considered Caroline's arguments.

"We need to see bank records," Caroline continued. "That's how we can find out how often the banks have cut checks to Oasis. If the numbers are higher than those for other charities, there might be something here. And if there is, you're a hero, right?"

After another long moment of consideration, Boyd lifted his phone.

"Fowler? Can you come on down for a sec?" he asked.

Seconds later, a young man with a patchy goatee entered. With wheat-colored hair and nondescript eyes of some unmemorable shade of blue, he reminded Caroline of a dozen law school classmates whose names she couldn't remember.

"This is our clerk, Gordon Fowler," Boyd introduced the man. "He'll help me begin to work up this case. If there's something here, we'll submit it to the deputy in charge, who will then submit it to the chief deputy DA." He shrugged apologetically. "It's a big bureaucracy."

Fowler perched himself against the wall and tried to balance a laptop on his thighs.

Caroline rose from her chair. "Why don't you take my chair?" she offered.

With a grateful smile, Fowler sat down to listen while Boyd caught him up on the case.

Caroline watched Fowler enter information into the DA's internal docketing database. There were drop-down menus for potential witnesses and contacts. There were places to enter information about anticipated targets for subpoenas. Whoever had written the software had been very thorough. Hopefully the human element at the DA's office would be as effective as the software.

"If there's really something going on here," Boyd said to Fowler, "there should be other people who've been taken by surprise by a loved one leaving money to Oasis. Other angry heirs. I'd like you to look for any internal records of complaints. Search our files. Search the police call logs. See if there have been any complaints from any members of the public."

"I'll jump right on it," Fowler said, typing notes on the laptop.

"I'm sure you will," Boyd said, apparently enjoying Fowler's earnestness as much as Caroline was.

"If your preliminary research pans out, will you subpoena bank records?" Caroline asked.

"Almost certainly, but let's not get ahead of ourselves," Boyd said. "Everything's digitized, so it shouldn't take long. We should be able to get through our internal search by the end of the day. I promise I'll run everything by you once we've completed our internal review."

"What about human intelligence?" Much as Caroline believed in and depended on tech assets, she knew that not every piece of data was likely to be recorded in the DA's databases.

"Good point. Maybe I'll bring Chief Deputy McFadden into the loop now," Boyd said. "He's a powerhouse. He knows everyone. He'll know if there have ever been any rumblings about Oasis."

Caroline warmed at Boyd's words. That he was willing to involve his boss at this preliminary stage struck her as significant.

"Please call me as soon as you've finished your internal review." Caroline took Fowler's laptop and inserted two phone numbers. "If you can't reach me, try my assistant, Amy. She knows as much about this matter as I do. She'll also know how to find me."

After Caroline finished typing, Fowler shut his laptop, and Boyd rose.

"I'll walk you out," Boyd said. He held up the badge he wore around his neck. "I need to swipe you through the security doors."

As she followed Boyd into the hallway, Caroline realized he was lucky. His tiny office with its stained blinds and sagging furniture had a window. The cluttered cubicles lining the interior of the floor were a type of grim that Caroline had only ever seen before on television. They made her meager office suite look luxurious.

When they reached the elevator, Boyd held the door open then entered after her.

"You seeing anyone these days?" he asked.

Before Caroline could answer, he shook his head. "No. You wouldn't be, would you? You really should give people a chance, Caro." His gray eyes were sympathetic, as if he could see some cracks in her personality that she couldn't see herself.

Caroline frowned. The conversation had careened from work to her personal life with all the grace of a drunk driver in a Formula One race. It was time to get the car back onto the blacktop.

"Let's see what happens with your initial investigation." She smiled in a way that left open the possibility of a date. Perhaps he'd grown in the year since they'd graduated. Perhaps they'd find community in their efforts to create careers. Or maybe she was leading him on to prove to him she didn't have whatever flaw he thought he saw in her.

When the elevator reached the lobby, the doors slid open.

Like two homing pigeons, Boyd's eyes landed on a group of people standing beside the adjunct DA office's security desk. A tall African American woman stood in the center, regaling the others with a story. Her voice dipped and rose as she spoke, holding her listeners enthralled. Everyone laughed when she finished.

DA Johnson, Caroline identified the woman. With her room-lighting smile, the DA looked the part of the politician–law enforcement official. Beside her stood Chief Deputy DA John McFadden, her second in command. A shadow of a beard clung to his chin, the only hair on his otherwise hairless head. His small eyes swept back and forth across the room with the regularity of a light on a prison watchtower.

McFadden's gaze settled on Caroline.

She shuddered with a sudden chill. She'd heard rumors about McFadden. He was well connected, if not well liked.

"I'll be in touch," Boyd said, striding away to join the high-powered group.

Watching him go, Caroline hoped Boyd's ambition would motivate him to pursue the investigation as far as her instincts told her it needed to be pursued. Without a criminal case, her legal options for investigating Oasis narrowed. And the prospect of crossing the line into less traditional means of gathering information filled her with apprehension.

She dismissed the worry.

Boyd would find something. The sheer elegance of the affidavit-withdrawal scam convinced her that it had to exist. Oasis's carefully constructed invisibility confirmed it. Boyd's search would yield evidence of other complaints or hints of some other wrongdoing. He'd take the risk of championing the case—for his own career, if not for her.

That's what she told herself, anyway, as she headed home to await his verdict.

CHAPTER 4

Caroline wiped the sweat from her forehead with the back of her hand.

She'd scrubbed the bathroom until her arms ached. She'd swept her downtown loft until the invisible motes of dust had sent her into sneezing fits. She'd even prepared a new batch of coding exercises for Amy. Now she'd run out of things to do.

Yet Boyd hadn't called. Or texted. Or e-mailed. Or sent up smoke signals.

Just to be sure that was still true, Caroline checked her phone.

Still nothing.

She wondered how much longer she'd have to wait before Boyd called.

She also wondered if she'd melt before he did.

Checking the weather app on her phone, Caroline shook her head in dismay. It was still eighty-five degrees at 9:30 p.m. The heat wave had taken meteorologists by surprise. The September Furnace they were calling it. Caroline agreed with the moniker. In her stifling apartment, even the fake houseplants looked wilted.

Pulling at the tank top that clung to her torso, she considered what else she could do to distract herself. Something outside preferably.

Her eyes fell on the lone object sitting on the coffee table by the door to her flat: the Guatemalan pouch she'd taken from her grandmother's room.

Grabbing it, she walked the length of the shotgun apartment to the kitchen.

An ancient refrigerator hummed along one wall. A row of metal shelves hung over a farmer's sink on another. The other two walls each had a large window.

The first window faced the street, giving a view of a gritty strip of downtown that glowed orange in the perennial city light. The neighborhood was slowly gentrifying. Still devoid of all but a handful of restaurants, the area north of Little Tokyo had attracted young professionals with large ambitions and meager down payments. Like many of them, Caroline was renting. For now.

The other window faced a fire escape. It was this window that Caroline approached, hands on hips, frowning. Beyond the pane, a rusted landing hung four floors above the street. The perch promised respite from the heat.

Unfortunately, the window never opened smoothly. Maybe the paint hadn't properly cured. Or maybe the window just hated her. Whatever the reason, it had always given Caroline trouble. She'd considered leaving the thing open. But she'd heard the fights on the streets. The occasional gunshots. She'd decided it was safer to keep the window shut. And locked.

Now, Caroline gave the window's molding a solid whack with her palm.

As expected, it didn't move.

Placing the Guatemalan pouch atop the stove, Caroline leaned hard into the molding, applying all of her 126 pounds to the task until the seal broke with a faint jerk.

Shouldering the window open, Caroline scrambled out onto the fire escape.

The air outside was as unmoving as it was inside the apartment, but the night sky arched overhead, the half-moon bright against the rusty firmament. There were no stars. There never were in Los Angeles.

Caroline opened the Guatemalan pouch and eased the pile of pictures out onto her lap.

The first image showed her grandmother as a young woman. Kate's hair had been dark then. She smiled into the camera, her right arm flung back, gesturing toward the Eiffel Tower. Next to her, Grandpa Jack stood with a glass of wine, toasting the unseen photographer. Caroline couldn't recall ever having seen her grandfather holding a drink. By the time she'd been born, he'd stopped.

Her eyes traveled back to her grandmother's face. It shone with elation.

She wondered at the source of that joy. Was it that Kate was standing before one of the world's great monuments after having come so far from her small town in North Dakota?

Or perhaps Kate smiled because she had no idea what was coming next.

The smile on Caroline's own face faded.

The woman smiling in the picture would face hard years. Kate's genes were as solid as the Sentinel Butte that stood guard over the town where she'd been born. Nothing in her life had prepared her for the wild element to which she'd tethered herself in Jack Hitchings. Still, she'd persevered. She'd found meaning by volunteering. She'd taken in Rayan Hafaz, the original owner of the heirloom watch. She'd created a family with an expansive enough sense of kinship to embrace a lost native from another continent.

Now that family had become far-flung to different worlds. Hitch to the streets. Caroline's mother to the Oregon fringe. And Caroline to a transitional neighborhood near Skid Row. They were dissolving into strangers, losing whatever cohesion had once made it possible to welcome a lonely man like Rayan Hafaz into the fold.

Somewhere in the distance, a siren echoed down the city streets. A personal tragedy to someone. A background noise to Caroline, as she lifted the pouch to replace the pictures.

In the heft of the empty pouch, Caroline felt something weighing down the corner.

She turned it over.

A medallion fell into her hand. It was the size of a quarter and strung on a silver chain.

On one side of the disc, there was a man wearing a robe and holding a staff. He leaned forward as if walking into a stiff breeze. A baby sat on his shoulders, pointing the way.

Saint Christopher, Caroline identified the old man. Patron saint of wanderers.

In a half-moon at the bottom of the medallion, Caroline found an inscription: PROTECT US.

"Protect us all," Caroline murmured, stringing the chain around her neck.

The metal settled against her chest, its weight cool against her skin.

Caroline closed her eyes, trying to feel some connection to her grandmother.

Instead, she felt the hairs on the back of her neck rising.

The sensation was familiar. She placed it: it was the same feeling she'd had it at court. The sensation of someone watching her. She couldn't say how she knew it, but someone's eyes traced her form. Someone's attention caressed the surface of her skin.

Peering into the darkness, Caroline scanned the urban landscape, trying to substantiate the hammering of her heart. Was there really someone out there? Or was the racing of her pulse just her own fears made manifest with the energy of her attention on them?

Suddenly, she saw it. A shape on the roof of the building across the alley. A silhouette, but human. Facing her.

Watching her.

Thrusting the Guatemalan pouch into her pocket, Caroline scrambled sloppily to her feet, her eyes still riveted to the shape on the neighboring roof.

A wave of nausea coursed up and down her gut.

She'd exposed evil before, just a year ago, and the experience had come with harrowing escapes from people trying to kill her. What had she been thinking, investigating Oasis? If they were running a scam, they wouldn't take kindly to her trying to drag it into the light.

But when she reached the open window, she stopped.

With deliberate slowness, she turned back toward the spot where she'd seen a person.

The shape was still there, but it hadn't moved.

With a flush of embarrassment, Caroline realized it wasn't human at all. It was just a cell tower. Or one of those other strange vestigial appendages that tended to adorn the tops of old buildings. A chimney or vent.

A chimera, then. The equivalent of the creepy tree, silhouetted atop a hill, shapes of limbs resolving into human forms with the suggestibility of an overactive imagination.

Gloom settled over Caroline as she climbed back into the kitchen.

She'd always prided herself for her rationality. For her ability to control her fears with logical thought. She hadn't had a full-fledged anxiety attack in a long time. But her recent performance on the fire escape didn't bode well for her mental stability.

Her grandmother's death seemed to have stirred up mud from the bottom of the bucket of her psyche. The disappearance of the watch had only exacerbated her disquiet. She'd stop sleeping soon, she knew. She'd stop thinking about anything except finding out whether Oasis had scammed her grandmother and others.

Opening the utility drawer, Caroline hunted around until she found what she sought: a strand of onyx beads. Called *komboloi* in Greek, the worry beads helped, Caroline had found. Their smooth roundness grounded her. The deliberate breathing as she moved through each stone calmed her. She hadn't needed them in months. But now that she was spooking at cell towers, the beads seemed like they might be useful.

A buzz in Caroline's pocket interrupted her spiral of concern.

Her phone.

She read the screen: Wallace Boyd.

Before answering, Caroline took a breath. She couldn't let Boyd hear her jangled nerves.

"What've you got?" she asked, skipping the chitchat. She'd been waiting too long to pretend she was interested in anything else.

"I've got nothing," Boyd said.

It took several seconds for Caroline to process his words.

"Turns out Duncan Reed was never much for paperwork," Boyd continued. "He didn't register Oasis as a charity or take tax deductions for his good works or anything. He didn't care about any of that stuff."

"Doesn't Oasis still have to file tax returns?" Caroline asked. There had to be a record of Oasis's finances somewhere, she figured.

"No. Oasis currently operates under the umbrella of a fiscal sponsor—Reed Philanthropy. They file tax returns, so Oasis doesn't have to."

"In other words, Oasis is invisible," Caroline said, making a mental note to look into Reed Philanthropy. "Someone really needs to look into this."

"I agree—and turns out we already have. Chief Deputy McFadden jumped in as soon as I told him about your theory. He pointed me to our files. Apparently the administrator of a skilled nursing facility out in North Hollywood complained a few years back about caregivers encouraging residents to leave money to charities. We investigated back then and came to the conclusion that Oasis is legit."

"Legit?" Caroline echoed. "Did you get bank records?"

"No, but—"

"Then you can't know whether Oasis is *legit*. Come on, Boyd, aren't you even a little curious how often people are giving their estates to Oasis?" Caroline asked.

"You need probable cause to subpoena bank records," Boyd said. "We don't have that here. It isn't unusual for someone to leave money to their caregiver. And in Oasis's case, this isn't even leaving funds to some corrupt caregiver unduly influencing an elderly person—it's folks leaving funds to a solid organization that's doing great work in the community."

"I don't care about the money—" Caroline's face flushed.

"There's nothing here, Caro," Boyd cut her off. "I promise you."

"But how can you promise?" Caroline asked. How could he promise anything? He hadn't done a real investigation. No one had. "Did Gordon Fowler find anything in the call logs?"

"He found nothing. Turns out we tried that angle before, too," Boyd said. "There aren't any records of any other complaints from disgruntled family members."

"But that just means that Oasis is targeting elderly residents who are estranged from their families—populations without relatives or friends who might cry foul if—"

"Stop, Caro. Just stop."

In the silence, Caroline forced herself to humor the possibility that her suspicions about Oasis were meritless. That they'd germinated from a seed of irrational anger. Or displaced grief.

All at once, she recalled Julie DeSotto, her second-grade classmate who'd been hurt when a car hadn't stopped at an intersection. Julie's parents had waged a campaign to get a stoplight installed at the intersection. It wasn't clear the intersection needed one, but the DeSottos had channeled all of their fear, all of their helplessness, and all of their guilt into their campaign.

Caroline realized she might be doing the same thing. Perhaps she was directing all of her sadness and guilt about her grandmother toward

an outward foe. Perhaps her campaign against Oasis was no more rational than the DeSottos' obsessive campaign had been.

As if following the arc of Caroline's thoughts to their logical ter-
minus, Boyd said, "Your grandma just passed. Anybody would be on
a hair trigger."

Caroline stayed silent. Boyd was accusing her of seeing ghosts.

"Why don't we focus on what's really going on here," Boyd continued. "Patricia stole your family's watch. There's a thief out there who's
got something that's yours. If this lady's got a record, she's going to be
in our database. You got a good look at her, right?"

Caroline recalled exactly everything about the manipulative caregiver. The long red braid. The green eyes. The sympathetic tilt of her
head. That Sanskrit tattoo on her wrist.

"Yeah, I know what she looks like."

"Great. If you can ID her, I've got some buddies on the squad
that could run her down." Boyd paused. "That would be nice, right?"
he asked, his voice conciliatory. It was the same tone she'd used with
Mateo, offering him the Xbox. Or the one that nurses in mental hospitals used to cajole patients into taking sedatives.

"Just tell me where to be," Caroline said quietly.

"I'll meet you at 8:30 tomorrow morning."

Caroline was only vaguely aware of Boyd's closing niceties before
he hung up.

Caroline stared up at the stained ceiling of her kitchen.

Was she wrong to think Oasis might be bilking the elderly?

The possibility that Boyd's investigation had been shut down
by someone at the DA's office who was trying to cover up the scam
wouldn't stop yanking at the hem of her shirt, but she refused to give
it her attention. Once she'd gone down the road of thinking she was
seeing a swindle, everything fit into that narrative. But what if she was
wrong?

Either she was the mythical Cassandra, telling the truth to nonbe-lievers. Or she was paranoid.

Both were possible, Caroline admitted.

She lifted the worry beads from the counter where she'd laid them when she answered her phone. After walking her fingers through a few of the round stones, she felt a little better.

She needed sleep. She needed perspective. She needed to grieve.

Going to bed would be a good start.

Before leaving the kitchen, she looked out the window one last time.

Her eyes traced the jagged horizon. She stopped at the spot on the rooftop where she'd thought she'd seen someone watching her. Someone that was just a cell tower or chimney.

But after looking and then looking again, she realized the shape she'd seen was gone.

CHAPTER 5

Caroline tried to rub the sleep out of her eyes as she approached the police station.

Boyd waited for her at the top of the steps. A stocky officer stood beside him, his feet shoulder-width apart. The officer's hat was tucked under one arm, leaving the man's full head of inky-black hair exposed to the wind. He eyed Caroline coolly as she approached.

Though she was careful not to let it show on her face or in her stride, the presence of a uniformed officer worried Caroline. Perhaps Boyd had arranged for an escort to make sure she didn't do something erratic. Perhaps he worried that she'd become consumed by the smoldering suspicions that had sent a thick cloud of irrationality across her mind.

She'd stood at the window of her kitchen for an hour, trying to decide if she'd really seen a shape watching her from a neighboring rooftop. To force herself to bed, she'd convinced herself she hadn't. It had been an optical illusion. A mistake, she told herself.

But as soon as she'd crawled under her covers, she'd recalled the human silhouette dimly seen from the fire escape. Its contours were still vivid in her mind's eye. The sensation of being watched still raised the hairs at the back of her neck.

Flip-flopping back and forth on whether there had or had not been someone watching her had taken the better part of the night. And then it was daybreak. And here she was.

Ignoring her exhaustion, Caroline jogged the last few steps up to the landing.

"This is Captain Nelson," Boyd introduced the dark-haired officer beside him. "He'll take care of you."

Captain Nelson shook Caroline's hand. "I've got to get back inside for a meeting, but I'll be around all day if you identify the perpetrator from the mug shots."

Watching the officer head back inside the police station, Caroline frowned. Captain was an awfully high rank to be babysitting her on her simple task.

"Sorry I can't stick around myself," Boyd said, causing Caroline to return her attention to her classmate. "I've got a new assignment and a new office."

The smile that blossomed on his face reached the highest recesses of his forehead.

"They're moving you over?" Caroline asked, happy for her friend.

Boyd nodded. "McFadden gave me the good news this morning. He wants me to second-chair a huge mail fraud case he's handling. An office opened up near his, so it's mine."

"Congratulations. That's great news," Caroline said.

"Oh, before I forget, I need to give you this," Boyd said, pulling a file from his briefcase. "Shaina Parker over in the gangs unit gave me the docket for Fernando Gonzalez's case, as well as some stuff from her files that you might find useful. These are the materials the judge considered in his criminal action—all of the information's public, but it takes forever for it to get uploaded and archived on the court's server. I know you don't have time to wait, so I went ahead and made copies of everything for you."

"Thanks," Caroline said, taking the file folder. She appreciated the peace offering.

"For what it's worth, I think you might be right that Rogelio Gonzalez is involved in his brother's drug business," Boyd said. "Rogelio and Fernando actually own Rogelio's apparel business together. Rogelio is the general partner. Fernando is the passive partner. Fernando's been bragging in prison that his brother owns a big compound down in Guadalajara."

"That's a lot of lingerie," Caroline mused. "If I find out anything useful about Rogelio, I'll let you know."

"If you find something, please tell Shaina Parker directly. She's been trying to figure out how to get at Rogelio. You'd be doing her a favor if you come up with anything."

"Understood. If I come up with anything, it'll be soon," Caroline said. Mateo Hidalgo's next hearing was in less than two weeks. If she didn't find something by then, she never would.

"Great, I'll show you to the mug shot room," Boyd said, holding open the door of the station. "Let's go find that woman who stole that watch of yours."

• • •

Caroline regarded the two computers sitting on the long wooden table. The pixelated screen savers attested to their age. She wouldn't have been surprised to learn they ran on DOS.

Behind the computers, an interior window faced the break room. Some joker had tuned the television to C-SPAN, where a row of senators silently debated something. The screen filled half the wall, a taxpayer expenditure devoted to the important purpose of ensuring the police could watch football at a scale similar to real life.

Boyd pointed her toward a battered chair in front of one of the computers.

"Our database is huge—it's statewide. I've put in some search parameters so you're not here until next Tuesday. You told me you're looking for a Caucasian woman, thirties, with red hair, correct?"

"She's got a tattoo around her wrist, too."

"Okay, so then you've only got a few thousand mug shots to flip through," Boyd said.

Caroline examined his face for sarcasm. She found none.

"Ring the bell whenever you finish." Boyd pointed to what looked like a doorbell affixed to the wall beside the computer table. "Captain Nelson will come see what you've got."

After Boyd departed, Caroline returned her attention to the interior window facing the break room. Captain Nelson had entered with a parole officer. They sat together at a white table with their backs to the television.

Soon, a third officer, a woman with lieutenant stripes, joined them. Apparently they would be enjoying a meeting over doughnuts and stale coffee. None of them watched the C-SPAN hearing.

Caroline viewed the soundless proceedings on the television for a few more seconds. Whatever was going on, it was clear the nays had it.

Exhaling, she sat down on the ancient chair.

The center sagged three inches, absorbing the weight of her butt like quicksand.

Giving up on comfort, Caroline focused on the computer's screen. She had a thief to find.

• • •

Two hours later, Caroline had seen a thousand faces. Some were green eyed. Some had red hair. Others had tattoos. None was Patricia.

Now they were blurring together.

It was time to stop.

Caroline rang the bell and closed her eyes.

Inside her eyelids, the parade of faces continued, phantom images cast up by her brain. One after another after another. Young women, their eyes wide with mortification at having landed in front of a camera at a police station. Older women, with resignation in their expressions, as if this were one of a series of photographs, taken over the years like school pictures in a yearbook.

But no Patricia.

The watch was gone.

The knowledge settled in Caroline's soul. She'd run out of places to look. Soon Captain Nelson would show her out, and that would be the end of her pursuit of Patricia.

The nays have it again, she silently mused.

When she opened her eyes, Caroline noted that Captain Nelson had left the break room. He was probably on his way to let her out.

The parole officer and the lieutenant still sat together at the white table in the break room. The broadcast behind them had moved on to a story about local government.

On the screen, a woman in a red suit stood at a podium, speaking to a small audience, some of whom held balloons. The crawl at the bottom of the screen revealed it was a ceremony dedicating a new affordable housing project in Pico Rivera.

Smiling, the red-suited woman stepped aside to welcome the main speaker to the podium, a man with hawkish features and a broad smile, wearing a suit without a tie.

Caroline's eyes narrowed.

Something about the man's face was familiar. Something in the pronounced cowlick of his auburn hair. Something in the set of his bright eyes and the enthusiasm of his delivery. Although Caroline couldn't hear his words, she saw how the crowd leaned forward, charmed by his infectious energy. It was an energy she'd seen before.

Suddenly, Caroline placed it: Duncan Reed. The man's face was younger and his stature much taller and broader, but the resemblance was uncanny. It had to be his son.

The eyes of the man at the podium shone with pride as he gestured toward a row of workers in green shirts standing behind him. Some wore tool belts and boots. Others wore hard hats. All wore the same slogan—HELPING YOU HELP YOURSELF—that Caroline had seen on that pamphlet at the soup kitchen.

A prickle ran down her arms.

Oasis was everywhere. On the streets. In nursing homes. And now, apparently, in the construction industry.

The sheer sprawl of Oasis tickled some instinct. Some concern about its benevolence.

Pulling her laptop from her bag, Caroline fired it up to confirm her suspicions.

Sure enough, Duncan Reed's Wikipedia page revealed that he had a son named Simon, who was a developer. Simon had launched Greenleaf Development ten years earlier, parlaying an initial investment from a handful of financiers into one of the biggest development companies in the city. In addition to handling high-end commercial projects, Greenleaf Development built affordable housing and other city buildings. It regularly partnered with Oasis to hire tradesmen.

Watching Simon's face on the break room TV, Caroline marveled that he hadn't been courted by some reality TV producer. He was naturally telegenic. Like his father in his prime.

Fascinated, Caroline opened a recent link on the KTLA local news website.

Simon sat with a journalism student at El Monte High School. The title of the interview, according to the website, was "Partnering with the City to Improve the Lives of Its Citizens."

"Most people don't ever see Skid Row," Simon said, sitting in a simple folding chair in the middle of a school auditorium. "They never drive down there. They never see the tents."

The student reporter across from him nodded.

"But I grew up there," Simon continued. "I spent my childhood working with my dad at Oasis—it was just a bunch of beds back then, plus all of these cardboard boxes filled with these little scraps of paper on which we'd record everyone who came in for help. It was absurd, really. My dad always meant well, but organization isn't his strong suit."

Simon smiled, and perhaps unconsciously, the reporter smiled back.

"My dad's been helping people all of his life," Simon continued. "Even though I've gone in a different direction, I like to think I'm carrying on his work."

"You mean your public-private development projects," prompted the reporter. "You've faced some criticism for some of those."

Simon inclined his head in a way that suggested he wouldn't deny the criticism existed.

"Some people get angry when we tear down an old building," he said, "but the city owns many properties that aren't being used for much. By partnering with us to develop those properties, we create value for the city."

"And make a profit for yourself and your investors?" the intrepid journalist pressed.

"Sometimes," Simon allowed. "But we also assume great risk. When the market tanks, as it did not too long ago, it can become difficult for us to sell our projects. We share profits with the city when our projects are successful, but we bear the risk of all losses when they aren't. It's a 'heads we both win, tails only I lose' deal with the city—the city always benefits from these arrangements, while we sometimes get stuck with the carrying costs."

As Simon droned on about the economics of his projects, Caroline minimized the interview and kept reading.

In article after article, Simon had been hailed as a real estate genius. He marshaled low-income housing tax credits and bonds, land swaps, and private investments to build projects that he sold, often at large profits, according to his public relations people.

His latest development would be his largest yet. A fifty-three-story building to be constructed on city-owned land on Bunker Hill.

Although the city council had yet to approve the project, it seemed a foregone conclusion that it would—and that Simon would benefit.

Five floors of the Bunker Hill building would house city offices, ensuring an anchor tenant. The rest of the building would service high-end clientele. Law firms. Private equity firms. Companies in the types of industries that were least affected by the economic downturn. Industries that might benefit, as well, from the close proximity to city offices and the powerful people that occupied them.

Caroline considered the information.

Like his father, Simon Reed appeared to be a do-gooder. But unlike his father, Simon was making a profit from his purported benevolence.

What about his investors? Who were they?

Caroline probed the Internet for the names of those who were getting rich with Simon. She ran searches for Greenleaf Construction and Oasis. She tried searching the names of the projects those entities had built together.

But she found nothing. She discovered no mention at all of Simon's investors except for an interview where he'd talked about the difficulties he'd faced finding money for his initial projects—apparently, people had been unwilling to take a chance on a new and unproven developer. In the interview, Simon had crowed about how grateful his investors were to him now. But he hadn't provided their names.

The dearth of information bothered Caroline. People who built popular projects took credit for them. Always. Goodwill was a valuable commodity in the business world. Simon knew that. He touted his projects and their benefits to the city at every possible occasion. He marketed himself as the guy with the good ideas who was doing good in the world.

What about Oasis's training program for CNAs? Had that been Simon's idea, too? Was it another cash cow he'd created and now was milking to great effect?

Caroline's searches yielded no answers.

Instead, she learned that ever since Duncan Reed had suffered a stroke, Simon had overseen management of his father's charitable endeavors, including Oasis. Rejecting suggestions to turn over the reins to an independent board of trustees, Simon had insisted on maintaining personal control, citing the fact that his disabled father was estranged from the other Reed child, Simon's sister, Mary, who apparently resented all of the years that her father had spent acting as the nation's father rather than as her own.

There was no picture of Mary on Wikipedia, just a short note about her existence. An afterthought at the end of the Wikipedia entry.

Caroline studied Simon's face on the minimized interview still running in the corner of her screen. The real estate developer exuded charisma. That he'd persuaded city government to support his projects wasn't surprising.

More searches yielded clips of Simon dedicating buildings and appearing at hearings before the city council. In each video, he brought the same infectious energy that he'd shown in the C-SPAN clip still playing on the police break room's television.

Caroline was just about to stop watching when something caught her eye.

The clip playing on her laptop showed the dedication of the newly restored County Law Library. In the video, Simon walked along a row of green-shirted Oasis workers, shaking hands. But it wasn't anything about the revamped building or the smiling workers that made Caroline pause. It was something on Simon's wrist.

A green glint. A square housing. A large face with darkly vivid hour and minute hands.

Caroline's scalp tingled with recognition.

It was the watch. Her family's watch.

She checked the date stamp on the video.

The County Law Library event had taken place on August 31.

That was two weeks ago. Eleven days before Grandma Kate had died.

A flock of goose bumps landed on Caroline's neck and skittered down her shoulders.

"Any luck?" came a voice from behind Caroline.

Spinning around, Caroline found Captain Nelson standing in the doorway, his inky-black hair reflecting the fluorescent lighting.

"Is anything wrong?" the police officer asked. His eyes held concern.

"I'm fine," Caroline said, her eyes traveling back to her laptop.

The video clip had ended. Beyond the computer, the meeting in the break room had ended, too. The lieutenant stood beside the parole officer, showing him something on a tablet.

But neither of their eyes were on the tablet.

They were on Caroline.

The hairs at the back of her neck rose.

"See someone familiar?" Captain Nelson asked.

Caroline opened her mouth to tell him about Simon Reed and the watch.

But the words froze in her throat.

Something was wrong.

The DA's obvious failure to conduct a complete investigation of Oasis.

Chief Deputy DA McFadden's sudden interest in the Oasis matter.

Boyd's promotion to the main office.

Some ancient neural patterning, tucked deep within her genes, hissed a warning. She was vulnerable. Or maybe she was paranoid—that other possibility shouldered its way into her mind like an unwanted party guest.

Captain Nelson raised his eyebrows in silent question.

"I found nothing," Caroline said. "Nothing at all."

CHAPTER 6

Hurrying away from the police station, Caroline tried to explain away what she'd seen. Maybe Simon's watch was just one of a similar style to the one her family had owned. That was a far more likely explanation than he'd gotten it from Patricia Amos.

And yet there was a clear connection between Simon and Oasis—and, therefore, a clear chance of a connection between Simon and Patricia. Plus, Caroline's grandparents had always described the watch as one of a kind. So it could very well be her family's heirloom.

The possibilities chased one another like fireflies at dusk.

Was it real? Was it paranoia?

There was no one to tell her. No one to calm her.

Her mother was at sea, literally. Unreachable and possibly manic even if she could be reached. And her father lived across the country. With his new wife. With his new family.

Seemingly of their own volition, Caroline's feet brought her back to her office.

Absently, she swiped her card to gain access to the elevator.

Unthinkingly, she keyed her password into the lock and entered the small suite.

She stopped short at the sight before her.

A cascade of ruby-red roses filled the entry, their silky petals strewn around the carpet.

Sitting at the desk beside them, Amy crinkled a wad of silver wrapping paper in one hand. In her other hand, she held a framed five-by-seven photograph. The smile on her face suggested that whatever she'd received was better than a puppy.

"Whatcha got there?" Caroline asked, tiptoeing through the flowers.

"Oh! Don't worry about this. This, on the other hand—" Amy opened her macramé purse. She withdrew what looked like a small key fob. Three inches tall, it was shaped like a black ninja, its plastic arms frozen midpunch.

Swinging on the ring beside the ninja, Caroline recognized her own apartment key. She had a copy of Amy's key on her own ring. It was a small concession to adulthood to have a backup key somewhere out there in the universe.

"I did all of those coding exercises like you said," Amy said, removing the ninja from her ring of keys.

Caroline raised an amused eyebrow at the tiny utilitarian action figure. "Thumb drive?"

"He's cute, isn't he? I just had to get him," Amy said.

Caroline smiled. Amy had a penchant for plastic junk, evidenced by the row of snow globes and fading magnets on her file cabinets.

Amy handed the ninja key fob to Caroline.

"If you could do your code review for me before Friday afternoon, that would be super awesome. Then I could go on to the next batch of exercises. If I have time this weekend—Hector and I have some plans . . ."

"Sure," Caroline said, pocketing the ninja. "You're almost ready to apply for a job."

She lacked the spirit to follow Amy's trail of bread crumbs to a fuller explanation of whatever good news Amy was hinting at. Caroline knew she couldn't eradicate the distracting sadness from her voice, and she didn't want Amy to think that she disapproved.

The fact was, she'd miss Amy when she left for a job in tech. What Boyd had said about her inability to trust wasn't totally true. She trusted Amy. Amy managed the practice's calendar. She caught Caroline's mistakes in pleadings. She provided another good mind to help think through thorny problems. And she was a friend.

"Don't get that look," Amy said. "Once I get a new job, I'll still come back and visit you and your totally subpar new assistant. You guys can share your new stories about your adventures."

"Yeah, speaking of those," Caroline said, deciding not to mention that she probably wouldn't be able to afford another assistant. Instead, she told Amy about her visit to the police station and what she'd discovered about Oasis.

"If they're running a big scam, you'd think someone would've sued them by now, right?" Amy said when Caroline finished.

Caroline heard the note of skepticism in Amy's voice, but for the first time, she also heard a hint of curiosity.

"I bet if we could see that Patricia Amos lady's personnel file at Oasis, we'd find out all sorts of useful information," Amy said, her eyes hopeful.

"No hacking," Caroline said.

Growing up, she'd hacked for fun with her father—until they'd gotten caught. Although her dad had avoided serving time for what had really been Caroline's ill-conceived effort to hack a hospital firewall, she still carried the shame of it close to her heart. In leaving software engineering for the law, she'd tried to leave her past transgressions in the past. She knew her dark skill set could still prove useful. But only when warranted.

"Sometimes you're the fun police," muttered Amy.

Caroline didn't wait to see Amy's frown. She knew how Amy felt. She felt the same tug. The ability to access hidden information was addictive. But it was fire, pure and simple. You didn't play with it unless you had to torch something. While that might be coming, Oasis didn't justify a conflagration. At least not yet.

Heading toward her office, Caroline called back to her assistant, "I just need to do a little research. Then we'll decide what to do."

• • •

When Caroline reached her desk, she paused. She had to decide where to begin.

The questions about Oasis had multiplied exponentially on her walk from the police station. There were dozens of avenues she could pursue. Scents she could follow. But only one of them burned in her mind like a need.

"Simon Reed" and "watch." She typed the search terms into the engine.

A cascade of results streamed down the page.

Numerous websites described Simon's watch collection. Considered one of the best vintage collections in the country, it was the envy of the United States Watch Society, which had published catalogs filled with effusive descriptions of his historical pieces.

But nothing explained how he'd gotten the watch. Or whether the watch was even hers.

Limiting her search parameters by date and file type, Caroline focused on a narrower question: *When* did he get it? She limited the results to videos.

She learned that, two months earlier, Simon had given a speech to the Rotary Club. In the video, he wore a white-faced Cartier with Roman numerals painted in black.

Six weeks ago, he'd attended a ribbon cutting of another Oasis-Greenleaf project.

Caroline zoomed in on Simon Reed's wrist on the hand cutting the ribbon.

Again he wore a watch, but it wasn't Caroline's. This one had a black face.

Narrowing the time parameters, Caroline tried again.

The results landed like a kick to the solar plexus: a month ago, he'd donned the green-faced watch. On August 16, he'd celebrated his birthday at a banquet. He'd worn it then for the first time. And he liked it. He'd worn it in every public appearance for the weeks that followed—far longer than either of his previous timepieces.

An unexpected tremor of anger quaked across Caroline's nerves.

Simon Reed was not allowed to like her family's watch.

She wanted to call him. She wanted to tell him that he was wearing stolen property.

But before making accusations about a well-connected man who happened to be the son of a much-loved television personality, she needed to be sure those accusations had some basis in reality. She needed to resolve whether the watch actually was her family's heirloom.

By the time another hour had passed, Caroline had learned about the heyday of the Glashutte, the so-called Silicon Valley of watchmaking in early twentieth-century Germany. She'd discovered that different craftsmen had different styles. But she'd found nothing conclusive about whether Karl Geitz had made other watches like the one Caroline's family had owned. She'd found articles suggesting that Geitz had made limited runs of certain designs, but nothing suggesting the watch Caroline's family had inherited was actually a one-of-a-kind piece.

She'd even tried calling the watch repair shop, but she'd been relegated to leaving a voice mail message.

Caroline walked to the window of her office.

Down below, at ground level, a patch of green surrounded a pond. She knew the pond was home to several turtles. When she'd picked the office, she'd imagined strolling down by the fountains and pond, hanging out with the improbable downtown wildlife. It hadn't happened. With her obsessive working style, Caroline wasn't the communing-with-turtles type, apparently.

She looked back at her desk, where her laptop glowed with information.

It wasn't clear that Simon was wearing her family's watch, but it was possible. And if it *was* her family's watch, the fact he wore it was proof that whatever was going on at Oasis went beyond a dodgy bequest policy and a poor job vetting CNAs. It was proof that there was a connection between Simon and Patricia. A direct one.

When Caroline emerged from her office, she found Amy smiling.

Caroline glanced at Amy's desk, where the new five-by-seven photograph was facedown, as if to hide it from Caroline's sight.

"What?" Caroline asked.

Instead of revealing the hidden photograph, Amy gestured with her chin toward the screen of her computer.

"I found the guy at Oasis who handles all of the job training programs, including the CNA program," Amy said. "His name's Conrad Vizzi."

Wordlessly, Caroline came to stand behind her assistant.

She read Vizzi's biography. The breadth of his accolades and the length of his qualifications suggested a man of at least fifty. But the slight, curly-haired man wearing a blue work shirt couldn't have been much older than thirty. Perhaps it was an old picture.

"I've got an idea for finding out why no one sues Oasis," Amy said.

She prompted the phone for an outside line. Then she dialed *82 to block caller ID and keyed in Vizzi's number.

"This is Conrad," answered a man's voice. A pleasant tenor.

"I'm calling about your CNA program," Amy began. "I'm the administrator of a fifty-bed skilled nursing facility that's just ramping up in Long Beach. We're putting together our staff, and I've heard good things about the people you guys train."

"Thanks for reaching out to us," said Vizzi. "What would you like to know?"

"If you just could tell me about your program, that would be great," Amy said, meeting Caroline's eyes. Social engineering worked best when the target had been induced to talk freely.

"As you may know, we focus on training folks who are putting their lives back together again after suffering domestic abuse or homelessness or incarceration for nonviolent felonies. We do careful background checks, but I just wanted to put that out there," said Vizzi. "Some facilities are uncomfortable with hiring people trying to get back on their feet."

"I understand," said Amy. "We like the idea of being a part of your mission."

"That's great," Vizzi said. The relief in his voice was palpable. "In that case, we have some great people, and you're right, we try to make it work for the skilled nursing facilities we partner with."

Scribbling on a piece of paper, Caroline pushed another question in front of Amy.

"How do you handle payroll?" Amy asked at Caroline's behest.

"Once you sign a contract with us, we handle all of the tax reporting, plus we pay the CNAs directly. We deal with all of the administrative hassles."

"Let me make sure I understand. Our facility would pay you guys, and then you'd handle all payments and tax withholdings and whatnot for the CNAs?"

"Exactly. It keeps things nice and simple for the nursing homes."

"Wow. That's great." Amy paused long enough for Vizzi to bask in the glow of her positive reaction. "There's one small thing I'd heard about from some colleagues that gave me just a little concern."

"Yes?"

"I've heard your CNAs sometimes talk to nursing home residents about Oasis, and that Oasis sometimes receives contributions from residents. Bequests and whatnot."

"That's true, but nursing home residents regularly leave money to all sorts of charities. It's entirely legal. We're very careful in how we train our CNAs. They never pressure residents."

Caroline noted that Vizzi had described Oasis as a charity.

"But what if someone complains?" Amy asked. "I really don't want to get sued."

"We go to great lengths to avoid anything like that. Our policy is to return bequests to families that complain rather than litigate over what a nursing home resident intended."

"This has been very informative. Thanks for the information. I'll be in touch."

Without waiting for Vizzi's response, Amy hung up.

Caroline gave a low whistle of appreciation. "That's one way of avoiding lawsuits. It's genius, really. Just treat complaints by heirs as a cost of doing business. Return the gift and no one has anything to complain about." Oasis's scheme suddenly seemed that much more devious.

"Or maybe they aren't doing anything wrong," Amy said, holding Caroline's eyes. "Maybe Oasis really isn't manipulating anyone to do anything. Maybe they're exactly what they appear to be. Maybe your boy Boyd is right—maybe Oasis is legit."

Caroline knew what her assistant was thinking. Amy knew her obsessive tendencies. Her sometimes irrational tenacity.

"But what about the watch?" Caroline asked.

Amy just shook her head.

"I'm going downstairs to get sandwiches for us. When I get back, we're going to call Vizzi back," Caroline said, heading for the door.

• • •

An hour later, Caroline took up Amy's seat at the desk. She hoped she'd waited long enough not to raise Vizzi's suspicions.

She hit speakerphone, screened caller ID, and dialed Vizzi's number again.

As soon as the on-site director had answered and introduced himself, Caroline started straight in, "I wanted to ask you some questions about one of your CNAs, Patricia Amos. I believe she might've stolen something from a nursing home resident."

"Is this The Pastures?" Vizzi asked. "I've already told Mr. DuBois, we haven't seen Patricia in months. We don't know where she is."

"I'm not calling from The Pastures' administrative offices. My grandmother was a resident of The Pastures before she died and left everything to you." Caroline paused to listen for Vizzi's reaction to the awkward fact. She waited for some hint of panic that he was speaking to a disgruntled would-be heir whose hopes of inheriting had been dashed by his organization.

But Vizzi just said, "From time to time, nursing home residents leave us bequests." His voice rose at the end of the sentence, as if beckoning for more information.

Caroline noted that he hadn't yet offered to return her grandmother's money. That probably came later.

"How long have you been training your CNAs to try to write Oasis into the wills of residents?" Caroline asked. The question was provocative. Deliberately so. She didn't expect Vizzi to admit to anything, but again, she wanted to judge how he'd respond to the accusation.

"Our trainees never pressure anyone. That sort of conduct would go against everything we stand for. Everything Duncan Reed stands for," Vizzi added with vehemence.

"How involved is Duncan Reed in Oasis?" Caroline asked. The television personality's stroke was common knowledge.

"Our whole mission has been shaped by his vision."

"How so?" Caroline pressed, noting Vizzi's dodge.

"Mr. Reed has always been deeply religious. He spent time in seminary as a young man. His mission throughout his life has been to make a difference in people's lives. That's everyone's goal here, mine included."

Listening to the earnest tones in Vizzi's voice, Caroline realized she was listening to a true believer. And yet, those tones were the same as so many pious voices through history whose piety had justified all manner of theft.

"I'll make the same promise to you that I made to the administrator at The Pastures," Vizzi continued. "If we find out anything about Patricia, we'll let the authorities know right away."

"Thanks, but I'd like to see Patricia's personnel file, or at least the information regarding how you vetted her," Caroline said.

"That information is confidential. If you believe a bequest was made in error, I can assure you we'll return it. And, of course, we'll cooperate with the police in any investigation. But we cannot share personnel records with the public."

"Even a member of the public who we both agree had something stolen by one of your residents?" Caroline pushed.

"We cannot turn over any records without a court order," Vizzi repeated, his voice hardening. "It's a busy day here, and I've got to go. I've got an appointment I can't miss. Have a good day."

At the sound of a dial tone, Caroline and Amy met each other's eyes.

Caroline spoke first.

"You heard what Vizzi said," Caroline said slowly, a grim smile forming on her mouth. "Oasis won't give us any records without a court order. Fine. We'll get a court order."

"What are you going to do?" Amy asked.

"I'm going to sue Oasis." Caroline was done giving Oasis the benefit of the doubt. The fact that the entity was encouraging elderly people to leave money to it was suspicious, no matter what Boyd or McFadden or the DA or anyone else thought. Someone needed to figure out how often it was happening, and to whom.

"Prepare a short complaint," Caroline continued. "Allege that Oasis is employing Patricia Amos and other employees to defraud elderly people. Assert claims for undue influence, fraud, and elder abuse."

Amy's eyes held uncertainty. "Do we really have enough evidence to file suit?"

"Sure. You don't have to know the whole story to sue someone. You just have to know enough of it. We've got that. Once we get that complaint filed, we can file discovery requests. Oasis will either tell us what it knows or they'll resist our requests, and we'll get the court to issue orders compelling Oasis to tell us. One way or another, we'll get what we need to see."

• • •

"Serve it personally," Caroline said, handing the signed complaint back to Amy twenty minutes later. The pleading was short, but it would suffice to start the legal proceedings.

"Will do," Amy said.

"You can figure out who Oasis's service agent is from the corporation's articles of incorporation," Caroline suggested. She knew that every corporate entity had an agent for service of process—the person to whom any legal complaints had to be given in order for the corporation to be deemed to have received them.

It took ten minutes of research before Amy figured out where Oasis had been incorporated.

"Nevada," Amy announced to Caroline as she downloaded the articles of incorporation from the Nevada secretary of state's website.

"Interesting," said Caroline from over her assistant's shoulder.

"Really?" Amy asked, half turning to meet her boss's eyes.

"Yes. Nevada corporations aren't required to list their shareholders or board members in their articles of incorporation." Caroline's eyes narrowed at the public filing that represented the birth of Oasis. Nevada's unusual disclosure rules provided yet another way that Oasis had shielded its operations from scrutiny. Yet more invisibility for the shady entity.

"Oasis's service agent is some guy named Mark Roe," said Amy, pointing at the screen. "His office is in an office building down on Figueroa Street."

Caroline's brow furrowed. Logically, the service agent should have been Vizzi or maybe Vizzi's secretary. Who was this Roe guy on Fig? And why wasn't he located on the Oasis campus down on Skid Row?

"I'm on it. Mind if I leave work after I serve the complaint?" Amy asked. "I need to do some shopping." The corners of her mouth curled in a little smile.

Caroline rolled her eyes. "Okay. Let's hear it."

Given permission, Amy squealed and finally turned the five-by-seven frame toward Caroline.

In the picture, she wore a sundress dotted with yellow daisies. Next to her stood her dour boyfriend, Hector. With his gunmetal-gray shirt buttoned up to the top and his domesticated loaf of neatly trimmed hair, he looked out of place next to the Spirit of Spring.

"He sent this, too." Amy held out a card to Caroline.

"'You are cordially invited to join me at Mitchell Cottage, Lake Arrowhead,'" Caroline read aloud. The flowery calligraphy lacked the panache of a real calligraphist. It occurred to her that Hector had probably done it himself. It was simultaneously cute and cringeful.

"He's taking me up to his family's cabin next Sunday for a week. Just as soon as he finishes some changes for his editor to some big story he's working on. He wants me to leave Liam with my parents so it'll be just us."

"Sounds fun," Caroline said, privately adding *for you*. Hector was a reporter. A self-impressed one. In the silver-framed picture, instead of smiling, he'd drawn his mouth into a serious line, as if practicing for the jacket photo of the Pulitzer Prize–winning novel he was sure he'd write someday.

"I can't wait." Amy smiled. "Only downside of staying at a private residence instead of a hotel is that there's no gift shop." She picked up one of the snow globes from the cabinet and wiggled it.

But then Amy's face grew serious.

"Maybe Hector could help us with this Oasis thing?" she asked.

Caroline considered the offer. She had little confidence in Hector's abilities. As a beat reporter covering the San Fernando Valley, he hadn't filed any stories of any real significance. But maybe he'd prove useful.

"Sure," she said.

Despite the audible lack of enthusiasm in Caroline's voice, Amy smiled broadly.

"Great! He's super busy, but I bet I can pry him away for coffee or something after work sometime in the next few days."

"I can't wait," said Caroline.

CHAPTER 7

"This isn't like the time I was investigating dangerous drinking water in rural Thailand with my J-school team," Hector said, stroking his goatee before taking a sip of his double macchiato. "We had the regional authorities up our asses, so we knew we were on to something. But who knows. Maybe this Oasis stuff is something."

It was a tepid endorsement, but Caroline took it. At least he hadn't called her paranoid. To express her gratitude, she restrained herself from pointing out the nonexistent impact of his only real investigative reporting endeavor. Thailand hadn't exactly changed its practices because of his journalism school's blog posting in a California news outlet.

"To know if this Oasis stuff is real, we need to see bank records— so we can see how often it's happening," Amy piped in from the chair beside Hector. She wore an aquamarine dress and matching aquamarine earrings. Her mother-of-pearl-shiny curls struggled to escape an emerald headband arrayed with starfish. Next to Hector in his untucked oxford shirt and wingtips, she looked like a mermaid who'd fallen in love with a Hollywood agent.

"Agreed," Hector said. "The fact there's no judicial oversight if you die with less than $150,000 creates an opportunity for bad people to do bad things. But to put together a story, we really need proof of some sort of abuse. Bank records would help," he concluded.

"We'll get them," Caroline said, resisting the urge to point out that Amy had just made the same suggestion. "We filed suit three days ago. Once we get discovery responses from Oasis, we can make a run at getting bank records."

Obtaining bank records would be hard, Caroline knew. But it was possible. Once she had Oasis's document production, she'd look for a justification for seeking the banks' records. She'd build her case. Brick by brick. Step by step.

"Speaking of filing suit, that Oasis service agent dude was creepy," Amy said, wrinkling her nose.

"Creepy?" Caroline echoed.

"He looked like a vampire. Pale and stringy and tall and weird. He was a dick, too. Just yanked the complaint out of my hand and slammed his door on me."

"Thanks for handling it," Caroline said. No one liked being served with legal papers. Getting a door slammed was probably one of the best available outcomes for a process server.

A waiter stopped at the table, pad and pen in hand.

His businesslike expression transformed into a smile when he saw Caroline.

"Hey there, stranger. I see you brought some friends down to try the new menu."

"Yep," Caroline answered, even though it wasn't true. Her reason for choosing Horus's Egyptian Café had nothing to do with the new menu. Horus's happened to be two miles from her apartment—the perfect distance to get a short run in on the way to meet with Amy and Hector. After the last week's unsettled happenings, she needed to burn off some of her nervous energy.

"Can I get something for you?" the waiter asked.

Caroline quickly scanned the menu. The owner's son harbored hopes of turning his family's restaurant into a gastropub, but the reality was now spread out in front of her in hipster sans serif font on oversize white bond paper, and it was a little depressing. Ra fries. Bess burgers. Anubis wings. My, how the Egyptian gods had fallen.

"Just some fries," she said. Hopefully those were still palatable.

"Sure thing," said the waiter before heading off.

Hector took another sip of his macchiato then fixed Caroline with his gaze.

"I can't promise anything," he said, "but I'll see what's what once you send me your complete files on everything you've found. The process of writing an investigative piece is different for each journalist, but mine requires extensive organization and deep focus. I've got a system for filtering information. It's one of the best systems there is."

Caroline fought not to roll her eyes.

"I'll get everything to you as soon as I get home," she said instead.

Hector began to stand up but sank down again, tapping his pen against his pretentious Moleskine. "You know, I'd have to check our research files, but Oasis did come across my desk once before. It was the last election cycle, and I was slammed, but I did some preliminary digging."

"But then you stopped?" Caroline asked.

Hector didn't have to answer. The answer was obvious.

"What was the story about? Nursing homes? The homeless?"

"That's the thing, it was going to be about unions and a fight with the developers of some city projects downtown. The union went on strike, and the scabs the developers brought in raised some hackles. But both projects came in *under* budget, and the developers and the officials who lobbied for the permits all came out looking like heroes."

"Let me guess," Caroline said, "the scabs were guys who came out of the Oasis program."

"Correct," said Hector. "At first I thought I had an angle there, but it turned out the city had passed a special resolution to allow nonunion workers on projects designed to aid the homeless."

"Do you remember the name of the developer? Was it Greenleaf Development?" Caroline asked.

"Could've been," Hector said. "I'd have to check my notes. When the story didn't come together, I moved on to other things. You know how it is."

He stood up and ran his hands down his shirt to dislodge any crumbs from his muffin.

"If I can find my notes, I'm sure I can find you some leads before Amy and I head up to Arrowhead," he said, giving a reassuring smile.

Caroline wasn't reassured. Her review of Hector's clips told her that his newspaper hadn't trusted him with any major assignments. Traffic accidents and potholes. Not exactly heavy-hitting journalism. He freelanced some features—in *Sunset* and *Powder*. But he'd never done any serious reporting. Never anything requiring real courage or grit. And even when he'd had the chance to do something interesting that took some tenacity, he'd backed down.

Now, he hurried out of the café with his laptop bag slung over his shoulder.

Watching him go, Caroline considered whether he'd be any use at all.

"I know you think he's kind of a douche," Amy said to Caroline when he'd gone.

"I don't," protested Caroline. She didn't dislike Amy's boyfriend. She just didn't think there was much to him. Just a pair of expensive shoes and a fashionably untucked shirt.

The waiter returned with the french fries and a round metal tray with a single sheet of white paper positioned on it, holding twelve glistening hot wings.

"They're on the house," the waiter said. "Omar insists."

"Please thank him," Caroline said, eyeing the virulent red mound of meat. She'd avoided most of Omar's spice experiments, but now, apparently, she was going to have to try one of them.

The waiter lowered his voice to a conspiratorial whisper. "They're kind of hot. You sure I can't get you ladies anything from the bar?"

"Nothing for me," Caroline said without even a glance at the bar menu.

In a show of solidarity, Amy waved the bar menu away, too. "At least you got those boring, solid Auden genes from your dad," she offered once the waiter had left the table. "Speaking of your dad," she continued, "I bet I know a way you could get those bank records."

"I'm not asking my dad," Caroline said.

"He's handling cybersecurity for a bank client, for god's sake," Amy said. "Those bank records would tell us how many times Oasis has gotten money from old people."

"Do you think I haven't thought of that?" Caroline snapped at her assistant, then regretted it. "I'm sorry," she quickly apologized. "I just don't want to call him."

It wasn't the fact that her father had left her mother that bothered Caroline. Not really. She understood the reasons he'd left—Joanne Auden's volatile brain chemistry created a roller coaster that made living with her difficult. Caroline knew that. She didn't fault him for deciding he'd had enough. What she faulted him for was how *normal* his life now seemed. She begrudged him his camping trips and barbecues. She resented his quiet nights and safety. She knew it wasn't fair. He had every right to find happiness. But it felt sometimes as if she was standing outside a window, watching another family opening her Christmas gifts.

"Is it your stepmom?" Amy asked.

"That's part of it." Caroline knew Lily didn't trust her. Perhaps she suspected her stepdaughter had something to do with her husband's brush with the law for hacking. Or maybe she wondered why Caroline had lasted only a month at a prestigious law firm. Whatever the reason, her interactions with Caroline had been cordial at best, frosty at worst.

"Isn't like you'd be asking your dad for money," Amy said, miscon-struing Caroline's misgivings. "He could do this so easily. He could just run a search and send us the results."

When Caroline didn't bite, Amy raised a mischievous eyebrow.

"You know . . . the bank's security isn't impossible. I bet you could—"

"I'm not hacking a bank," Caroline cut her off. "We'll serve discovery on Oasis and see what happens."

"Fine." Amy exhaled a huff of air. She pointed with her chin toward the mound of hot wings growing cold on the metal tray in the center of the table. "You gonna try one? Sounds like the owner's son might be bummed if we don't, and I'm a vegetarian, so it's all on you."

"Fine," Caroline said, grabbing a hot wing.

As promised, it was hot. Blazingly, irrationally, stupidly hot.

Caroline's eyes began to tear up.

She picked up her plastic cup of water with the palms of her hands, her stained, sticky chicken-wing fingers exposed. She drank it down in a few gasping gulps.

While Caroline bounced her knees in agony, Amy paid the check. Then she gestured for Caroline to follow her.

"Come see the new car?" Amy asked.

Without waiting for an answer, Amy continued, "Actually, you should let me give you a ride home. It's getting dark, and you don't look like you're up for running anywhere."

Unable to protest verbally, Caroline followed Amy to the parking lot.

• • •

The cars in the parking lot were mostly hybrids. Priuses and Volts and Escapes. Other than a couple of late-model luxury cars—a white Mercedes, a black BMW, and a silver Lexus—the only other vehicle in the lot was a bright-red convertible.

Caroline easily guessed which car belonged to Amy.

Red as an apple shined by an obsessive-compulsive on speed, the small convertible was much nicer than Caroline's Mustang GT, which had recently started to smell like old socks.

"Sweet," Caroline managed, still coughing from the hot wings.

When Caroline had settled into the passenger seat, Amy gunned the engine and headed out of the lot. She drove north on San Pedro, past the homeless encampment.

In the fading light of dusk, dark shapes moved among stained tents and tarps strung up on the sides of buildings. Caroline knew that somewhere close by in a similar encampment, Uncle Hitch was preparing for bed. Or to eat. Or maybe he was sleeping off a hangover in a doorway. Wherever he was, it was a world away from a sleek red convertible.

Coughing across her still burning throat, Caroline had an idea.

"Drop me off at Il Centro Paletería. I can just walk the rest of the way home."

"How cute, you want a Popsicle," Amy said.

She turned the corner onto Crocker and stopped across the street from the popular *paletería*.

Caroline climbed out.

"Will you be okay?" Amy asked.

Caroline nodded and smiled, because talking was painful. She'd only have to walk six blocks to get home. The canister of Mace in her pocket ensured she'd make it.

She waved as Amy sped off down the street, then she entered the shop.

It wouldn't have surprised Caroline if she'd learned the owner of Il Centro Paletería had sold her soul to the Devil for the secret of how to transform fresh fruit into a frozen bar that tasted more like the fruit than the fruit itself. The place was addictive, as evidenced by the fact that Caroline found herself standing at the counter at least twice a week.

The proprietress was a morbidly obese woman with tired eyes but a ready smile.

"Qué le gustaría?"

"Una paleta de sandia," Caroline answered. Same order every time.

The shop's owner fished a watermelon *paleta* from the freezer, a gasp of liquid nitrogen swirling up around her thick hand as she shut the door.

Caroline attacked the paleta.

As the blaze in her throat subsided, she gave silent thanks that the paletería stayed open late and that she lived in a neighborhood of culinary riches. She had grown up in a world of prepackaged American-food blandness. Mac and cheese. Take-out pizza. Hot dogs prepared in a microwave. The intense flavors of her adopted neighborhood—Salvadoran, Oaxacan, Korean—were the antithesis and antidote to that childhood wasteland.

Caroline exited the paletería at a stroll.

Behind her, she heard the door of the shop close as the owner shut down for the day.

Even without the sun, the residual heat in the air warmed Caroline's skin.

She decided on a route home that would take fifteen minutes. Twenty if she really lollygagged. She wanted time to think.

Hopefully her conversation with Hector had rekindled his interest in Oasis. At the very least, perhaps Amy would find his investigation notes. If Hector wasn't going to pursue his leads, she and Amy could. Unlike Hector, tenacity wasn't something she lacked.

Across the street, another source of light caught Caroline's eye. A car. The dark BMW sat parked on the side of the road thirty yards ahead, its shape etched against the rough backdrop of brick buildings, its shiny black paint reflecting light like a beetle's carapace.

There was movement in the driver's seat as a shadow detached itself from the headrest, shifting slightly. Humanly.

A shiver skittered down Caroline's arms.

There was someone there. In the car. Watching.

No. Caroline stopped the arc of her thoughts. This was the same irrational fear she'd experienced on the fire escape. She'd fought it then, and she needed to fight it now. And if she couldn't, she needed to see a doctor about some meds.

Despite her efforts, her back tickled with the sensation of someone's eyes. Someone's attention, like electricity across the surface of her skin.

And then a quiet but insistent voice spoke to her. A whisper from the infallible part of her soul that noticed small things of great significance reminded her: she'd seen the car before.

The knowledge hit her almost immediately: the parking lot at Horus's Egyptian Café. There had been a black BMW there, too.

Caroline's heartbeat kept time with her quickening pace.

But then she reminded herself that the person in the car might've, like her, developed a hankering for Il Centro Paletería. In a city of millions, more than a few owned black BMWs. Some were bound to be brave enough to seek out the best paleta in town, never mind the time of day. Or the neighborhood.

Taking a calming breath, Caroline forced her feet to slow.

A man in a car eating a Popsicle was no cause for alarm.

But then she heard a soft mechanical growl as the BMW's engine turned over.

She felt rather than saw the headlights sweep over her as the car began moving down the street. Slowly. Keeping pace with her.

She turned a quick corner, and then another.

Behind her, the car followed, turning each corner, remaining far enough back to avoid coming parallel with her, but pacing close enough to keep her in sight.

Caroline's mind cast around for a refuge. A police car. An open store. Anything.

Dropping the paleta on the sidewalk, she reached into her pocket to grab the canister of pepper spray. She flipped the safety off the top. She wasn't going down without a fight.

But then, up ahead, she heard the clang and whine of a trash truck. The sound echoed down one of the small, snaking side streets that crisscrossed the Arts District.

She hurried toward the cacophony.

Soon she saw the truck, blocking the road, its hazard lights blinking, casting amber strobes across the seedy surroundings. Groaning, the trash truck lifted a stinking dumpster up from beside a warehouse. With a reverberant crash, the dumpster reached the apex of the truck's arm's arc, and a cascade of foul-smelling refuse tumbled down into the open top of the truck.

Hurrying until she was beside the truck, Caroline squeezed past the warehouse's stained metal siding. There was just enough room for her to fit, the grease of the truck smearing onto her tank top.

Once she was through, she ran. Until the trash truck moved, the BMW would not be able to follow. But that didn't mean the driver couldn't ditch the car and follow on foot.

Fueled by terror, she sprinted the last four blocks home.

Before entering her building, she risked a glance behind her.

No BMW. No one on foot. No sounds beyond the ambient hum of the city.

Still, she slammed the key into the lock so hard she feared she might break the tumblers.

The metal door clicked open.

She slid inside the entryway then pulled the door closed behind her.

CHAPTER 8

"How was it?" Amy asked from her desk. She wore a peasant blouse and jeans. The splay of red roses that had covered the office floor were now corralled into a glass vase that glittered on her desk in the morning sunlight.

Amy's words reached Caroline as if across an alpine crevasse.

"How was what?" Caroline asked.

"My code," Amy clarified. "Did you look at it?"

"Oh. Yeah. It was great." Caroline dug in her purse for the ninja thumb drive.

She handed it to Amy before continuing her zombielike walk to her office.

She could feel Amy's gaze on her back. She imagined the wrinkle forming between Amy's eyebrows, deepening with concern that the assistant had done something to anger her boss.

But it couldn't be helped. Not now.

Sitting down in her chair, Caroline closed her eyes. She allowed the hum of the traffic outside to calm her. Even the stir of activity in the suites next door registered as comforting, like cavemen rustling in a shared cave, telling her she was safe now. In her own domain.

She'd stayed up late the night before. Again and again, she'd run through the cascade of events that had caused her to run from the BMW. And still, she couldn't decide if her terror had been warranted or if she'd been running from another imagined ghost.

She'd tried to relax with meditation exercises and worry beads. And when that had failed, she'd turned to research. She'd poured her restlessness into her laptop until morning light had tinged the sky.

Unfortunately, the anemic leads she'd followed for hours and hours had resolved nothing. Reputable organizations like the Red Cross regularly trained caregivers to work at nursing homes or home-care agencies. Other good charities used homeless people and ex–gang member labor to build public-private projects. None of these other charities had any blight of scandal. All served the public good.

After a full night of research, Caroline still didn't know what was real. She was just tired. Really damn tired.

At the tap on her office door, Caroline opened her eyes.

"Come in," she called.

Amy stepped inside the office. She held a file in her arms.

"I found out some interesting stuff on Mateo's case." The assistant raised her eyebrows, as if hoping some good news might cheer up her grumpy boss. "Remember that guy Stanton Escovar, the owner of that warehouse where Rogelio Gonzalez keeps inventory for his apparel business?"

"Yes," Caroline said, "the place where Gonzalez has Mateo playing that spot-the-cop game."

Amy nodded. "I asked Escovar how many pallets can fit into each storage unit—you know, in case I wanted to rent a unit myself." She smiled slyly at her cover story. "The answer's twenty-five, not that it matters."

"Okay," Caroline said, her voice rising in question.

"I got Escovar to tell me how many pallets of lingerie Rogelio Gonzalez ships to Mexico every year."

Caroline decided not to ask how Amy had induced the warehouse guy to share the information. She hoped it didn't involve Amy promising to go on a date with Stanton Escovar. There were limits to what a person should do to acquire information.

"Escovar told me that Perez Shipping does two shipments a year," Amy continued. "One in July and one in December. Each time, Perez takes six pallets down to Mexico. The shipping manifest reflects this. Plus, Rogelio Gonzalez told Escovar the same thing."

"Okay," Caroline said again. It was sounding like a math problem. Or a logic puzzle.

"Now look at this." Amy handed the file in her hands to Caroline.

Caroline looked at her assistant with a question in her eyes.

"That's the police report your friend Boyd gave you for Rogelio's brother, Fernando. You know, the file Boyd got from that woman Shaina in the DA's gangs unit, detailing the evidence supporting Fernando Gonzalez's conviction for drug dealing."

Caroline remembered. It was the file Boyd had handed her before she'd gone to the mug shot room to try to find Patricia Amos.

"Read the report from Immigration and Customs Enforcement," Amy said. "It describes a search the Border Patrol did at the Otay Mesa, California, border crossing in December 2015."

Caroline flipped to the page.

In succinct prose, the Border Patrol described stopping an eighteen-wheeler on its way south to Mexico. The truck was operated by Perez Shipping. Federal agents had opened containers from Rogelio Gonzalez's apparel business. They'd found nothing but lingerie.

"They didn't find any drugs," Amy said, "but that's not the point."

Caroline kept reading. Apparently, the Border Patrol had attempted a bust as part of the investigation into Fernando's suspected drug dealing. The bust had failed. The Border Patrol had found only a bunch of panties and bras. Nothing different than what Rogelio had already copped to: selling lingerie both at home and abroad. *Rogelio Gonzalez, Panty King.*

But then Caroline's eyes fell on the number of pallets the Border Patrol had searched.

Twelve.

"This isn't right," Caroline said. "Escovar says Rogelio only shipped six pallets in December 2015."

"Exactly," said Amy. "There's a discrepancy. Someone's numbers are wrong. Either the shipping manifest from Perez Shipping or the Border Patrol report miscounted the pallets. I just don't know what it means."

Caroline just shook her head. She didn't know what it meant, either.

"It's not like Rogelio got caught shipping drugs," Amy continued. "He wasn't. That's why he escaped conviction when his brother went down. And anyway, the shipments are going in the wrong direction— Rogelio is shipping goods to Mexico, not the other way around. He isn't bringing anything into the country."

Caroline frowned. Her headache was coming back.

"I'm inclined to believe the Border Patrol's numbers," Amy continued, "which means Rogelio lied to the warehouse manager and on his shipping manifest. At the very least, he's dishonest, right?" She raised her eyebrows hopefully.

After a moment's thought, Caroline nodded. It was better than nothing.

Satisfied, Amy withdrew.

Alone in her office, Caroline continued studying the file. Rogelio Gonzalez's shipping manifest clearly stated a number of pallets that the Border Patrol had found to be false. But why? Perhaps with enough passion, she could persuade the court to give her just a little more time to keep looking for the answer.

She drafted a quick declaration and attached the materials Amy had found. Then she prepared a request for judicial notice, asking Judge

Flores to review the indictment file from the Fernando Gonzalez matter, including the Border Patrol's records of its search in Otay Mesa.

As an afterthought, she forwarded her filings to the assistant DA in the gangs unit, Shaina Parker. Perhaps the information would prove useful to the DA.

Thanks, came the e-mailed response from Shaina Parker. I'll take a look at what you found and follow up as needed.

Caroline raised an eyebrow. Shaina was a quick draw. After having been blown off by Boyd, Caroline found Shaina Parker's responsiveness gratifying. And encouraging.

Rubbing her eyes, she forced herself to focus on the screen. Mateo's guardianship hearing was in less than a week. She didn't have much time to find out the truth about Rogelio Gonzalez's business. No matter how tired she was or how distracted she'd been by the mystery of the missing watch, she needed to keep searching for answers for Mateo.

She opened the file she'd created about Rogelio Gonzalez. It contained several documents. The guardianship petition. The excerpts from Rogelio's tax return that he'd included as support for his petition. The materials she'd scanned from his brother's criminal files.

Her gaze fell on Rogelio's declaration in support of his petition. In it, he'd described the success of his business, his devotion to his family, and his favorite hobbies, including his newfound passion for boating—something he promised to share with Mateo, if he was awarded a guardianship over the boy.

Caroline navigated to the Department of Motor Vehicles website.

Using Rogelio's address and name, she pulled up his records.

The results were interesting. Rogelio owned a boat: a sixty-eight-foot 2015 Sunseeker Predator 68.

He also owned two cars. A 2015 Tesla and a 2016 Escalade.

Neither car could be cheap.

What about the boat?

A quick search provided the answer: the price of a Sunseeker was $2 million.

"That's a lot of lingerie," Caroline murmured as she prepared another short declaration to file in the Hidalgo matter. Unusual property holdings or assets were an indication of drug money. Judge Flores might find that suspicious, too.

Another tap on the door broke Caroline's reverie.

"Sorry to bug you again," Amy said, poking her head into the office.

"It's all right," Caroline said, waving her inside. "What's up?"

"Oasis filed a demurrer," Amy said.

Caroline grabbed the pages.

She scanned them for the highlights. Or rather, lowlights. The fake charity had filed a pleading that argued that even if the court assumed that everything in Caroline's complaint was true, she still hadn't stated any possible legal claims against Oasis.

Caroline shook her head.

The arguments were almost laughably bad. No court would be persuaded by them.

Her eyes traveled up to the upper left-hand corner of the caption page.

"This is embarrassing work from Buckner, McKinnon & Thibodeaux." She wasn't surprised to see a high-end firm handling the case—it was a reminder that she faced a powerful foe. But the quality of the papers was miles below the firm's blue-chip reputation.

"Totally," Amy agreed, tucking an errant blonde curl behind her ear. "We stated viable claims. An Oasis employee manipulated an old person into giving money to Oasis. That's undue influence. Easy-peasy. Why bother filing that kind of junk?"

"Buckner McKinnon's just churning," Caroline concluded. She hated big-firm tactics, including the meritless motions designed to force the other side to waste resources responding. For Caroline, who was representing herself, the cost in money wouldn't be felt, but the cost in time would be.

She handed the pages back to Amy.

"When's the hearing calendared?" The deadline for filing an opposition to a demurrer was always the same: nine days before the hearing. She'd have to put aside some time to prepare her opposition. Even though Oasis's motion was trash, she couldn't risk failing to oppose it.

"Friday—September 23," Amy said.

Blood rushed past Caroline's ears.

"What? That's impossible. That's three days from now." The deadlines weren't flexible. They were etched in granite by the legislature. And by statute, a hearing on a demurrer had to be at least thirty-five days from the date of the demurrer's filing.

"Apparently, Oasis went into court ex parte the day after we filed our complaint to ask the judge to hear the demurrer on shortened time," Amy said. "The judge granted their request."

"Why didn't we get notice of that request?" Caroline asked.

"I don't know," Amy said, her expression pained. "I was checking the docket so I could create a caption page for our opposition for the demurrer—you know, so I could get the case number and the judge's name. That's when I saw the notation on the court's docket about Oasis's notice of motion to shorten time to hear the demurrer. Maybe they didn't serve on us?"

In answer, Caroline turned to her laptop and brought up the civil court register. The other side's failure to give proper notice of the ex parte hearing was a problem, but it was a mere speed bump compared to the bigger issue she faced: she had a judge who'd thought he or she could alter a statutory notice period. The Los Angeles Superior Court had many capable, committed jurists. It also had a handful of boobs. She feared she might've drawn one.

When the court's register flashed onto Caroline's screen, it confirmed what Amy had said: the demurrer hearing would be in three days.

"Oasis's proof of service shows they personally served us with the motion to shorten time," said Caroline, shaking her head. "More like gutter service."

She released a long breath. She could argue in court that Oasis had lied about serving her. But she also needed to oppose the motion on its merits. One way or another, she had to defeat Oasis's effort to shut down her case.

Caroline closed her research file on Gonzalez.

Mateo's case would have to wait. So would everything else on her desk. The judge's mistake in calendaring the hearing so soon didn't leave her much time to write an opposition.

The arguments would be simple enough. But the stakes demanded that she get them right. Without Boyd, her only avenue for investigating her suspicions was her civil suit. She could not allow the court to dismiss it.

CHAPTER 9

Three days later, Caroline entered the courtroom with the same vomit-on-her-shoes nervousness she always felt before a court appearance. She accepted the queasiness as normal. After a year in practice, she no longer worried that she might pass out at the podium. Instead, she tried to relax while she waited for the battle to begin.

She checked the calendar set out on a fake wooden table at the back of the gallery.

Hitchings v. Oasis Care Co. was first.

Good. Less time for panic attacks.

She caught the bailiff's eye.

He waved her forward, inviting her to get her materials prepared at counsel's table.

Caroline took her seat at the thick wooden table. She opened her laptop and pulled up the relevant pages of the cases describing the elements of undue influence and elder abuse. Beside her laptop, she mounted her tablet, where she'd loaded the demurrer papers.

Ready to go.

Taking a calming breath, she pulled the strand of worry beads from her pocket. Looping them around her hand, she closed her eyes and let her fingers travel through the onyx stones.

Behind her, the low door that separated the gallery from the counsels' tables clicked.

A shuffle of movement told Caroline her opponent had arrived.

She turned to see a man in a navy suit towing a rolling briefcase topped with a small bronze tag with the firm name and address. With his gray hair trimmed close against his scalp, the lawyer had the half-asleep poise of someone who'd been to court thousands of times. A poise that Caroline could only hope to achieve someday.

Suddenly, something occurred to Caroline: Oasis didn't have an associate or even a junior partner handling the hearing. Oasis had a senior partner presenting argument. Perhaps he'd come to do damage control? Maybe he'd seen the sorry state of the demurrer that some associate had filed and he'd come to try to salvage the situation?

When the gray-haired lawyer reached his chair at the table across from Caroline's, he snapped open his briefcase. With practiced movements, he removed a thick book, which he positioned in front of him.

Even without seeing the title, Caroline knew it was *The California Reports*. The book was one in a series that had reported California case law for more than a hundred years. No lawyer under fifty years old read anything in hard copy anymore, now that Westlaw and Lexis and a dozen other web-based services published all California case authority online. But the library at Hale Stern had been filled with the tan volumes.

At another click from the gate, Caroline turned to see Conrad Vizzi.

She recognized the job-training director from his picture on the Oasis website's biography. With curly brown hair and a slight physique, he cut a decidedly unimposing figure. Instead of a blue work shirt, he wore an inexpensive suit—the kind of humble garb that endeared litigants to judges and juries.

Ignoring Caroline's presence, Vizzi handed a note to his lawyer, then retreated to his seat in the gallery.

The senior litigator tilted his gray head as he read the note.

With a hint of a smile flickering across his wrinkled features, he glanced at Caroline.

Flushing, Caroline looked away.

"Good morning," the senior litigator said in her direction, forcing her attention to him and to her own awkwardness.

"Good morning to you, too," Caroline answered, meeting his eyes.

The senior lawyer leaned back confidently in his chair.

He looked Caroline over.

Then he cocked his head and raised an amused eyebrow.

"How old are you?" he asked. A note of paternalistic scorn colored his voice, and Caroline heard the parade of indictments tucked like time bombs in the question. She was too young. Too inexperienced. Too inadequate to sit opposite him.

Caroline weighed how to respond.

She eyed the tan volume of *The California Reports*.

Then she met the senior litigator's smug half grin.

"How old are *you?*" she asked, forcing every negative implication she could pack into the four words.

She watched the senior litigator's eyes drop to the volume on his table, then come back up to meet hers. The grin had left his face.

At the front of the courtroom, the bailiff stood.

In Pavlovian response, the courtroom hushed.

"Come to order. Court is now in session," the bailiff called, his voice formal and the words formulaic. "The Honorable Beatrice S. Chandler presiding."

Judge Chandler emerged from her chambers.

Caroline recognized her from the court's website. The official judicial biography indicated that Judge Chandler had graduated from some no-name law school and received her appointment after only three years as an assistant district attorney. Must be nice to be the daughter of the governor's biggest campaign contributor, Caroline reflected.

Judge Chandler sat down on the high-backed leather armchair.

"Please state your appearances," she ordered the waiting attorneys.

"Caroline Auden for plaintiff."

"Francis Thibodeaux for the defense."

"I'd like to hear from the defense first," said Judge Chandler. "Since it's your demurrer."

Caroline poised her ballpoint pen above her legal pad, preparing to take notes. In longhand. Despite her love of technology, she'd learned that handwritten notes worked better than trying to navigate on an iPad or carry a laptop up to the podium when it came time for her to argue. With practice, she'd gotten fast at jotting down her opponents' arguments so that she could rebut them, one by one.

Now she readied herself to summarize Thibodeaux's arguments. They'd be strong. Presenting them had to be why he'd come to court himself rather than sending an associate.

Caroline had considered just arguing waiver—that Oasis's failure to previously raise whatever arguments Thibodeaux was now going to make barred the court from hearing those new arguments. But she'd decided that she'd need to be ready to answer whatever new arguments he made, as well.

Thibodeaux rose from his chair. He made no move to approach the podium that stood between the two counsels' tables.

"I'm comfortable submitting on our papers," he said. Then he sat down.

A rush of blood sped past Caroline's ears.

Had she heard right? Was this senior litigator from a well-respected firm just submitting on the weak arguments in the demurrer itself? His firm's arguments leaked like a torpedoed World War II cargo convoy. He couldn't possibly win on his papers.

"Okay, Mr. Thibodeaux. That's fine. Thank you," said the judge, turning to Caroline. "Please go ahead."

Caroline left her blank legal pad at counsel's table and went to stand at the podium. She tried to divine why Judge Chandler wanted her to present argument when everything had already been briefed in her papers and the other side had essentially abdicated.

"Thank you, Your Honor," she began. "First, I'd like to bring up the obvious defects in service—we received no notice of the ex parte hearing."

The judge shrugged. "Your appearance here today cures any defect in notice."

Caroline's face flushed. An attorney's appearance couldn't waive a defect in service.

But Judge Chandler was already thumbing through the next file on her desk.

"All right, then I'll reach the merits of our opposition to Oasis's demurrer," Caroline said, "I'd like to take a moment to review the elements of an undue influence cause of action."

"Let me stop you right there," said Judge Chandler, holding up a well-manicured hand. "I know the elements of the claim. I have a different question for you."

Caroline waited to hear what that question was.

"Don't you have to present evidence that the decedent's will was overborne?" asked the judge.

"Yes. That's my trial burden."

"But not now?"

"No, Your Honor. At this early stage, we need only allege a cause of action. We don't have to prove it yet. A demurrer just asks whether, assuming the truth of everything I've said in my complaint, I've properly stated my causes of action. I don't have to put on proof until trial."

"I'm not sure I can agree," said Judge Chandler.

Caroline blanched. How could the judge not agree? Those were the governing standards. Demurrers didn't require evidence. Proof of a claim came later. Surely this judge knew that.

"Can you give me an offer of proof?" the judge asked.

"An offer of proof?" Caroline echoed.

"Yes, please tell me what evidence you plan to proffer to prove that Katherine Hitchings didn't intend to leave her estate to Oasis Care."

"Your Honor, with all due respect," Caroline began, even though she knew that any statement beginning *with all due respect* usually connoted anything but, "offers of proof aren't relevant at the demurrer stage. This court must decide only whether my complaint alleges facts satisfying each of the legal elements of undue influence. The answer is indisputably yes. If it's helpful, I can go through each of the paragraphs of our complaint to explain which element it satisfies—"

"That won't be necessary," said the judge, holding up a hand. "I just want to know if you've got an offer of proof you can make here today."

"We're just beginning to conduct discovery, Your Honor, so we can—"

"I'm not interested in what discovery you're serving. I just want to get a picture of what kind of showing you plan to make."

"But finding evidence is the whole point of discovery. It's the plaintiff's means for marshaling evidence to support the allegations in the complaint." When the judge didn't respond, Caroline continued, "We ask that the other side turn over documents or respond to requests for admission. The other side's responses to those discovery requests become the backbone of our evidentiary presentation at trial."

"So you don't have an offer of proof," said the judge.

Caroline was mute for a moment, in disbelief she was having to explain this to a sitting judge. "No, but I don't need one—"

"I've got a busy calendar today, so I'd like to move on," said Judge Chandler. She turned to the other counsel's table. "Mr. Thibodeaux, do you have anything you'd like to add?"

The senior litigator half rose from his chair.

"No, Your Honor," he said before sitting back down.

"Well, okay, then Oasis's demurrer is sustained without leave to amend," the judge announced. "Defense to give notice." She glanced at her clerk. "Please call the next case."

Caroline remained standing. Just like that, her case was dead. Unbelievable.

She was dimly aware of the clerk calling the next case. She watched her hands gather her things. As if underwater, she vacated counsel's table so that the next attorney could take her spot.

What had just happened?

The whole hearing had gone horribly wrong. Somehow, the court had twisted, abused, and shot her case in the head. She'd appeal Judge Chandler's ruling, of course. An error this egregious might even rouse the affirming machine that was the court of appeal and compel it to reverse. But the appellate process was slow. It would take a year—maybe more—to undo the damage that one incompetent judge had wrought in five minutes.

Ahead of Caroline, Francis Thibodeaux paused at the short little swinging door that separated the counsels' tables from the gallery. Someone held the door open for him.

Vizzi.

As Thibodeaux pulled his rolling briefcase through the swinging door, Vizzi put a hand on his shoulder, clasping it in congratulations.

Following the two men out of the courtroom, Caroline watched their interaction as they stopped to chat beside the elevator. This wasn't the first time these two men had met, she realized. Their body language was too comfortable. Too at ease. They joked with the rapport of old friends, not the semidistant cordiality of client and attorney.

Perhaps they'd been here before? Perhaps they'd defeated other efforts to probe Oasis?

Caroline made a mental note to try again to see if any beneficiaries had ever sued Oasis. Some jurisdictions didn't have their records online. Maybe sending an attorney service down to the courthouse could yet yield evidence of past complaints.

Thibodeaux's phone rang.

Pulling it from his pocket, he stepped aside. He waved for Vizzi to go ahead down the elevator without him.

Alone in the hallway, Caroline felt suddenly conspicuous standing beside the courtroom's doors. She had little excuse to linger.

Steeling herself, she approached the elevator and Thibodeaux, who stood a few feet away from it, talking on his cell phone.

She pressed the call button and hoped the elevator came quickly.

But in a continuation of the morning's bad luck, Thibodeaux's call ended.

Pocketing his phone, he came to join Caroline in front of the doors.

"Nice try in there," Thibodeaux said, his eyes watching the elevator floor indicator.

Caroline had no ready retort. He'd won ugly, but he'd won.

The elevator doors opened onto an empty car.

More bad luck.

Caroline entered. Thibodeaux followed, positioning himself as elevator decorum required—in the opposite corner of the back wall, facing the doors.

As the elevator descended at glacial speed down the ten floors to the courthouse lobby, Caroline prayed to whichever deities would listen that Thibodeaux wouldn't say anything more to her. She prayed he'd parked in a different parking structure than she had.

Didn't matter, she decided. Whichever way he went, she'd go in the opposite direction.

But when the elevator's doors opened, Thibodeaux turned toward Caroline, forcing her to meet his eyes. A sympathetic little smile played at the corners of his mouth.

Caroline braced herself for another dose of condescension.

But Thibodeaux's words shocked her.

"Sometimes who you know is more important than what you know," he said with an unmistakable smirk.

Then he turned and walked away, leaving a stunned Caroline alone in a crowded lobby.

• • •

Caroline had planned to return to her office. But she couldn't.

Thibodeaux's words prevented her. They required rumination. They required study.

Sometimes who you know is more important than what you know.

Had Oasis's attorney just confessed to buying the judge?

Caroline turned Thibodeaux's words over like a child examining a seashell in the sun. She could divine no other possible meaning.

The lame demurrer. The terrible judge. The smug, high-flying attorney.

The whole thing smelled of conspiracy.

The weight of the debacle carried Caroline down to Spring Street. The court of appeal building was there, just a few blocks away. Someday, her civil suit might rise from the dead in that building. But for now, she had nothing. No criminal suit and now no civil suit. Add to that an icing of potential judicial malfeasance at best, and corruption at worst, and Caroline could not return to the office.

She needed to walk. She needed to think.

As she left the towering buildings of Bunker Hill for the grittier flats east of downtown, Caroline's back warmed with sweat. She contemplated heading back to the cool refuge of her office, with its calming familiarity. Its familiar light filtering into its familiar spaces. Its familiar hum of office equipment. Its distant rattle and thump of the elevator.

Its rustle of tenants in the suites beside hers. All would soothe her, she knew.

But even though the day scorched and her feet begged for release from her pumps, she ignored the temptation to flee to her office and shut the door.

She slung her jacket over one arm and kept marching.

She needed someone to talk to.

CHAPTER 10

"Am I crazy to think they bought off the judge?" Caroline asked.

She stood in the corner of the bedroom, watching Amy pack. The number of dresses alone suggested Amy would be changing outfits three or four times a day in Lake Arrowhead.

"I'll admit there have been some times in the last week when I've thought you were obsessing a little too hard over Oasis," Amy said, lifting another pile of clothes into the suitcase on her bed.

Caroline nodded. She'd suspected as much.

"But I keep thinking to myself that a lot of people might've said you were acting crazy before you pulled off that last win at Hale Stern," Amy continued. Her eyes flickered up to the picture of her son, Liam, smiling from a frame on the dresser.

Caroline nodded again. She'd never told Amy the details of how she'd defeated the biotech company whose deadly product almost killed Amy's son. She'd never revealed the risks she'd taken. The information she'd stolen. None of it mattered to Amy. In her eyes, Caroline was a hero. Liam's survival was the proof of it.

"I don't think you're crazy to think they bought off the judge," Amy said, finally answering Caroline's question. She gestured with her chin toward the computer on her desk. "It's time," Amy finished simply.

Caroline stayed still. She'd put Amy off before when the assistant had suggested hacking. After almost getting caught in high school for breaching a hospital firewall for fun, Caroline was circumspect about invading anyone's privacy. But she'd run out of options. She'd grown certain not only that Oasis was engaging in criminal activity, but that no one would ever bring the fake charity to justice.

Wordlessly, Caroline sat down at Amy's desk.

Before she could begin, she heard the padding of feet approaching.

Seconds later, a small boy entered the room. With white-blond hair and large green eyes, Liam reminded Caroline of one of the angels painted on the ceiling of the Sistine Chapel. In his hand, he held a piece of paper, which he offered to her.

Caroline smiled down at it. Liam had drawn three bigheaded people standing in front of a building. His mom and himself, standing side by side. Another form stood behind and to the side, wearing glasses, the mouth drawn in a slim, serious line. Hector, Caroline identified him.

"Is this your house?"

"Uh-huh," confirmed Liam. "And my family."

"Liam's hoping if he kisses up to Hector, he'll get to come with us to Arrowhead the day after tomorrow."

The little boy's head came up fast, his eyes widening.

"Moms just know stuff, baby," Amy said, placing her hand on her son's head. "Now go pack up for Grandma and Grandpa's house."

With a huff, Liam left, casting a backward look toward his mom.

Caroline watched Liam fondly as he departed. She treasured the drawings he'd given to her during the last year. She knew others did, too. His grandparents. Amy's sister. Even the landlord.

It occurred to Caroline that Liam was close in age to Mateo Hidalgo. But unlike Mateo, whose fate would be decided at a hearing in four days, Liam had a stable home. He had a mother who thought his every utterance was worth recording. Every piece of art worth saving. Every fart worth bottling. And he had grandparents. Cousins. Even Hector had taken the boy into his heart.

Caroline wished Mateo had that kind of support. Instead, he had a distracted lawyer who hadn't found any solid proof that his would-be guardian was a criminal. Beyond the discrepancy in the shipping records and Rogelio Gonzalez's ownership of suspiciously expensive vehicles, she'd found nothing casting aspersions on his character, let alone doubt on his story. She'd try her best at Monday's hearing, but she faced the prospect of another legal failure on the near horizon.

"Liam will come back in a few minutes," Amy said, shaking Caroline from her reverie.

Caroline understood. If they were going to do any hacking, it needed to happen quickly.

She placed the drawing aside and brought her fingers to the keyboard.

She began by routing through a VPN to hide her IP address. Then she navigated to Oasis's website: www.oasiscareco.org.

An image of two men in green shirts and tool belts building a house anchored the homepage. A list of Oasis's good works crawled across the top: *Jobs. Support. Housing. Counseling.*

But Caroline wasn't interested in hearing about how great Oasis was. She was interested in finding out what Oasis knew about Patricia Amos.

She typed "www.oasiscareco.org/admin" into the URL pane.

A sign-in panel popped up, asking for the website administrator's username and password.

Caroline typed "admin" into the username.

For the password, she tried the most obvious six-digit passwords—"123456," "111111," and "passwd."

None of them worked. That meant she needed to find another way to access the site.

"Could be an old PHP application," she muttered, cocking her head at the website.

To test her hypothesis, she typed a semicolon into the username field and hit "Enter."

The resulting error message came back instantly:

Microsoft OLE DB Provider for ODBC Drivers error '80040e14'

[Microsoft][ODBC SQL Server Driver][SQL Server] Unclosed quotation mark before the character string ".

/target/target.asp, line 113

Although indecipherable to most people on the planet, the message was a gold mine of information for Caroline. The "SQL" in the code told her it was written in Structured Query Language, the standard language for communicating with a database. Properly manipulated, she could use it to retrieve data from Oasis's database.

But first she had to get inside.

She brought up the log-in panel again. This time she focused on the username field.

There, she typed in a short line of SQL code: *admin' OR 1=1;*

"I'm going to use SQL injection to trick Oasis's website into letting us in as though we're the website administrator," Caroline said, glancing at Amy.

"How?" asked Amy.

"Whenever you log into a website, the site confirms that the credentials you've provided match ones it has in its database. To get around the fact that we don't actually have a password or username, I'm writing code telling Oasis's website that so long as one equals one, it should let us in."

"But one always equals one," Amy said.

"Exactly." As Caroline spoke, the screen changed, allowing her into the site.

"Now what?" Amy asked.

"Privilege escalation," Caroline said, feeling the rush of having cracked the first layer of security. "Once you get access, you find ways to deepen that access. It's like being an archaeologist. You keep digging down into the information you've got available so that you can come up with ways to dig down to the next layer."

Caroline hunted around until she found a configuration file on the server with the name "uniform protocol for credentials." She eyed the admin's list of how to construct usernames. Beside each employee's username, there was a long series of numbers.

"The passwords are hashed," Amy said, pointing at the numbers.

"Damn," Caroline said. The passwords had been mathematically transformed into random-looking strings of characters. There was no easy way to decipher the passwords.

She'd have to find Vizzi's password some other way.

Opening another tab, she searched online for data from the LinkedIn hack. Over one hundred million passwords to the popular business networking website had been compromised in 2012. Although LinkedIn had tightened its security since the hack, there were still lists of old LinkedIn credentials floating around the Internet.

It took only five minutes to find Conrad Vizzi's old LinkedIn password on one of the lists. Caroline figured that even if he'd changed his password on LinkedIn, he hadn't changed it for any other sites. Most people didn't like to remember more than a couple of passwords, after all.

Caroline navigated back to Oasis's e-mail server.

She inserted Vizzi's old LinkedIn password into the password field. It worked.

"Let's find all e-mails containing the name Patricia Amos," Amy said.

Caroline heard the excitement in Amy's voice. She shared it. The open access to information that had been guarded was intoxicating. The sense of power invigorating.

Her search retrieved a long list of e-mails containing one or both parts of the name.

Reading the e-mails would take time, but she'd learn whether Vizzi had told the truth when he'd said no one had heard from Patricia in months, that he didn't know where she was, and that Oasis hadn't had anything to do with the theft of the watch.

Caroline moved to exploit the data breach, beginning with the most recent e-mail, a correspondence between Vizzi and Simon Reed, dated a little over a week ago.

No luck yet, Vizzi had written.

Tracking backward in time through the e-mail chain, Caroline found the question by Simon that Vizzi had answered: Find Patricia Amos?

Caroline calculated the timing. Apparently, Vizzi and Simon had lost contact with their nursing home mole soon after she'd quit her job at The Pastures.

But why? What was Patricia Amos's reason for disappearing?

Lifting her hands back to the keyboard, Caroline prepared to open the next oldest e-mail containing the caregiver's name.

But suddenly, the screen changed.

"It dumped us!" Amy said.

Caroline blinked at the rejection notice on the screen.

"We got null routed," Amy said, stating the obvious. "They must have an intrusion detection system in place. They're probably dropping all packets from my IP."

Caroline tapped her upper lip. "So let's come at them from another IP."

"Tor routing?" Amy asked.

"Yes, that should work." She'd taught Amy that Tor used so-called onion routing, where communications were encrypted and then bounced through a network of relays around the globe. Tor routing would let her obscure her identity from Oasis. No suspicious IP address. No null routing.

Bringing up the same admin log-in page that she'd started with, Caroline tried the same SQL injection she'd tried before.

Access denied.

Caroline stared at the message. "They're not just sensitive to my IP address. They must be reacting to the SQL injection."

"Really? How would they know you're doing it?" Amy asked.

Caroline sat back. She could think of only one possibility.

"They must have a contract with Signal Sciences or one of the other good security engineers that'll customize security for clients. I bet Oasis got a security alert and shut down their log-ins. Or maybe they've already patched the hole." She shook her head. "Whatever happened, we're not getting in."

A kernel of dread lodged itself in her gut.

A contract with a highly sophisticated security engineering firm was unwarranted for an entity that had nothing to hide. It was like hiring armed guards to protect a vegetable garden. Or like hiring a $1,000-per-hour shark like Thibodeaux to represent you in what looked like a nuisance lawsuit filed by a newbie lawyer.

Amy lifted her phone. "I'm texting Hector to get his old research notes from that Oasis investigation he was doing last year."

"Thanks," Caroline said, her voice flat. She knew Amy was just trying to help.

When Amy finished her text, she eyed Caroline.

"I'm sorry I'm going out of town."

"Don't be sorry," said Caroline.

"No, I feel really bad about leaving you like this."

"I'm fine," Caroline insisted. Was her consternation so evident? "I'll be okay. I promise."

Liam reappeared in the doorway of Amy's room. He held a blue elephant under one arm and a stuffed leopard under the other.

"I'll be right there to tuck you in," Amy said to him.

"That's my cue," Caroline said, forcing a smile. She'd have to continue her research on her own once she got home. Perhaps she'd try hacking Oasis's server again. There was more than one way to beat security, even sophisticated security.

Amy regarded Caroline with a probing expression.

"Don't bite my head off, but I really think you should try your dad," she said. "That's what family's for, right?"

Caroline didn't answer. She couldn't tell Amy that her father had almost gone to prison on her account. She couldn't tell Amy she'd hacked a hospital firewall but he'd taken the blame. There was no way she could ask her father to risk himself.

Rising to her feet, Caroline headed for the door of Amy's room.

"Are you going to be okay?" Amy called after her.

"Don't give me another thought," Caroline said. "I'm okay, I promise."

• • •

Caroline's ears buzzed with anxiety. Stress. The ambient hum of an unsettled mind.

It was Saturday night, and she wasn't going out.

Instead, she was sitting on the couch by her front door, staring down at the phone in her hands.

What she'd said to Amy wasn't true. She wasn't sure she'd be okay on her own. Since leaving tech, she'd become less active on Slashdot and the other hacker havens. The community of lawyers she'd expected to create at a law firm had dissolved, too, with her abrupt departure from Hale Stern. And her friends from childhood were immersed in careers or children. She knew she needed to begin to reach out. To connect.

She'd spent the day resisting the urge to bother Amy. She knew Amy would be happily chirping around her apartment, waiting to head up to Lake Arrowhead with her boyfriend. She didn't need her boss calling to obsess about Oasis. And anyway, Caroline knew her assistant didn't have the key to unlock more information about Oasis. Only one person that Caroline knew did.

With her pulse throbbing in her ears, Caroline dialed.

"What's wrong?" Caroline's father asked when he heard his daughter on the phone.

Caroline hadn't meant to alarm him, but her voice must've sounded a discordant note.

Taking a breath, she told him about the theft of the watch. She told him about her efforts to discover whether Oasis was preying on the elderly. She described her campaign against a many-tentacled specter that no one else seemed to care about. Except perhaps Amy, who had to care, because Caroline was her boss.

When she finished, she exhaled, feeling some of the tension leave her shoulders.

"I'm glad you called," said William Auden. "This sounds like a lot to be dealing with on top of Grandma's passing."

"It is." A sob threatened to rise in Caroline's throat. She hadn't realized how raw her emotions were. The kindness in her father's tone seemed to call to that rawness.

"You don't have to do this," William said. "I'm not saying I don't believe you," he added quickly, "but you've taken on so much here."

Caroline weighed how to respond.

It had been so long since they'd spoken about anything of substance. They'd tried, but things had been strained ever since he'd moved back east with his new wife. A year ago, she'd seen glimmers of reconciliation. She and her father had edged closer together. But those tentative steps had ended after she'd left Hale Stern. She didn't know if the distance was his fault or her own, but it didn't matter. The effect was the same: she missed him.

"This is real, Dad," Caroline said. "It's real, and no one else can see it."

"I wish there was something I could do to help you," William said, dodging the implicit request for validation in Caroline's question.

"Actually, there is one thing. I need to see some bank records." When she'd dialed her father's phone number, Caroline had told herself she was calling primarily for connection and understanding. But she couldn't avoid the other reason she'd called, too. "I want to get a sense of how often the banks have cut cashier's checks to Oasis. I just need to know if this thing is real. Only the banks will have any records of these transactions."

William remained silent.

"You do have bank clients, don't you?" Caroline asked.

"Yes. BanCorp's one of my biggest." William said *biggest* in a way that let Caroline know he'd really prefer not to lose that client.

"You run routine scans and searches all the time, right? This would just be another one." It was a favor that Caroline didn't want to ask, but all other paths had been closed to her. She couldn't do anything about the theft of the watch, the DA's refusal to investigate, the judge's misconduct, or Patricia Amos's disappearance, but she could still investigate Oasis. And as long as she could do that, she could bind the worry that coursed through her limbs.

"I swear if nothing turns up, I can chill out," she continued. "But if BanCorp has a bunch of these transactions, it'll tell me I'm not wrong. Please. If you could just run a search—"

"I can't just *run a search*," William interrupted, his voice tight. "You more than anyone else should know there are privacy rules."

A spasm of guilt ricocheted around Caroline's chest, but she couldn't stop. A report showing how often Oasis was receiving bequests would either end her investigation or prompt some branch of law enforcement to do something. BanCorp was just one bank. But if it had handled an unusual number of affidavit withdrawals, that fact might prod the police to subpoena other banks' records.

"I wouldn't ask if it wasn't important," Caroline said quietly.

When her father said nothing, Caroline frowned. Once she'd started hunting for information, it tugged at her like a riptide. She could sense the end point. She had to try to get there.

"I suppose I could try to hack—" she began.

"No, Caro. Don't." William's voice was sharp.

Caroline could feel his consternation across three thousand miles. He'd risked going to jail to protect her from an ill-fated hack. In his voice, she heard his fear that he wouldn't be able to protect her again.

"Do you really think there's something going on here?" he asked.

"I don't know for sure, but I think so, yes."

"And you don't think you're displacing emotions about Grandma's death onto this Oasis thing?"

"That might be part of it," Caroline admitted, "but I also think there's something here. I can feel it. I just need bank records to know for sure. One way or another."

Caroline knew that nothing her father gave her would be admissible in a prosecution, but she didn't care. She needed the information for herself. She had to confirm her suspicions about Oasis or stop her obsession. Because that's what it had become. Short of resolving whether her paranoia was founded, she didn't know how to stamp it out and scatter its ashes.

Finally, William exhaled. "I can't give you anyone's names."

"Fine. No names," Caroline agreed quickly. "Just a list of how many times in the last five years BanCorp has cut a check to Oasis based on a death certificate, an affidavit, and a will."

"Give me an hour, and promise me, Caro, if you think this is getting out of hand, you'll go see someone."

Caroline knew from his tone that *this* didn't mean Oasis. It meant her inability to let it go.

But William hung up before she had a chance to give him her promise.

CHAPTER 11

The phone pinged and vibrated in Caroline's hand.

The arriving text surprised her, even though she'd carried her phone everywhere for the last few hours. From the kitchen to make dinner, to the bathroom, juggling to keep her eyes on the screen while she tore off toilet paper, she'd kept it glued to her hand like a new appendage. She'd known that at any moment her father would give her fuel for her investigation or an antidote to her paranoia. Either way, she didn't want to miss it.

Caroline read her father's text: File too big to send via text. Check e-mail.

When Caroline touched the link to retrieve the file, it began loading. Slowly.

Perhaps the connection was bad?

Caroline pulled at her shirt where sweat tickled down her back.

While she waited for the file to download, she headed down the hallway that separated the couch by the front door from her kitchen.

When she reached the kitchen, she faced off with the window that faced the fire escape.

She pushed on it with one hand.

No luck.

Placing her phone on top of the printer that lived on a small table beside the refrigerator, she leaned hard into the window frame until it creaked open and she could scramble out onto the metal slats of the fire escape.

A warm wind blew—soft at first, but then much harder.

Caroline identified the gust: the Santa Ana winds. Given the name by a reporter in the early 1900s who'd misheard "Santana," the Devil Winds had been the bane of the city since before the Spanish conquest. Animals bit their owners when the winds blew. Murderous embers sparked to full flare, filling emergency rooms with indirect victims of the winds' howls. Heat loves heat, and fire loves the Devil Winds. House fires. Brush fires. Car fires. Any small spark fanned into conflagration under the demonic attentions of the winds.

Only those who weren't raised in Los Angeles found joy in the warm nights and unseasonable heat. The city-born knew better than to revel in the warmth that could turn dangerous with a shift of the breeze.

Tying her hair back to keep it from blowing in her face, Caroline looked at her phone.

Her eyes widened.

The list her father had sent was pages long. In the last year alone, BanCorp had cut four dozen cashier's checks to Oasis in Los Angeles County. It had cut thirty-five in Phoenix. Twenty-six in Scottsdale. Eighteen in Las Vegas. And the list continued.

"What the—" Caroline said to no one.

The math wasn't hard. Oasis had harvested millions of dollars from vulnerable nursing home residents over the last five years, with the frequency and number of transactions increasing, especially in the last year. All over the Southwest, the elderly were surrendering their small estates to Oasis. And these were just BanCorp's records. The same thing was probably happening at other banks that Caroline's father didn't have access to.

Whatever was happening, it was much bigger than one woman named Patricia Amos operating at one nursing home in Los Angeles. The scam was massive.

And yet the DA had shut down an investigation before it got started.

Despite the warm night, a cold shiver ran through Caroline's body.

Was the DA covering it up? Were the police involved?

And if they were, who could Caroline talk to?

Maybe a federal prosecutor from the US Attorney's Office. Like DAs, federal prosecutors brought criminal suits against people engaged in wrongdoing. While DAs prosecuted violations of state law, federal prosecutors prosecuted violations of federal law. Caroline just needed a federal-law hook to attract the interest of a federal prosecutor.

She hoped a case involving widespread financial elder abuse triggered some federal racketeering or bank-fraud law. Bringing in the US Attorney's Office might also bring in the FBI.

Caroline's eyes drifted back to the telephone in her hand.

The affidavit withdrawals desperately needed to be investigated. But what if they weren't? What if she was dismissed as a meddling crackpot, and the scam rolled on and on?

Still stung by the DA's rejection, she needed to make sure the evidence compelled an investigation. What additional information would convince a prosecutor to issue subpoenas to pry into bank records?

She dashed off a text to her dad: Names, please.

She hated to ask for more information, but she had to try. If she could give a prosecutor the names of those who'd left their estates to Oasis, the prosecutor could contact the families. Interview would-be heirs. Look for connections to Oasis caregivers at nursing homes.

Seconds later, her father responded: No can do. Privacy regulations.

"Damn," Caroline murmured. She'd expected his response.

Climbing back through the window into her apartment, she hoped the sheer number of affidavit withdrawals would be enough to spark the curiosity of some earnest federal prosecutor.

She wandered into her bedroom and perched atop her featherbed. She let the soft cloud of goose feathers cushion her tense shoulders. She took a deep breath and let it out slowly.

Tomorrow, she'd begin the quest for a federal prosecutor.

On her bedside table, her phone buzzed with an incoming text. Her father.

Got time to Skype? Want to talk to you about Xmas.

Caroline's brow wrinkled at the bizarre message.

Okay, she responded.

Almost immediately, the bubbling tones of a Skype call trickled out of the speakers of her phone. She opened the connection, and there was her dad, sitting in his office at work.

William Auden wore his usual open-collared button-down shirt. Although others in his security firm favored T-shirts, he insisted on maintaining a certain level of decorum.

"You're there late," Caroline said.

"Bunch of us got some stuff to finish up before we can leave." He glanced over his shoulder. "I'm going to be here so late tonight that I think I'm going to have to grab some coffee down at the kitchen. Should take me about five minutes." He chuckled softly. "At least it's easier than the old days when I used to walk our old dog down to the coffee shop. Remember that?"

"Yeah. Lola hated the cold." Caroline smiled at the recollection of her dog cowering against her leg while her dad tried to cajole the canine out the door to join him for his morning walk to get a latte.

"I don't think Lola ever liked New Jersey much. Do you recall what year we moved out to LA?"

"I do, 1998," Caroline answered. It had been sixth grade. She'd lost touch with so many friends when she'd moved. But why was her dad asking her this? He already knew what year they'd moved out to California.

"Anyway, I need to go. I need some coffee, then I'll stop by a colleague's office to give him a report. Like I said, I'll be back in five minutes," William Auden repeated pointedly. "When I get back, I've got a ton to do, so let's talk about Christmas another time."

He stood up and walked out of the frame of the picture, leaving Caroline looking at her father's empty office. His desk in the foreground. His clock ticking on the wall in the background.

"Dad?"

William Auden wasn't old, but perhaps he was under too much stress at work. This seemed at first like a senile moment.

Then Caroline noticed what her father had left on his desk: his phone. It sat next to the keyboard, turned toward the camera on her dad's computer so she could see the small screen. Easily.

Lunging across her bed, Caroline grabbed her laptop and pulled it onto her pillow. She had to move quickly. Five minutes wasn't much time.

She brought up the log-in page for her father's security company. She knew his username was just his name. And now she knew his password—Lola 1998.

But that wasn't enough to get in. The rest of the information would come soon.

She kept her eyes trained on her own phone, looking at her father's empty office.

William Auden's phone lit up with an incoming text.

Caroline's heart pounded.

The string of letters and numbers was the second half of the security firm's two-factor authentication.

Using thumb and forefinger to bring the image of her father's phone into larger relief, Caroline quickly typed the letters and numbers into the authentication pane of the log-in panel.

She was in.

The list of her father's clients appeared in the upper left-hand corner of the home page.

She navigated quickly to BanCorp.

Using her father's configuration file, she found the credentials she needed to access BanCorp's server. Hopefully a single database would contain everything she needed.

She glanced at the clock.

Her dad would return in three minutes. She needed to get in and out fast.

Hurdling rapidly over the last few security barriers, Caroline set her search parameters to capture every account that BanCorp had emptied and given to Oasis via affidavit withdrawal in the last five years. She grabbed all data on the withdrawals. Names. Dates. Bank branches.

When she had what she needed, she sent the data to a point of retrieval and then logged out and killed the video-conference connection.

Smash and grab.

She was out.

With her heart still beating hard in her chest, she navigated to the retrieval point. It was a remote location on the Internet, unconnected to her IP. After opening the files she'd just sent to herself there, she saved the information onto her laptop then got out, hiding her tracks.

Caroline's chest surged with hope.

Now she had a way to prove that Oasis regularly used caregivers to induce residents to leave estates to it. She had the volume of bequests.

She also had the data that Harold had provided—the deaths at The Pastures' facilities in the last five years. She could compare that list to the list of BanCorp affidavit-withdrawal transactions. Not all residents of The Pastures would've banked with BanCorp, but it would still be interesting to see what percentage of deceased residents had left their estates to Oasis.

Her eyes traveled back to her laptop's screen.

The information from her father spanned many pages.

She needed to find a way to corral it.

Opening a spreadsheet, Caroline began inserting each piece of data from each page. Name. Date of will. Bank branch. Amount.

The process of creating the spreadsheet and then cross-checking the information against The Pastures' records would take hours, but it didn't matter. Caroline wasn't tired.

The thrill of the chase still pumped through her veins, enlivening her senses and honing her awareness until there was nothing in the world except the screen glowing before her. This was what it felt like to hack: as if she had cracked through time itself, taking her outside it. While the clock whirled, she felt nothing. No hunger. No fatigue. No interest in anything but the data in front of her face.

Caroline's hands paused above the keys as she realized the risks her father had taken for her. He'd risked his job. Possibly even his freedom. Sure, he'd created some plausible deniability for himself with his trip to the kitchen for coffee and his visit to his coworker, but he had to know it was flimsy.

The significance of his sacrifice settled around Caroline.

Her father had seen the number of hits—the number of times that Oasis had received a bequest in the last five years. Something evil lurked in the volume. He'd let her retrieve the list of names so she could keep trying to bring that evil into the light.

He believed in her. He believed in what she was doing.

Now she needed to vindicate his belief.

• • •

The early morning found Caroline still hunched over the spreadsheet, which she'd privately dubbed "the Spreadsheet of Death." She'd discovered thirty-seven hits at The Pastures' facilities. Thirty-seven times in the last five years, a resident of The Pastures had died and left his or her estate to Oasis. The number was suspiciously high.

And there was a pattern, too. While there were instances of gifts to Oasis from residents of The Pastures' facilities all over the state, all of the transactions in the last year had been performed at a single BanCorp branch. Every month, someone from Oasis went to the Hope Street branch and made a large set of affidavit withdrawals. There was no pattern to the dates, but it was clear that Oasis was doing the errand regularly.

Caroline hadn't been able to fit every piece of data that her father had given her onto the spreadsheet, but it contained plenty of leads. It would be rocket fuel for an investigation.

Glancing at her phone, Caroline noticed a new text. Amy.

Call me.

The time stamp showed Amy had sent the message hours earlier.

Through the window, the first hint of daylight brushed the top of the horizon. But it was still too early to call Amy.

Putting the phone aside, Caroline tried to focus on the screen in front of her. Exhaustion crested, making her eyelids heavier and heavier, but she had one last thing to do.

She hit "Print" to generate a hard copy of the Spreadsheet of Death. The numbers and names. The dates and times. Every entry pointed at a wrongdoing. Each was a possible link to a disgruntled would-be heir who had been surprised by a loved one's gift to Oasis.

She just had to find the right federal prosecutor to hand the spreadsheet to.

Tomorrow, she'd do that.

In the kitchen, the remote printer whirred to life.

Even before the spreadsheet had finished printing, Caroline had fallen asleep.

• • •

The cell phone's ring floated toward Caroline's consciousness as if across a chasm.

It took long seconds to identify the sound.

With a start, Caroline lifted her head from her bed, hair plastered to her cheek.

Light streamed into her bedroom. The position of the sun suggested late morning. She'd slept in. Her featherbed felt warm and comfortable, and the phone was in it somewhere.

She dug through its folds until the sound grew louder. When she finally found the phone, she wrinkled her brow at the caller.

Tracy Garber. Amy's sister.

Tracy had been Caroline's college roommate—Caroline had met Amy through her years ago. Now Tracy lived in Boston. It had been ages since they'd caught up.

"Hey, Tracy," Caroline said.

"There's been an accident," Tracy said in the strained tone of emotional agony.

Caroline's heart stopped.

"Amy's alive. She's in critical condition. Hector's dead."

The words landed like a blow to Caroline's diaphragm. She couldn't breathe.

"Where is she?"

"Central Hospital. Room 205."

CHAPTER 12

Amy's parents sat slumped in the waiting room. Both looked haggard, their eyes haunted.

When they saw Caroline, they stepped toward her, arms outstretched. Even though she'd never known the Garbers well enough to move beyond pleasantries when they called the office, Caroline now buried herself in a hug.

Stepping back, she asked, "How is she?"

"She's sleeping right now," Mrs. Garber said.

"Is she really going to be okay?" Caroline asked. Nothing seemed real. The hospital. The news that Hector had died. That her friend and assistant had been gravely injured.

"She's got a shattered pelvis, a broken leg, a couple of broken ribs, and a punctured lung. She lost some blood. She's got a long road ahead, but the doctors say she'll recover," Mrs. Garber answered.

"In body, anyway," added Mr. Garber. "She's devastated about Hector."

"What happened?" Caroline asked, swallowing the bile that had crept up her throat.

"Accident. Someone ran them off the road up on Highline. You know, the part of the climb up the mountain to Lake Arrowhead where there's that steep drop on one side. Hector tried to stay on the road, but that little car that Amy bought was too light." Mrs. Garber broke off, a harrowed, ragged edge to her voice. "They went over the edge."

"Oh my God." Caroline had driven that road before. She'd clung to the center divider to avoid getting too close to the abyss. She imagined Amy's terror at passing over the lip.

"Their car rolled until it hit a tree," Mr. Garber said. "They'd have tumbled down the hill even farther if the tree hadn't been there. The car caught fire."

Caroline's head swam with dizziness at the horrific description.

"How'd she get out of the car and away from the fire with a broken leg?" she asked.

"Hector saved her," Mr. Garber choked out. "That boy dragged her clear of the car. He got her away from the fire. He died doing it. He'd lost so much blood . . ."

Caroline put her hand on Mr. Garber's arm. He didn't need to say more. It was enough.

She bowed her head at the determination—the love—it had required for Hector to ignore his wounds and put Amy's safety ahead of his own. She regretted every bad thing she'd ever thought about him. His family had to be devastated.

"Can I see her?" she asked Mrs. Garber.

"Yes, of course. She's on pain meds. She's been in and out of consciousness, but you can try. She's been asking for you."

• • •

Caroline entered the hospital room quietly, as if her footfalls could harm her friend.

She almost gasped aloud at the sight before her.

Amy was unrecognizable. Bandaged and broken. Hooked up to tubes and monitors. Her hair was bloody, and her face was swollen.

Caroline's vision blurred with tears.

As if sensing someone near, Amy opened her eyes.

Caroline swiped the moisture away from her own eyes.

She sat down on the chair next to the bed.

"Hey, there," Caroline said, taking her friend's hand. That bit of Amy's body, at least, didn't seem injured.

Amy slowly turned her head to face Caroline. Her eyes struggled to focus.

"Caro?" Amy's voice scratched out the question across a dry throat.

"I'm here." Caroline grabbed the cup of water on the tray beside Amy's bed and offered the straw to her to drink, but Amy shook her head.

"He did it," she croaked.

"Don't talk, honey," Caroline said, offering the water again.

"He did it," Amy whispered again, more insistently.

"Yes, I know. He got you out."

"No. Roe." Amy struggled with the name on her bruised lips. "Mark Roe. Service agent. Oasis."

Though her eyelashes fluttered, Amy kept her gaze trained on Caroline, her eyes holding a desperate need to be understood.

"Roe?" Caroline echoed.

"Drove car," Amy said.

Caroline's pulse quickened.

"The one that ran you off the road?" she asked.

Amy nodded slightly. "Saw him. Blond. Vampire."

A shiver ran down Caroline's arms.

"What kind of car was it?" Caroline asked. She already knew the answer.

"BMW."

"A black one," Caroline finished for her. The car from the parking lot at Horus's Egyptian Café. The car that had followed her from Il Centro Paletería. She knew the driver now. Mark Roe. Oasis's service agent.

But how had he found Amy? Had he run Amy's license plate? Or maybe—

"Did you try to hack Oasis?" Caroline asked.

Amy closed her eyes, squeezing out tears between her blonde lashes.

"I'm so sorry," Caroline said, knowing the words were flimsy. What was she sorry for? Sorry the world could be brutal? Sorry bad things could happen to good people? Sorry that she'd ever taught Amy about hacking? Or that she hadn't taught her enough to avoid getting traced?

Caroline stroked her friend's hand, murmuring words of empty comfort. Amy had always been like the sun. A halo of blonde curls as unruly as her spirit. Her bright, shining friend, always there for a smile, now lay here battered and bruised, with her eyes dark and dull.

"They did this," Amy said, her eyes still closed.

"I know," Caroline said, nausea creeping up her throat again. Oasis had been willing to kill to protect itself, and she'd brought its wrath down on her friend. She'd brought Hector to his death.

With obvious effort, Amy turned her head to face Caroline.

"The ninja drive. In my apartment. Everything I found."

"What did you find?" Caroline asked, her spiral of guilt temporarily arrested by the urgency in her friend's voice.

"Oasis. I found out about them," Amy said, half rising. "Tried calling. Tried telling you—"

"I understand. The ninja," Caroline said, urging Amy back down to the bed. "I'll get it."

Amy let her body sink back into the covers.

"Thank you," she murmured as her eyes finally slipped shut.

Soon, her breath lengthened, growing regular with sleep.

Rising to her feet, Caroline looked down on her friend.

The flash drive seemed irrelevant in the face of the human tragedy in the room behind her. But she owed it to Amy to retrieve it. Hector had died because of what was stored there. Whatever was on it was dangerously valuable.

• • •

Caroline blinked in the bright hall outside Amy's hospital room.

At the nursing station, there were two uniformed police officers and a detective in plain clothes talking with Mr. Garber. The detective leaned against the wall, jotting notes on a pad.

When he finished writing, he handed a business card to Mr. Garber.

Amy's dad looked down at the card, then back up at the detective. He gave a curt nod before turning to walk away, back toward the family waiting room.

At the sight of the law enforcement personnel, Caroline changed her plan.

"The guy who did this is named Mark Roe," Caroline said, stopping in front of them.

"Slow down, miss," said the detective, turning his notepad to a blank page.

He leaned back against the wall, positioned his pen over his pad, and then met Caroline's eyes. He raised his eyebrows in invitation.

"This wasn't an accident," Caroline began again.

"That's what your friend says, yes."

Caroline's face prickled with heat. It was clear from his inflection that he didn't believe her.

"It isn't the meds. She's not deluded. She knows what she saw."

The detective inclined his head in a way that let Caroline know he'd decide for himself. "Please just tell me everything you know."

136

The halfhearted, skeptical invitation was enough. In a rush, Caroline described her previous encounters with the black BMW. She explained how Amy had seen Mark Roe when she'd served him with a complaint against Oasis—such that Amy could've positively identified him as the man who'd run her off the cliff.

"We'll do our best to follow up," the detective said when she finished.

"Thank you," Caroline said. She couldn't ask him to do anything more than that.

But then her eyes fell on the notepad.

It was still blank.

The detective hadn't taken a single note.

Frustration sparked in Caroline's chest. He'd been humoring her. He'd decided Amy was drugged and Caroline was just a distraught friend, mindlessly crediting Amy's story.

She opened her mouth to describe the affidavit-withdrawals scheme and Simon Reed and the watch and everything else she'd discovered. Perhaps if he understood the larger context, he'd shed the indifference he wore like armor. Perhaps he'd feel some echo of his police academy days and the reasons he'd gone into law enforcement. He was supposed to protect people like Amy. Like Hector.

But then she stopped as a different explanation for the detective's disinterest in the details of the accident occurred to her. She recalled the sensation of being watched from the police break room. Captain Nelson's attentiveness. Boyd's convenient promotion.

As he had with Mr. Garber, the detective reached into his pocket and withdrew a business card.

"I've got to go," Caroline said, ignoring the card.

She hurried away down the hall.

• • •

When she reached Amy's block, Caroline slowed her steps.

Her eyes swept the street for suspicious cars. Dodgy people. Hidden lookouts.

She saw nothing amiss.

Still, her ears buzzed with adrenaline.

Amy lay in a hospital. Hector was dead.

The two facts reverberated in her mind like twin explosions. She could scarcely think over the din of them.

She had to get the thumb drive from Amy's apartment. That little black ninja held the key to slaying the monster who'd committed these crimes. Amy had been sure of it.

A shiver coursed down Caroline's back.

If Amy had been run off the road by someone trying to stop her from uncovering the scam, it was highly likely that person knew where Amy lived.

With her heart pounding in her throat, Caroline ducked into the doorway of a Laundromat. The red awning dipped low enough to conceal her presence from the upper-story windows of Amy's building.

Leaning out, Caroline cased the block one last time.

The redbrick facade of the converted biscuit factory where Amy lived looked calm and solid in the morning sun. Other than a handful of Priuses carrying their yuppie owners to work, there was no one around.

It was time to go.

Pushing off from the Laundromat's doorway, Caroline jogged across the street and into the alley between the apartments and the biscuit factory. The insistent odor of trash emanated from the dumpsters of the neighboring lofts. Decomposing burrata, artisanal breads. Overripe summer fruit and rare roast beef. The discarded staples of the hipsterati.

In one fluid movement, Caroline slid her copy of Amy's key into the lock, opened the external door to the apartment building, and entered the service porch.

A row of bikes sat chained to a long rail that traveled the length of the half-finished room. Drywall stopped five feet from the ceiling, exposing a system of pipes and ducts.

Caroline paused again, listening.

The hum of a half dozen laundry machines vibrated the walls, obscuring any other sounds beyond the room. She had no way of knowing whether Amy's assailant waited outside the door. Or in the apartment.

With a shaking hand, Caroline pulled the Mace canister from her key chain. It wasn't much, but perhaps it would give her a chance to flee. If it came to that.

Taking a deep breath, Caroline opened the door of the service porch.

There was no one in the hall.

Exhaling, Caroline stepped onto the well-worn carpet. She commanded herself to walk like a normal person. A friend. A random visitor to someone in the apartment building. Not a freaked-out lawyer who'd just come from seeing her half-dead friend in a hospital.

She hurried up the five flights of stairs to Amy's floor.

When she reached the door of her friend's apartment, she paused one last time.

She glanced down the hallway.

Seeing no one, she opened the door and slipped inside.

She froze, listening.

The blinds were down. The curtains, drawn.

It was dark but quiet—the kind of hush that felt solitary. A relief.

With a scarcely audible puff, Caroline released the breath she'd been holding.

But when her eyes adjusted to the dim space, she gasped.

Drawers lay all over the floor, their contents spilled out in puddles of belongings.

Winter clothing from the storage bins.

Silverware and tablecloths from the sideboard.

Even jars and cans from the recycling bin.

Amy had always been disorganized. She'd prided herself on being able to find anything in her creative chaos. But whatever slapdash organizational system Amy had once imposed no longer existed. In the carpet of objects, Caroline could feel the malevolent energy of the intruders who'd probed the private corners of Amy's domain.

Caroline's throat tightened.

Her arms chilled, prickling with fear.

Run, her mind shouted, almost drowning out rational thought.

She forced herself to think. How long ago had the apartment been ransacked? She'd seen no one coming up the stairs. She'd heard nothing out of the ordinary. Trashing Amy's apartment couldn't have been a quiet endeavor. Whoever had done this must have finished some time ago and gone. There would've been no reason for anyone to stay. And no reason for anyone to return. She had time to look around. She was safe. More or less.

Despite the flawless logic of her internal pep talk, Caroline remained frozen.

Somewhere in the building, something thumped. A metallic sound. A vibration.

Caroline's fingers tightened on the canister of pepper spray.

Closer now, laughter in the hallway.

The rise and fall of voices approached, then receded.

Neighbors. No one dangerous.

Caroline repeated the words to herself until her pulse slowed.

Exhaling, she scanned the defiled apartment again. Get the ninja and get out. Don't linger.

Up ahead, she saw Amy's bedroom. Bathed in light, the small room glowed even from across the living room. The windows of the bedroom faced the side of the building, and perhaps for that reason, the intruders had not bothered to pull down the blinds.

Tiptoeing through the field of debris, Caroline moved carefully toward the light.

But when Caroline arrived in Amy's bedroom, her face flushed with disappointment.

A shaft of light lit the desk . . . a desk devoid of a computer.

Where the high-speed computer had once been, there was now a small mountain of files. Car lease information. Frequent-flier miles. Old tax returns. All yanked haphazardly from the file cabinet and thrown onto the desk.

Moving closer, Caroline tried to fathom the destruction. She'd been in this very room so recently, watching Amy pack for her trip. She'd sat at the desk, researching. Hacking. Now the space barely resembled the place where Caroline had accepted the gift of a picture from Liam.

Poor Liam. He was probably still at his grandparents' house, worried about his mother.

With a bolt of recognition, Caroline spotted her firm's name on a tax return, sitting atop the pile of papers on Amy's desk.

Whoever had trashed the apartment knew where Amy worked. And for whom.

Caroline's hands tingled, cold and slippery with nervous sweat.

Why hadn't she gotten the name of the investigator handling Amy's case? Why hadn't she talked to him more at the hospital? She should have told him everything . . .

No. Caroline imposed the word like a dam against the torrent of doubt.

No.

She needed to remember why she'd come: the ninja.

Her eyes swept the bedroom. The intruders had taken the computer, but Amy's clutter of figurines and knickknacks and snow globes and souvenirs from vacations still littered the space. The ninja didn't look like a thumb drive. So long as it hadn't been plugged into the laptop's USB port when someone grabbed the computer, it might still be somewhere in the apartment.

Caroline didn't need to look far. There, beside Amy's tambourine and finger drum—treasures from her trip to Cuba—the little black shape lay on its side punching a maraca.

Crouching, Caroline lifted the ninja drive from the mess.

The silly figurine held data, every bit of which could be an answer. An indictment.

Pocketing the drive, Caroline fled the violated space.

CHAPTER 13

Caroline didn't go home immediately. Instead, she walked.

She wandered through Little Tokyo, hoping the crammed storefronts and scents of udon would distract her from the foreboding that had settled around her. The destruction in Amy's apartment had confirmed every paranoid suspicion she'd ever had about Oasis. There was nothing accidental about what had happened to Amy and Hector. Oasis was a killer.

Wind blew swirls of napkins in the hot air. Food. She knew she ought to find some sustenance, but her stomach rejected the thought of eating while panicked.

Her office address. Those who'd invaded Amy's apartment knew where she worked.

She couldn't go back to her office. At least not until she talked to the police.

But could she talk to the police? The detective at the hospital had been plying her for information, hadn't he? Or were his questions innocent? She had no way of knowing.

Walking east, Caroline found herself standing at the Los Angeles River. Paved almost completely from source to mouth, the "river" was always misleadingly drawn in some cheerful shade of blue on maps.

The concrete reality resembled no river anywhere in the world. Spray-painted tags blighted the walls on both sides of the concrete trough.

Beyond the barbed wire separating the city streets from the river, Caroline saw a man with a shopping cart. He pushed it down the center of the bone-dry channel. Every so often, he crouched to gather something from the ground. Cans? Bottles?

His deliberate, unhurried movements soothed Caroline.

No one knew where she lived. Other than a lease and some utility bills, there was no record anywhere of her address. She didn't need to run away and check into a hotel.

She watched the man until he'd disappeared under a bridge, probably to find a place to sleep.

It was getting dark, Caroline suddenly realized.

She needed to head home.

She needed to figure out what to do.

But who could she talk to? Who could she trust?

• • •

Five blocks and four flights of stairs later, Caroline stood inside her apartment.

She paused at the threshold, scenting the air for danger, trying to determine whether all was just as she'd left it. She listened hard for some wrong note, some sign that the dark forces that had ransacked Amy's apartment had found their way into her private sanctum.

In the silence, Caroline found nothing amiss.

She exhaled.

Her apartment was safe. Empty.

Before some new fear could seep into her consciousness, turning every shadow sinister, she flicked on the lights.

Her eyes swept the familiar contours of her possessions.

The couch beside the front door beckoned. That she'd left her laptop charging on the coffee table seemed an omen. She needed to go no farther to access a USB port.

Slipping off her shoes, Caroline sat down and tucked her legs underneath her.

She pulled her phone from the back pocket of her jeans. She had a call to make before she opened the thumb drive that now burned like a radioactive isotope in her other pocket.

Thumbing her phone, she dialed the number. Tracy Garber. Amy's sister.

As expected, Tracy didn't answer. Caroline left a message. She told Tracy what had happened to Amy's apartment and warned her of the danger. She urged Tracy to impress on her parents the importance of keeping a close eye on Amy. Caroline realized her message would be cryptic, but she had to try to explain the threat.

After imploring Tracy to keep Amy safe, Caroline hung up.

She exhaled. It was time to find out what the thumb drive held.

Flipping open the laptop, Caroline inserted the ninja into the USB port.

She found one file: "Oasis."

A flurry of goose bumps rose on her bare arms.

"Okay, Amy. What'd you find?" she murmured as she opened the file.

Her computer seemed to slog.

Finally, the contents of the Oasis folder appeared on the laptop's screen.

Caroline's eyebrows knit. The first batch of documents contained Hector's notes from his investigation into whether Oasis had secured a no-bid contract to restore the County Law Library. He'd collected the names of disgruntled general contractors who'd found themselves frozen out of the bidding. He'd recorded their gripes that the city had cut sweetheart deals for Oasis, circumventing union rules on the basis that Oasis was putting the homeless back to work. He'd also made a memo to himself to try to find the full name of a worker who'd been injured on the County Law Library job and who was rumored to be planning to sue Oasis.

Caroline reread the notes to find the name of the injured worker but found a reference only to the man's first name: Jessie.

The second batch of files came from Amy's own hack. Apparently after dropping Liam off at her parents', she'd found an unpatched database vulnerability and accessed Oasis's server. She'd zeroed in on a set of files describing Oasis's construction projects.

The contracts that Amy had downloaded onto the thumb drive showed that Oasis crews were, indeed, being used on city jobs. Among those contracts was the one between Oasis and the city to reconstruct the County Law Library. Its terms were fairly standard. The public-private partnership allowed Oasis to hire contractors as it saw fit and to run the project in its discretion, so long as it stayed on time and within budget. A final accounting for the job showed Oasis had performed well and earned a modest profit. Nothing that raised any red flags, certainly.

A juicier, separate document detailed problems on the jobs. OSHA violations. Union threats. Plus, the injury on the County Law Library job to a worker named Jessie Tuttle.

Caroline glanced back at Hector's notes.

While Hector hadn't found the worker's full name, Amy had. The name Jessie Tuttle had appeared in an e-mail chain Amy had found. Unfortunately, other than the name, the e-mail had contained little information. Tuttle was a fairly common name. It could be difficult to find the right person. But at least it was a lead.

The last file from Amy's hack was a directory of city employees. Parole officers. Beat cops. Court clerks. It read like a who's who of government jobs. Some had asterisks or other cryptic notations beside them.

Then, apparently, Amy had gotten null routed, and that had been the end of it.

The only other files in the Oasis folder were two title reports. After getting locked out by Oasis's security, Amy had fallen back on her skills as a title officer. She'd chased down Oasis's property holdings. The first report reflected Oasis's ownership of its downtown campus. Nothing surprising there. But the second title report was interesting. It showed that Oasis owned property on Parrino Court, on the edge of the Los Angeles River. Oasis had purchased it a year ago.

Caroline cocked her head at the screen. As far as she knew, there were only warehouses in that industrial stretch to the east of downtown. Why did Oasis own property there?

She hit "Print." The property purchase wasn't proof of any wrong-doing, but it was weird—and weird, in Caroline's experience, usually meant something.

A whirring at the other end of the hallway, in the kitchen, told Caroline the printer had spat out the title report. She'd retrieve it later to study more closely.

Leaning back on the couch's cushions, Caroline considered what she'd found.

After Amy's breathless plea to find the thumb drive, Caroline had expected bombshell evidence of wrongdoing. Two title reports, a directory of city employees, a contract to restore the County Law Library, and a vague reference to an injured worker didn't exactly qualify.

Even so, Caroline stashed virtual copies of the documents at the retrieval spot. Then she closed her laptop and rose to her feet.

She needed a break from research.

At the end of the hallway, the kitchen beckoned, its familiar contours faintly visible in the ambient light cast from the neighboring buildings.

Tucking her phone in her back pocket, she left the laptop on the coffee table and headed down the long hall.

When she arrived in the kitchen, Caroline opened the refrigerator and removed the large bottle of water she kept there. She held the moisture-beaded glass to her forehead for a long moment before uncorking it and drinking half.

As she closed the refrigerator door, her eyes fell on the printer.

The title report was still warm to the touch. Under it, Caroline found a second document. The Spreadsheet of Death. That had been the last time she'd deigned to use expensive ink to print something out in hard copy.

Lifting the spreadsheet, she considered what to do with it. She'd have to create a Redweld file to preserve the materials she'd printed out. But even more than that, she'd have to find someone to give it to. As a civil litigator, she had no power to bring criminal charges. She had to find a federal prosecutor to do that for her.

Caroline's stomach knotted around the cold water she'd just consumed.

If Oasis's service agent was the guy who'd run Amy and Hector off the road, Oasis had shown itself to be far more sinister and far more deadly than a monster of benign neglect by nursing home administrators. Finding a prosecutor brave enough to take on slaying that monster with her could prove difficult.

The logistics of finding the right person were thorny, too. Sending an e-mail to her law school classmates seeking a referral would prompt another flurry of questions about why she'd left her job at Hale Stern. Though packaged as good-natured curiosity, the root of those questions would be prurient interest—the same prurient interest that made people slow down to get a good look at a car wreck. In the year since she'd left her first law job, Caroline had avoided those questions. She'd have to dodge them again—a prospect she didn't relish.

Best to get started now, she decided. Her best friend was in the hospital. Hector was dead. A little embarrassment was nothing in comparison.

Replacing the bottle in the refrigerator, she tucked the spreadsheet into her front pocket. She'd create a hard-copy file of the materials she'd found. Something she could hand to a prosecutor.

But before she could move, Caroline heard an engine in the distance.

A motorcycle. Approaching slowly from somewhere down the street.

It stopped outside her building, its engine shutting off with a guttural purr.

Caroline looked out her kitchen window, the one that fronted the apartment building.

Four stories below, a man clad in leather climbed off a Ducati. His long leg easily cleared the top of the bike as he dismounted. Straightening to standing, he hunched his shoulders in the habit of those accustomed to shrinking slightly to fit through doorways not built for height.

He took off his helmet, and long blond hair fell to the middle of his back.

Even before he turned enough for the streetlights to reflect off his pale skin, Caroline knew who he was: Oasis's service agent. Mark Roe, or whatever his real name was. The man who Amy said had run her and Hector off the mountain road.

Caroline's arms prickled with warning.

She watched in fascinated horror as he approached the apartment building's outer gate and cocked his head at the buzzer panel of names.

Using the flats of his hands, he pushed all of the call buttons for all of the residents.

A chorus of hellos erupted from the intercom, audible to Caroline even four stories up.

Then some careless resident buzzed the gate open without waiting for an answer.

The hit man was inside the building.

• • •

Backing two steps away from the window, Caroline tried to think.

She needed to get out. She needed to run.

But if she fled into the hallway, she'd run into the hit man.

She had to call the police.

There was no time. The police couldn't respond fast enough.

Caroline's eyes raked the kitchen for a weapon.

A cooking knife?

The man who'd gotten off the motorcycle had to be close to six feet five inches. She couldn't beat him in a knife fight.

She grabbed at the nearest drawer, yanking it open with so much force that the contents skittered to the back as if trying to escape her hand. Tape measure. Pens.

She couldn't fight. She had to escape.

She lunged toward the other window, the one that faced the fire escape. Below Caroline's landing, a rusted staircase extended two stories down to another landing, and then to a ladder, and then, below that, to the alley.

She flipped open the lock and pushed hard at the frame.

It didn't move.

Caroline heard a distant thumping. Heavy footfalls. Man size. Moving with purpose down the hall outside her apartment.

She leaned into the window hard, pushing with all her weight, grunting with the effort.

But the barrier remained solid as a wall.

Grabbing a dish towel, Caroline wrapped it around her hand, ready to shatter the glass.

But then she paused. She was barefoot and the window was large. The shards could injure her, hampering any chance of escape. She needed a different plan.

A tapping came from the door of her apartment. Quiet at first. Growing insistent.

Caroline froze. The man who'd killed Hector was standing right on the other side of the thin wooden door that separated her apartment from the hallway.

With keening desperation screaming in her ears, she slammed the palm of her hands against the frame of the window.

It didn't move.

Frantically, she tried again. And again.

At the other end of the apartment, Caroline heard a rustling. Then the faint tickle of metal against metal. Lock-picking tools, Caroline identified the likely source of the sound.

She only had seconds before the man was inside.

She had to get out now.

Caroline turned back to the window.

But this time, she took a slow breath. The window had never beaten her before. It would not beat her today. It needed to open. Right. Now.

With a sharp pop, she slammed both palms into the top of the frame, concerted effort, directed energy. And the seal separated.

She shouldered the window frame open and scrambled outside.

The warm Santa Ana winds swirled her hair, lifting it in updrafts from the alley below.

She gripped the railing and swung around. Inside her apartment, at the far end of the hall, the front door swung open and the tall, blond man entered.

His head snapped up as he spotted Caroline on the fire escape.

Predator and prey locked eyes for a timeless moment, burning up the air between them. Sizzling with concentrated attention.

And then Caroline ran.

Vaulting down the first three stairs of the fire escape, she flew downward.

She hit the second floor, landing hard.

Her gaze pivoted toward the window of the apartment beside her. She didn't know who lived there, but maybe they could help.

The apartment was dark. No one home.

She felt rather than heard a heavy rattle from above as the hit man stepped onto the fire escape. The stairway vibrated with his steps as he came after her. Thumping, shaking footfalls, like the Giant coming for Jack, who'd dared to climb the beanstalk.

Caroline hurtled onward, her plunge down the stairs a controlled fall through space, her hands tracking the banister to keep from stumbling.

Her bare feet scurried down the metal risers, nerve endings oblivious to the uneven metal slicing flesh.

Cortisol hopped up her senses. Fight or flight. Her mind had been engineered for both, and now flight was all she knew.

Reaching the end of the metal-slatted risers, she stopped. A ladder on a pulley hung suspended in the air above the alley. She'd seen the setup before in movies. The ladder needed weight on it to descend. But she wasn't big. She hoped it worked.

Jumping onto the ladder, she begged the counterweight to acquiesce, to let her down to the relative safety of the alley below.

There was a sharp ping, and a shower of sparks blossomed inches from Caroline's face as a bullet ricocheted into the night.

Flinching, she instinctively crouched and felt the phone squirt loose from her back pocket. It plummeted twenty feet down and shattered on the ground.

But Caroline had no time to mourn its destruction.

She flexed her legs and thrust downward. Hard.

The ladder groaned. The metal wheel began to turn.

Slowly at first, then faster, Caroline rode the ladder down, the gears clattering like trash cans until the ride stopped with a metallic jerk that almost threw her from the rungs.

Thrusting hard, she leaped off the bottom.

Her bare feet startled at the sensation of pavement, rough and still warm from the day.

She took off running, away from her building. Away from the man with the gun.

CHAPTER 14

When Caroline reached Alameda Street, she looked for help.

She saw no one. Just warmly lit apartments far above, sheltering people who, like her, ignored disturbing sounds in the night. The yells of the homeless. The gunshots of gangbangers.

How many nights had she taken solace in the impenetrable gates of her apartment, knowing none of the dangerous elements outside could reach her? Now those same barriers prevented her from seeking help. She was on her own. Being chased by a killer.

The broad boulevard provided no respite. But she knew the neighborhood's winding streets and narrow alleys. If she could duck into one.

Racing around the corner ahead of her, she hurtled toward the Fashion District. The shops were closed, sealed up tight for the night. She wished she could take refuge in one, but steel-slatted gates covered the fronts of most of the stores. Others had bars so close together that scarcely a ferret could've squeezed between them.

Caroline flashed past makeshift showrooms where bolts of fabric were piled from floor to ceiling. Outside, rows of mannequins were chained to posts. The human forms gave the illusion of people. But they were nothing more than fabricated witnesses to Caroline's frantic flight.

Up ahead Caroline spotted a branching alleyway, curving away from the sleeping stores.

She darted down the nearest alley.

The odor of food rotting in dumpsters rode a wave of warm air, nauseating and sick, but she kept going, deeper into the alley. There, she found kitchen bags of food clippings and mounds of discarded fabric.

Broken-down boxes mounded the gutters. Carpet remnants. Old pieces of equipment.

Finding a large pile of fabrics and boxes, Caroline squatted low and ducked into it.

Quickly, she pulled pieces of cardboard over her.

Soon, she heard footsteps. Running. Coming closer. Definitely coming her way.

A wave of nausea climbed Caroline's throat, clawing at her esophagus.

She clamped down on the sensation.

Struggling to control her panting, she imagined herself as lifeless as the plastic mannequins in the store windows beside her.

A sense of déjà vu washed over her. The hiding. The waiting. The fear of discovery. There had been times when her mother had raged. Those times had been infrequent, but often enough to keep her on edge, always vigilant for the demon that would appear, occupying her mother's body, poisoning everything her mother said. When the rages came, Joanne Auden's posture changed, as though her limbs were threaded with crooked wires and charged with a sharp electric current. Her voice would become acid edged and cutting. And Caroline would hide. Blending into the curtains in her father's study, trying to reduce her human profile, hoping she'd avoid becoming a target for her mother's free-floating fury.

Now, Caroline willed her shape to appear as just another haphazard lump.

There's nothing here. There's nothing here. There's nothing here.

She let the words fill her mind, repeating them, thrusting them out into the universe, begging them to take hold, gathering force with her will. She hoped the man would see nothing.

A flashlight beam swept over her hiding place, strafing her tank top and the leg of her jeans. Light leaked through the cracks in the cardboard, painting stripes all around Caroline.

Caroline held her breath. She waited for the hit man to kick the cardboard box aside and point the muzzle of his gun at her.

But then the flashlight switched off and her rank hiding place fell into darkness again.

With a soft scraping, the footfalls withdrew. Slow at first, then faster. The man was backtracking to find her. He was leaving.

Caroline exhaled, the tension leaving her limbs.

But she knew she couldn't stay where she was. Nor could she go home. She needed to keep moving. The man would return as soon as he realized she wasn't ahead of him.

Pushing out of the pile of trash, Caroline stood up.

Her tank top, now streaked with dirt, still reflected streetlamps. Too visible. Too distinct.

Atop her pile of refuse were tattered pieces of fabric. Spotted with dark green and brown blotches, they reminded her of the backdrops she'd helped paint for school plays in grade school.

She pulled a jagged bolt of it from the heap.

She slung it around her shoulders like a shawl.

Then she ran.

• • •

The first people Caroline encountered were homeless. Standing together in an abandoned construction site, the six shapes clustered around a trash can filled with fire.

A bearded man with an army surplus jacket stood closest to the fire, his hands outstretched for warmth even though the night was easily north of eighty degrees. Beside him stood a woman with a baseball hat pulled low over her forehead. The other four were all men.

They looked up as Caroline approached.

"I'm . . . I'm being chased," Caroline said. Her voice sounded small and wrong in her ears.

"Yeah, me, too," muttered one of the men from the dark.

"No, really," Caroline said. "He's got a gun. Do the police . . . Are there any around?"

The man beside the fire spat. "Fuck the police."

A murmur of agreement rippled through the group.

The sound of a motorcycle echoed down the street, the whine and whir of the engine approaching. Growing close.

With a wave of cold terror, Caroline realized the hit man might've retrieved his bike so that he could hunt for her.

"You sure got a pretty ass," said a voice from behind her.

She resisted the urge to look at the speaker, because doing so would force her to face the street, where the motorcycle was slowing down.

A hand alighted on her right triceps.

She tensed but didn't move.

As the sound of the motorcycle came parallel to the construction site, Caroline made a decision. Steeling herself, she leaned into the unwanted caress.

Encouraged, the homeless man put his arm around her.

A wave of stale sweat coursed up into Caroline's nostrils—the musky funk of a human without the benefit of regular showers during the Santa Anas.

The man leaned in until Caroline could feel his warm breath behind her ear.

"Let's go, baby," he said. "There's a mattress back in the alley," he added to sweeten the offer.

Instead of answering, Caroline tracked the crunching of the motor-cycle's wheels as the vehicle left the paved road and rode closer and closer to where she stood. A chain-link fence separated the unfinished driveway from the half-completed building. The hit man wouldn't be able to enter with the motorcycle. He'd have to climb off and go on foot, Caroline knew.

She considered her options.

Should she run? No. It was too late for that.

A flashlight flipped on.

A wide, white beam of light swept across the landscape, touching the mounds of dirt and locked equipment before settling on the group by the trash can. The light seemed to settle on Caroline's back, glinting in the hairs of the arm circling her shoulders.

"Get that fucking thing out of my eyes!" snarled the bearded man by the fire.

"Yeah, you're ruining the ambience," added the man's girlfriend.

Caroline stood frozen, hoping her silhouette—a woman in a long shawl, embraced by an amorous suitor—looked sufficiently different from the hit man's prey that he'd move along. There were hundreds of homeless souls in the area. He wouldn't search them all. Would he?

After another moment, the flashlight turned off.

The motorcycle's engine revved.

With a crunch and thump, the bike rejoined the paved street, then sped off.

After the motorcycle had gone, Caroline's body tremored with exhaustion.

"Come on, baby," said the hot voice in her ear.

Spinning away from the embrace, Caroline ducked through the gap in the chain-link fence and ran down the street.

• • •

Caroline's feet screamed in agony—a strange, uncomfortably deep pain from her flight down the fire escape. Then the flight down an alley. Then the walk through a construction site. Then the jog down Towne Avenue. The grit and broken glass had penetrated and shredded whatever meager calluses she'd developed from running. She needed shoes. Even more than that, she needed somewhere to regroup. But the farther she ran, the fewer people she saw.

At first, she'd tried to flag down cars. All had given her a wide berth, a wild harpy flapping her makeshift shawl on the roadside. She wouldn't have stopped for herself.

The memory of her apartment sucked at her thoughts, promising all sorts of comforts if she gave up and went home. Her closet full of shoes. Her laptop. Her wallet. But the hit man knew where she lived. She couldn't go there. Not safe. So she had no phone. No purse. No money. Nothing.

Fear stretched her in odd directions—cramping in her guts, aching through her legs, tugging at the edges of her psyche, threatening to drag her down to the lower depths of herself. Sweating and terrified. Rational thought threatened to leave her.

Grandma Kate had always said, "Get out of the problem and into the solution."

She needed a solution now. She hurried on into the night to find the only person she could reach on foot.

• • •

"You didn't bring me another one of those AA flyers, did you? Because I'm really not interested," Uncle Hitch slurred at Caroline.

She'd found him sitting on the steps of a defunct factory on East Second Avenue. Slumped against a wrought-iron banister whose curlicues and fleurs-de-lis clashed with the dilapidated structure it adorned, he'd been regarding the rising moon when she approached.

"Someone's trying to kill me," Caroline said. The words sounded hyperbolic and strange in her ears, but she knew she wasn't exaggerating. Her presence here alone was confirmation enough of their truth. Her destination had been a reflection of her desperation.

In response, her uncle looked down at the empty bottle beside him, as if frustrated that he could not dispel this vision of a blood relative who was intruding on his oblivion.

"I can't stay here," Caroline said, looking over her shoulder. "Too exposed."

Hitch took long, languid blinks as his eyes fought to focus on his niece.

"You're serious, aren't you?" he said.

Caroline just nodded. Her chest felt scooped out and hollow as a drum. Her face was crusty with sweat and grime. And she was standing in front of her drunk, homeless uncle, looking for help.

"Okay, okay," Hitch muttered, hauling himself up to his feet.

He walked into the building's shadow and pulled his shopping cart out onto the street with a clatter. Mounded with possessions, the cart steadied him. A poor man's walker.

"Come on," he said.

He headed down the street, leaning hard into the cart, one step at a time.

Unsure what else to do, Caroline followed.

CHAPTER 15

The blanket that covered Caroline stank of urine and ash. The over-size flannel jacket that she wore smelled of Uncle Hitch. The chaparral beneath her head poked into her cheek.

She turned her head away, and when she did, the sound of traffic invaded her senses. Unbuffered by walls or windows, the whoosh of cars on the 110 freeway was deafening. Trucks and buses. Cars and motor-cycles. All roaring past the spot where Caroline had spent the night. All oblivious to her presence.

She didn't feel rested. Instead, she felt . . . numb.

Beside Caroline, her uncle groaned.

Caroline regarded his profile. Stubble covered his chin, speckles of black against the tanned skin of his face. He'd thrown his right arm across his eyes, blotting out the light. The gray fabric of his sweatshirt made a ratty sleep mask.

As if sensing his niece's eyes on him, Uncle Hitch roused.

Shifting, he settled on his right side, facing Caroline.

His eyes opened slowly. A muddy shade of pond bottom, they regarded Caroline for a long moment before closing again.

Then Hitch rolled over onto his back again.

"This can't be good." His puff of breath swirled white in the cold morning air.

Caroline nodded. *Uncle Hitch, King of Understatement.*

Over the din of traffic on the morning commute, Caroline recounted what had happened. She'd already told him the night before, but he'd had trouble standing, let alone focusing. Teetering, he'd guided Caroline to this ditch beside the freeway, where he'd stashed some supplies. The rough brown blanket from an old electrical box. The tarp from a hollow in a gnarled tree. Three half-eaten apples, mealy and dirty, but still edible. She'd forced herself to take a bite of one before settling down to try to sleep.

Now Hitch listened attentively as Caroline described how she'd come to seek him out in a doorway on the edge of Skid Row.

When she finished, he shook his head in annoyance.

"I just need a phone," Caroline said, cutting off whatever snarky comment he was going to make. She didn't have time for it. She had to call the police. Or her dad. Or Joey, her best friend from New Jersey. Or the ship where her mom was.

Without answering, Hitch sat up.

He brushed pieces of blond grass from his arms. Teetering slightly, he stood and gathered the blanket and tarp, then tucked them inside the basket of his shopping cart.

Wheeling the cart over the uneven scrub brush, he tucked it into a nook under a bridge beside the freeway. The spot was mostly invisible.

When he returned to Caroline, he kept walking past her.

"Where are we going?" she asked.

"To see a friend."

• • •

When her uncle had said they were going to see a friend, Caroline had expected someone with a phone. Or maybe a few dollars to spare.

But the man they approached looked as destitute as Hitch. Thick as an ancient oak tree and just as weathered, he squatted on a slab of concrete in a grove of half-dead willow trees overlooking the Los Angeles River. The elements had burnished his skin to a deep mahogany.

In his left hand, the man held a piece of wood. In his right hand, he held a bull knife, which he used to shave thin slivers onto the dry grass. Though he did not look up, Caroline had the distinct sense he knew they were approaching.

"Yo, Hitch," the man's voice rumbled when they reached the edge of his clearing.

"I need a favor," Uncle Hitch said.

Still whittling, the big man grunted his assent.

"I need you to keep my niece safe," said Uncle Hitch.

Caroline flushed. Her uncle was ditching her with an ox of a man with a knife.

"That's Jake," said Uncle Hitch from beside her. "He's an Army Ranger. He served a tour in Iraq. You'll be safe here with him while I . . . try to, um, function."

"I don't need a babysitter. I need a phone. I need someone on the police force I can talk to. Someone honest." Caroline knew there had to be honest police officers. In fact, her rational mind told her most of them were likely honest. But Captain Nelson's eyes still haunted her.

Hitch let out a mirthless laugh.

"These people . . . they're the government and the police and corporate America," he said. "They're all out there. They're all working together. All the time. Can't trust anyone."

Paranoia. Caroline saw it smoldering in her uncle's eyes. That it might have some basis in reality this time only made it harder to judge.

"Do you have any money?" Caroline asked. She could get a burner phone. With a phone, she could call a friend to wire her some money. Then she could work on finding her way to an honest member of law enforcement.

Hitch turned out the pocket of his trousers. "I'm a little short on cash at the moment."

Caroline exhaled her frustration.

She regarded the clearing. She'd have to find a friend or colleague who could give her shelter while she figured out her next move. It would be dangerous for anyone to harbor her, and it would be humiliating for her to have to ask. But she needed help—help her wild-haired still half-drunk uncle couldn't give her.

"You can't go." Hitch's voice echoed across the clearing, stopping Caroline's steps. "They know where you live. Lord knows what else they know—your friends, your classmates. They could come after you anywhere. There's going to be an APB out on you, too. The police are going to come looking for you. And Oasis clearly has people inside the department."

The possibility of rotten cops made Caroline pause. She had little time to find refuge, she realized.

"How soon will the APB come out?" she asked.

"As soon as you miss an appointment or something, someone's going to report you missing, and that'll trigger the APB," said Hitch.

Caroline's heart lurched at the mention of missing appointments. Mateo's guardianship hearing was today. In five hours, Judge Flores would call his afternoon calendar. He'd expect her in court, presenting evidence of Rogelio Gonzalez's gang affiliation or drug activities. He wouldn't expect her to be sitting beside the Los Angeles River, trying to figure out who was trying to kill her.

"I need a phone. Right now," Caroline said.

Hitch chuckled again. "Sorry, but my iPhone's out of service."

"You don't understand. I need to attend a hearing telephonically. A little boy's life depends on it." Caroline had never attended a hearing by phone, but she knew it was allowed. Standing in court, she'd often heard attorneys call in to the court's phone line rather than attend in person.

It seemed irresponsible, or at least bad form, but it was an accepted practice. And now, for her, it couldn't be avoided.

"No one has a phone out here," Hitch said, his face growing serious.

"What about at a shelter or residence hotel or something?" Caroline asked, scanning the jagged skyline of downtown. She didn't know the landmarks of the homeless world, but there had to be a place with a phone.

"No chance you're going to get through a whole hearing at one of those," Hitch said.

"This isn't negotiable," Caroline said, setting her jaw. She couldn't miss the hearing.

"What isn't negotiable is that you need a federal prosecutor," said Hitch.

Caroline nodded. Even still smelling of the previous night's bender, her uncle was right. He'd been a detective long enough to know how the system worked.

"I might know how to find a prosecutor. An honest one," Hitch continued. "But you need to stay out of sight. I'll try to reach him for you, but you need to stay off the grid."

Caroline heard the implication in his words—he thought she should stay on the street with him. She was about to tell him there was no chance of that, but she stopped at the evident concern in his eyes. He cared. He was trying. In his own way, he was offering her a place to stay where he thought she'd be safe.

"I'm sorry," she said, "but I need to find a phone. I know it puts me at risk of being seen, but there's just no other way. I have to do this."

Hitch exhaled.

His eyes settled on Caroline's bare feet. He'd watched her pick splinters and glass out of them before she'd painfully risen to follow him to the clearing where they'd found Jake.

"I suppose we do need to get supplies for you if you're staying out here with us," Hitch said.

"Distribution center?" Jake asked.

Those two words were only the third and fourth utterances Caroline had heard the big man make, but they seemed promising.

"There's a phone there?" she asked.

"Sho' is," Jake said. "Oasis don't operate those centers, either. Could be okay. I could take you there."

Caroline regarded Jake. She wasn't a fool. Having a burly Ranger watching her back would probably increase her chances of surviving her current nightmare. Even if that Ranger looked like a shell-shocked homeless man whittling a figurine that looked like a poodle.

"Sounds good," Caroline said. She looked at her uncle. "I promise it'll just be a quick call." *Or calls,* she amended silently.

Standing up, Jake shook the wood shavings off the creature he had carved. A sheep. The likeness was impressive, Caroline decided. Jake had followed the whorls and curves of the piece of wood, sculpting them down to reveal a reclining sheep.

He tucked the carving into the pocket of his army jacket—probably the real thing, not a surplus item, though he'd torn off his name tapes and rank. Then he bent down to lift a rucksack to his shoulders. A sleeping bag and tent dangled from the faded green nylon. Neither was new, but both looked carefully compacted and secured with well-executed knots.

"I'll try to reach this federal prosecutor I know," Hitch said.

"Great," Caroline said. "We can do that after the distribution center."

"Naw," Hitch said, "I gotta do this alone. Could take me some time."

He looked to the side, not meeting Caroline's eyes.

He was thirsty, Caroline realized, and not for water.

Did he really even know a federal prosecutor? Or had he just left her with a babysitter so that he could go slake his thirst for booze?

"Let's just meet up later at East Seventh," Hitch continued, facing Jake, still not meeting his niece's eyes. "You know the spot, right?"

"East Seventh," Jake confirmed.

Caroline watched her uncle shuffle off, his feet crunching on twigs until he disappeared.

She tried not to think about where he was going, what he was doing, and whether he'd return.

She didn't have time to worry about him. She had Mateo Hidalgo to worry about.

Not to mention her own survival.

• • •

Caroline regarded the small auditorium. Someone had arranged supplies by category. Blankets piled at one wall. Shoes and clothes organized in boxes at another. A row of bagged lunches topped a table along the third wall. On the fourth wall, an open door led out to the street and the park beyond that.

A picture of DA Donita Johnson and Police Chief Donald Park hung over the door. Apparently the two city officials had helped set up the distribution center to address the reality of the two hundred thousand homeless people living in Los Angeles.

Caroline walked to the boxes of clothes and shoes. Another patron squatted in front of the shoes—a slight woman with long ebony hair and tanned skin. At odds with the morning hour, the woman wore a bias-cut red dress and satin ballet slippers. Apparently she, like Caroline, was looking for more appropriate footwear.

The woman looked up sharply as Caroline approached. Her hands, which had been rummaging through the shoe box labeled "7–7½" stilled. Her large, dark eyes held worry.

Instinctively, Caroline slowed her step.

"Mind if I join you?" Caroline gestured down at her own feet. Dirt stained and scratched, they spoke eloquently of her reasons for needing what the box offered.

In answer, the small woman scooted to the side to make room for Caroline.

"Find anything good?" Caroline asked, noting the row of paired shoes the small woman had organized on the floor beside where she squatted.

"There aren't any size sevens in here," the woman said. "They're all too big for me. What size are you?"

"Seven and a half."

In her periphery, Caroline could see the woman studying her feet.

"Maybe try these," the woman said, reaching to offer one of the pairs she'd put aside. "They're the best ones I've found."

Taking the pair of faded Converse high-tops, Caroline pulled them onto her feet, then stood up. Though ill fitting and old, the shoes were a vast improvement over bare pavement.

"Thanks," Caroline said to the still-squatting woman.

Then she glanced up at the clock.

It was 12:35.

She still had a little time before the one o'clock hearing. Under ordinary circumstances, she'd be sitting in a corner of a courthouse, studying her argument notes, jotting down a few last-minute ideas. But now, instead, she was collecting shoes and hoping the lady shouting into the phone would vacate it before the hearing began. She was also trying to forget the other worry that pulled at her mind.

"Do you happen to know whether Oasis has anything to do with running this place?" Caroline asked the slight woman still crouching by the shoes.

Jake had already said Oasis didn't operate the distribution center, but Caroline could not erase the image of Amy's battered face from her mind. Oasis had done that. Being out in the open was dangerous. But it was necessary. She had to attend the hearing.

Not that it would matter, some part of her mind whispered. She still didn't know how to thwart Rogelio Gonzalez's guardianship petition. She'd filed bits of evidence. Hints of subterfuge. She'd found a whiff of drug dealing. But no actual proof. Nothing that would convince Judge Flores to prevent Mateo from living with Gonzalez.

"Oasis? I've been told they don't usually run distribution centers," said the woman. "Thank God," she added, frowning.

Caroline cocked her head at the negative reaction to Oasis.

But before she could ask about its source, there was a shout from outside.

The woman's head snapped up. Then she rose and hurried toward the door.

Caroline watched her go with a furrowed brow.

"Here," Jake said from behind Caroline, causing her to turn.

In one hand, he held a child's sleeping bag, a castoff from some middle-class family.

"Thanks," Caroline said.

As she took the bundle, her stomach sank.

The prospect of spending another night outside settled around her. She had no close friends in Los Angeles except Amy. Even if she could convince her building manager that she was stuck in the hospital, say, with a hurt friend, she'd still need someone to enter her apartment and gather her wallet and computer—something someone would have to do at the risk of his life, and even if the hit man wasn't watching the apartment, that person would have to meet her to deliver her possessions and observe her state, not ask questions, not spread gossip about her sanity among her colleagues or neighbors.

If Hitch came through with his contact, she'd have a prosecutor who could help her find refuge. But for now, all she had was a kid's sleeping bag decorated with little red fire trucks.

Caroline held it to her nose.

It smelled like wooden bunk beds and fabric softener. It smelled like . . . a home.

A loud voice from outside made Caroline look up from her musings.

"Stay right here! Daryl says you've got to wait for him," a man said. It sounded like the kind of order someone would give to a child, but this was no place for a kid.

Caroline met Jake's eyes.

He shrugged.

Tucking the sleeping bag under one arm, Caroline walked to the door to investigate.

Outside the distribution center, a man wearing a white T-shirt advertising Bud Light stood in front of the same small woman Caroline had met moments earlier by the shoe box. The kind woman who'd given her the Converse she now wore on her feet.

"Please. You've got to let me go," the woman said, hugging her arms around herself.

"After Daryl comes, you can. He's gonna be here real soon. You just have to talk to him." Mr. Bud Light was no longer shouting. Instead, he spoke with a tone of reasonableness wrapped in condescension. A babysitter's voice.

A cluster of onlookers gathered to watch the altercation. People in ragtag clothes. Some from the distribution center. Some from a homeless encampment in the nearby park.

"I need to go." The woman took a half step away, her full mouth quivering with urgency, but Mr. Bud Light grabbed her arm.

"Just stop right there, Lani," he said. "I told you—you've got to stay here."

Caroline drifted closer, shrugging off Jake's hand.

"Hey," Jake called after her. "Too exposed out here—" His low voice carried, but it wasn't enough to stop her.

"Is there a problem?" Caroline asked, approaching the scene. She stopped three feet away from the man. Hopefully far enough that he couldn't reach her.

The small woman called Lani froze, her eyes sharp with concern, her gaze flitting from Caroline to Mr. Bud Light to the park beside the distribution center.

"You should stay out of things that aren't your business," Mr. Bud Light growled at Caroline, his jaw tightening.

Fear sparked in Caroline's breast. She'd taken a risk by getting involved. Perhaps a foolish one. She hadn't been able to watch without trying to help, but now she was a target, too.

In the near distance, the sound of an engine approached.

Seconds later, a pickup truck came into view, tearing down the road in front of the distribution center.

With a bump and a screech, it jerked to a stop in front of the trio.

The door clanged open, and a lanky man climbed out. A gold chain glittered around his neck, swinging from side to side with the motion of his long strides.

"Lani!" he shouted.

The woman's eyes widened. Twisting her hand free of Mr. Bud Light, she spun and ran toward the park. The satiny soles of her ballet slippers blurred with the speed of her retreat.

"I tried to keep her here, Daryl—" Mr. Bud Light began as Daryl approached.

But Daryl ignored him. Instead, he watched Lani, as if doing the math. She was only twenty yards ahead and veering toward the trees.

He launched off after her.

But as he came parallel with Caroline, she stuck out her foot. It wasn't a premeditated act. She didn't like him, and she didn't like his friend. And suddenly, there he was, right in front of her at the exact moment that it occurred to her that he should not be allowed to catch a woman who was running away from him.

Daryl's boot snagged on her ankle.

He plummeted forward, his momentum carrying him to the ground.

He landed hard with a huff of expelled air.

When he looked up, the gold chain had looped across his mouth.

"Damn it!" Daryl shouted, spitting out his chain and struggling to his feet. His eyes followed Lani, who had now reached the trees—too far to catch.

Daryl rounded on Caroline, glaring at her with wide, angry eyes.

He took a half step toward her but then stopped.

In her peripheral vision, Caroline saw the hulking shape of Jake move forward to stand beside her. With deliberate slowness, the Ranger crossed his forearms across his chest.

"I'm so sorry," Caroline said to Daryl. "Are you okay?"

Daryl eyed Jake.

"That was my girlfriend," Daryl said, apparently deciding that excuses were the better part of valor. "I just wanted to talk to her."

"She didn't look like she wanted to talk," Caroline ventured, looking in the direction Lani had disappeared.

Instead of answering, Daryl turned away from Caroline and Jake.

He tromped back toward his truck, his footfalls hard and petulant.

Mr. Bud Light followed, climbing in the passenger-side door and slamming it overly hard. Then, with a roar of impotent rage, the truck tore away from the distribution center.

Soon, peace reigned again. A few tentative birds chirped their joy at the end of hostilities. The cluster of onlookers began to disperse now that the show was over. Some gathered backpacks or shopping carts. Others shuffled off into the encampment in the park.

"What do you think that was about?" Caroline asked, glancing back at Jake.

"Dunno," Jake said, his eyes still watching the access road where the pickup truck had departed. "Haven't seen her before. Probably that guy beats her. None of my business."

The words hung in the air like a challenge. It was none of anybody's business beyond a moment of entertainment—don't ask questions, Caroline supposed.

Beside her, she sensed Jake's unease. He wanted to get out of the open.

Rather than waiting for him to insist, she retreated back inside the distribution center. She needed to get to the phone anyway. The hearing would begin soon.

"What's going to happen to Lani?" Caroline asked. It might not be her business, but she couldn't help wondering.

Jake grunted. "Getting off the street's hard. Can't get no job if you got no address. Can't get no apartment if you got no money."

"There must be a way for someone like her to earn some money or find a bed." But even as she said the words, an obvious answer occurred to Caroline. Perhaps Daryl was Lani's pimp.

Meanwhile, Jake shook his head.

"Money?" he repeated. "You don't want no cash on the streets. People get robbed all the damn time. You get cash, you turn that cash into something else. Something you can barter with." He jutted his chin toward the piles of shoes and blankets bordering the sides of the distribution center. "You turn them shoes into cigarettes or whatever. Something you can trade for toilet paper."

It was the longest soliloquy Caroline had heard from Jake. His effort to educate her in the ways of the homeless struck her as both kind and depressing. She hoped she wouldn't need the knowledge he sought to impart.

Eyeing the piles of supplies, Caroline contemplated Jake's words. Her gaze settled on the pile of shoes . . . shoes that could be traded for cigarettes . . . that could be traded for toilet paper. Metamorphosis. A transformation of one good into another in a world where cash was unusable.

A shiver ran down her arms.

Where cash was unusable . . .

She swung around to face Jake.

"I need that phone. Now."

CHAPTER 16

"What's that sound I hear in the background?" the court clerk asked.

Caroline winced at the homeless woman raging twenty feet from where she stood. It had taken ten minutes to pull the ranting woman off the telephone. Now Caroline risked losing the hearing because she couldn't hear herself think over the sound of shouting. She wished the ancient phone had a mute button that worked.

"Nothing," Caroline answered, hunkering closer around the phone. "It's just someone out in the hall of my firm. How long before the Hidalgo matter is called?"

Caroline waved frantically for Jake to give an assist.

Jake bit the inside of his cheek as he regarded the woman. Then he took her by the arm and guided her out of the distribution center, diverting her attention with some question that made her ravings grow in intensity as she disappeared out the door.

"Case number 579297. In re *Matter of M. H.*," called the clerk. "Caroline Auden appearing telephonically on behalf of Mateo Hidalgo. Rogelio Gonzalez in pro per."

"Welcome, Ms. Auden," said Judge Flores's voice, coming onto the court's speakerphone. "Welcome, Mr. Gonzalez."

Caroline heard Rogelio Gonzalez's muffled greeting in response.

"When we parted company," the judge continued, "Ms. Auden was going to gather evidence of Mr. Gonzalez's gang affiliation or drug activities. I see that she has filed certain materials, including a declaration describing conversations with the warehouse manager. Plus, she has asked the court to take judicial notice of certain Border Patrol records in Mr. Gonzalez's brother's criminal file."

"Yes, Your Honor," Caroline confirmed the recitation of the evidence she'd proffered.

"There's no such thing as guilt by association, Ms. Auden. That Mr. Gonzalez's brother is currently serving time for drug activities will have no impact on this court's determination of the guardianship petition currently pending before it."

"I understand, Your Honor, and that is not my argument." Caroline took a breath. She had only one chance to persuade the judge there was a reason to stall granting Rogelio Gonzalez's guardianship petition.

"Then what is your argument, Counsel? You can't see it, but I have a full courtroom sitting here today."

"Floriana Perez's family owns a shipping company. Perez Shipping. They're the company that ships lingerie down to Mexico for Rogelio Gonzalez."

"Yes, I saw that in your papers," the judge said. "So what?"

"Perez Shipping has misstated the amount of lingerie it shipped for Mr. Gonzalez."

"And we know this how?" the judge asked.

"Border Patrol records. They searched Mr. Gonzalez's shipment of lingerie to Mexico in December 2015."

"And they found no drugs or any other sort of contraband," the judge noted, his voice flat. Caroline could hear a frown in it—she had stood in his courtroom often enough to read impatience in his studied ambivalence.

"Yes, but Border Patrol did find there were twelve, not six, pallets of lingerie in the shipment. That's six more than Perez Shipping's manifest states. Why does this discrepancy matter?" Caroline asked, preempting the judge's question. "It matters because this may be how Rogelio and his brother are turning drug money into something else."

"I'm not following," Judge Flores said.

"If you sell drugs in the United States, you end up with a bunch of cash, right? You can't deposit that cash in a bank without raising red flags. As a result, you can't move that cash out of the country. So what do you do?"

"I'm sure you will tell me."

"Transactional money laundering," Caroline said, talking quickly. Outside the distribution center, the woman who had monopolized the telephone now spoke emphatically to a tree. Caroline hoped the tree was holding up its side of the conversation.

"I'm not familiar with that," said Judge Flores.

"Transactional money laundering is how you turn illegal profits into clean money," Caroline said. She'd heard about the technique in her criminal law class. "The way it works is, you buy some sort of easily transportable, easily sold thing. Like lingerie. Now you've turned your drug money into—"

"Undergarments," the judge finished, his voice holding a hint of prim amusement.

"Exactly. You take those undergarments down to Mexico and sell them there—essentially turning them back into cash."

"Pesos."

"Right. Then you can use those pesos to buy more drugs." Caroline paused. "Or a big house in Guadalajara. Or some fancy cars and boats."

This was where a trained attorney would object to her speculation. But in place of an objection, Rogelio's outraged sputtering drew a sharp word from Judge Flores.

C. E. TOBISMAN

There was silence on the line while the judge considered Caroline's theory.

Caroline wished she could see Judge Flores's face. She couldn't gauge his mood.

If she'd been in court, she would have pointed to each page of evidence, handing the judge the shipping manifest, then the Border Patrol report, leading him through her line of thought. But with only an earpiece and a receiver connecting her to the courtroom on Hill Street, she could only try to persuade the court with her words. And she couldn't gauge whether those words were landing squarely or missing the mark.

"If Mr. Gonzalez is understating the amount of lingerie he's purchasing wholesale in the United States and then shipping to Mexico to sell, it would certainly raise the specter of money laundering," Caroline pushed. "Understating the amount is a way of obscuring just how much money you've turned into other goods."

"Has the DA's office looked into any of this?" Judge Flores asked.

"I've been in touch with them, so it's possible. Given more time, I would be happy to find out, Your Honor." Without a phone, laptop, a good meal, or clean clothes, she added silently.

"Mr. Gonzalez, are you willing to make your shipping records available so we can get to the bottom of this?" the judge asked, evidently now turning to Caroline's opponent.

"No," Rogelio answered quickly.

Caroline resisted the urge to cheer. The reflexive response suggested something to hide. Surely the judge had heard it, too.

"Then you leave me little choice, Mr. Gonzalez." The judge shuffled through the printouts on his bench. "I will continue this matter again, pending contacting the DA's office to determine the status of any investigation."

A smile blossomed on Caroline's face. The judge couldn't see her anyway, so she could fully express her joy.

But then the judge exhaled.

"Unfortunately, this means we will need to move Mateo to another temporary home."

"Excuse me, Your Honor?" Caroline asked.

"The proof of service here says you got the notice of Mateo's temporary guardians' emergency filing this morning," the judge said.

"I apologize. I must've missed it. I've been out of the office."

"Mateo's temporary guardians have run into some issues. Mateo needs tutoring. Counseling. They've been doing their best, but now Francisco Castillo has some immigration issues, as well. It's all become too much for them."

Caroline resisted the urge to ask for specifics. It was bad enough that she hadn't seen the papers the temporary guardians had filed.

"I'm willing to assist the Castillos with whatever I can in order to stabilize the situation," she said. "I've got some experience with immigration matters, and I'm willing to help them at no charge—"

"I'm sorry, Ms. Auden, but this family's guardianship obligation has ended. They're asking to be relieved. Although we have not yet resolved the question of whether Mr. Gonzalez will be a suitable placement, we must move to another temporary home in the interim."

"Please, Your Honor, I can help." Caroline felt like she had a front-row seat to the fraying safety net. Mateo. The Castillos. Uncle Hitch. The other lost souls she'd seen on the streets. People without the legal or social services. Never enough resources. Never enough help.

"I'll tell you what, Counsel. I will extend your offer of pro bono assistance to the Castillos and let them decide how to proceed."

"Thank you, Your Honor," Caroline said, even as she wondered how she was going to provide help to the Castillos while she was fighting for her life.

"We'll meet back here in two weeks. Anything further, Ms. Auden?"

A half dozen answers ran through the gates of Caroline's mind, all impulses to beg for justice in the matter of her current predicament. But if she told the judge what was happening, she'd sound insane. She'd hurt her credibility and undercut her ability to represent Mateo.

"Nothing further, Your Honor," she said quietly.

"Good. We'll meet back here on October 11 at 1:30 p.m. I'm moving to Department 17, so please be sure to go to the right courtroom," Judge Flores added.

As he gave the information, Caroline looked for something to write on. She reached into the back pocket of her jeans for a scrap.

There, she found two sheets of paper. The first was the Spreadsheet of Death. The second sheet was the first page of the title report. The one for the property on Parrino Court that Oasis owned. Crumpled into her pocket, the two documents gave testament to how far she'd fallen. In the short time since she'd stood in the kitchen of her apartment studying those pages, she'd been locked out of her entire life.

Hanging up, she noted Jake leaning against the door frame, chewing on his lip. His expression exuded impatience.

Ignoring his consternation, Caroline turned her attention back to the phone. Western Union could take delivery of a wire transfer from her father or a friend. She could get off the street and regroup. She could get a room somewhere. Maybe even a rudimentary computer.

She considered whom to call.

Sudden movement from the corner of Caroline's eye made her freeze.

Through the open door, she watched a green van pull up in front of the distribution center. Although the door frame blocked her view of all of the words on the side of the van, she knew what they said: HELPING YOU HELP YOURSELF.

"I thought you said Oasis didn't sponsor this place," said Caroline.

"They don't," said Jake, reaching for her arm.

But Caroline was already in motion, hurrying out the opposite door. The one farthest from the goons in green shirts.

• • •

Caroline and Jake sat beneath the bridge at East Seventh Street. A graffitied shelf provided them with shelter from the wind, if not the noise of cars passing overhead.

But it wasn't the noise that weighed on Caroline. It was the time. It was almost 6:00, and her uncle still hadn't appeared.

Caroline considered her predicament. She hadn't planned to spend the night in the fire truck sleeping bag. She'd planned a dozen other futures, none of which involved climbing through a break in a fence and scrambling down a concrete embankment toward a sleeping spot located steps away from the Los Angeles River.

But despite waiting for over two hours, her uncle was a no-show.

She considered leaving to try again to find someone who would loan her a phone or money, but she nixed the plan. Her earlier efforts had been thwarted by the same sorts of rebuffs she'd given panhandlers in the past. Everyone she'd tried to approach had walked the other way. She'd needed a moment of kindness. Instead, she'd found indifference.

Plus there was another problem: she was depending on her uncle to find a prosecutor. He'd promised he'd known someone who could help. She wasn't confident he'd find someone, but she had no leads, no phone, and no money. And so she was doomed to wait. With each passing minute, her chances of arranging some other place to sleep were slipping farther away.

Beside her, Jake opened his rucksack.

With methodical movements, he untied his sleeping bag and tent.

When he finished setting them up, he straightened.

"Hitch's got his own tent," Jake said, gesturing with his chin toward Caroline's sleeping bag.

Caroline nodded her understanding. Apparently her uncle had been too hammered the night before to manage his tent. At least if he showed up, she'd have shelter for the night.

"Hungry?" Jake asked.

Caroline nodded again. They'd eaten nothing since their visit to the distribution center.

Jake pulled two crumpled brown paper bags from his backpack. More bready sandwiches from the distribution center, plus two bottles of water.

"Thanks," Caroline said, taking one of each. The thin slice of ham was slimy, and the lone piece of lettuce was limp, but she ate the sandwich anyway. She didn't know when she'd eat again or where the meal would come from.

Another hour passed, and the sun sank behind the curvature of Earth. Darkness fell in earnest. Soon, only the strobes of light from passing cars and the ambient glow of the rising half-moon provided any light.

In the darkness, Caroline reconciled herself to another night outside. It seemed inconceivable that she'd remain there, and yet her options had narrowed with the setting sun. She only hoped her uncle returned with his tent.

Jake pulled a candle from his rucksack. He struck a match on the concrete wall beside him then touched it to the wick. With a guttural hiss, it caught fire.

Placing a plastic bottle with the top and bottom torn off over the candle, he shielded it from the wind that stirred the trash under the bridge.

Caroline watched the candle lick at the sides of the old soda bottle.

The situation would be laughable if it wasn't so tragic. She'd left the tech world and gone to law school, renounced a plush firm and hung out a shingle as a solo practitioner. She'd worried about attracting enough clients to pay the rent, worried about finding time to go to the grocery store. About eating too much fatty meat and about where to run for exercise. And here she was anyway, waiting to see if her homeless uncle joined her under a bridge.

But why not? some dark part of her mind queried.

Her mother had disintegrated into periodic madness. Her uncle had caved to alcohol. Caroline had lived the fantasy that she was different, but she'd never had any proof of it.

She tried to push the despair away. Corrosive and dangerous to the soul, it would weaken her when she needed strength. She had no choice but to shackle herself to the investigation that had put her in her dire straits. Somehow, she had to find the proof she hadn't been able to locate even when she'd had all her resources.

A scraping sound brought her out of her reverie.

Jake had taken out his knife. In the wavering dance of the candle's golden glow, he whittled a tree branch he'd found under the bridge.

"What are you making?" Caroline's voice echoed under the bridge.

"Snake," Jake answered.

"What kind of snake?" Words flowing between her and another human being would provide a sense of normalcy, something to cling to like a life raft in shark-infested waters.

"He hasn't told me yet," Jake said. "Could be poisonous. Could be a garden snake."

Caroline considered his words. She'd heard about sculptors who peeled away stone to reveal the image that hid within.

A shuffle of movement from the fence up by the road made Jake's whittling stop.

The knife in his hand pivoted slightly, facing the fence.

But then he grunted. "Hitch," he said and began whittling again.

Moments later, Caroline's uncle stumbled down the slope looking like a troll with gray hair frizzing around his head. He used his right hand to steady himself as he reached the encampment. In his left hand, he held the cords of a sleeping bag and tent.

Caroline's shoulders relaxed, releasing a tension knot she hadn't known she'd been carrying.

He hadn't left her. He'd returned.

She rose to help him set up the camping equipment.

Right away, the putrid-sweet scent of alcohol poured off her uncle. It permeated his clothes and emanated from his skin.

Her joy dissipated.

"Have any luck at the bar?" She heard the bitterness in her own voice.

"I had to go to a bar," Uncle Hitch said. "That's where the guy is who knows the prosecutor I'm trying to reach. It was nec . . . necessary . . ."

Caroline imagined her uncle sliming into a bar and sidling up to some off-duty police officer or public defender drinking buddy to ask a favor. Asking some currently employed civil servant to hopefully, maybe, get in touch with some other guy. She'd bet her uncle had mooched some booze off whomever he'd contacted. A twofer.

Uncle Hitch looked down.

"I'm glad Jake's here," he said quietly.

Taking in her uncle's bedraggled appearance and unsteady posture, Caroline understood: Jake was her uncle's fail-safe. Hitch knew he was a mess, and he was still sentient enough, still caring enough to be worried about what that would mean to his niece's survival. Jake was the proof that Hitch expected his own failure.

"What did you find out?" She extended the question like an olive branch. "Did you reach your friend?"

Hitch's muddy eyes came up to meet hers. He weighed her expression. Finding no further criticism, he nodded to himself. "Yeah, I talked to my buddy. He's going to try to reach this guy I know in the US Attorney's Office and ask him to meet you in Pershing Square at 7:30 tomorrow morning."

"An assistant US attorney?"

"Yes. His name's Albert Khaing. I knew him back . . . before. Anyway, we got to know each other during an investigation I was working on with the feds. He was new at the US Attorney's Office and pretty wet behind the ears. I helped him out. Steered him away from some shady evidence in a case. Fruit of the poisonous tree and all that."

Caroline knew the fruit-of-the-poisonous-tree doctrine. A prosecutor could not present evidence at trial that stemmed from an illegal search. Doing so would result in the exclusion of the evidence and, probably, the career-damaging embarrassment of the young prosecutor who'd tried to introduce it.

"Tell me more about him," Caroline said. "Anything you know." She needed her uncle to be clear about the specifics. Without a computer, she was depending on her uncle's relationships, as old and shaky as they were, to lead her to evidence and to safety.

Hitch rubbed his eyes, as if trying to focus despite the alcohol still buzzing in his veins.

"He's about five feet six inches tall. One hundred forty pounds. Slight build. Short hair. Balding. Brown eyes." Hitch rattled off the description like a cop describing a witness.

"No, I mean what do you know about his character? His history?" Caroline realized she was looking for reassurance.

"He's from Burma," Hitch began slowly. "He told me about it once. His parents were involved in the 88 Generation Students Group—that's the prodemocracy movement that got hammered by the military government in 1988. His parents fled. They got asylum here when Albert was only five years old."

Caroline nodded encouragingly. She knew her uncle had a good memory for people. It had made him an effective cop . . . before he'd fallen apart.

"I remember being impressed that he'd made his own way," Hitch continued, fighting to enunciate his words. "He had to teach himself English. He became a Christopher Scholar in high school. The best of the best get that scholarship."

Caroline warmed at her uncle's description. Albert Khaing sounded good. Maybe too good. She'd heard people describe federal prosecutors as arrogant. While she had little choice in the matter, she hoped this one wasn't.

"Anyway, he always struck me as a stand-up kid," Hitch finished.

Caroline hoped the feeling was mutual. She reminded herself that her uncle had once been a good detective and a good man. Maybe someone else saw him that way, too.

If Albert Khaing did, he'd meet her on a park bench in Pershing Square at 7:30.

CHAPTER 17

"You're in major trouble," said Albert Khaing over his shoulder, where he sat on the back-to-back bench in Pershing Square.

"What's wrong?" Caroline wished she could turn around and see the prosecutor's face. When she'd arrived, he'd already been sitting on the park bench in navy-blue suit pants and a collared shirt with a tie. His face had been an inscrutable mask of professionalism when he'd asked her to take the spot behind him.

Caroline, for her part, had tried to ignore the dust that covered her after another night sleeping in the rough. Even in the tent, the Santa Ana winds had pushed the dirt and the grime up into her nose and over the surface of her skin.

A hand passed Caroline an iPhone low and around the edge of the bench.

Taking the phone, Caroline read what had caused Albert's grim assessment. On the screen, the lead story in the local section of the *Los Angeles Times* website was accompanied by a photograph of a car, the front of which was buried in the doorway of the paletería. Chunks of wood and a spray of glass from the store lay shattered all around the accident site.

It took Caroline several seconds to register what she was seeing. A Mustang GT. Hers. Although the front of the car was crumpled, she recognized familiar body damage to the side panels. The familiar rims her father had put on the tires twenty years earlier.

"I didn't do this," Caroline said, realizing that Albert might think he was talking to a hit-and-run criminal. A fugitive from justice.

When Albert didn't respond, Caroline's eyes flew down the article.

The crime had occurred the previous night. Neighbors reported hearing a crash shortly after 10:00 p.m. The owner of the paletería happened to have been in the shop despite the late hour. Now she was in the intensive care unit in a coma. She had a fractured skull. Brain swelling. Her family asked the community to please pray for her survival.

The driver of the car had disappeared, but the car had reeked of alcohol, and an empty bottle of vodka had been found under the seat. There were no security tapes. But there'd been a witness. An anonymous tip.

"Someone reported seeing a woman matching your description fleeing the scene," Albert said.

"This wasn't me. I swear. I left my keys in my apartment when I ran away from that guy with the gun. He must've done this. My uncle can vouch for where I've been for the last forty-eight hours. So can Jake—"

She trailed off. Her alibi depended on the credibility of her alcoholic uncle and his homeless friend. The tenuous nature of her position struck her with a shudder that reached the core of her soul. She was one false accusation away from destruction. Forget about Amy. Forget about elders like her grandma. Forget about everyone. She couldn't even protect herself.

A wave of nausea climbed up Caroline's throat.

"I believe you," Albert said.

With those three words, Caroline's world began to right itself. Slightly.

"I know your uncle," Albert continued. "He's got his issues, but he's an honorable man."

An honorable man. The words echoed in Caroline's mind. Whatever else Hitch had done when he'd been a police detective, he'd kept his honor—at least in the eyes of this one federal prosecutor. Thank God.

"The police are looking for you," Albert said over his shoulder.

The information didn't surprise Caroline. Of course the police were looking for her. Scrunching her head down, she wished she could disappear in the too-large flannel coat she'd borrowed from her uncle.

The Santa Ana winds still swirled through the park, warming the pavement and baking the dried leaves clustered at the struts of the bench. The sounds and movement around her only added to the dizzying sense of the world falling apart around her. How was she going to get out of this one?

"Why don't you tell me what happened," Albert invited, his voice gentle.

Taking a breath, Caroline told Albert everything that had led her to be sitting back-to-back with him on a park bench: the many-tentacled Oasis with its soup kitchen volunteers and promise of free services, its scab construction projects and its nursing home scam. She told him about Oasis's hit man service agent who'd put Amy in the hospital for her prying. The same hit man who'd chased Caroline out onto the streets, presumably because Oasis had even more to hide. And she told Albert about the watch on Simon Reed's wrist.

Albert listened without comment, but she felt his attention on her story.

"The police will be contacting your friends and family," he said when she finished.

Caroline's stomach churned as she considered the humiliations ahead.

She reconciled herself to them. The spreadsheet she'd handed to Albert when she'd arrived in Pershing Square contained proof that Oasis was harvesting money from elderly people on a massive scale. She had no choice but to see the investigation through from the safety of protective custody. As a suspect in a hit-and-run crime, she couldn't take refuge with friends or family—she couldn't put someone she loved in the position of being implicated in a crime or accused of hiding a fugitive.

"I think you should stay out here," Albert said.

"What?" Caroline wasn't sure she'd heard right.

"If you come in, you're going to end up in police custody. You'll end up in the system."

The knot in Caroline's gut pulled a little tighter. She'd seen the system at work. Sometimes it yielded justice, but often, it didn't. If she ended up in police custody, she'd put herself at risk of incarceration for a crime she did not commit. Even worse, she'd lose the ability to fight back. To investigate Oasis. She'd be left trying to exonerate herself with little evidence, up against a powerful foe that likely had agents in law enforcement.

Caroline's hands began to shake on the iPhone.

She was trapped.

Someone had engineered the paletería accident to flush her out. The plan was elegant and ruthless.

"That bust down in Commerce showed there are some dirty cops," Albert continued, as if reading the arc of her thoughts.

Caroline remembered the City of Commerce scandal. The industrial area south of Los Angeles had become a hotbed of gambling activities. Free from zoning restrictions, organized crime had thrived there. The police officers who'd abetted their activities had been suspended, but that didn't mean there weren't other corrupt cops.

"I'm not sure there's much I can do to help you right now," Albert said.

"Yeah, I get it, you can't risk it," Caroline said, not bothering to hide her disdain. Physically, Albert was the opposite of Boyd. Where the assistant DA was tall and Nordic, Albert was short. His face was all angles and planes. In a capitulation to early male-pattern baldness, he'd cropped his hair short, leaving only a shadow of black hair curving across the top of his tanned head. But under flesh and bone, Albert was just another Boyd—afraid to take a stand. Gutless. Useless.

"That's not it," Albert said. "Those bank records suggest there's something going on here. I just can't use official channels to help you— especially in the current political climate."

Suddenly, Caroline understood. The new DA had promised a return to community-based policing and an emphasis on prosecuting crimes against marginalized communities. Too long neglected by law enforcement, the minority communities had celebrated DA Donita Johnson's election. A drunk white girl crashing her car into a family-owned paletería and gravely injuring the Hispanic proprietress would be slaughtered in the court of public opinion, regardless of the merits. Meanwhile, the DA would feather her political nest with a conviction.

"If I can pull together enough evidence, I'll get this done," Albert promised. "But if you want to remain free, you've got to stay out of sight. Trust me on this."

Caroline nodded to herself. Albert's parents had been political dissidents. He knew something about staying out of sight to continue fighting against corrupt, oppressive authority.

Exhaling, Caroline considered the days ahead of her. She'd have no federal protection. No warm shower. No roof over her head.

"I'll find out what I can, too," Caroline said. Even if she didn't have an apartment, a phone, a laptop, or anything else, she'd find a way to fight.

"How are you going to do that from the streets?" Albert laughed.

"I'll figure it out," Caroline shot back. "Just tell me what you need."

"Links in the chain," Albert said, his voice growing serious. "Money trails. Documents. Who's pulling the strings? Where's the money going? It can't just be to buy some land near the LA River. We need to know how the scam works and who's benefiting."

"What about the information on my spreadsheet?" Caroline asked.

"It's a start. But proving that Oasis coerced people into giving it gifts is going to be a challenge. The elderly residents are dead. Plus, Oasis is a favorite of city government. Everyone loves public-private partnerships these days. Everyone loves Duncan Reed. We're going to need a lot on Oasis if we're going to nail it."

"We'll nail it," Caroline said. If she was right, Oasis was a soft monster slowly digesting society's most vulnerable fringe, then funneling resources to . . . to somewhere. Without knowing who Oasis's shareholders were, she couldn't know who profited from the closely held private corporation. But one thing seemed likely: it was enriching the Reed family. What they needed was someone who'd be willing to talk about Oasis's secrets.

"See if you can track down Jessie Tuttle," Caroline said, recalling Hector's notes from his investigation into Oasis's construction enterprises. "Tuttle got injured during the restoration of the County Law Library. I'm assuming he came out of the Oasis training program. He might be willing to talk—he could have some information on how Oasis operates and how it keeps its workers in line. I believe he was planning to sue Oasis. He could be friendly to us."

"I'll see what I can find," Albert said.

"I'm going to do my own looking, too," Caroline said.

This time Albert didn't laugh.

Caroline looked down at the iPhone still cradled in her hands. Flipping it over, she noted the colorful case adorned with a peacock with the number 88 woven into its tail feathers. The emblem of the 88 Generation Students, Caroline surmised. The Burmese dissident group Albert's parents had belonged to—and perhaps still did.

"Things have gotten better in Burma—Myanmar—haven't they?" she asked.

"Only on the surface. But the repressive mind-set's still there. The fight goes on," Albert said. "There's still a need for the 88 Generation."

With her eyes still on the phone case, Caroline nodded to herself. Albert came from a family where freedom and justice mattered. She hoped those values were in his DNA, too.

She knew it was time to give Albert back his phone, but still she clung to it. An irrational part of her wanted to take the phone and run. A more rational part wanted to call her parents. To preempt the questions the police would be asking. At least her mother was still on a cruise. But what would her dad think when he got the call from the cops? Even worse, what would her stepmother, Lily, think?

Caroline hands tingled with sudden apprehension.

She had to reach her dad and stepmom before the police did.

She lifted her finger to dial.

But then she stopped. If she was the target of an active investigation, her parents' numbers could not be found on Albert's phone. She couldn't get him in trouble.

She slowly handed the phone back over her shoulder.

As it left her grip, something in her soul withered.

Behind her, she heard the click of Albert taking pictures of the spreadsheet and the first page of the title report for the Parrino Court property that Oasis owned.

Then Albert handed the pages back to her.

"I've got some contacts in the banking sector that might be able to feed me some information in a form I can use at trial—or at least to get subpoenas." Albert's voice held a kind of earnestness Caroline had rarely heard in a fellow lawyer. She wanted to believe his words. She wanted to believe in him. But nothing in her past suggested anyone could help her.

There was a rustle of movement behind Caroline. Then Albert's hand passed something back to her over his shoulder.

A business card and some cash. A five and two ones.

"It's all I've got on me," Albert said. His tone was apologetic.

Caroline looked at the crumpled bills. She wished she were in a position to refuse.

"You've got my card," he said. "I'm going to be in trial and then in meetings with my trial team, but I should be able to talk by 8:30 p.m. every day this week. You'll have to call me."

"I will," Caroline said. She considered asking Albert to make arrangements to bring her more money or a burner phone or clean underwear, but she stayed silent. She didn't know him well enough to push. For whatever reason, Albert believed in her, in her theories about Oasis. She couldn't jeopardize his good opinion.

And yet, there was one favor she had to ask.

"I'm handling a guardianship case for a boy named Mateo Hidalgo," she began. She quickly told Albert about the status of the proceedings. "I can't let Mateo end up in a bad spot because I'm in one. If you could make sure that Shaina Parker in the gangs unit at the DA's office is looking into the *Hidalgo* case, I'd be grateful."

"I'm on it," Albert said. "I'll put in an informal inquiry about the *Hidalgo* case as soon as I get into the office. I'm also going to check on your friend in the hospital. If she was the target of a hit, we've got to keep a close eye on her. I'll set something up."

"Thank you," Caroline said, and she meant it. It was horrible enough that Amy was in a hospital and that Hector was dead. That something could still happen to Amy and that she couldn't do anything to prevent it hung over her like a cloud of inevitable doom.

"No problem," Albert said over his shoulder as he pretended to tie his shoe and leave.

Just as they'd planned, Caroline remained on the bench.

Watching the day unfold at Pershing Square, she wondered how three street people could bring down a powerful entity whose motto taunted her.

Helping you help yourself.

CHAPTER 18

Jake, Caroline, and Hitch huddled together in the trees on the edge of Pershing Square.

"We're going to need to work fast," Caroline said, thinking about the paletería accident. "It's only a matter of time before someone sees me." She ran a hand over her head, wishing for a shower to clear her mind. She paced the small clearing instead.

"We need to solve this damn thing," she continued. "Caregivers in nursing homes are getting elderly residents to write wills leaving their money to Oasis."

"Where does Oasis find these caregivers?" Hitch asked, playing along.

Caroline noted the clarity of his diction. He hadn't had anything to drink since the night before. She hoped he managed to make it through the day without drinking again. She needed all the focus the ex-cop could muster.

"That's easy," Caroline replied. "They're sending ex-felons and people off the street to these nursing homes. These people train at Oasis's nursing program."

"But why do these people cooperate?" Hitch asked. "What's in it for them besides a free meal and a roof?"

"Maybe that's enough. Maybe these people think they're doing a good thing by steering old people into leaving money to Oasis." Caroline was thinking out loud, editing herself as she went. "But Oasis seems pretty corporate. Corporations don't rely on people's consciences to meet a bottom line. There's got to be something more to it."

"Agreed," said Hitch, following Caroline with his eyes. "Where's the money going once Oasis gets it? What's it being used for? Who's benefiting?"

"Oasis is Duncan Reed's company, but he had a stroke. His son, Simon, is the obvious culprit, especially since Duncan is—"

"—incompetent," Hitch finished. "I agree, Simon's the suspect. Our problem is one of proof."

Caroline stayed silent. Proving the criminal involvement of the charismatic son of one of the city's most beloved citizens remained an intractable problem. How could they connect the dots that had eluded Hector? While Caroline had seen the hazy outlines of the beast she fought, she had not yet seen its true contours.

"What about the affidavit-withdrawal transaction itself?" she asked. "There's a moment where some Oasis officer goes to a bank and cleans out an elderly person's account, right?"

Hitch's muddy eyes ignited with interest. He nodded, urging his niece onward.

"That person's going to show up at the bank with a Probate Code 13100 affidavit and a copy of the dead person's will," Caroline continued. "The bank cuts a cashier's check to Oasis and then hands it to that person." She paused. "Who's the person standing there?"

"It has to be someone pretty high in the Oasis food chain," Hitch surmised. "Handling money requires trust."

"We need to figure out who that person is," Caroline said.

"How are we going to do that?" Hitch asked.

Caroline leaned back against a tree. She pulled the Saint Christopher medallion out of her shirt. Warmed to body temperature by its contact with her chest, its uneven ridges soothed her like the worry beads that were a million miles away in her apartment. That the medallion once belonged to her grandmother calmed her, as well.

Her mind traveled to the watch. The quest for it had once seemed irrational. Her anger at its theft and her visceral discomfort at its absence had been all consuming. But that form of obsessive grief had moved aside to leave room for desperation. She wasn't running on despair anymore. She was running on fear for her life.

Dropping the medallion, she thrust her hand into her back pocket and pulled out the Spreadsheet of Death. The list of BanCorp customers who'd left money to Oasis.

Her eyes scanned the columns of information. "Oasis does all of its affidavit withdrawals each month from the same branch in Los Angeles. They aggregate all of the death certificates and make one trip of it."

"Maybe we could ambush him or her?" Hitch suggested.

Caroline studied the dates of the transactions. Most recently, someone from Oasis had visited BanCorp's Hope Street branch on July 17, August 21, and September 13. It wasn't the same day each month. That meant there was no way to predict when he or she would show up again to make the next batch of affidavit withdrawals.

But then something caught Caroline's eye.

"The most recent batch of affidavit withdrawals was just a couple weeks ago. September 13. There's a time stamp—10:35 a.m." She tapped the page.

"The security camera would have taken a picture of whoever it is, right?" she asked, meeting her uncle's eyes.

"Definitely." Hitch nodded. "I had a case involving a bank heist once. Most banks use a contractor called Security Images to store and maintain footage from the security cameras."

"In other words, there's a centralized database," Caroline said. "Or, more likely, each bank's got a cloud account connected to Security Images."

"Something like that," Hitch confirmed. "Standard operating procedure is that contractors only keep footage two weeks before destroying it."

"The last withdrawal was two weeks ago," said Caroline. "When does the data purge happen?"

"Midnight, usually," said Hitch.

"That footage still exists," Caroline said. "I need a laptop."

"We're a long way from any computer here, kiddo."

The answer wasn't acceptable to Caroline. Her mind flew in a half dozen directions. She could try to contact Albert, but he'd already said he couldn't bring her into protective custody. And anyway, he might not be able to get her what she needed—a computer she could use for the three to four hours necessary to hack the security company and then review reams of video files.

She'd face the same problem if she tried to use a computer at a library or some other publicly available computer lab. Even assuming she could overcome whatever restrictions on Internet access she found at a public lab, she wouldn't have the time and bandwidth necessary to retrieve what she needed from Security Images.

Maybe she could try to reach someone who could wire money or lend her a computer, but how and whom? No, she was a suspect in a well-publicized crime. Who could she contact that would be willing to harbor a fugitive? Who could she even ask to take that risk?

"We gotta talk to Floyd," said Jake, interrupting Caroline's flood of ideas.

"Who's Floyd?" she asked.

"The mayor," Jake said without any trace of irony.

• • •

Caroline ran her hands down her shirt to make it more presentable, which was impossible, because her tank top had turned more brown than white.

"Does he know we're here?" Caroline asked.

"Yes," her uncle answered, his eyes trained on the hillside in front of them. "But he might not be willing to talk to us."

Caroline squinted up the scrub-covered hill. It didn't resemble any other mayoral mansion. But her uncle's description during their walk across town to this hillside on the edge of Vista Hermosa Park had convinced her that in the decentralized world of the homeless, Floyd was something between an ombudsman and the yellow pages. Everyone knew him. Everyone trusted him. Some even imbued him with some sort of mystical importance. It was said he could leave the streets if he wanted, but he'd decided to stay.

"He's coming," Jake said, his eyes tracking the shadow of a man approaching.

Hitch's posture shifted to readiness. He stood on the balls of his feet, poised. For what, Caroline didn't know.

Soon a man came into view. Barefoot but wearing dress slacks and a button-down shirt, he picked his way down the hill until he stood seven feet from the group. Though he was not tall, his jet-black eyes commanded attention. They moved from Caroline to Uncle Hitch to Jake.

Then Floyd raised an eyebrow: an invitation for the group to state its business.

Jake reached into his jacket pocket and withdrew a wood carving. He offered it to Floyd.

With long, graceful fingers, Floyd accepted the figure. He turned the object over in his hands, his brow crinkling.

"An albatross." Floyd's voice was eerily singsong, and it floated on the wind. "Yes, I am very much the albatross around my family's neck." His soft observation held an echo of regret.

"No," Jake said. "The albatross flies across great distances. Over oceans. But he always comes back to the same place. He's committed to his home. To his people. He mates for life."

Floyd tilted his head as if considering this new interpretation.

Caroline had watched Jake whittle late into the night without realizing he'd been creating a tribute. A poetic, thoughtful one.

Floyd cradled the carved albatross in his hands.

After a long moment, he turned and began walking back up the hill.

Jake followed.

Hitch and Caroline fell in behind him.

• • •

Floyd led the group to a clearing. High above, an electrical tower rose over the eucalyptus trees. The loading lines hummed at a pitch barely audible to human ears. There were no birds.

Floyd stopped in the shadow of the electrical tower. Beside a fraying green tent, a string between two trees held an assortment of blankets and jackets. A closet in the wind. Farther back, at the edge of the woods, were two sky-blue tents visible against the silvery eucalyptus trunks.

The only other sign of civilization was the table. Small and square, it sat atop a carpet of fragrant leaves. It had been set with a red-and-white-checkered tablecloth and mismatched plates, saucers, and cups. Finishing off the settings, two silver candlesticks held two half-burned white tapers. An Italian café in the woods.

Floyd gestured for them to sit.

Once everyone had picked a chair, he disappeared into one of the tents.

He emerged moments later. In his hands, he held a box of Walkers Shortbread cookies.

With precise movements, he pulled a clear plastic tray out of the box to reveal a neat row of golden-yellow cookies. Accompanied only by the rustle of the eucalyptus trees and the hum of electrical wires, he placed a single cookie before each person.

"Thank you," Caroline said, grateful for the strange hospitality. The sweet, buttery flakiness was decadence on her tongue. After three days of slimy ham sandwiches and old apples, she knew she'd never think of shortbread the same way again.

"I wish I had tea to offer, but I don't," Floyd said. His voice held genuine regret. "The city finds me and throws my stuff away every month or so. Then I have to start again. I haven't found more tea yet. I take what I can when the police come, but it isn't always possible to take much. Sometimes I have to leave everything." Floyd touched the base of the silver candlesticks. "These are the exceptions. I always take these. They remind me of my family . . ." A grimace tugged at the corner of his mouth.

"What happened?" Caroline asked, ignoring the cautionary glare from her uncle.

"To my family? They're much the same as they always are, I imagine. Work, work, working in the family business."

"Family business?" Caroline pulled her legs in to avoid the kick she knew would be coming from her uncle. When she found something—or someone—worth knowing more about, her curiosity was relentless. In Floyd she'd found a fascinating specimen.

"My family owns a controlling share in one of the largest fast food franchisors in the country. But it wasn't for me. The pressures of family can be intolerable," Floyd said, as though that explained everything.

Caroline remained silent. In her experience, people tended to fill the gaps in conversations.

"I don't have a head for business," Floyd continued. "My family thought tough love would make me more . . . What was their word?

199

Ah, yes, *serious*. But I didn't do well without the intravenous drip, drip, dripping of cash, either."

In Floyd's singsong voice, Caroline heard a downward spiral. Had Floyd fallen down a pit of addiction? Or mental illness? Dual diagnosis seemed to be de rigueur on the streets.

"My father gave me a franchise to run for myself. But times aren't great for the small-business owner." Floyd shook his head. "Payroll taxes. Health care costs. Liability insurance. All of it was far too much to care about or manage. By the time my franchise went under, I'd come to understand some very important things."

"Like what?"

"Like, I detest the scent of frying potatoes. Also, I didn't need the corrupting influence of my family. You can't escape the greed that goes with money. Why do you think so many people are so stingy about handing a homeless veteran even a dollar at a stoplight?"

Caroline resisted the urge to point out that some people assumed the dollar that went to the homeless veteran went to buying alcohol or drugs.

"So you stayed on the streets," she said instead.

"It rather works for me. I much prefer being outside." As he drifted off, the wind pushed through the eucalyptus grove, showering thin silver-green leaves onto the table.

"People come to me for advice," he continued, focusing his attention on Caroline again. "They call me the mayor." A smile tugged at the corner of his mouth.

He liked the moniker, Caroline realized. Was it really ego that kept this man on the street? A need for respect so deep that the adulation of lost souls, addicts, and mentally ill vagrants was enough to justify living permanently in transit?

"I know everyone out here," he continued. "Who they are. What they're good for. How honest they are. How addicted they are, and to what." He smiled a full row of even, white teeth, the lasting legacy of a wealthy upbringing. "I am . . . respected."

A Craigslist. A Yelp. A Google. All rolled up into one small-boned little man sitting in a clearing on top of a hill.

"When someone gets off the streets, I'm happy for them," Floyd continued. "But I have no desire to leave."

"Really?" Caroline asked. She thought of Lani, the slight woman in the red dress who'd fled the distribution center in terror. She remembered the echoes of late-night fighting outside her apartment building. And she recalled the prostitute she'd once seen slip into a portable bathroom in the shadow of Skid Row to turn a trick. None of those people had found a comfortable home on the streets. That anyone could belong outside was ludicrous. It was a sad fantasy, at best. A dangerous illusion, at worst.

As if to prove her musings correct, the distant shout of a man's voice echoed up the hill, rising in crescendo until tapering off in murmured babbling.

"That's just Ansel." Floyd chuckled. "My Minister of Madness. He's harmless."

"He's probably schizophrenic," Caroline shot back. "Medicine would help him."

"Schizophrenics are drowning in the same ocean that mystics are swimming in," Floyd said. "Some are enlightened or touched. Some are just stark raving mad. Some are broken. Some were never whole. Some are sojourning here. Some are just passing through." He paused. "Which are you?"

Caroline resisted her lawyer's instincts to debate Floyd. Her goal was to get off the streets, and she needed Floyd's help.

"Passing through, I hope, but I really need a computer." If Hitch was right, the security camera contractor would delete the bank's video footage soon. They had to hurry.

"There's a whole unseen universe out there." Floyd gestured with one long hand, around the grove. "Filled with everything you need."

Caroline wondered if he meant the urban wilderness or the spirit realm.

"So what do you *really* need?" he asked.

Caroline exhaled her frustration. She needed to dance with Floyd's demons, apparently.

"Justice. Safety. A way to make the people who are chasing me disappear," she said.

"Good, good." Floyd nodded, gesturing for her to continue. "And a computer will make you free?"

"It'll help me make myself free," Caroline said. The distinction seemed important.

"Ah, taking initiative. Good!" Floyd slapped the table with both hands.

"So you'll help me?"

"No," he said.

Caroline's hopes fell.

"But I know someone who can," Floyd said. "His name's Curtis. He's even crazier than I am."

"Where can I find him?" Caroline asked.

Floyd looked up at the sun, then met Caroline's eyes again.

"He'll be at the doughnut shop on Jefferson and Orchard right now, if you hurry. I think you'll find that the dog is saner than his master."

CHAPTER 19

They found the dog first. With black-and-white markings like a Holstein cow and the compact frame of a pig, he stood at the edge of the alley behind Stanley's Doughnuts. He looked up at the group, then cocked his head as if asking whether they'd made an appointment.

From somewhere deeper in the alley came a crash and a shuffle. The sound of dumpster diving.

After licking Caroline's offered hand, the dog trotted into the alley, leaving the sun-heated pavement for the alley's humid, putrid shade.

Caroline followed with Hitch, while Jake took up a post at the mouth of the alleyway.

Approaching the cacophony at the end of the alley, Caroline's body felt jerky and wrong. Hunger. Fear. Nerves. All had conspired to diminish her capacity to function.

But she had to keep going. The clock in the window of the doughnut shop said it was 11:05. That meant she had less than twelve hours to find a way to hack Security Images' server and uncover the identity of the person handling the affidavit withdrawals for Oasis. Though Caroline had worked under tight deadlines before, this one seemed impossible to meet.

Pushing despair from her mind, Caroline forced herself to focus on the task in front of her. Or rather, its rear end. The dog had stopped beside a man whose head was buried in a dumpster, his long legs dangling down the front of the rusted green metal.

"Excuse me," Caroline said.

She waited for the man to dislodge his face from the trash.

Beside her, Hitch shifted from foot to foot. Evidently, he, too, knew they were running out of time.

After another moment, the man emerged from his explorations. He had long black hair that hung down below his shoulders and teeth with too much space between them. In his hand, he held the crumpled white paper bag he'd fished from the dumpster.

"Are you Curtis?" Caroline asked, though his identity was obvious based on Floyd's physical description.

Curtis kept his attention on the bag. He peered at it intently, as if building anticipation for opening a birthday present. Then he opened it, jutting his long neck down to gauge its contents.

"Damn! Just scones." He dropped the bag at his feet and dived back into the dumpster.

"Floyd sent us," Caroline said to Curtis's butt. "He told us you had a computer I might be able to borrow. It's a matter of life and death. It'll save lives." And quietly, "Mine included."

But Curtis continued rummaging through the dumpster's contents, the occasional swear words resonating in the metal box.

"What are you looking for?" Caroline asked.

"Doughnuts and their holes. Most eat them because they are sweet."

"That's true," Caroline agreed. "But you don't?"

Curtis withdrew his face from the dumpster.

Straightening to his full height, he towered over Caroline like a basketball player.

"Why do I eat doughnuts?" he echoed.

"Yes. You said most people eat them because they are sweet. That suggests that isn't your reason." Caroline knew how to talk to crazy people. She was related to a few. She'd logged many hours navigating the distorted dimensions of their realities.

"I eat doughnuts because they are the perfect Zen snack. Round and endless on the outside, the empty space in the center is there to remind you of the missing piece, which is also fried in oil. Together they are whole. Yin and yang."

He brought his two hands together in a thunderous clap.

"How about computers? Can we talk about computers?" Caroline asked.

"I don't eat computers."

"Of course not," Caroline agreed. "That would be nuts. But if you have a computer I could borrow for just a half hour, I'd—" She tried to think of something she could trade.

"You'd what? Tell the authorities where I live, and then they would confiscate my computer along with all of my belongings?" Curtis returned to his hunt for doughnuts. "Only I know the undisclosed safe location where the computer lives. Where the movies play."

"Movies?" Caroline echoed. The word hummed with significance.

"Yes, but the evil Comcast thinks that I am a torrent freak, so they keep throttling my flow so I can only watch one movie at a time," Curtis said, his voice echoing in the dumpster. "One screen at a time. It is a hateful choking."

Caroline considered the information. This mad hatter of a man apparently had access to electricity and a computer. She sent silent thanks to Floyd.

"You mean you don't have the bandwidth you want," she said.

Pulling himself from the dumpster, Curtis frowned and brought his hands together. "My reach is oh, so, so, so short. And there are so many movies. So many images that I cannot reach."

A tear formed at the corner of his eye, and he used the bottom of his shirt to dab at it.

"Now go." He waved his other hand away.

"It's not a permanent problem," Caroline ventured. "It's just the, um, evil Comcast throttling your flow."

Curtis looked up from his shirt.

With tears still in his eyes, he nodded.

"What if I could get you more bandwidth?" Caroline asked.

Curtis raised his eyebrows, hope igniting in his gaze. From his expression, Caroline could tell that bandwidth was even better than doughnuts in Curtis's Pantheon of Favorite Things.

"Yes, much more bandwidth—huge, long bandwidth," Caroline offered, lowering her voice to a deeper register. "What if I could get you a constant torrent?"

"You can do this?" Curtis asked.

"Oh yes," Caroline said. "But only if you'll let me use your computer."

Curtis rubbed his hands together again like an addict being offered his favorite vice.

"If you can bring me the torrent, then you may use my computer," he announced.

"No, I need to use the computer first," Caroline said. She was running out of time.

But Curtis shook his head. "I have told you what I need. You must bring me the torrent. Then you may use the computer."

"But you can wait for bandwidth. I need a computer now. You don't understand—"

"No, you do not understand. My computer. My rules. Either you're in or you're out."

Caroline controlled her desire to scream at the clearly insane man.

"Do you have a wireless router?" she asked instead, caging her temper.

"Yes, yes. I have all manner of only slightly old tech. People are fickle. Oh, so very fickle. They throw away things. Monitors. Ethernet cables. Routers. All of it is mine now." When Curtis smiled, the spaces between his teeth reminded Caroline of a small child.

"You want movies?" she asked again, her mind working hard to figure out how to get Curtis what he wanted. There were many ways to pirate bandwidth. But without seeing Curtis's setup, it was difficult to determine how to augment it. She needed more information from him.

"Yes. But not only that," Curtis said. "I am also wanting legal things."

"Legal things?" Caroline echoed, exhaling in exasperation. The deal the tall man had struck was apparently now growing an amendment.

"Yes. I am studying all the time. All, all, all the time. Except when I am gathering doughnuts," he added. "Professor Graverstein is my favorite for studying." Now Curtis's voice dropped to a lower register, suggesting the sort of interest beyond the merely academic.

"Professor Graverstein? You mean the Con Law professor at Southwestern Law School?" Caroline had owned a textbook authored by Professor Graverstein. The professor was not only brilliant, she was beautiful, as Caroline had learned from the book jacket. She could understand Curtis's interest, if not how he'd managed to watch one of the professor's lectures. Law schools guarded their intellectual property. Otherwise, there'd be little point in charging tuition.

"Professor Graverstein is teaching always about the government's powers," Curtis continued. "What it can do. What it can take away. What it cannot do. Listening to her . . ." He closed his eyes and rocked back and forth.

"Did you find something on YouTube about her?" Caroline asked.

Curtis bobbed his head up and down. "She gave only one interview on CNN, and I have learned all there is to learn from that interview. Now I must learn more. I also saw her in person once, too, but I stayed away so that I would not frighten her. She is too important to be frightened. Instead, I tried to talk to the students to find where the video lectures are hiding."

The corners of his mouth turned down.

"You talked to students at Southwestern Law School?" Caroline asked.

"Some would not talk to me. One did. He confirmed there are dozens, hundreds, thousands of videos of Professor Graverstein. But they are caged." He frowned more, the light leaving his eyes. "They are not on the Internet."

Judging by the location of the doughnut shop, Caroline had an idea where Curtis lived. She knew how to help him pirate bandwidth for watching movies. But she still had to figure out how to give him access to a law school professor's video lectures that resided solely on Southwestern Law School's server.

"Find me a wireless router and some Ethernet cable and I'll get you your bandwidth," Caroline said. "I'll need a few hours to get your access to Professor Graverstein's lectures."

"But you can do it?" Curtis asked.

"Yes."

"If you do this, you can come to the undisclosed safe location where the computer resides."

Caroline's heart thrilled. Right now, it was better than an invitation to the White House.

But then she realized something.

"How will I know where the undisclosed location is?"

"Enzo will bring you," Curtis said. "You will find him at the soup kitchen near City Hall. He is always there when he is not here. Or somewhere else."

Caroline frowned. Find some dude named Enzo at a soup kitchen he was at sometimes. Except when he wasn't. What could possibly go wrong?

• • •

Caroline flexed her toes in her ill-fitting shoes. The fifteen-block walk to her destination had ensured that the blisters growing on her heels would take weeks to heal. She hoped she'd be able to hitch a ride back to Julian Street, where she'd meet up again with Hitch and Jake. But right now, she had other things to worry about.

Looking up, Caroline regarded the building she needed to figure out how to enter.

The exterior of the Bullocks Wilshire building hadn't changed since Caroline had last been there, but the inside had been gutted and turned into Southwestern Law School. Still, the shell of the structure remained exactly as she remembered it from childhood. The Art Deco edifice rose a half dozen stories from the street, its taupe and mint walls harkening back to an age of elegance. But the doors that had once welcomed high-end shoppers in overcoats and fedoras now teemed with students in backpacks and blue jeans.

Feeling like an interloper, Caroline circumnavigated the school until she found what she sought: the side entrance. It was right where she remembered it. She'd passed through it many times with her mother. Joanne Auden had been allowed to use the special entrance reserved for Bullocks Wilshire's best customers. As a child, Caroline had thrilled at the special treatment. The smiles of the uniformed staff as they held open the door. The cheerful attentions of the personal shopping assistants waiting on the other side.

Looking back, Caroline recognized her mom was a "best customer" because she went on manic spending sprees. She recalled her mother grabbing fistfuls of shirts from the display tables, the personal shopping assistant gleefully suggesting accessories to go with each. The mood had been elating. Festive. Hours after entering the special side door, Joanne Auden would leave with a valet carrying a half dozen full shopping bags to the car.

Now, the door that had once allowed her mother to mainline her shopping addiction allowed Caroline to avoid the security desk at the front of the school. A desk where she'd be asked for an identification card.

Caroline had no time for questions. Hence, the side door.

Leaning back against the side of the building, Caroline opened the newspaper she'd found in a free kiosk on the corner near the bus stop. She scratched at the back of her neck, where the tag of the shirt she'd grabbed from an open locker at the YMCA bothered her neck. She'd risked the trip to the public pool to use the showers. The clean T-shirt had been a bonus. Both were necessary for what she had planned now.

Soon, the door opened. A student emerged, backpack in hand, cell phone in the other. He hardly missed a step as Caroline brushed past him, through the open door.

Once she was inside, Caroline stopped to get her bearings. While she was familiar with the building, she wasn't familiar with the law school's build-out.

Gone were the mannequins. Gone were the clothes. Gone were the helpful assistants, waiting to ply her mother with compliments and stoke her mania. But Caroline could still guess where to find the server. It would be somewhere near the library or the administration center. Somewhere at the nexus of information. The layout would be predictable. She just needed to find the landmarks that would tell her where to look.

A sign listed the faculty and their offices. Below the directory, arrows pointed in different directions.

Caroline followed the arrow that pointed toward the Sonesseri Computer Lab.

• • •

As Caroline had hoped, the server room was located two doors down from the computer lab. A keypad was mounted at face level beside the server room—a layer of security that Caroline would have to figure out how to crack.

But first she had to write some code. She glanced at the clock in the hall.

It was 1:58 p.m. She needed to move quickly.

Inside the computer lab, Caroline found six desktop computers available to any student who had a password. It was an artifact of earlier computing days when not all students had their own laptops. The room's only occupant was a woman with ebony skin and an amber dress.

A jar of memory sticks sat atop a small table by the entrance. A note card informed students that the memory sticks were complimentary from The Sonesseri Firm, which was also hiring unpaid externs for work during the summer. Another business that wanted cheap, desperate labor.

Slipping a memory stick into her pocket, Caroline approached the ebony-skinned woman.

"I'm new here," Caroline began. "I mean, I'm a first year."

"Me, too," said the woman with a French accent. She didn't take her eyes from the computer.

"My laptop got stolen," Caroline volunteered. It wasn't entirely untrue.

"That's terrible," the woman commiserated, looking up.

Caroline warmed at the reaction. Though she disliked preying on compassion, it was a useful human emotion for someone in desperate need of a favor.

"I came from Ghana two months ago," continued the woman. "I'm waiting two months already for my stipend so I can buy a laptop. Until then, I am here."

"At least you can get into your account and get your assignments," Caroline said. In the African woman's eyes, she noted the restrained urge to press for more information. Curiosity. Another malleable human emotion.

"The truth is," Caroline continued in a low voice, "I haven't prepared for my Contracts exam. My professor posted a bunch of stuff we were supposed to read, and unfortunately I forgot my password for these." Caroline gestured to the computers in the lab. She paused another beat. "I never wrote down my computer lab password. I thought I wouldn't need it." She looked down, as if acknowledging she'd been chastised by the fates for her arrogance.

"Contracts?" the African woman asked, her eyes brightening. "Who's your professor?"

"Fesler," Caroline answered. She was glad she'd read the staff directory.

"Oh, I'm in Culberson's class," the woman said, her face falling. "But if you want, you can get in on my account."

"Really? Thanks so much." Caroline hurried to sit down at the computer farthest from the African woman.

With swift keystrokes, she brought up the log-in panel.

As soon as the woman gave her a username and password, Caroline jammed the memory stick into the USB port and began her work. Instead of navigating to the course directories, she opened a document and began writing code. Once loaded onto the law school's server, it would create a back door that she could open remotely for Curtis so he'd have endless access to Professor Graverstein's lectures.

The sensation of keys beneath her fingers gave Caroline the illusion of having reached her goal of securing a computer to hack Security Images, but she knew she couldn't use the law school's computers for that task. She needed a private computer with unfettered Internet access and hours of uninterrupted time—something the computer lab didn't offer, but that hopefully Curtis could provide. If she could earn his trust.

Writing swiftly but carefully, Caroline constructed the series of commands she needed the law school's server to obey.

From the corner of her eye, Caroline noticed the African woman looking over at her, probably wondering why someone who was supposed to be downloading course materials was furiously typing on a keyboard.

Caroline hurried to finish her code. Just a few more strings of commands should do it. Just a few more orders to the server, telling it whom to let inside. Who was friend and who was foe.

When she finished, Caroline forced herself to proofread her code. She didn't want to spend any more time in the server room than she had to in order to load her work onto the server. Better to get it right now than stay in the server room where her presence would raise alarms.

"What are you doing?" came the woman's voice from directly behind Caroline.

"Just printing out the law review article now," Caroline said, pointing at the screen, where she'd pulled up Professor Fesler's current reading assignments.

She hit "Print," then logged off before yanking the memory stick out of the USB port and pocketing it.

"Thanks. You're a real lifesaver," Caroline said, hurrying out of the computer lab.

CHAPTER 20

Instead of trying to break into the pass code–protected server room, Caroline wandered the halls of Southwestern Law School. Despite the ticking clock, Caroline forced herself to slow down. She had an idea how to get inside the server room, but she'd need to use the computer lab again. This time, she had to make sure she had no witnesses.

So she drifted past the library and watched the students study.

She strolled by the mail room and grabbed a law school newsletter, which she tucked under her arm to use later.

Finally, she reentered the computer lab.

To her relief, she found it empty. The African woman must have finished her work. Hopefully she wouldn't return soon.

Placing the newsletter on the desk beside one of the computers, Caroline crouched low and followed the cord from the nearest computer to the lab's router. Routers were used to connect computers to the Internet or, in this case, to the law school's server.

She discovered that the computer router was an outdated Cisco. In her software engineering days, Caroline had written articles about the common vulnerabilities and exposures—or CVEs—for routers. She knew Cisco routers were vulnerable to denial-of-service or DoS attacks.

Inserting a string of characters into the log-in prompt would crash the router, resulting in a denial of service to everyone using the server.

With deft keystrokes, Caroline inserted the characters.

Then she waited.

Ten seconds later, the screen of her computer flashed an urgent message: *No network access.*

Twisting around in her chair, Caroline checked the screens of the other five computers in the computer lab.

They all showed the same message: *No network access.*

Everywhere around Southwestern Law School, people would be getting the same error.

Moving quickly, Caroline exited the computer lab. She hurried down the hall to the door of the server room.

The red light on the keypad beside the door told the tale: the keypad was down.

Even though the door remained locked, Caroline lingered nearby. She knew that soon the administrator would come to try to fix the downed router. And when that happened, she'd learn the last bit of information she needed to gain access to the server.

Picking up the school newsletter, Caroline leaned against a wall and pretended to read.

Her patience was rewarded by the sound of swift footsteps hurrying toward her.

A woman with short, spiky hair and glasses stopped beside her. The woman scowled at the keypad and then stabbed at it with her index finger: *5-8-9-1-5-2.*

Watching her over the top edge of the newsletter, Caroline memorized the sequence.

Then she drifted closer to the door and gave the woman a concerned look.

"I was working in the computer lab and got kicked off. Are you here to fix the server?"

Without looking over, the short-haired woman nodded. "Router went down."

The woman tried the password one last time then exhaled. She pulled a physical key from her pocket and used it to open the server room.

"It'll be just a second," said the administrator. "Sit tight and I'll have it fixed soon."

Nodding, Caroline withdrew.

Walking down the hall, Caroline stopped in front of a display case that used to hold clothes back in the building's Bullocks Wilshire days but that now held a visual history of the building. She waited, her eyes unseeing, her body attuned to the server room door twenty paces down the hallway from her.

Finally, the door opened, and the administrator strode away in the opposite direction.

Even from where Caroline stood, she could see the light on the keypad was green again.

Time to get in.

• • •

The warmth of the school's servers hung thick and buzzing in the room.

Caroline took quick stock of the setup. A single computer sat on a metal desk surrounded by thick ropes of cords and connectors that threaded off to an array of humming machinery. The single terminal ran on a KVM switch so that one keyboard, video, and mouse controlled all of the servers in the room. Now she just needed to tell the KVM which server to bring up.

Sitting down, Caroline pulled up the interface.

As she'd hoped, the servers contained no further layers of security. Most admins were lazy when it came to that extra layer. They figured that once you'd gotten into the server room, your credentials had already been checked. And so Caroline easily accessed the server containing the faculty accounts allowing professors unlimited access to one another's lectures.

She slipped the memory stick into the USB port and ordered the computer to run the code she'd written. A bar across the center of the screen appeared, tracking the upload's progress. The code she'd written was short. It wouldn't take long.

Her eyes darted to the door, begging it not to open. There was nowhere to hide if someone entered the server room. And there was no possible explanation she could offer for her presence. No student should be inside.

A sound from the hallway made her freeze.

Voices. A laugh.

A pause. More muffled conversation.

Students, Caroline decided.

She eyed the screen. Just another couple of seconds and she'd be done.

But then there were louder voices, coming near the door. A fragment of conversation. Close enough that Caroline could make out words. Something about a football game.

Caroline's eyes flickered back up to the screen.

The server had stopped loading her code.

Something was wrong.

Pushing the sounds in the hallway from her mind, Caroline opened her code, then scanned the letters and numbers, looking for the flaw. She forced herself to focus until there was nothing but coding. The hum of electricity fell away. The voices fell away. Even her awareness of herself fell away until all she knew were the commands she wrote.

When she finished, she tried loading again.

As her eyes obsessively tracked each pixel of movement on the upload bar, Caroline recognized her mother's mania in herself. A furnace of energy lived within her, every bit as much as it lived within her mother. When directed toward a goal, it made Caroline effective. An effective hacker. An effective lawyer. But the raw materials were the same as the restless intensity in her mother. Her brilliance was harvested madness.

Finally, the upload bar filled and disappeared. The malware was in.

Now Caroline just needed to get out of the server room unseen.

Stretching out her senses, she listened for the voices on the other side of the door.

They seemed to have gone.

She crept to the door and peered through the small window.

The pane was too tiny to provide a view of anything except an empty patch of hall directly beyond the door. She couldn't see in either direction. There was no help for it, though. She had to take a chance. So long as no one else was coming down the hall when Caroline exited the server room, she'd be safe.

Gathering her courage, Caroline opened the door.

The hall was empty.

She ran for the exit. She needed to find Enzo at the soup kitchen near City Hall and get back to Curtis in time to hack Security Images before the video feed was dumped.

• • •

"It's the damn APB," Uncle Hitch grumbled, ducking back behind the tree twenty yards from the tarped area next to City Hall where a line of homeless people waited for food.

It had taken Caroline almost two hours to hitch a ride downtown, collect her uncle and Jake, and head to the soup kitchen. Their meeting spot with Enzo had been in sight, but they'd stopped their progress toward it upon sighting the two police cars parked nearby.

"They've figured out you could be on the street," Hitch said. "Someone must've told them about me."

"Do you see anyone you know?" Caroline asked.

"No uniforms. Just cars."

At the reassurance, Caroline risked another look at the food line. Dozens of people in stained clothes and old hats waited to be served from a row of plastic folding tables. Three black-and-whites sat parked on the street next to the temporary pavilion erected by Oasis's Homeless Services branch. No officers were visible, but Caroline knew they couldn't be far away.

"You stay here," Jake said. "I'll go find Enzo."

Though his offer worried her, Caroline didn't protest. If someone had seen her with Hitch, they'd probably also seen her with Jake. And yet, she didn't have a better solution.

She watched Jake approach the food line. His head swung back and forth as he studied faces, looking for someone who might be named Enzo.

Caroline considered the prospects.

Not the short white guy with the drooping mustache and Dodgers cap. Not the black guy holding a dog. Perhaps the portly Latino guy wearing the flannel jacket? The one Jake was talking to now, his head bent down close enough to communicate with the man without anyone overhearing?

When Flannel Guy shook his head no, Jake continued down the line.

"That guy isn't homeless," Hitch said, breaking Caroline's reverie.

"Who?" Caroline asked.

"The big guy. Toward the front," Hitch said.

Caroline focused on the people gathering milk boxes from a bowl of ice water before gathering sandwiches from Oasis volunteers in green shirts.

"With the beard," Hitch continued. "Look at his pants."

"They've been ironed recently," she agreed. With his fresh crease and neatly trimmed beard, he wasn't ratty enough to be standing in a food line.

"Plainclothes detective?" Caroline asked.

"Maybe. I don't know him," Uncle Hitch said.

As Caroline watched, someone else came to join the bearded man. Even before she saw the newcomer's face, she recognized him. His posture. Shoulders hunched to offset his height. His hair. Long and blond, lashed back in a ponytail. When he turned toward the grove of trees in the park adjacent to the shelter, Caroline's blood froze in her veins. It was the hit man.

"That's him," she managed, ducking back behind the tree.

"The man from your apartment?"

Caroline nodded, her head filled with sudden dizziness. They needed to get away. Jake could find them later, but they had to leave. Now.

"He's coming," Hitch said.

Caroline's heart squeezed up into her throat.

"Jake, I mean," Hitch added, but not quickly enough.

Seconds later, Jake came into view, holding two sandwich bags in one hand. Behind him, a skinny kid with wavy dark-brown hair followed. His muscle shirt showed off biceps that were no wider than his triceps. A constellation of blue-black bruises darkened the inside of his left elbow. Heroin addict.

"You got what Curtis wants?" said Enzo.

Caroline gathered herself and nodded again.

"Yeah," she said, glad her voice didn't quaver.

"Cool," Enzo said. "Come on."

• • •

Hurrying away from the shelter in the wake of a teenage heroin addict, Caroline frantically raced through the possibilities. How had the hit man found her? The food line at City Hall was one of Hitch's regular lunch spots, so it was the logical place to look for him—and therefore her. It meant the hit man had deduced she was living on the street . . . which meant she needed to get off it.

But how?

Until she'd found a way to exonerate herself of the paletería crash, she couldn't go to Albert without turning herself in to the police. But her dad could still help, she decided. As soon as she reached Curtis's computer, she'd call him. Nothing else mattered. Not her stepmother's bad opinion. Not her tenuous relationship with her dad. Survival was all that mattered right now.

Up ahead, Enzo walked, high on the balls of his feet, a rocking motion that made him look jaunty despite his stained clothes. Caroline wondered at the combination of brain chemistry, circumstance, and bad luck that had doomed him to the streets. Where once she might've asked, now she kept her eyes focused on the narrow path she walked, hoping it didn't lead to her doom.

The University of Southern California soon came into view, its red brick warm and inviting against the tan-grays of the city streets. The area around the school thrived, spawning rows of fast-food joints and Laundromats, late-night munchie hangouts, doughnut shops, and sports bars. But Caroline didn't see student hangouts. She saw possibilities. Each place contained people that might be manipulated. Phones to borrow. Computers. If Curtis didn't come through, she'd need to try something else. Her mind formulated contingency plans. None were great, but she'd try every one of them if she had to.

Enzo stopped in front of a dilapidated Victorian mansion. Four stories tall, it had a facade like a mouse-eaten gingerbread house. At least eight labels plastered each of its mailbox slots, the names torn off, replaced, erased, or scratched out every other semester.

"This is it," Enzo announced.

Caroline regarded the house. It had been owned by some prosperous family in the 1800s. But as harder times had fallen on the neighborhoods to the south of downtown, the once-grand dame had fallen with them. Then, finally, the most egregious disrepute of all: it had become a boarding house for an ever-changing menagerie of USC students.

"He lives here?" Caroline asked.

Enzo answered with one word: "Under."

Without further explanation, he headed around the exterior of the house, into the backyard. The legacy of its occupants lay mounded amid overgrown weeds. Old bikes and discarded lawn furniture. Empty kegs. An agave cactus, baking in the sun, its spiked fronds wilting and withering, untended.

At the edge of the property, he crouched. Embedded in the ground, there was a set of double doors that looked as old as the house. They were invisible except to someone standing directly before them.

Reaching down, Enzo looped a finger in the metal hasp that kept the door shut.

With a muffled groan, one side of the door opened against its hinges until it lay back against the weeds. A row of dusty stairs dipped into a subterranean world.

Enzo gestured for Caroline to enter first.

"Seriously?" Caroline asked.

Enzo shrugged.

As Caroline stepped gingerly onto the first of the wooden risers, Enzo put a hand on her shoulder. "Be real quiet when you're under there, 'cause no one knows he's down there."

Once Caroline, Jake, and Hitch had cleared the door, Enzo closed it behind them. Then his footsteps receded aboveground as he left, off to go find a fix or food or whatever he was doing when he wasn't leading beleaguered ex-hackers to a man who lived beneath a student rooming house.

CHAPTER 21

The scent of the earthen passageway sparked a sense of déjà vu for Caroline.

Where had she smelled that loamy odor before?

Her grandmother's funeral.

Shivering, Caroline forced herself to focus on the faint light at the end of the passageway. Judging by the length of the tunnel and the direction they were walking, they were now directly beneath the house.

The passageway broadened into a low-ceilinged basement, supported by two-by-fours and unfinished redwood planking. The space was rough, but what Caroline beheld in it was almost beautiful: screens from the early 2000s. Dot-matrix printers. Stained keyboards. Dozens of desktop computers, some missing their sidings, their motherboards opened to the dust.

Everything was held together with cords and duct tape, snaking like tree roots across the earthen ground, and up the posts and unfinished interior siding of the house.

At first glance, it was a mess. A trash heap of burned-out leftovers retrieved from dumpsters across the city. But the more Caroline looked, the more she could see there was a method to it. Curtis might be insane, but he knew what he was doing.

She tracked the cables to where they disappeared into the ceiling and realized that Curtis was borrowing power and bandwidth from everyone in the house. It struck Caroline as impossible that no one above had noticed the drain. But perhaps there were so many unrelated people that everyone blamed someone else or no one at all for why their Internet ran so slow. No one guessed they had a torrent freak living under the floorboards.

At the center of the tangled mess sat Curtis himself. He hunched over a keyboard atop two repurposed road barriers and a plank of plywood. His glowing screen illuminated his craggy face. His dog curled at his feet, unbothered by the arrival of strangers. Or perhaps trained not to bark at them.

"This is impressive," Caroline said. She wasn't sure whether she meant the computer setup or the fact that Curtis had created a home in the basement of a college boardinghouse.

"Have you brought me what I want?" Curtis asked.

"I've got Professor Graverstein." Caroline stepped toward the terminal. "May I?"

Curtis rose and moved aside.

Caroline navigated to Southwestern Law School's faculty log-in page. Using the code she'd inserted into the server, she generated a fake account. Now—at least until some savvy admin noticed the dummy account—Curtis would be able to log in just like the rest of the faculty.

Behind Caroline, she heard Curtis lightly clapping his hands.

But then the clapping stopped.

"What about my movies?" Curtis asked.

Caroline looked at the piles of discarded junk in the corners of the basement. When Curtis had mentioned at the dumpster that he collected old equipment, she'd hoped he'd have the rudimentary materials she needed. Now it was time to find out.

"I need some Ethernet cable, a wireless antenna, and"—Caroline scanned the dimly lit space until she found the last item she sought— "that Pringles can over there."

"I'll be right back." Hunching over, Curtis disappeared into the darkness.

He returned wearing a pair of blue-tinted, wire-rimmed John Lennon glasses.

He put them on his face and smiled broadly.

"Ah, the Blueniverse," he said, seeming to mean the entire world.

Then he gestured to the far corner of the basement space.

"Everything you need is there," he said, "or not."

Ducking to avoid hitting her head on the low ceiling, Caroline retrieved a coil of Ethernet cable and a wireless antenna. Neither was new. Both were covered with dust. But they'd work. Last, she retrieved the can and popped the top off.

"Do you have anything I can use to punch a hole in the side of this can?" Caroline asked, holding up the empty Pringles can.

"I have many tools." Curtis pointed toward the brick substructure of a fireplace. In front of it, there was a row of discarded tools. Screwdrivers. Hammers. And a rusted hand drill.

"What are you doing?" asked Hitch, coming to squat beside Caroline as she measured the Pringles can, judging how far down the chamber to make a hole for the antenna.

"I'm making a cantenna," Caroline said, beginning to drill. "I'm going to use this Pringles can to focus the Wi-Fi signal from USC."

"Will it work?"

"We're only about a mile away from the campus," Caroline said, digging through a pile of adapters. She needed something she could use to hold an adapter in place. Her eyes fell on the insulation lining the unfinished walls. "So long as I build the cantenna right, it'll work."

"Cantenna?" Hitch's eyebrows rose in amusement.

"Sometimes low-tech does the trick." Caroline threaded an adapter into the Pringles can and then plugged the space around the hole with putty she'd scraped off the wall's insulation. Once she'd gotten the adapter set firmly into the hole, she hooked it up to the Ethernet cable. She plugged one end of the Ethernet cable into Curtis's computer, then began backtracking down the dirt-sided hallway.

"I'll be right back," she said to the group as she headed toward the cellar doors, unfurling the cable as she went. She figured she had about fifty feet of it. She hoped that would be enough.

In the bright light of day, Caroline's vision went white, but she didn't slow down. She needed to provide Curtis with his torrent quickly or else lose her window to hack Security Images. Examining the backyard, she looked for something to climb.

The fence overgrown with ivy in the corner of the backyard would work.

She glanced at the house across the yard, saw no one. If she got caught, she had some lame excuses she could use. Or try to use, anyway. She hoped not to find out how bad they were.

Tucking the cantenna under one arm, she scaled the fence until she was high enough to see the top of USC's redbrick administration building in the distance, amid a gaggle of low-rise offices and apartment complexes. She wedged the cantenna into a tangle of vines, facing USC, then hopped back down into the yard.

When she returned to the cellar, she found Curtis sitting in front of his monitor.

"Now?" he asked, his eyes hopeful behind his blue glasses.

Caroline nodded.

Curtis navigated to eight different websites on four different screens.

He brought up YouTube videos of pets performing unexpected acts of heroism.

He brought up a group of Swedish musicians who played an array of vacuum cleaners like bagpipes.

He brought up a montage of flash mobs from India.

All of the programs and images ran unimpeded.

"Huzzah!" Curtis said in a stage whisper. "I've dreamed of watching *The Fugitive*, *Bill & Ted's Excellent Adventure*, and *The Care Bears* at the same time."

He closed his eyes and bounced his head up and down in satisfaction. "It will be a perfect symphony of ideas and sound."

"We have a deal," Caroline reminded him.

"Yes, a deal." Curtis stood. He removed his glasses and offered them to her.

"I'm cool for now," said Caroline, waving away the offer, "but thanks."

"If you need them, they are here." Curtis folded the glasses, put them at Caroline's elbow, and gave them a gentle pat-pat.

Hitch drifted up to Caroline's shoulder. "Now what?"

"I make sure no one can trace us," Caroline said. Enough people had already been hurt on her account. "Then, once I get into Security Images, we'll need to find a way to narrow the segment of surveillance footage we need to review. I'm hoping the website has decent search capabilities so we're not stuck watching days of footage."

Reaching Security Images' website, Caroline prompted the password page.

Finding the username would be fairly simple. Permutations of "BanCorp" would probably yield a hit. But hacking the password could take a while. She needed an effective algorithm but didn't have time to write her own.

She opted for a brute-force attack using a bot. She set the parameters, using every possible combination of corporate-identifying information. Combinations of letters and numbers, symbols and underscores. It would work. Eventually.

The next hours passed slowly. And silently.

Whenever anyone started to speak, Curtis held up an index finger and glared at the would-be speaker, who'd fall back into muteness.

Occasional sounds of shuffling from the ceiling above gave testament to the presence of Curtis's upstairs neighbors and hammered home the rational nature of Curtis's caution.

Soon, more of those neighbors would be arriving as students came home from class.

Caroline wondered how long Curtis had lived beneath the house. Not that she'd ask him, lest she receive The Look and dreaded finger wag.

And so the group waited.

Jake sat on a pile of unused cables and discarded keyboards, petting the dog.

Hitch hunched his shoulders, pacing, probably wishing for a drink of something stronger than the water they'd subsisted on for the last forty-eight hours.

Caroline chewed her dirty cuticle, watching the brute-force attack flicker by at many thousands of attempts per minute.

Finally, the screen froze.

Then everything changed.

They were in.

Caroline retook her seat at Curtis's workstation. It was time to figure out how Security Images arranged its data.

The answer was a relief. The company saved the footage for each bank client's account by bank branch, date, and hour—all relatively searchable, once she found out what time the last Oasis withdrawal had occurred at the Hope Street branch.

Pulling out the spreadsheet of information about the affidavit withdrawals, Caroline read the list of transactions until she found the information she sought: the last Oasis withdrawal from the Hope Street branch of BanCorp had been at 10:35 a.m. on September 13.

She navigated to the archived footage for 10:00 a.m. Though that was the time stamp on the withdrawal, the person she sought would've entered the bank sometime before then to begin his or her transaction. She needed a good image of a face.

Caroline hit "Play."

Black-and-white footage of the bank appeared on the screen.

There were no patrons at 10:00 a.m., just a handful of bank employees, getting ready for the day. Preparing coffee. Placing cookies at the private banking desk.

Caroline advanced the feed. In fast motion, the employees scurried, zooming from one side of the screen to the other in efficiency the directors of the bank could only hope to imagine.

At 10:22, a man entered the door of the bank. He wore a pinstriped suit, and his hair had been neatly combed to one side. He carried a briefcase in his right hand.

When the man in pinstripes reached the teller, he pulled a wallet from his back pocket and removed his driver's license. He slid it under the Plexiglas wall for the teller to inspect.

Looking up from the driver's license, the teller gestured toward the private banking desk.

With a nod, the patron joined the teller. He sat down with his back to the camera.

"Come on," Caroline muttered. She still hadn't gotten a look at the man's face.

The man opened his briefcase and removed a stack of papers. He arranged them in two piles in front of the teller.

"The wills and affidavits," Caroline surmised.

The teller took the papers with him back behind the Plexiglas wall.

"Now he'll cut the checks," Caroline said.

Sure enough, the teller returned minutes later, holding a pile of thin pieces of paper.

One by one, the teller presented them to the patron, who placed the whole pile inside his briefcase. Rising, he locked the briefcase and rose to his feet.

As he exited the bank, the man finally looked up toward the camera, which must have been located near a clock.

Caroline froze the image.

"Gotcha," she said.

The man's face, tilted up toward the camera, was bland. Eyes neither too far apart nor too close together. Chin neither too pointy nor too round. A neatly combed side part gave him the visage of a Republican congressman.

Moving quickly, Caroline copied the clip and sent it to herself at the retrieval point she'd used to store the BanCorp data her dad had let her swipe. She'd access it again later, when she had time to study the image. For now though, one thing was clear.

"It isn't Simon Reed or Conrad Vizzi," Caroline announced. The fact was surprising. She'd expected either the operating head of Oasis or the on-site director of Oasis to be the bagman—the guy that handled the money. Clearly, that was wrong. This new man with the bland face and fancy suit was someone she hadn't yet encountered. Identifying him wouldn't be hard for Albert. He had facial recognition software at his disposal.

Glancing toward Curtis, Caroline loaded FreedomPop onto the computer. After running it through a VPN server to hide the source of the call, she dialed the number printed at the bottom of Albert's business card.

At the sound of the buzz and pause of the Internet phone trying to connect, Curtis emerged from the shadows, frowning.

"I promise to make it fast," Caroline said, her eyes pleading.

A creak of the floorboards above her head reminded her of Curtis's other stakes.

"And quiet," she added, turning down the volume.

With a single nod, Curtis gave his assent.

Exhaling, Caroline prepared to explain what she wanted from Albert.

But instead of hearing Albert's voice, Caroline heard his secretary's prerecorded voice mail greeting, advising callers that Mr. Khaing was in trial. Caroline recalled Albert saying he'd be in court each day and would not be available to talk until close to 8:30 p.m.

She hung up. She couldn't leave the prosecutor a voice mail without risking getting him in trouble. In the silence, Caroline realized there was one other person whose voice she desperately wanted to hear. Someone who might bolster her spirits, which presently felt about as buried beneath the earth as the cellar where she now sat.

Caroline dialed her father's phone number.

A woman's voice came onto the line. "Hello."

Caroline's stomach sank. She'd called her father's cell phone number, but the voice on the line wasn't William Auden's. It was Lily's. Caroline's stepmother.

"Is my dad around?" Caroline asked, trying to keep her tone light.

"The police are looking for you," Lily said.

Caroline restrained a groan.

"I know, but I didn't do anything wrong—"

"Then go to the police." Lily's tone brokered no dissent. Unspoken, but as loud as an air horn was her judgment that turning oneself in was what any law-abiding citizen would do.

"I can't," Caroline began but then stopped. Any effort to explain herself was doomed to failure. While she strongly doubted her father had ever told his new wife about his daughter's hacking exploits—and his near incarceration because of them—Lily seemed to have some kind of sixth sense for dishonesty.

"Can I just please talk to my dad?" Caroline asked.

"No," Lily said.

"No?" Caroline echoed, her voice rising slightly.

A pop of floorboards overhead bespoke the presence of upstairs neighbors.

"Why not?" Caroline lowered her voice, controlling her tone.

"I saw the police reports from your father's probation."

Caroline exhaled. So much for Lily having no basis for her poor opinion of her.

"I wasn't going to bring that up," Lily continued. "I'm not your mother, and I don't need to scold you for what's in the past, but this latest incident—"

"But I didn't do it," Caroline said, her voice rising again.

"You need to learn to play by the rules, Caroline. You're not better than the rest of us. The sooner you learn that, the easier life will be for you."

Caroline's face flushed.

"Please tell my dad I called," she said, trying hard to control the fury that roiled her soul and threatened to break her composure.

"No. I won't let you destroy him." Lily's tone let Caroline know she'd block her calls, lose the phone, or do whatever else she needed to do to keep her wayward stepdaughter from contacting her husband. "Turn yourself into the police. It's the only way."

"Please, Lily—"

The line went dead.

Caroline's chest flared with anger. She'd planned to talk to her father. To receive his succor. Instead, she'd received a full measure of Lily's heartless wrath. Turning herself in to the police was absurd. Leaving the streets for a holding cell was a death wish. It was wrong— all wrong—and Lily was a jerk to demand it when she knew nothing. Absolutely nothing.

Fueled by rage and humiliation, Caroline brought her hands back to the keyboard.

If no one could help her, she'd help herself. Lily was right about one thing—the rules would be no impediment. She'd e-mail her father. She'd hack Oasis. She'd do whatever she needed to do to bring down Oasis and save herself.

But then the floorboards creaked again overhead.

The sounds were followed by a rhythmic series of thuds.

Footsteps. Growing closer.

Caroline froze.

A shroud of dread, heavy and horrible, descended on her. She'd been too loud. So late in the day, the house was full of residents. Residents upon whose obliviousness Curtis's shelter depended. She wished she could undo the horrible conversation. She wished she could go back in time and hang up when Lily's voice had answered the phone, but it was too late.

The ceiling creaked again. Directly overhead.

A flash of terror reflected off the faces of everyone in the basement.

Caroline imagined someone squatting low, head tilted to one side. Listening.

She willed the steps to move away.

Finally, the creaking ceased and the footsteps retreated, fading into the distance.

The residents of the basement let out a collectively held breath.

But Curtis rose from the beanbag.

"It is time for you to go," he said, jabbing a finger toward the cellar's entrance.

Caroline looked around for something to waylay him, some other tool she could offer, some inducement to give her more time at the computer. There was one essential task she hadn't yet accomplished. She needed more time.

But then a better idea occurred to her.

Standing up from the makeshift computer desk, she held her hands up, palms facing out in the universal sign for surrender.

"We're leaving right now," she said in a soothing tone. "Soon, you'll be all alone with Professor Graverstein with all of your new bandwidth. You'll be able to watch whatever you want." As she spoke, Caroline edged toward one of the piles of junk that filled the cellar's corners. "There's just one last thing I need from you before we go away and leave you with the professor."

CHAPTER 22

Standing on the sidewalk outside the Victorian house, Caroline smiled for the first time in days. Not the grimace she'd worn upon finding decent leftovers in a dumpster. Not the half grin of satisfaction she'd allowed herself after hacking Southwestern Law School. No, this was a real smile.

It wasn't the first stars appearing in the early evening sky that sparked Caroline's joy.

It wasn't the fresh air, enjoyable after the dank mildew of the cellar.

It was the laptop she held.

Sure, it was ancient and weighed close to seven pounds. Sure, it would run slow and have a pixelated screen. But it would allow her to research and communicate and hack. Once she'd loaded Ubuntu onto it, the world would open up to her. Some people went to war with planes and guns and tanks. Caroline would go to war with her weapon of choice—a computer.

"I need a café with Wi-Fi," Caroline said, turning to her uncle.

• • •

Caroline ignored the smell of coffee. She ignored the baseball game on the TV behind the barista. She ignored the flyer she'd pulled off a telephone pole outside the café, showing a picture of her and inviting the public to contact the authorities with any information about the prime suspect in the paletería incident. All that mattered was the laptop.

She typed as fast as she could. She had to wire funds from her bank account to Western Union. Though the steps weren't complicated, each took time. Use a proxy server to access her account. Set up a link to Western Union. Authorize the wire transfer.

While she was taking those steps, she remained out in the open. Exposed.

Caroline consoled herself that she'd be back underground soon. As soon as she'd secured the funds to finance her war against Oasis, she'd become invisible again. But for now, she sat with her head down, her hair falling across her eyes, trying to look like an antisocial college student cramming for a test.

With a final command, Caroline authorized the transfer. Jake would be waiting to collect the cash when the wire hit. It would be almost all of the money in her account, but she couldn't worry about that now. She needed cash. As much as she could get. As fast as she could get it.

Meanwhile, Hitch was gathering their meager belongings from the alleys and nooks where they'd stashed everything before going to Curtis's house. They'd all meet at the Royal Residence Hotel at 7:30.

They'd passed the hotel on the edge of Skid Row as they'd departed Curtis's underground lair. Sandwiched between a marijuana dispensary and a pawnshop, most of the hotel's windows faced a windowless establishment that advertised NAKED GIRLS ALL DAY LONG. Caroline could almost smell the syphilis.

Her choice of lodging wasn't driven by penny-pinching. It was driven by administrative realities. Reputable hotels required credit cards. Disreputable hotels didn't. And anyway, Caroline didn't need luxury. Just enough space for three people to sleep. And Wi-Fi. The clerk had promised they'd find both when they returned with the cash to secure the room.

Caroline checked the time.

She still had twenty-five minutes before she was supposed to meet Jake and Hitch.

She had time to do one more thing.

Linking back to the virtual retrieval point, she grabbed the video clip she'd taken from Security Images. Then she sent it to the e-mail address on Albert's business card, along with a request that he run it through the Department of Justice's facial recognition software. Unlike static images, video clips were easy to match against the state driver's licenses that populated the government's facial database. She knew Albert would be able to identify the man in pinstripes who was handling the affidavit withdrawals for Oasis.

As soon as the clip finished loading and sending, Caroline snapped the laptop shut and shoved it into the reusable grocery bag she'd snagged from a trash can. It wasn't the most elegant laptop bag she'd ever owned, but it would do.

She looked up, ready to leave.

And froze.

New patrons had entered the café. Two uniformed policemen.

With her heart slamming against her rib cage, Caroline took quick stock of the café.

There was no back door. Just the screened entryway at the front, by the register. An entryway that the two police officers now blocked.

Caroline knew they weren't looking for her. They were just two cops ordering coffee and muffins. But in seconds, they'd notice her. There were probably dozens of those flyers with her photo all over the neighborhood. The likelihood that the cops hadn't seen one recently enough to recognize her was next to nil.

She was trapped. A waterfall of self-recriminations followed the realization. She'd survived a hit man. She'd survived sleeping on the streets. She'd survived old food and bad shoes and loneliness. And now she was going to get caught because she'd lingered too long instead of just waiting to send Albert the video clip from the safety of the hotel.

The first police officer leaned back against the counter, making himself comfortable while he waited for the barista to make his coffee drink. The second police officer pulled a dollar from her wallet to put into the tip jar.

Caroline turned her face away, wishing she could disappear into the patterned wallpaper.

Perhaps she'd get lucky. Perhaps the police would leave without ever casually glancing up to see who else was in the café. Perhaps pigs could fly.

A shout from outside intruded on Caroline's terror. A woman's voice, loud and frantic.

"My bike! Someone just stole my bike!"

The screen door flew open with a crash. A small woman lurched into the café. She looked around until her eyes found the police officers.

"Oh, thank God! I thought I saw cops come in here. You've got to help me. A guy with a blue baseball hat and a silver jacket just took my bike. Grabbed it right out of my hands."

Caroline sat transfixed by the woman's familiar face. It was Lani—the woman she'd helped at the distribution center. The small woman wore the same stained dress and red scarf she'd been wearing the last time Caroline had seen her, but now she'd paired them with combat boots and a fleece jacket. Fortunately, in the edgy neighborhood, she came off as fashion forward, not homeless.

"He took off down East Thirty-Sixth Street," Lani continued. "You can still catch him if you hurry. Please. You've got to help me!"

The police officers left their coffees and muffins to hurry with Lani through the door.

Through the screen, Caroline could hear her say, "There—you see him? He's at the end of the block. Oh, you've got to get him. Please!"

The sound of footsteps attested to the police officers' belief in Lani's ruse and their efforts to catch the phantom fugitive.

Half a second later, the screen door clattered open again.

Lani caught Caroline's eye.

And then they both ran.

• • •

Caroline and Lani didn't stop until they reached a spot behind a dumpster in an alley four blocks away from the café. Both women leaned forward, hands on knees, panting hard.

"I don't know how you did that, but thank you," Caroline said when she could talk again.

"I've been following you," Lani said. "I saw you and your friends, and I wanted to thank you for what you did to Daryl, but then I just followed. And I felt safer near people who helped."

"How long have you been following us?" Caroline asked.

"About four hours. I saw your big friend—he was at that food line near City Hall."

Caroline remembered. Jake had gone to find Enzo to lead them to Curtis's underground lair.

"There was a guy asking about you. A blond man," Lani continued. "Offering money for information. Usually the volunteers would tell people like him to leave, but their manager let him stay until he'd asked everyone. It seemed wrong."

A shiver scurried down Caroline's arms.

"Anyway, I followed you. I'm good at making myself invisible," Lani said, looking down.

She was right, Caroline realized. The way Lani's shoulders curved forward, the way she ducked her black-haired head, she seemed to disappear into herself.

Caroline noted the dark circles under Lani's eyes. She had to be exhausted. To Caroline, a night on the street had meant sleeping in shifts. Jake, Uncle Hitch, and she took turns, watching to make sure no one sneaked up on them. But Lani? She'd been all alone.

"When I saw you go into that café, I was going to come and talk to you. But then—"

"—you saw the police," Caroline surmised.

Lani nodded. "I wanted to help."

Suddenly, something occurred to Caroline.

"You knew the police were looking for me, didn't you?"

Lani nodded again.

"But you still helped me," Caroline said.

"Someone who did what you did to Daryl wouldn't have hurt that lady at that shop."

Caroline warmed at the unexpected compliment. It had been a long time since anyone had given her the benefit of the doubt about much of anything.

"Do you want to come with us?" Caroline asked impulsively. "We're going to a hotel."

Lani looked uncertain. "What's there?"

"A war room," Caroline said.

CHAPTER 23

Caroline sat at a small Formica desk in the corner of the hotel room. Beside her laptop, she'd placed the burner phone she'd bought with the money Jake had retrieved from Western Union. Just knowing she now had the capacity to make untraceable phone calls calmed her nerves as she turned to marshaling the information she'd need to bring down Oasis.

With Lani in the shower and Jake out doing "some more reconnaissance," she had time alone to concentrate. Hitch had gone down to the lobby to offer the desk clerk a little money to store his shopping cart in the hotel's garage. Though she'd hesitated to give her uncle any cash, the plan to secure his possessions had been the only way she could coax him indoors.

Caroline glanced at the clock humming beside her—7:52 p.m.

She still had a little time until she could call Albert. Before she spoke to him, she wanted to crack the firewall that had defeated her. She wanted to find the information secreted in Oasis's server—information she'd trawled only briefly before getting shut out.

Not this time, though, Caroline silently vowed. Oasis had run her out of her life. Now, Oasis would answer for it.

But when she tried to reach Oasis's server, Caroline retrieved an error message: *Service unavailable.*

It could mean only one thing: Oasis had taken its server off-line.

The move wasn't unexpected, Caroline realized. Perhaps after Amy's and her hacks, Oasis had gotten scared. Or maybe the charity's security service had recommended the drastic measure in an abundance of caution until it could patch the holes that had been breached. Whatever the reason, Caroline needed some other way to find out more about Oasis.

Fortunately, she had other sources of information.

Linking again to the retrieval spot, she copied the BanCorp affidavit-withdrawal transactions onto her laptop. The Spreadsheet of Death had been only an abbreviated version of her haul. Now she had the complete data set, plus the title reports Amy had found.

Once she'd sent Albert copies, she turned back to the raw data glowing on the screen. Like an ancient mystic examining strings of numbers, she tried to discern shapes and meaning from the information her father had allowed her to retrieve from BanCorp.

Gradually, a pattern began to resolve itself from the columns of numbers and dates. There was something about the frequency of the affidavit withdrawals. Though the data stretched back five years, most of the bequests had occurred in the last two.

Before she could study the pattern more closely, the lock on the hotel room's door clicked open and Jake entered.

"Only one ingress and egress, plus the back gate near the empty pool. Secured parking garage. One desk clerk," he said, as if reporting up the chain of command.

Caroline stifled a smile. Once a Ranger, always a Ranger.

His mission accomplished, Jake settled himself on the bed closest to the door.

"Did you happen to see my uncle down there?" Caroline asked. Hitch had gone almost forty-eight hours without drinking, by her count. It probably wasn't enough to have trusted him with cash.

"No, but he'll be back," said Jake.

Caroline appreciated the certainty in his voice. She wished she shared it.

Jake lay back on the bed with a sigh that seemed to last for a full minute.

"I forgot," he said, closing his eyes.

Caroline understood. The sight of a bed had brought her close to tears, too.

"Have you ever tried to get off the street?" she asked.

"No," Jake answered.

"But you want to?"

With his eyes still closed, Jake nodded. "I'm not like Floyd."

Caroline studied the Ranger's face. When she'd first met him, she'd seen only his mass. The corded muscles of his forearms. The knife. Now, she saw a shyness. And a quiet eloquence, both in his speech and in the shapes he fashioned out of wood.

"What happened to you?" Caroline asked, almost to herself. She imagined the answers he'd give if he decided to answer her open-ended query. He'd probably seen combat. Maybe he'd seen friends die. Maybe he'd killed someone.

"After 9/11, I joined the service," he began with his eyes still closed.

Caroline nodded to herself. His story began like so many others.

"I wanted justice for those who'd died," he said, his eyes open now but trained on the stained ceiling of the shabby hotel room. "But I just wasn't down with it."

Cocking her head, Caroline listened for the story to get back on the rails. The expected path.

"I was a combat fatigue casualty," Jake continued, "which is just a stuck-up way of saying I was a coward."

"What? No." Caroline had never heard the phrase *combat fatigue casualty*, but whatever it meant, she didn't think it applied to Jake. Sure, he could seem withdrawn, but he'd never shown any fear at the horrors of living on the street. And there were so many . . .

"Every time we were out on patrol, every sound was an IED. Everyone I saw was an enemy combatant. When we actually came under fire, I couldn't sleep afterward. Or eat. My commander ordered me to a critical event debriefing so I could get my head together."

"Did it work?"

"No. But I completed my deployment anyway." There was a trace of pride in Jake's voice. Or masochism. "The army wasn't like I thought it would be." He paused and shook his head. "What I mean is, I wasn't how I thought I'd be."

Caroline understood. His private mythology hadn't matched his reality.

The bathroom door opened, and Lani emerged. She wore the same stained red dress, but now her hair was wet. As if sensing the serious conversation still hanging in the air, she sat down on the rollaway bed farthest from the door. She tucked her feet under herself, making herself small.

"Coming home—it's been hard," Jake continued, as if oblivious to Lani's presence.

"Didn't the government take care of you when you got back?" Caroline asked.

Jake let out a bitter laugh. "I had a good doc at the VA—so good, he got transferred."

"What about a new doctor? What about counseling?"

Jake just shrugged. "You can't run from what's inside."

"No, I suppose you can't," Caroline agreed quietly.

"The only thing worse than worrying about getting killed was worrying about having to kill somebody. Those people in Iraq—they wasn't the ones that hit us on 9/11."

"I don't think it's a bad thing that you couldn't kill people," Lani volunteered from the rollaway bed.

"It is when you're a Ranger," Jake said.

Though Caroline agreed with Lani, she knew Jake would not be convinced.

"Why are you helping me?" she asked instead.

"I owe Hitch," Jake answered simply.

Caroline's face grew warm with annoyance. She'd just finished demonizing her uncle and the addiction that eclipsed everything else in his life. She didn't want to entertain the possibility that someone could depend on him when she didn't trust him to come back to the hotel room.

"Some skinheads was out bothering homeless people one night. Hitch helped me. He's a good man." Seeing Caroline's scowl, Jake continued, "He don't hurt no one. He pays his debts."

Caroline knew that a person's word counted for a lot in the non-cash world of the streets, but she still couldn't accept that her uncle was worthy of his good reputation. Or that Jake wasn't deluded in thinking he owed risking his life to help Hitch's wayward niece.

"But what if they get you?" she asked. She wasn't sure who "they" were. Aside from the hit man, she wasn't sure who else was trying to find her. But she did know she didn't want anyone else to get hurt on her account. Especially this strangely gentle giant.

"I'm already a dead man walking," Jake said. "People say you can't ever really come home from a war. That's the truth. You come home all messed up. There's no fixing that."

"That's not true. There are always choices." Caroline heard the vehemence in her voice and knew where it came from. In her mother and uncle, she'd seen cautionary tales. She'd felt the same tugs toward oblivion. But she'd clung to the belief that she had free will. Genetic predisposition was a reality, but so was self-determination.

Jake's deep, rolling laughter filled the hotel room.

"What?" Caroline asked, suddenly embarrassed by her speech.

"You don't even know your privilege."

"And you don't know me. I might not have gone to war, but I've seen darkness."

"Nah, you're a rich white girl who only thinks she's seen the dark."

"And I also think I see a good man who's given up."

Jake grew quiet.

"You always so damn optimistic about human nature?" he asked finally.

"No," Caroline admitted, the fight going out of her. "But what's the alternative?"

Jake shook his head, his lips pursed.

Caroline looked away. She'd said something wrong, off base. She'd presumed things about Jake and made judgments. She'd revealed her own cluelessness and presumptuousness when she'd lectured the ex-soldier on how to make his life better. No wonder he'd dismissed her as an errand he was doing for her uncle.

"I'm sorry," she said. "I didn't mean to sound like an Oasis pamphlet. I'm still learning to mind my own business."

He snorted—the joke was her peace offering, and his laugh was an acceptance.

"So, you gonna figure out how to end this damn thing with Oasis?" he asked.

"Yes," Caroline said. Her voice held resolve. She had no alternatives now. No other options. The only way forward required her to slay the beast. And so even if she had to do it alone, she'd find a way to bring Oasis down.

"Cool," Jake said. "I've got your back."

• • •

At 8:16, Hitch returned. In his right hand, he held a large paper bag.

He paused at the door and looked down.

"Everything okay with your cart?" Caroline asked. He'd been gone more than long enough to pay the desk clerk to stash his belongings in the garage.

"Yeah." Hitch's eyes remained down on the ugly brown carpet.

Opening the bag, he removed the contents, setting each on the small table beside the door of the hotel room.

"There was a mini-mart two doors down that had some supplies. Orange juice. Ding Dongs. Ho Hos. Coca-Cola. Froot Loops," he narrated in a whisper.

Then he took the last item out of the bag: a six-pack of Pabst Blue Ribbon.

One can was missing.

Wordlessly, he put the cans beside the junk food.

Eyeing the blue label of the cheap beer, Caroline swallowed thickly. As she'd feared, he'd caved to his addiction. And yet, he hadn't slunk off to drink the whole six-pack. And now he was offering the remainder to her. The act was as honest as it was unexpected.

"I've tried to pinpoint when it went wrong," he began in a quiet voice, his eyes still downcast. "You know, the moment when I had to numb things."

Caroline wasn't sure if he was referring to the last twenty-four hours or the last fifty-six years. So she stayed silent, waiting to hear the rest of what her uncle wanted to say.

"That watch that got stolen from your grandma—it came from my best friend's dad," he continued. "You know that, right?"

Caroline nodded again. She remembered the story. The tragedy of a boy who'd escaped war only to die too young.

"I'm not sure I ever really trusted the world again after Nazim died," Hitch finished.

Then he fell silent.

Caroline tried to decide what to do with the confession. The introspection it suggested was heartening, but she'd long ago ceased thinking of alcoholism as a lock that could be picked with a revelation or two. The disease was far more complicated. And far more intractable.

"Thank you," she said, making up her mind. "You are an important member of this team." She knew the words were professional-sounding, not at all familial. "If we're going to survive this, we're all going to need to function at our very best."

In her peripheral vision, she saw Jake look down at his hands.

"I don't have to tell you what we're up against," Caroline finished softly.

Her eyes settled on the puke-colored walls. The clunky computer. The comforter that looked like it had escaped one of the dumpsters downstairs.

She compared her surroundings with Simon Reed's. His lavish development offices. His state-of-the-art tech. He was building a skyscraper in the middle of LA. He was hobnobbing with politicians and charming the public. What was she doing? She was relying on a wheezing laptop and a crew of homeless people, hoping not to get bedbugs from the cigarette-stained sheets. The odds of prevailing felt daunting.

Giving a curt nod, Hitch came to stand beside Caroline at the desk.

"What have you got so far?" he asked. His tone was professional.

Good. She needed the ex-cop in her uncle to bring his trained eye to the data set.

"I've got a pattern," Caroline said. She brought up the records of the affidavit transactions in chronological order. "Look at the frequency of the transactions five years ago. Now compare that to the frequency four years ago, then three years ago."

"It's happening more often," Hitch said. "There are more transactions each year."

"Exactly," Caroline said.

"Somehow they've expanded their operations each year. Maybe they've gotten more nurses or CNAs into nursing homes?" he mused.

Flipping back to the page showing the gifts from The Pastures' residents to Oasis, Caroline looked for information about the names of the caregivers. She'd cross-referenced The Pastures records against the BanCorp data to see the number of bequests, but she hadn't looked for names before. Perhaps The Pastures had kept track of some sort of identifying information?

No, there was nothing there. No names or codes for names. Just the amounts of the bequests. The dates on the wills. The dates of the affidavits. The dates of the deaths. The dates of the withdrawal transactions.

"Jesus," Hitch breathed behind her.

Twisting back so she could see her uncle's face, Caroline watched him tilt his head to one side. Then he reached for the mouse.

With quick movements, he zeroed in on the last pages of the data.

"What do you see?" Caroline asked. While she waited for him to respond, her heart began to pound, though she couldn't say why. Perhaps it was the sight of the color draining from Hitch's face, leaving him pale and haunted.

"The gap," he managed. "Look at the interval between when people at The Pastures made their wills and when they died."

When she looked back at the data, Caroline saw it.

"The interval's gotten shorter," she said. "In the last twelve months. People are making their wills. Then they're dying." Her eyes tracked through the data. Five weeks. Six weeks. The gap between the dates on the wills and the dates of death were all in the same range.

The implications were ominous. And unavoidable.

Caroline didn't have to remind her uncle that Grandma Kate had had an IV placed in her arm shortly before she died. Nor did she have to tell him that an air bubble pushed into an IV line could stimulate an embolism.

She brought up the most recent data. The data that included her grandmother.

Katherine Hitchings had signed her new will on August 3.

She'd died on September 11.

Five weeks. The interval was similar for most of the deaths at The Pastures' facilities.

Caroline felt as though someone had thrown her into an icy lake. Once she'd seen the pattern, she couldn't unsee it.

"That woman—Grandma's caregiver. She's the one—" Caroline trailed off, remembering the New Age hippie CNA. She'd been worse than a sham. She'd been worse than a thief.

At the mention of the woman, Hitch clenched and unclenched his hands. The small muscle at the corner of his jaw began to work.

"She's still out there somewhere," he began, his voice low and angry.

Although Hitch hadn't been loud, Lani roused on the bed.

She sat up, rubbing her eyes.

"What's wrong?" she asked, looking back and forth between Caroline and Hitch.

"Everything," Caroline said.

She waved away Lani's baffled look.

It was 8:30 p.m.

It was time to call Albert.

CHAPTER 24

"I'm so sorry," Albert said. If he'd entered the conversation hoping for evidence from Caroline, he'd gotten a full truckload of emotion along with it. "I'll continue to analyze the data, but I agree with your analysis—the timing cannot be a coincidence."

At his words, another shiver of nausea coursed through Caroline's esophagus. Her grandmother had been murdered. The realization was so huge and so horrible that she could scarcely touch it.

"You do understand that I'm not going to be able to use any of this stuff you've sent to me in a trial," Albert added quietly.

"I know. I was hoping you could obtain the data from other sources—legal sources."

"I'll do my best," Albert promised. "But we're in a bit of a bind—to subpoena documents from a bank, I need evidence. But to get evidence, I need to subpoena the bank."

"You just need a good judge to give you a warrant." Even as she said it, Caroline recalled Judge Chandler's brutal treatment of the civil suit against Oasis. Frustration welled in her breast. Oasis had obscured its operations. It had bought influence. Even the judicial system, which was supposed to be designed to unearth the truth, seemed impotent to breach Oasis's fortress.

Across the room, Lani looked at her with sympathetic eyes.

"I do have some good news for you," Albert said. "I got a positive ID on the guy in that video surveillance footage you sent me from the bank. The man who's handling the affidavit withdrawals for Oasis is named Gregory Parsons. He's a real scumbag. He's a lawyer, but he doesn't practice anymore. He got tagged for liability in a civil fraud action about fifteen years ago. He runs a financial consulting company now."

"What were the facts of the case against him?" Caroline asked, glad to have something to distract her from the queasy feeling in her esophagus.

"Parsons altered some appraisals in a partnership dissolution action. His defense was that he was an appraiser. Turned out he was never licensed as such. There were also claims for accounting irregularities, misrepresentations, and other matters."

"How'd he get wrapped up with Oasis?" Caroline asked.

"I don't know. Maybe he's one of Simon's investors," Albert speculated.

Caroline shook her head slowly. Despite her efforts, she'd never been able to identify any of Simon's investors.

An unsettled churning quaked through her gut.

Her inability to discover Simon's investors bothered her. People who invested in do-gooder projects usually liked getting credit for their charity. They put their names on plaques. They memorialized their gifts in their annual reports. Anonymous giving was unusual. It didn't make sense that Simon's investors would hide.

Maybe the reason they'd never come forward was simple: maybe Simon's entire cohort was as sketchy as he was.

"Okay, so this scumbag Gregory Parsons is a major investor and collects the money," Caroline mused. "Simon is the big-picture guy and the front man—he makes nice with the city so it'll green-light his development projects and give him city funds for them. Meanwhile, Conrad Vizzi handles the training of the CNAs."

At the mention of Vizzi's name, Lani's eyes widened.

Lani knew Vizzi, Caroline suddenly realized. She made a mental note to ask her about it.

"That sounds possible," Albert was saying, drawing Caroline's attention back to the phone line. "Maybe the CNA scam's a nice little side business Simon's got going. When they're not milking the public treasury, they're milking the nursing homes. But we still need evidence. Proof."

"Agreed," Caroline said. "Have you found anything?"

"I looked at that property that Oasis owns on Parrino Court, down near the LA River," Albert said. "Like you suspected, it's a bunch of nothing. Just some trailers and empty warehouses."

"Why does Oasis own it?" Caroline asked. She could think of no reason for the fake charity to own a large tract of useless land on an undesirable side of town.

"Wish I knew," said Albert, "but it seems like a dead end. Speaking of which, I tracked down Jessie Tuttle—that Oasis worker who got hurt on the County Law Library restoration job."

"What did he say?" Caroline asked. Hector had believed the injured man might have information about Oasis's dark dealings. He'd sought—but failed to find—Jessie Tuttle. Perhaps Albert had achieved what Hector had not.

"He's dead," Albert said.

"Dead?" Caroline echoed. She knew the news shouldn't have surprised her, but Tuttle's demise still filled her with dread.

"I found his lawyer," Albert said. "The guy was trying to put together a wage-and-hour suit against Oasis. Jessie Tuttle was going to be his lead plaintiff. He filed suit and propounded discovery, asking for all records of the Oasis construction projects. A month later, Tuttle was found in a ditch with a needle hanging out of his arm. Apparently Tuttle had a smack habit that he'd kicked."

"Or not," Caroline said.

"Or not," Albert agreed. "The lawyer couldn't find another plaintiff. The case died with Tuttle."

"Of course it did," Caroline said, exhaling her frustration. Inquiries about Oasis always went nowhere. People with knowledge disappeared. Trying to see Oasis's workings was like trying to view a construction project through a hole in a tarp covering a fence. Although Caroline could hear the movement of heavy machinery and see part of the works, she couldn't make out the whole operation. But one thing was sure: Oasis was deadly serious about avoiding scrutiny.

"If I don't come out of this, Mateo Hidalgo is going to need other counsel. Please make sure he gets that," she asked quietly. The boy whose representation she'd undertaken could not be left without an attorney. He deserved an advocate. Someone somewhere in the system needed to make sure he was safe.

"Let's not go there quite yet," Albert said.

Caroline exhaled. He was right. She still had a laptop. She still had her freedom. While the odds remained heavily weighted against her, she wasn't out of the fight yet.

"That assistant DA in the gangs unit, Shaina Parker, told me she's on top of the Gonzalez matter," Albert said. "I told her we were working on a case that could be affected by any prosecution. She promised to keep me apprised."

"Thanks," Caroline said. That Albert had been willing to contact the assistant DA was a gift. Being on the run was bad enough. That a little boy might be harmed because of her troubles was unacceptable.

"Your friend Amy's doing better," Albert said, his voice bright in a way that let Caroline know he was trying to cheer her up. "She came home from the hospital."

The news had the desired effect, warming Caroline. She wished she could call her friend. She wished she could make sure she was going to be all right. But Caroline knew that until she'd found some way to clear her name, she was toxic to anyone she tried to contact.

"We're keeping an eye on her," Albert continued, "just to be on the safe side. We believe she's likely safe now—since she's given whatever information she had to us."

"She could ID the hit man," Caroline mused aloud. "That would be a reason to continue pursuing her, if I were Oasis." She hated discussing the ways in which her closest friend might still be a target for a hit man, but she needed Albert to provide protection.

"Agreed, which is why we're keeping someone on her, but she doesn't have any information beyond that. She isn't a witness to Oasis's CNA program or other wrongdoing, so she's probably fine."

Caroline exhaled again. Albert was right, of course. And that was the problem. They desperately needed a witness. Someone inside Oasis who could act as a whistle-blower in a criminal prosecution.

"Any leads on finding the hit man?" Caroline asked.

"Unfortunately not," Albert said. "He's underground."

Underground. The word gave Caroline no solace.

"I'm going to keep working on the Gregory Parsons angle. If we can find something on him, maybe we can get him to turn state's evidence," said Albert.

"Good thought," Caroline said, though she wasn't optimistic about anyone within Oasis turning on Oasis.

"Check back in with me tomorrow," Albert said.

"Will do," Caroline agreed.

"Are you doing okay at your current location?" Albert asked.

"Yes," Caroline said. "I'm good for now." Her meager funds wouldn't last long. She'd be back on the street soon if she didn't get back to work. But she had enough to deal with now.

"Good luck," Albert said, hanging up.

Caroline turned to find Lani staring at her.

The small woman's eyes were filled with trepidation.

Caroline thought she knew the reason.

"You know Conrad Vizzi, don't you?"

Instead of answering, Lani glanced over at Jake, who lay on the bed watching TV.

"Jake's a good guy," Caroline said. "You heard what he said about his service in Iraq. He's a gentleman, truly." She noted a small smile twitch at the corner of Jake's mouth.

"I always guess wrong about men," Lani said, "especially my last boyfriend."

"Daryl," Caroline surmised. "The guy at the distribution center."

Lani nodded. "Things were always bad with him. The first time I left Daryl, I stayed at a friend's house. But he found out where I was from Facebook—someone posted a picture with me in it. He came after me. I was going to try to disappear—you know, go to a new city or something. But I didn't have any money. Daryl always paid for everything."

Although Lani's story was meandering, Caroline's instincts told her to let it unfold. Lani hadn't denied knowing Conrad Vizzi. Caroline was confident Lani would circle back to him.

"I called one of those domestic violence hotlines," Lani continued. "They mentioned that Oasis campus downtown. You can get retrained. They'll feed you and give you a bed. So when I left the second time, I went there."

Nodding, Caroline realized how Lani had crossed paths with Conrad Vizzi.

"How long were you at Oasis?"

"For about a month," Lani replied. "I lived on that huge campus they have."

"Why'd you leave?" Caroline asked.

"I didn't want to do one of those training programs that the Oasis people push you into." At Caroline's quixotic expression, Lani explained, "They promise you'll get fast-tracked for employment if you sign up for their courses. You know, car repair, welding, framing, food service, nursing, whatever. But then they slap you with this program fee that you're supposed to pay back. And then your wages suck, so you're paying it back pretty much forever."

"Why don't people just leave?" Caroline asked.

Lani paused before answering. When she spoke again, her voice was lower, almost a whisper. "If you try to leave Oasis without paying back your program fee, things happen to you. Bad things."

A faint buzzing began in Caroline's ears, as if the pieces of the puzzle had edged a little closer to one another.

"What kind of bad things?" Caroline asked.

Lani twisted her hands together and looked away.

"Please," Caroline said. "I need to know."

When Lani met Caroline's eyes again, her own held fear. "Like if you're supposed to report to your parole officer, he's suddenly recommending a longer parole period or he's come up with some reason you've broken parole. Or if you served time for drugs, you get pulled over, some cop plants coke on you. Or maybe you try leaving town and getting a job, you know, like trying to make a new life for yourself, and then some pictures from your juvenile files that were supposed to be sealed suddenly appear in the local paper. You got to pay your debt to Oasis if you take them up on their services or they screw you."

"What happened to you?" Caroline asked.

"I started helping out in the kitchen at Oasis, you know, learning about being a cook—that's a nice, useful skill, right? But when I found out about the whole program fee thing, I bailed. I've got enough debt. I tried going to another shelter that wasn't run by Oasis."

"But Daryl found you there," Caroline surmised.

"He didn't find me. Oasis told him where I was."

"How do you know that?"

"Because that's how Oasis works," Lani said, her small jaw setting in repressed rage. "You got to pay your debt one way or another. Work those construction projects for minimum wage. Tell those old people at nursing homes about Oasis. That's the way a lot of girls did it. And anyways, lots of people don't mind paying Oasis back. They get into the whole thing—Oasis is your lifeline. Your chance at a future. But to me, it all seemed too wrong. Oasis promises to take care of you, but then they never let you go."

After spending nights on the street, Caroline understood the attraction of making any available deal with the Devil. And yet, not everyone's connection to Oasis was about coercion. Oasis provided training but also context. Connection. It satisfied needs strong enough to tie a soul to Oasis. But were those needs strong enough to drive someone to murder to protect it?

"You met Vizzi at Oasis," Caroline said.

Lani nodded. "He's the one that's running things over there on that big campus."

Caroline had already assumed as much.

"What about other people connected to Oasis? Did you ever meet Simon Reed?"

"I don't know. What does he look like?" Lani asked.

Instead of trying to describe him, Caroline pulled the laptop toward her.

When she found the page she wanted, she carried the laptop to where Lani sat in bed.

"This is Simon Reed," Caroline said, sitting down beside the small woman.

On the screen, Simon was standing in front of City Hall. The accompanying article described his ambitious development plans, including the fifty-three-story building to be built on city land on Bunker Hill.

"I've seen pictures of that guy at the Oasis campus. His picture's all over the place there. But I never met him," Lani said.

Caroline swung the laptop back in front of herself. With a few more keystrokes, she brought up an image of Gregory Parsons. The man in pinstripes from the bank's security footage.

"What about this guy?" Caroline asked. "We think he might be Oasis's money guy."

Lani shook her head. "Never seen him. I was in the Oasis dormitory or the kitchen, so if that guy worked in the back office, I wouldn't have ever come across him."

Putting the laptop aside, Caroline tucked her legs under her, getting comfortable. Though it wasn't exactly a slumber party, the sensation of sitting on a bed, chatting, felt soothingly normal. She hoped the same was true for Lani. She needed the small woman to talk freely and hopefully provide some useful information.

"Tell me about the dorm," Caroline said.

"There's nothing much to it. Just a big room with a bunch of cots. Better than being on the street, I guess." Lani shrugged. "There are a lot of girls there—we have a harder time on the streets than the men do."

"Did you get to know anyone at the dorms?"

"Sure. I hung out with a few."

"How about Patricia Amos?" Caroline asked. "I'm not sure that's her real name, but she's the CNA that cared for my grandmother. She went through the Oasis training program."

"I don't remember any Patricia," Lani said. "What does she look like?"

"Red hair. When I met her, it was tied back in a long braid. She's got a tattoo on her wrist," Caroline added, pointing at her right wrist. "I think it's Sanskrit. She told me it was her mantra."

"Oh, that's Rica," Lani said, her eyes lighting up. "Federica Muller."

Caroline's heart hammered. A name. She had a name.

"I don't know why she'd be going by 'Patricia,'" Lani continued, "but that's definitely Rica."

"She used a fake name because she's a murderer." Caroline had wondered before whether Patricia Amos was a fake identity. Now she knew it was—and she knew why Federica had used one.

Lani's eyebrows knit. "No," she said, her tone decisive. "Rica would never kill anyone. I mean, the woman meditates and shit. She loves animals. When I knew her at the Oasis dorm, she had this little dog named Baby. Oasis wouldn't let people have pets, so she had a homeless friend bring that dog by for her to walk so he wouldn't forget about her."

Caroline was far from convinced. Just because a person liked animals didn't mean they weren't capable of murder. Even criminals had pets, after all.

"How'd she end up on the street?" Caroline asked.

"I remember her telling me how she dropped out of school to follow some band. You know, traveling around, having fun. Except she got hooked on Oxy, and then the Oxy got too expensive, and so she ended up shooting up smack. You know how that shit goes." Lani shook her head mournfully, as if she'd seen or heard about the trajectory numerous times before. "Rica was just a messed-up kid who went down a bad path."

Caroline found herself growing angry. Patricia, or Federica or whatever her name was, had duped everyone. The proximity between Grandma Kate's will and her death was unavoidable. Maybe Federica had been coerced into doing it, but Caroline had no doubt that she'd committed murder. And not just any murder. She'd killed Caroline's own grandmother.

"Do you know where Federica Muller is from?" Caroline asked. She hated that she had to find Federica, not to bring her to justice but to try to get her to cut a deal to testify against Oasis. Much as she hated it, she couldn't think of an alternative. Albert needed a witness.

"Desert Hot Springs. Her parents are still there, I think."

• • •

"Hi, there," said Caroline into the burner phone, "I'm on the Desert Hot Springs High School reunion committee. I'm putting together a list of alumni, and I'm just trying to track down a current address for Federica Muller." Despite the anger coiling in her gut, Caroline kept her voice light and pleasant.

"Rica hasn't lived here in years," said Federica's mother.

"Do you know her current address?"

"Sure, it's 135 South Slauson Avenue. Apartment 12-B."

Caroline thanked the woman and hung up.

Opening Google Maps, she quickly found the address.

Zooming in on the street-view image, she noted the property management company's name printed on a large sign in front of the apartment building.

Finding Federica was going to be easy.

• • •

"If you see her, please let her know that the reunion committee is trying to get in touch with her," Caroline said.

"No problem," the property manager said before hanging up.

Placing the burner phone beside the laptop, Caroline turned to meet the expectant eyes of Lani, Hitch, and Jake.

"The property manager hasn't seen Federica," she told them. "He says no one has. Her mail's been piling up for weeks." Caroline considered the timing. "She must've dropped out of her life around the same time she quit her job at The Pastures."

"But why?" Lani asked.

Caroline just shook her head. The caregiver's behavior made no sense. Even if Federica had been rattled by her encounter with Caroline at the nursing home, she had to know that Oasis would protect its own. The CNAs were valuable members of Oasis's operation, as Caroline understood it. That Federica had gone missing was inconsistent with Oasis's modus operandi.

As the questions piled up, Caroline realized Albert was right—she was functioning almost entirely on suspicion. The pattern of wills and transactions was circumstantial evidence of something, but she had no direct proof of anything. Even Lani, who'd lived at Oasis, had only heard rumors—she wasn't a firsthand witness to any of Oasis's crimes.

But Federica was. If Caroline was right, she'd even committed some of them.

The fact that Federica had disappeared hinted at a deeper story— one that Caroline's instincts insisted she discover.

And yet, looking for Federica would mean leaving the sanctuary of the residence hotel—and risking capture by the police.

Exhaling, Caroline confronted an unavoidable conclusion: She had to find a way to exonerate herself of the paletería accident. Problem was, there'd been no witnesses to the accident. Plus, the cascade of news reports Caroline had seen since arriving at the hotel room had mentioned only one suspect—her. How could she find the identity of the person who'd driven the Mustang into the front of the paletería?

Pulling her laptop to her, Caroline considered how to begin.

She closed the useless tab showing the Google Maps image of Federica's apartment building. That had been another dead end. She'd hit so many . . .

But then her eyes fell on the frozen image that now filled the screen of her laptop. Gregory Parsons. The man in pinstripes that Albert had identified from the surveillance footage.

Suddenly, Caroline knew exactly what she needed to do to prove her innocence.

CHAPTER 25

Caroline began the next morning at a pawnshop.

Ten minutes and twenty-six dollars later, she had what she needed in her pocket. The binoculars weren't new, but they'd be powerful enough for her purposes.

She ran a hand through her hair. The short strands were a surprise to her fingers.

If things went well, she'd exonerate herself of having had any involvement in the destruction of the paletería. But to find that exoneration, she'd need to spend hours in the open. Even worse, she'd have to walk the streets near her apartment. The haircut and cheap sunglasses gave her confidence she'd accomplish her mission without being detected. She'd get the hack job she'd done on her hair fixed once she wasn't being hunted by the law.

When she reached Traction Avenue, she stopped.

A quarter of a block ahead, in the late-morning sunshine, she could see the brick facade of the building that housed her apartment. She was close enough to see her kitchen window. Close enough to imagine her couch. Her clothes. Her bed. She'd slept better the previous night than she'd slept in the previous week, but it was still a hotel bed. She longed for her own.

Turning her back to her apartment, Caroline began walking toward the paletería. She took the shortest, most direct path.

As she moved slowly down the sidewalk, Caroline scanned the buildings on either side of her. Every once in a while, she'd stop and use the binoculars to better study the tops of fences and shops, scouring them for the one thing she knew would conclusively establish her innocence.

She finally found what she needed at a bar on the corner of Fourth and Crocker.

Replacing the binoculars in her pocket, she stepped inside the bar.

The proprietor sat on a stool by the door, watching television. His generous backside drooped over the edges of the wooden perch. In his hand, he held a glass of flat Coca-Cola.

He looked up at Caroline, who stood blinking in the doorway.

"Can I help you?" he asked, not bothering to rise from his stool.

To see anything in the dim light, Caroline removed her sunglasses.

The bar was empty except for a wrinkled woman cleaning highballs with a rag.

"I see you have an AngelView cam outside. I was hoping you'd let me take a look at your footage from Sunday, September 25. Around 10:00 p.m." Caroline knew that unlike bank security footage, footage from personal security cameras was not warehoused in a single, commonly used server. Businesses contracted with any number of smaller cloud-based services to record and save footage—footage that was accessible only on the account holder's phone or computer. Hence, her house call to the owner of one such camera.

The big man shifted in his seat.

"Why do you need it?" he asked.

Caroline had prepared for the question. "I got into a car accident the other night, and I was hoping your footage might show that I wasn't at fault."

The man squinted at Caroline.

"Aren't you that girl they keep showing on the news?"

Caroline's heart froze rock solid in her chest.

She considered denying the accusation. But the tone of the proprietor's voice and the expression in his eyes let her know it would achieve nothing. He'd spent hours in front of a TV. He knew exactly who she was.

"I didn't do it," Caroline said, dropping the act. "Someone stole my car and crashed it into that shop."

She braced herself for the next question and the judgment that would inevitably follow. He'd ask why she hadn't turned herself in and then, like Lily, he'd treat her failure to do so as an admission of guilt.

"You think my video's gonna show the guy?" The man raised his eyebrows.

"Yes. That's exactly what I think it's going to show."

"Cool," said the man, rising from the stool. "Let's go see if you're right."

• • •

"You got this from a bar?" Albert asked on the phone.

In the hopes that his trial broke for lunch each day around noon, Caroline had taken the risk of calling the prosecutor in the middle of the day. Fortunately, he'd answered.

"Yes, they had a camera trained on the sidewalk," she explained. "The top of the frame included the intersection." As she spoke, Caroline watched the footage she'd just sent to Albert. A blond man drove her black Mustang GT down East Fourth Street. He stopped at the stoplight at Crocker Street and then drove onward. The scene was commonplace and innocuous but utterly incriminating with the license plate on the car, plus the date and time stamp on the video.

"Nice trick." Albert whistled appreciatively on the line. "Once the investigating detective at LAPD sees this, they'll definitely call off the search for you. It shouldn't take long for them to verify the provenance of the footage."

"I've tried to expedite that process. Check your e-mail. I've sent you a declaration from the bar owner, attesting to the chain of custody of the video footage and authenticating it. His number's on there, too. He's happy to talk to the detective or you or anyone else."

"Really?" Albert asked.

Instead of answering the obviously rhetorical question, Caroline waited while Albert looked at the short declaration she'd scratched on the back of a bar menu. She was glad the proprietor had been so willing to help. Everyone wanted their fifteen minutes of fame, apparently, and his would surely come now. When the police dropped their search, the news trucks would follow. The publicity would probably elevate the bar's profile and make the proprietor a local celebrity for a news cycle or two.

"I'll make sure this doesn't fall through the cracks over at LAPD. They'll be embarrassed enough that they didn't already obtain this footage themselves. They won't want to sit on it. Just give me a couple of hours."

"Hurry. I need to go to Desert Hot Springs, and I'd really rather not be arrested."

"You really think that caregiver's parents are going to tell you where she is?"

"No, but I'll think of something."

"I'm sure you will," Albert said. There was a smile in his voice.

Caroline found herself smiling, too.

"What are you going to do if you find her?" Albert asked, his tone growing serious.

"I don't know, but I'll think of something there, too," Caroline said, and it was true. She knew they needed a witness. Someone Albert could use to build a criminal case against Oasis and Simon Reed. That's what they'd been missing all along—an informant who might be willing to testify against Simon. But she dreaded the moment when she would meet Federica Muller.

The sun outside the hotel room was still high in the sky, but she had much to do.

Hanging up with Albert, she got to work.

• • •

The 1983 Cadillac Eldorado wheezed as Caroline stepped down on the accelerator as she headed east on the I-10, into the dusk.

In the passenger seat, Lani sat with her feet up against the dashboard. With ninety-eight thousand miles on it, the car rattled and hummed, which was why it had cost Caroline only $1,800 at the used car lot—the most she could allow herself to spend of the Western Union funds she'd wired to herself.

Beside Caroline on the Eldorado's spacious front seat, the laptop sat uncharged. She didn't have an adapter to turn the cigarette lighter into a USB port, but thankfully she didn't need the laptop at the moment. Instead, she held the burner phone. Its glow lit the side of her face.

"You're lucky you caught me," said assistant DA Shaina Parker on the line. "I was actually just putting the finishing touches on the charging document."

"What have you decided to do?" Caroline asked. She'd been eager to call the assistant district attorney handling the *Hidalgo* case. Now that she'd been exonerated of any involvement in the paletería incident, she finally could.

"We might add other charges later, but we've got Rogelio Gonzalez for money laundering for sure."

"That's great news," Caroline said. Her money-laundering theory had been a Hail Mary, a desperate reach to keep Judge Flores from rubber-stamping the guardianship petition. And it had worked. That she'd come up with the argument in a distribution center while on the run made her feel like her trip to Desert Hot Springs, winging it as she went along, might not be a total bust.

"None of Gonzalez's manifest numbers add up right, and there are a number of other suspicious transfers on top of the ones you've identified," continued the assistant DA. Then she paused. "Wally's been telling everyone in the office that he knew all along that you didn't crash your car into that shop."

Caroline doubted that Wallace Boyd had been convinced of her innocence until he'd personally seen the security footage from the bar, but she gave Shaina Parker a charitable, noncommittal *hmm*.

"I'll send a courtesy copy of the charging document to the dependency court, just to let Judge Flores know the status of the case," the assistant DA finished.

"Thanks so much. Please keep me posted."

Hanging up, Caroline dialed the next number. She had one last task to complete to ensure Mateo's safety.

"Mr. Castillo?" she asked when a man's voice answered. "I'm the guardian ad litem for Mateo Hidalgo. We've talked once before, when Mateo was placed with you. I know you've run into some problems and wanted to check in personally to see whether you're amenable to keeping Mateo in your house until his father is released."

"If you are able to help us with our legal troubles, we are willing," said Mr. Castillo.

"I am. I will stick with you until we get it all sorted out. No charge."

"Mateo is a good boy," Mr. Castillo said. "We are doing what we can to help him."

"We all are," Caroline said. "Thanks for taking care of him."

Hanging up, Caroline released a long, slow breath.

She might be driving into Hell, but at least she'd left a patch of grace behind her.

That Mateo Hidalgo was in a safe home, where he'd remain, was a consolation as she entered the stretch of freeway where big-box stores mingled with warehouses and outlets. The monotonous urban land-scape would continue until they reached the mountain pass that marked the divide between city and desert.

She glanced in the rearview mirror.

The headlights behind her were too numerous to identify, but she hadn't seen any motorcycles. That, at least, was encouraging. Their errand would go much more smoothly if they weren't also trying to avoid getting killed by a hit man.

Without Hitch and Jake along, the car was quiet except for the rattle of the engine. Both men had objected to being left behind. But Caroline had worried that her irascible uncle might throttle Federica Muller, and Jake had agreed that the least threatening way to approach the caregiver's parents was for Lani to do it—someone who'd known Federica Muller from her days in the Oasis dormitory.

"I've never been to the desert," Lani said, watching the landscape change in the twilight, growing drier and scarcer of foliage. "I grew up outside Oahu." In thrift-shop blue jeans and a loose blouse, she no longer looked like she'd stepped off a party bus and lost her way home.

"What brought you here?"

Without turning from the windshield, Lani answered, "We were going to be in the movies, my ex-boyfriend and me. My parents hated him. They called him 'that silly haole.' 'Big dreams in your eyes, what do you know?' they told me. 'You gonna come back here with big regrets.'" Lani parroted the words in a way that let Caroline know they were not her own.

She glanced over at Lani. With almond-shaped eyes and deeply tanned skin, Lani could've been part Polynesian, part Filipino, part Japanese, and a mishmash of a half dozen other genetic lines, all of which had come to mix in the Hawaiian Islands. And she was beautiful. It wasn't inconceivable that some talent agent somewhere would've plucked her out of obscurity. Serendipity had more than a little to do with fame.

"I never wanted to prove them right," Lani finished quietly. "How much farther?"

"We'll be in Desert Hot Springs in another hour," Caroline replied, allowing Lani to change the subject.

"Then what?"

"We'll wait until morning to visit the Mullers," Caroline said. It hadn't been difficult to find an address for Federica's parents. The Mullers had purchased their home forty-three years earlier. Plus, they were the only Mullers in the town.

"Hotel?" Lani asked.

"We'll sleep in the car," she declared the grim verdict. After bank-rolling the residence hotel and meals for a small village of people, plus purchasing the car, her funds were running low. As it was, she'd have difficulty covering her next month's rent. She'd worry about that if she survived her current adventure.

Lani accepted the decision without comment. After nights on the street, a night in an Eldorado's front seat didn't sound so bad, Caroline realized.

"Have you figured out what you're going to say to Federica?" Lani asked.

"No, but I think she's on the run."

In her periphery, she saw Lani turn to study her face.

"No one at Oasis knows where she is," Caroline said. During the hours she'd waited for Albert to ensure that the LAPD had called off its hunt for her, she'd reviewed all of the evidence she'd gleaned about the woman that everyone at The Pastures had known as Patricia Amos. She'd found her notes about the e-mail she'd seen when she'd hacked Conrad Vizzi's account.

"Vizzi lost track of her—they can't find her," Caroline said.

"But you think her parents know where she is?"

"I do." Caroline couldn't explain exactly how she knew the Mullers would know where their daughter was hiding except that she knew if she had good parents, she'd go to them, too, if she found herself on the run.

"Are you going to tell the Mullers what happened to your grandma?" Lani asked.

Caroline shook her head. The gesture was equal parts uncertainty and disbelief. That she was trying to find the woman who'd murdered her grandmother was unfathomable. That she needed to find her was undeniable, though. She tried to imagine what she'd say to Federica.

Hello, you killed my grandmother. Will you be a witness in a criminal prosecution?

Maybe Lani would do the talking.

CHAPTER 26

The sun rose crisp and clear. Though it shed no warmth at the early hour, it reflected bright and blinding off the small house. A garden of rocks covered the spot in the front yard where people from more temperate climates might've planted grass. A pickup truck sat in the driveway, its wheels caked in white dirt.

Behind the dwelling, hills rolled into the distance, dotted with tan tufts of dried plants. The Santa Ana winds that still plagued the city had left the desert pleasant. The sky was an electric blue, stark against the hills.

Caroline stretched her arms and heard something pop back into joint in her neck.

A night sleeping in the Eldorado in a residential neighborhood ten miles away in Palm Springs hadn't done good things to her back. And yet, the discomfort of spending a night in a car seat had been at least a partial boon—it had distracted her from the dreaded task that now lay a mere twenty yards ahead of her at the end of the driveway.

"You ready for this?" asked Lani.

"No," said Caroline, walking up the front walkway toward the front door.

When she reached the door, she knocked before she could change her mind.

A chorus of dog barks let her know their arrival had been duly noted by the occupants.

Soon, there was a shuffling and then some clicks as someone unlocked the door.

It swung open to reveal a woman with auburn hair streaked with gray.

Federica Muller's mother.

At the sight of her, Caroline's mouth went dry as the desert hills.

Fortunately, Lani spoke.

"Are you Mrs. Muller?" she asked.

"Who wants to know?"

"I'm a friend of Rica's, and I was hoping she might be here."

The auburn-haired woman squinted at Lani in distrust. Behind her, a tabby cat slunk by, slowing its step to regard the strangers. The suspicion in the cat's golden eyes mirrored the owner's.

"I lived with Rica," Lani continued. "We were in the dorm together at Oasis. Nobody's heard from Rica in a couple of weeks, and I got worried. I thought maybe she needed help."

Lani's tone was convincing, and Caroline realized it was because she was telling the truth. She really was worried.

Mrs. Muller stepped back, making room for Lani and Caroline to step into the foyer.

The dwelling was modest. The foyer and living room were covered in thick brown carpet. The ceiling was made of acoustic material. Sandwiched between the cottage cheese and the shag, Caroline felt like a hamburger inside a bun. The effect was stifling.

"I haven't seen my daughter in quite some time," Mrs. Muller said, glancing toward the cat, which had turned to slink back toward what Caroline guessed was the kitchen.

"When's the last time you spoke with her?" Caroline asked, finding her voice.

"Oh, let me see," said Mrs. Muller, looking away again. "We must be going around two months ago now. But that Rica has always been an independent-minded gal. She calls whenever she calls. Always been like that."

The woman was lying, and not very well, Caroline decided.

Mrs. Muller was protecting a murderer. That Federica happened to be Mrs. Muller's daughter didn't matter to Caroline.

"Who's there?" came a man's voice from somewhere in the house.

"Just some friends of Rica's," said the woman, her voice still artificially cheery.

"Did you tell them we don't know where she is?" asked the man, who stepped into view. Tall and wiry, he stooped slightly. At his side, a large golden retriever panted. The dog's mouth stretched into a wide smile that Caroline wished his owners might have greeted her with.

"I sure did, honey," answered Mrs. Muller.

"Good, then I'm sure they'll want to be on their way now," said Mr. Muller, his lips pursed together tightly.

"I know Rica's had some trouble in the past," Lani said. "She used to tell me about how she'd left town to follow that band and then things kind of went downhill from there."

Caroline watched Mr. Muller's lips purse even more tightly. He was bristling at the implication that he should have done something to prevent his daughter's downward slide—a slide he didn't realize involved taking people's lives.

"We really need to speak with her," Caroline said. "She might've gotten wrapped up in some . . . bad stuff." The last two words were so dense with understatement and euphemism that she almost choked on them.

"I heard Rica got herself together," Lani piped in, shooting Caroline a warning look.

Caroline understood. She was pushing too hard. The edge in her voice was too evident. Vowing to let Lani do the talking, she took a calming breath and tried not to focus on Charles Manson's parents.

"She's been doing really well," Lani continued. "I know she even got herself an apartment and everything. That's why I wanted to make sure she's okay. Are you sure you can't help us find her? We just want to help."

Caroline saw a glimmer of something in Mrs. Muller's eyes. Remorse. Or longing.

She wanted to talk, Caroline realized. But she couldn't.

The awkward silence stretched out, filling the brown-carpeted living room.

"That's a beautiful dog," Caroline said finally. At least the dog hadn't killed anyone. "What's his name?"

"Max," said Mrs. Muller.

"Do you mind if I pet him?" Caroline asked, squatting.

Mr. Muller opened his mouth to speak, but Mrs. Muller answered first.

"Sure, honey. He's a friendly one."

Caroline squatted. "Come here, Max."

The dog obliged, trotting over to Caroline for a rub between the ears. The sensation of soft fur under her hands calmed Caroline. The Mullers hadn't killed anyone. Regardless of what they thought or didn't think about their daughter, regardless of what they knew or didn't know about their daughter's job at Oasis, they were innocent of the wrongdoing that Caroline laid at their daughter's feet.

Caroline reminded herself she'd come to the desert for a reason.

"We really just want to talk to her," Caroline said. "I understand what it's like to have a loved one end up places you wish they'd never gone. I know how hard that can be."

Mr. Muller eyed Caroline, his jaw working.

A bark from the other room caught the golden retriever's attention, and the dog trotted off, apparently having found the human drama unfolding by the front door uninteresting. At the dog's arrival in the kitchen, there was another chorus of barks, punctuated by some hissing.

Mr. Muller took a step toward Caroline and Lani, forcing them to back up toward the front door.

"Please," Lani said. "We just want to help."

Caroline heard the desperation in Lani's voice, but she wasn't looking at Lani. She was looking at the two dog bowls by the door of the kitchen. Two large ceramic bowls with the name *Max* stenciled on their sides sat beside a small metal mixing bowl that had clearly been repurposed as a dog bowl.

Giving a low whistle, Caroline was gratified to see the golden retriever return.

But this time, he'd brought a friend. A Jack Russell terrier. Trotting gamely behind the larger dog, the terrier paused to regard the newcomers.

Again, Caroline squatted low.

"Baby, come," she commanded.

There was a short pause.

And then the Jack Russell terrier trotted over to Caroline.

The looks of mortification on the Mullers' faces told Caroline she'd guessed correctly.

"Hey, that's—" Lani began.

"We're just leaving," Caroline cut her off.

As she rose to her feet, Caroline kept her eyes on Mrs. Muller.

"I'm going to give you a note," she said in a cool tone. "I want you to give it to your daughter—you know, if you by chance just happen to see her."

Taking a scrap of paper from her makeshift laptop bag, Caroline wrote three short lines of text. Then she folded the page in half and handed it to Mrs. Muller.

Federica's mother opened the note and read the text.

When she met Caroline's eyes, her own held curiosity.

"Thank you for your help," Caroline said rather than answering.

Then she allowed Mr. Muller to usher them out the door.

• • •

"That was Rica's dog," Lani said, throwing her hands up in exasperation.

"I know," said Caroline, opening the driver's side door of the Eldorado. In the time since they'd been in the Mullers' house, the day and the interior of the car had heated up. Neither fact could keep her from getting away from the house as soon as possible. It had already been a risk to come to Federica's parents' house. That the hit man had not made an appearance, too, was a blessing. But it didn't mean he wasn't near.

"If you knew it was her dog, why'd you let them kick us out?" Lani asked, climbing into the passenger seat.

"They served their purpose." Caroline sat down behind the big maroon steering wheel of the Eldorado and turned on the engine. She pulled away from the curb and hung a U-turn before hurrying away from the Mullers' house.

Lani fixed the side of Caroline's face with a stare.

"What do you mean?" Lani asked.

"I mean I'm going to meet Federica Muller for lunch."

• • •

"I'll get out here." Caroline moved over to let Lani take the wheel of the Eldorado.

"Really?" Lani eyed the restaurant Caroline had stopped in front of. "Mexican food?"

"I saw it on the way into town. Casa Blanca Mexican Feast. Nice name, right?"

"Are you going to tell me what's going on?" Lani asked.

"As I said, I'm meeting Federica Muller for lunch. Now please go park in the alley behind the restaurant." Caroline had driven a lap around the restaurant to confirm it had a back door on the alley. "We could be here a little while, but I need you to be ready to help us get away fast if things go badly. I'll bring you a burrito."

• • •

Caroline sat in the back booth of the Mexican restaurant for almost an hour before the bells on the door tinkled and a woman entered. With shoulder-length hair hidden beneath a hat, she looked more nondescript than the last time Caroline had seen her, but Federica Muller's green eyes were the same, as was the tattoo that encircled the hand that held the door open.

Federica wore a long sweater, handwoven and hanging down to her midthigh. The hiking shoes on her feet were covered with the same white dirt that Caroline had observed on the tires of Mr. Muller's truck.

Seeing Caroline waiting for her, Federica blanched. Her face drained of color. Her eyelids let loose a rapid-fire staccato of blinks. A nervous twitch, Caroline noted. Knowing that Federica was anxious didn't do much to quell Caroline's own nerves. Her heart rate increased with each step Federica took down the aisle.

When Federica reached the booth, she stopped.

With her left hand, she pulled a piece of paper from her pocket and put it on the table.

In the half-unfolded sheet, Caroline could see the message she'd scrawled.

8-3-16, 8-16-16, 9-11-16,
Casa Blanca Mex—11:15 today

"Sit down. Please." Caroline gestured to the seat across from her.

With halting movements, Federica obliged, sinking into the red vinyl booth, hands clasped in her lap, her eyes downcast.

"Can I call you Rica?" Caroline asked. "Seems like that's what people call you."

Federica winced at the words. She made no attempt to explain why she'd introduced herself as Patricia Amos when they'd met at The Pastures.

"You messed up, didn't you?" Caroline asked.

Federica just blinked.

Caroline pointed at the dates. "My grandma made her last will on August 3. She died on September 11. But by that day, you'd already given Simon Reed the watch for his birthday. There's video footage of him wearing it at a birthday banquet on August 16."

When Federica didn't disagree, Caroline continued, emboldened.

"You gave it to him too soon, didn't you? My grandmother was still alive," Caroline said. It had bothered her when she'd realized that Simon was wearing her grandma's watch. But when she'd focused on the dates, her concerns had deepened. There was only one explanation for it: Federica had given Simon the watch as soon as Kate had remade her will.

Instead of answering, Federica shrank down in the booth, looking as if she wished she could disappear into the floor.

"Even if you killed my grandmother later, you couldn't undo the timing. Or the videos documenting it. The fact that Simon was wearing that watch before it became Oasis's property incriminates him." Much as she despised facing the woman who'd killed her grandmother, it gave Caroline a malevolent thrill to see her squirm.

"That's why you've run away," Caroline pressed. "You knew they'd come for you. Even killing my grandmother later couldn't fix what you'd done to Simon by exposing him."

As Federica blinked her fears in a wave of nervous tics, Caroline felt no sympathy. All of the chapters with her grandmother were finished. No more would be written. She'd have memories, but there would be no new material. And this was the woman who'd stolen that from her.

"I didn't kill her." Federica's voice was tiny but insistent. Her green eyes, which had fluttered throughout Caroline's cross-examination, now held a surprising earnestness.

"The timing of my grandmother's will and her death speaks for itself," Caroline said. She'd seen the pattern. Once her uncle had pointed it out, the pattern had become an irrefutable indictment of the woman who'd called herself Patricia Amos.

"I'm not saying I wasn't supposed to kill her," Federica began, "but I didn't. I couldn't. They tried to tell us these are mercy killings—you know, euthanasia for old people with dementia whose lives are hell. But even an old person who's having trouble remembering stuff has a right to live, right?"

"Um, right," Caroline agreed.

"Well, I couldn't do it. I couldn't kill anyone. I've been living in a yurt the last few weeks up in the hills. My parents know where I am, but that's all." Federica twisted her hands together in her lap. "I've got some granola and some lentils and rice, and a camp stove and some tanks of water, but it's cold and there are coyotes at night and—"

"Wait, go back to the part where you didn't kill my grandma," Caroline said. "You're saying she died of natural causes?"

"Yes. I swear that's the truth. Your grandmother was really great. I meant it when I said that to you. She was so warm and giving and nice. When I told her about Oasis, she wanted to help with the homeless program. She said something about wanting to help people like her son."

Caroline couldn't deny that her grandmother might've done and said exactly as Federica's words suggested. That was the kind of woman Grandma Kate had always been.

"She wrote that new will," Federica continued, "and then I went and picked up the watch. I knew Simon liked watches, so I gave it to Vizzi to give to him. I thought it would make Simon like me and that would be good since he's the guy running everything and he's got all kinds of connections, too." As the ex-caregiver's fire hose of words petered out, she looked back down at her hands and fluttered another cascade of nervous blinks.

"So what you're saying is, you chickened out," Caroline said, her mind still reeling with Federica's assertion of innocence in the death of her grandmother, if not the theft of the watch.

Federica nodded. "I didn't tell Simon. I didn't tell anyone anything. I just hoped this whole thing would all go away—you know, that no one would notice. But then you came to The Pastures and I realized everyone was going to know. Simon was going to find out about the watch and you were going to find out about the will and the fake name and—"

"Tell me how it works. The caregiver program. I need to know," Caroline said calmly. She couldn't let herself be roiled by the swirl of emotions that buffeted the red-haired caregiver. She had to remain on the outside, coldly dissecting the truth of Federica's story.

Federica nodded to herself. "When you come to Oasis off the street, they figure out what they can do for you. But that's not all they do. They also figure out what you can do for them. I didn't really have any skills. So they put me in the caregiver program. They give you all this literature about how great they are. Then they send you off to tell old people about it. It's really not that hard."

"I suppose not," Caroline agreed, just to keep her talking.

"I turned out to be good at connecting with people. My heart chakra is really open. Also, I remember someone saying it's easy to sell something you believe in, and I believed in Oasis. They saved my life. They got me clean. When I went to them, I was a smack addict living on the street. They got me treatment."

"They helped you," Caroline noted. Whatever evil Oasis had committed, it had also done a little good, apparently. At least in the life of the nervous woman sitting across from her.

"Yeah. They did. So I was good at getting people excited about Oasis and many of my patients ended up making gifts to it. I guess Vizzi noticed, because he asked me to join a special program. He said I'd make more money. That sounded good to me because I was trying to get my own apartment and I had to get a security deposit together and—"

"How does this special program work?" Caroline interrupted, trying to keep Federica focused.

"At first, it just seemed like they wanted to train us to become better caregivers. We got extra training on how to connect with residents— you know, how to tend to them emotionally, as well as how to take them to the commode and whatnot. We also had to take some medical training. It was a lot of work and it took a bunch of time, but the good part is, you make more money, plus you get to pay off your program fee to Oasis really quickly."

Caroline recalled the program fee that Lani had balked at owing. The debt that no one seemed to be able to repay—and the negative consequences of trying to avoid it. The setup had sounded like sharecropping to Caroline. A racket rigged to keep the poor man poor.

"I was really happy to be picked," Federica continued, "but then there were some strange things about the special program. Like, we had to work under a fake name."

"Patricia Amos," said Caroline.

Federica nodded. "Oasis handles payroll so there's no problem with the nursing homes—the facilities pay Oasis, and then Oasis pays us."

"Weren't you concerned?" Caroline asked.

"Sure I was. But what choice did I have? And anyway, everything was fine for a while. The money was good. Things were going well." Federica looked down at her hands that still lay cradled in her lap. "But then they told me what I was expected to do."

"You were supposed to kill."

Federica nodded and looked down.

At the admission, Caroline's hands tingled. In this beleaguered caregiver, she'd found what she needed: proof. Testimony by a firsthand witness to Oasis's scheme would become the centerpiece of a prosecution that would end Oasis.

"Your grandma was going to be my first," Federica continued, "but when it came time to do it, I just couldn't." She let out a long puff of air. "Everyone in the special program's supposed to be producing results. But I . . . I just couldn't."

"How many people are in this special program?" Caroline asked.

"I'm not sure. Maybe a couple dozen? I've never seen a list, but I've been to those trainings and I've talked to some of the others. I don't know anyone's names. Not their real names, anyway."

Caroline considered the ramifications of a couple dozen people out trying to induce nursing home residents into leaving money to Oasis. A couple dozen people pushing those residents off cliffs.

"Where does Oasis get these fake identities?" Caroline asked. Fabricating identities that would pass muster at a nursing home was no easy feat. It took years to perform the sort of theft necessary not just to create a fake identity but to populate it with enough history to get a job that required a background check.

Federica shook her head. "I don't know, but I'll tell you one thing— I'm not the only person who has ever used the name Patricia Amos. I overheard someone mentioning another one. Another Patricia Amos."

The hairs at the back of Caroline's neck rose at Federica's words. An image of the brown-haired, glasses-wearing woman who worked as a nurse in Burbank formed in her mind's eye. And a theory began to form in Caroline's mind. She made a mental note to pursue it later.

"The reason I'm so good at connecting with old people is that I really like them," Federica continued. "They've lived long lives. They have stories. They have heartbreak and they have love. All of that. Your grandmother had the loveliest stories before she got too confused to tell them anymore. I'd sit there for hours just listening to her sometimes."

Federica's words froze Caroline's interrogation. All of her efforts to remain dispassionate dissolved as tears welled in her eyes. She'd come to the restaurant planning to have a war. Instead, she was having a wake.

"There's no way I could've killed Kate," Federica said. "Honestly, I'd rather die than kill anyone. That's why I ran."

Caroline found honesty in Federica's eyes. Against all expectations, she found herself believing Federica wasn't a murderer. Doomed once by her own addictive biochemistry and again by the manipulative charity that had preyed on her, Federica had gone down a bad path. But she was trying to right the listing ship of her life. The Sanskrit mantra around her wrist made sense, Caroline realized. The lotus grew from brackish water. The heart of the lotus was within. Federica was trying. In her own nervous, halting way, she was striving to be good.

Caroline knew she should have been mad about Federica's role in remaking the will, but the fact that Grandma Kate had died of natural causes eclipsed any anger Caroline might've felt.

Federica looked down at her hands again. "I think giving the watch to Simon too early and chickening out and messing up the timing wouldn't have mattered so much to Oasis except that Simon's trying to get that big project going. You know, the one on Bunker Hill?"

Caroline nodded. She recalled reading about it.

"Simon's got all these approvals and meetings and hearings with public officials and stuff going on," Federica continued. "He couldn't have anything bad happen. Vizzi made that really clear to all of us."

The guilt Federica wore, even for messing up a criminal's plans, only reinforced Caroline's belief that her story had been true. Federica had balked when it came time to kill.

"You're not a screwup because you couldn't go through with it," Caroline said, stating the obvious.

Raising her eyes again to meet Caroline's, Federica exhaled and nodded to herself.

"I know I've messed up a lot in my life, but I'm figuring things out now that maybe I should've figured out before. I . . . I had some problems." Exhaling again, Federica looked at Caroline squarely. "Ever since we talked that day in your grandmother's room at The Pastures, I've been carrying a weight on me. The karma—I needed to resolve it. Now that weight isn't so heavy. You can feel that, too, right?"

Caroline wasn't sure she felt any lighter, but she'd gained new insight.

"I'm ready to go talk to the police," Federica said, sitting up straighter in the booth. "I'm ready to not be running anymore."

"I'm ready for that, too," Caroline agreed, her mouth pulling into a grim smile.

CHAPTER 27

"I have your witness," Caroline told Albert over the burner phone.

In the backseat of the Eldorado, Federica curled up with a duffel bag. It hadn't taken long for her to gather her things from the yurt. The ride up into the backcountry had been a different matter, however. The Eldorado's suspension had not enjoyed the bumpy dirt road. Now they were on the freeway, heading back to Los Angeles.

"You've got to get her into protection," Caroline continued to Albert.

"I'm in court today, so I can't do much, but I'll contact my section chief right away to get the ball rolling. I know she'll want to bring the witness in immediately."

"Sounds good to me," Caroline said, glancing in the rearview mirror.

Federica lay across the backseat, wearing earbuds. At first blush, the ex-caregiver looked like a thirty-something chilling out on a long road trip. But in the short time Caroline had known Federica, she'd realized she was highly anxious. Lying across the seats wasn't about relaxation. It was about not being visible through the windows of the car.

"I'll call you once we've gotten things set up," said Albert. "I promise it'll be soon."

"Thanks," Caroline said before hanging up.

Although she felt Lani's eyes on her, Caroline didn't look over at her. She had no words of comfort to offer. Lani's presence had calmed Federica when they'd climbed into the Eldorado waiting in the alley outside the Mexican restaurant. The two ex-Oasis residents had rejoiced at their reunion and found strength in each other's company. But Federica had quickly sunk back down to her baseline—fear. The caregiver's dread was infectious. In Lani's wide-eyed apprehension, visible in Caroline's peripheral vision, Caroline now felt it, too.

She checked her rearview mirror again to confirm that the constellation of vehicles behind her hadn't changed since the last time she'd looked. There were a couple of motorcycles in the mix, but they'd maintained constant speeds. No one had tried to approach.

She wanted to believe she'd managed to make the trip to and from Desert Hot Springs without being noticed. But it seemed unlikely. The hit man had tracked her and those she loved, even on the streets. While she enjoyed the fantasy that she'd escaped his scrutiny, she couldn't treat it as anything other than a fantasy. She had to stay vigilant.

"What's going to happen?" Federica's voice came from the backseat. She'd pulled the earbuds out and sat up, keeping her shoulders below the level of the windows.

"We're going to a hotel where some friends are waiting. They're nice. You'll like them. We'll wait for this federal prosecutor I know to set things up—then we'll bring you to wherever he says."

Panic flashed across Federica's face. Her green eyes widened.

"It's going to be okay," Caroline said. "This prosecutor is a good guy. He'll make sure nothing bad happens."

She hoped she was right.

• • •

The first minutes at the Royal Residence Hotel had been tense. Caroline had entered the hotel room first, followed by Lani and then Federica. Hitch's eyes had skipped past the two people he already knew, landing on the one he didn't know—except by reputation.

"She didn't do it," Caroline had said, stepping between her uncle and the terrified ex-caregiver. Speaking quickly but persuasively, she'd told Hitch what she'd learned from Federica. As he'd listened to the reasons why Caroline believed Federica had not murdered Grandma Kate, Hitch had gradually unclenched his hands. His jaw had relaxed.

But Federica had not relaxed. She still blinked in cascading flutters. She twisted the strands of her hair with her finger in a manner that would no doubt create dreadlocks if allowed to continue unchecked.

"I'm going to die. I'm a nobody and if I get killed, no one's going to care," she said.

"I'd care," Lani piped in from the rollaway bed, where she sat.

"You are the key witness," Caroline said, fixing Federica with her gaze. "You're incredibly important. You're the one who heard what Vizzi said. Your testimony will end this. Everyone is going to do everything they can to protect you."

Federica stopped twirling her hair around her finger.

Her apprehensive green eyes held Caroline's, unblinking.

"But if that's true, you're important, too, right? I mean, you saw that hit man guy and you did those hacks and stuff and you talked to Vizzi and you found me. You're going to have to testify, too."

Exhaling, Caroline looked away. She preferred not to think about the fact that the best-case scenario involved her testifying at a criminal trial. When she'd gone to law school, she'd planned to be on the other side of the cross-examination.

To avoid answering, she turned back to her laptop.

She'd logged into her private e-mail via a VPN server and found dozens of e-mails since she'd last checked. Some were from clients, wondering why she hadn't responded to their calls. Some were from concerned friends. Some were spam. There was only one that needed to be answered immediately. Caroline's father had written:

> I'm so glad to hear everything's okay re: that car crash. Please let me know whether there's anything I can do with the other stuff you've got going on. BTW, Lily feels horrible about what she said. She wants to talk to you when you get a free moment.

Though they were just words on a screen, they touched Caroline. Her father knew she hadn't resolved the Oasis mess yet—he'd have seen it in the newspaper if she had. Yet here he was, offering to help. That Lily was feeling bad was nice, too, though Caroline had no desire to talk to her stepmother quite yet.

> Will call when I can.

She hit "Send."

If she survived the next twenty-four hours, she'd think about reconciling with her stepmother. Until then, she needed to remain focused on Simon Reed.

Beside her hand, the burner phone rang on the desk.

She met Federica's eyes.

It was time to go.

• • •

Caroline chewed at her cuticle. The no-name gas station on the corner of Third and Butler gave her a bad feeling. Maybe it was the suspicious attendant who kept looking out the tiny window of the station at her. Maybe it was the dilapidated surroundings. The pockmarked concrete ground, covered in dirt and dust. Or maybe it was the fact that she was alone.

She'd left Jake and Lani at the residence hotel with the laptop. And she'd left Hitch with Federica in the Eldorado parked a block away. It had seemed like a good idea at the time. But now she found herself wishing she'd kept Jake with her, at least.

After another few minutes, an early-model Volkswagen came driving down Palmetto Street. When it reached the service station, it turned, bumping onto the uneven pavement. Silver beneath a layer of grime, the vehicle bespoke a salary somewhere south of what a lawyer could earn at a large firm. It came to a stop fifteen yards away from Caroline.

Albert climbed out of the driver side door. He wore a suit.

When Caroline had last seen him, they'd been seated back to back on park benches at Pershing Square. Now, she studied his stature. He wasn't tall, but he held himself with a self-possession that gave him a presence that exceeded his physical mass.

"How's it going?" he asked as he approached.

"Super awesome." Caroline smiled to release some tension.

"Sorry I'm late. I came straight from court as fast as I could. Don't worry—my section supervisor's got everything set up for us. As I expected, she wants to get the witness into protective custody as soon as possible. Speaking of the witness . . . where is she?"

Albert looked around.

"Nearby," Caroline said. "She's with my uncle."

"Trust but verify, eh?" Albert's voice held amusement but also disappointment.

Caroline knew she had trust issues, but the present situation seemed like a completely reasonable time for them.

A black-and-white police car pulled into the far end of the service station.

Flinching at the squad car's arrival, Caroline looked back at Albert.

"The plan is for local PD to escort the witness to our offices," said Albert as an officer approached.

The newcomer wore the dark-blue uniform made famous on decades of television shows about Los Angeles police departments. The sharp crease down the side of his pants and the shiny badge told Caroline he was probably a rookie.

"I'm Officer Charles Grady," he said, extending a hand.

Taking it, Caroline resisted the urge to ask where he'd be taking Federica. She knew he wouldn't tell her. That was the whole point of protective custody.

"You should come along with us, too," Albert said, turning his attention back to Caroline. "Once we move on the suspect, things are going to happen very quickly. It's going to be a full-on shit storm."

"Is that a technical term?"

"Absolutely," Albert confirmed, matching her smile.

Caroline considered the offer of protection. After a week on the run, it was tempting.

"How long will the witness be in the program?" Caroline asked, taking her lead from Albert. Apparently they were using euphemisms to avoid letting the local police know too much about the investigation. Probably a good precaution, Caroline decided.

"Hard to know. Unless the suspect is a flight risk, we take our time putting things together and convening a grand jury," said Albert, "and I don't think this suspect's a flight risk."

Caroline nodded her agreement. Simon Reed wouldn't run. His latest project was the capstone of his career. And to make that project happen, he had to show up at meetings with redevelopment officials. Hearings with the city council. Press junkets. He'd only run if he thought he had no chance of stamping out the small fire Caroline represented to him. That he'd stamped out so many other conflagrations meant he probably felt confident about his ultimate success with her. He was a well-connected man with many ways of destroying his opposition.

"It could be a month before we seek indictments," said Albert.

A month in protective custody. Caroline had a hard time signing up for that.

"Let's deal with this witness first," she said.

"Okay, let's get on with it," said Albert, looking to the rookie. "My section chief wants the witness delivered to our Alameda Street office. We'll take it from there."

"The witness is a bit fragile," Caroline said. The protective urge that rose in her was unexpected, but powerful. She knew that Federica was emotionally ill equipped for the intensity of what was coming. The interviews. The hearings. Caroline's impotent urge to shield Federica from the stress wasn't unlike what Caroline had experienced with her own mother. Life was especially hard for those who'd won the dark lottery of bad brain chemistry.

"I promise she's in good hands," said Officer Grady. "We often cooperate with the US Attorney's Office in sensitive situations. We receive extensive training in determining how and where local police and the DA have jurisdiction, and when the marshals and feds run the show. It's more complicated than you'd think," the rookie continued before launching into a description of the criteria used to make such complex determinations.

Ignoring the rookie's exegesis, Caroline scanned the surroundings for danger.

The only vehicles at the station were Albert's Volkswagen and the squad car.

Caroline squinted to see the rookie's partner. He sat in the driver's seat of the black-and-white with his elbow propped in the open window. He rested his head against his hand. Even wearing sunglasses, Caroline could see his pained expression. He was probably wishing he'd brought some duct tape to use on his partner's mouth.

Seeing nothing amiss, Caroline reached into her pocket for the burner phone she'd use to call her uncle. They'd picked up a second phone on the way over for her uncle for this moment.

As Caroline watched, the officer in the squad car took off his hat. He wiped his inky-black hair off his forehead before replacing his hat and tipping his head back against his hand.

With a pang in her stomach, Caroline realized she'd seen him before. It took a moment to recall where.

Then it hit her. That captain. The one who'd been so solicitous when she'd gone to the police station to look at mug shots. Captain Nelson—that was his name.

The coincidence seemed fortuitous for half a heartbeat.

But then Caroline realized what was happening.

She had walked into a trap.

With sudden certainty, she knew if she handed Federica over, Captain Nelson would find a way to lose her, most likely to the hands of the hit man waiting somewhere nearby.

Officer Grady was still talking, but Caroline no longer heard him. Her mind raced, her focus narrowing down to the critical path before her. She needed to escape. She needed to extract herself from the conversation and run.

But how?

The rookie didn't know anything. Caroline was sure of it. He exuded that special species of cluelessness reserved for newbies of all stripes who've had a little training and think they know everything. Could she warn him? Could she enlist his help? Or would his partner simply close the gap between the squad car and where she stood in the few seconds it would take for him to step down on the accelerator?

Turning her attention to Albert, Caroline weighed whether she could say anything to him.

He'd said his supervisor had arranged things. Did she believe Albert had not been involved in the arrangements? She'd trusted Albert. She'd shared information with him. She'd treated him as an ally. A friend, even. But she'd been betrayed before by people she trusted. She needed to decide whether she was being betrayed again.

Caroline realized that Albert had stopped paying attention to the rookie.

He was watching her.

The tips of his dark eyebrows dipped toward each other in question.

In answer, Caroline shifted her balance to her left foot. With a nonchalant sweep of her right foot, she carved a shape in the dirt in front of her. The number 88.

Then she waited.

Albert's brow knit for another moment.

Then understanding blossomed in his eyes.

The number 88 was the symbol of the dissident Burmese group that Albert's parents had fought for. The number symbolized freedom to him, Caroline hoped.

She glanced at the rookie, who still wasn't paying attention to anything except his own voice. Good. Time to give meaning to her code.

With a small, almost imperceptible step, she slid her shoe through the 88, crossing it out.

Then she let her eyes drift over to the black-and-white squad car.

When she looked back at Albert, his eyes held apprehension. And fear.

"That's great, Officer," said Albert, cutting off the rookie's monologue. "You certainly do know a lot about interoffice cooperation. But I need to get back to the office. I think it's time to have Ms. Auden retrieve the witness."

"Right. Of course," Officer Grady said, a flush of red rising from his cheeks up to his pale ears as he probably realized he'd been talking too long.

"I'll go get her now," Caroline said. "The witness is understandably terrified. It could take me a moment to bring her over here. Please be patient."

"No problem at all," said Albert with a forced smile.

The buzzing of Caroline's blood racing past her ears drowned out whatever the rookie said after that as she turned and walked away. If the police car followed her, she'd run in another direction, she decided. She wouldn't lead them to her friends.

She consoled herself that Lani and Jake were safe at the residence hotel with the laptop. If she didn't make it back—if Hitch and Federica didn't make it back—at least Lani and Jake would have all of the information on the laptop. They could take it to someone. An honest cop. A good detective. The contingency plan was weak, but it gave Caroline some solace as she walked away from Albert and the squad car, aware of everyone's eyes on her back.

Caroline strained her ears, scanning the auditory landscape for any sounds behind her.

She heard nothing. But she knew she wasn't safe yet.

Now, everything came down to what Albert did. This was the moment when he'd either protect her or betray her. With a word, he could bring the police down on her and, almost certainly, on the Eldorado that was parked nearby.

Caroline tried not to let her fear show in her pace.

Just another few yards until she reached the edge of the service station's sight line.

When she cleared the corner, she ran.

CHAPTER 28

Caroline caught up with the Eldorado on Colyton Street and East Fifth.

Hitch slowed the car, and Caroline scrambled into the backseat. She yanked the door shut.

"Go," she panted, clasping her uncle on the shoulder.

"What happened?"

"Bad drop."

"Was it Albert?" Hitch swerved away from the curb. His worried eyes darted up to the rearview mirror.

"Drive like a normal person," Caroline said. "Don't stand out."

When Hitch had let the car slow to the speed of the other cars, Caroline leaned back against the cushioned seat and released a long breath. She was safe. For now.

"It wasn't Albert," Caroline said, answering her uncle's question. "Could be his supervisor, though. Or maybe someone at the hotel."

"The desk clerk?" Hitch asked.

"Maybe." Caroline recalled the suspicious expression on the face of the desk clerk who'd watched their strange comings and goings. Had someone paid him for information? She had no way of knowing.

She had one consolation, though. No one had followed her from the service station. Albert had kept Officer Grady talking long enough to let her escape. Albert hadn't betrayed her. She still had an ally. And she still had Federica. The ex-caregiver sat forward in her seat, her hands over her head, in crash position. Terrified, but alive.

"We need to reschedule the drop," Caroline said, taking in Federica's horrified visage. The woman wasn't safe and knew it. She'd narrowly avoided capture.

But Hitch shook his head. "You've got to give Albert time to regroup. He's going to have to separate himself from local PD and figure out who he can trust at the US Attorney's Office. He can't bring Federica in yet."

Caroline ran a hand through her hair. She'd thought she had all of the pieces necessary to end the nightmare that Simon had wrought for them all. Protective custody for the key witness. Criminal prosecution for Simon and his cohorts. But now all the neat little pieces lay scattered on the floor. She was still on her own. Federica was still in danger.

Her uncle was right. She needed another plan.

The cityscape drifted by in the Eldorado's side window. People going to the market. People out for walks. Tourists. Laborers. Just the normal denizens of downtown.

Caroline's eyes settled on a half-built condominium project. The skeletal frame of the building stretched up five floors, then stopped. Its girders suggested more floors had been planned, but the construction site held no workers. No equipment. Where there should've been cranes, there were pigeons.

It was just one of many abandoned jobs that riddled the edges of downtown. Projects that developers had started in better economic times, only to abandon later.

Caroline's mind turned to Simon.

Somehow he'd survived the downturn. If anything, he was thriving. The city was poised to approve his Bunker Hill project. The planned structure would accommodate city offices and high-end clientele. Was it impervious to the economic downturn? Apparently the city thought so, or it wouldn't be contemplating supporting the project.

But what about Simon? Was he impervious to the downturn? Or had the declining real estate market hurt his business?

Caroline knew that some unscrupulous developers used the capital from their newer projects to service debts on their older projects. Was that what Simon was doing? It was possible. But presumably the city was checking Simon's books to make sure that wasn't happening.

A tingling sensation spread down Caroline's arms as the kernel of an idea lodged itself in her mind.

Tipping her face down so that she was parallel with Federica's, Caroline put a hand on the ex-caregiver's shoulder.

"I know you're scared, but everything's going to be all right," she said.

A gap in Federica's red hair parted so that one green eye peeked out. It held disbelief.

"I'm going to get us out of this," Caroline insisted, "but I'm going to need your help."

Now Federica's eyes held curiosity.

"I want you to tell me everything you know about Simon Reed," Caroline said. "Tell me what you've heard Vizzi say about Greenleaf Development and the Bunker Hill project."

• • •

Caroline sat in a corner of the pool hall, avoiding the eyes of the gangsters that populated the bar and leered at the small woman sitting alone in a corner booth.

The information that Federica provided had led to inquiries that had yielded a plan: at 7:30 p.m., the city council would host a public hearing on Greenleaf Development's Bunker Hill project. Simon would be there. And so would Caroline. But first she had to prepare.

She had five hours to trace the intricate web that Simon had spun. Five hours to learn what she needed to know to bring Oasis and Greenleaf and Simon down. It wasn't much time.

Caroline's fingers flew across the keys of her laptop as she began with the idea that had taken root in the backseat of the Eldorado. Linking to the cache of documents she'd retrieved from Amy's Oasis hack, Caroline found what she sought: the contracts among Oasis, Greenleaf Development, and the city.

Her eyes scrutinized the pages of each contract until she found the default provisions—the terms governing the parties' failure to abide by the contract's terms. In each contract, the terms were the same—if Greenleaf or Oasis fell behind, the city had the right to conduct an audit and, if irregularities were found, the city had a right to back out of the project with a payment by Greenleaf and Oasis equal to the city's investment.

Leaning back in the red vinyl booth, Caroline considered the information.

Contrary to her hunch, the city didn't have a mechanism to prevent Simon from using the city's money to pay his debts on his other projects. But the city did have a way to recoup city funds if Simon failed to hit his benchmarks or if he fell behind on his commitments.

Again, Caroline contemplated the abandoned projects dotting the skyline. Most developers had been hit by the declining real estate market. But the fact that the city was moving forward with its hearing on the Bunker Hill project suggested that Simon had stayed in the city's good graces. And that meant his financial footing had remained secure despite the downturn.

But how? Was he just a better businessman than the other developers? Or had he had some help remaining afloat?

To try to answer the question, Caroline turned toward the part of Simon's life that he'd kept out of sight. Away from the politicians who extolled him. Away from the publicly revered father who'd raised him. She turned to the early days of Greenleaf Development. The days when the fortunate son of a beloved television star had launched his new venture.

Simon had bragged about his investors—that dogged crew of brave do-gooders who'd launched his career. But he'd never named them. And Caroline had never found them.

Now, Caroline tried again to determine their identities.

Again, she ran searches designed to unearth the people who'd been the key to Simon's career and perhaps to his continuing financial fortitude.

But again, she found nothing. Not a single investor's name appeared anywhere.

Exhaling, Caroline ran a hand through her short hair.

Names. The absence of names had been a theme in Simon's scheming. Federica Muller. Patricia Amos. All of the other CNAs, whose names were undoubtedly fake. That the investors were nameless, too, tickled some instinct. It bespoke a greater plot, one whose shape she was only now beginning to see in its entirety. But one that she needed to grasp quickly.

She tried not to think about the Eldorado that was safely ensconced four blocks away in the self-park lot of the Millennium Biltmore. She'd figured the fancy hotel was the least likely place anyone would look for a group of homeless people.

She also tried not to think about the hit man. She'd avoided his trap at the service station, but she knew what the close call meant: Simon's minions had figured out where she was.

She only hoped that the public spot—the loud pool hall—would provide her with some measure of safety while she used the establishment's Wi-Fi connection to finish her research.

Giving up on Simon's investors, Caroline turned to her next concern: the Parrino Court property that Amy had discovered Oasis owned. Zillow showed the price the property had fetched each time it had changed hands over the years. Although the real estate market had gone up and down, the price of the industrial property near the Los Angeles River had remained low. It was a piece-of-junk asset with no obvious purpose for Oasis.

But Caroline knew it had to be important. Simon's purchases were always deliberate. Each was a playing piece on his chessboard. That Oasis had bought the land a year earlier meant something, and Caroline had a hunch what it was.

Caroline reviewed her notes about the structure of Simon's most publicized deals. Greenleaf Development had built its projects by using creative combinations of bonds, debt financing, and investments. For his public-private partnerships, Simon sometimes also utilized one more tool: land swaps—trading private property for the long-term use of government land.

Perhaps Simon planned to use Parrino Court for a land swap in the Bunker Hill deal?

There was an easy way to find out.

Caroline navigated to the City of Los Angeles website and she found the link she sought: *Agendas for Public Hearings.*

The upcoming hearings were arranged chronologically.

She opened the top one.

Details of the Bunker Hill project filled the screen. Pages of architectural specifications. Proposed approval documents from the city. Environmental impact reports and traffic reports. Somewhere in the documentation, she hoped to find some mention of a land swap.

Disregarding the glances of the men playing pool, she scanned page after page until she found what she sought.

"Bingo," she murmured.

She smiled to herself before turning to the next piece of the puzzle.

• • •

Caroline looked at the neon clock hanging over the bar—6:25 p.m.

Exhaling, she closed her laptop.

She'd used the time as well as she could. She'd satisfied her curiosity about Parrino Court. She'd hacked another server. She'd even made calls to the people whose help she needed in order to ensnare Simon.

Slinging her bag over her shoulder, Caroline walked to the bathroom at the back of the bar. It was better to go to war on an empty bladder.

The bathroom smelled almost as bad as the food being served at the bar. Stale bread and cold fried chicken. The drunk patrons didn't care so long as it was salty.

To protect her nostrils, Caroline breathed through her mouth. It was a trick she'd learned in the last week. Along with a great many other things.

By the time Caroline headed toward the back door of the bar, she was at peace.

A week of running had left her nerves raw, but the sensation that flowed across them now wasn't fear. It was acceptance. She had no ability to control the people she'd called to assist her. She could only hope they understood the stakes and cared enough to show up.

And if they didn't?

Then she'd figure something else out. But for now, there was nothing else she could do.

Exiting the side door of the bar into the alley, she paused and looked around for danger.

She saw nothing amiss.

She'd have to walk all the way back to the Millennium Biltmore, but that was fine. She needed to gather her thoughts.

Somewhere deeper in the alley, Caroline heard the rustle of can collectors trawling the dumpsters. She identified the odor of discarded restaurant trash. She could tell rot from nourishment, she realized. The alley had become familiar in a way she'd never expected it to be.

In fact, the dichotomy of downtown no longer struck her as strange. The elegance of the Millennium Biltmore was mere blocks from the gritty pool hall and stinking alley. The gentrifying apartments were adjacent to slums. Where once she'd embraced the hip parts and fled the edges, now she accepted both. She also accepted that while the Millennium Biltmore wasn't far, the people there might be miserable, too. Joy or fear, hatred or love. Where each resided had little to do with location. The heart of the lotus was within, indeed.

Unbidden, Caroline's thoughts turned to her father.

She'd never told him why she'd left her last job. She'd remained silent to protect herself. To protect those she loved. Knowledge could be dangerous, she'd told herself. But the fortress of silence she'd constructed to protect herself and those she loved had become a prison.

No wonder Lily had assumed the worst about her.

Caroline was so preoccupied that she didn't notice the shadow approaching.

Her chest froze as a man stepped toward her.

Blond and tall, he exuded the same menace that Caroline had felt from a distance when she'd seen him climbing off his motorcycle outside her apartment. But this time, there was no fire escape. There was nowhere to run.

Caroline's heart slammed in her throat. Her hands went numb with terror. One careless moment of not making sure she had a way out, and now she was trapped.

"Tell me where she is," the hit man said, his pale eyes piercing Caroline's soul.

"Who?" Caroline asked, though she knew the hit man's other target.

"Federica Muller," said the man.

"I don't know what you're talking about," Caroline said. "I think you've mistaken me for someone else."

She took a small step backward, trying put distance between herself and the hit man.

"Nice try," the hit man said, "but I've been following you for hours."

Glancing sideways, Caroline scanned the alleyway for something heavy. Or sharp.

She saw nothing.

"Your friend screamed when she fell down that cliff," the hit man continued with a small smile. "I could see her mouth moving even though I couldn't hear the sound."

Caroline's chest surged at the sadistic reminder of what he'd done to Amy and Hector. But she stayed silent. She couldn't afford any distractions. Her survival depended on the hit man making some error. Some miscalculation.

"I have no idea what you're talking about," Caroline said, still backing up, step by step.

The mouth of the alley was twenty-five yards behind her.

As if to stop her progress, the hit man reached into his pocket.

"I need Federica Muller," he said, withdrawing a long-muzzled gun.

A silencer, Caroline identified the three-inch tube screwed onto the end of it. She'd seen them in movies. She'd never expected to see one in real life, especially aimed at her head.

"I want to know where Federica is," the hit man continued. "And I want you to tell me. Right now."

"I don't know where she is," Caroline said, giving up on subterfuge. Her fingers tingled with adrenaline.

The hit man gave another smile, and Caroline realized he was enjoying the power he held over her. Her terror was his pleasure.

Controlling her breathing, Caroline forced her features into equanimity. She would not let him see her fear, if she could possibly help it.

"If you don't want to tell me where Federica is, then you give me no reason to let you live," the tall blond man said.

Caroline knew it was true. Her only bargaining chip was Federica, and there was no way she'd play it. Judging by the threatening step the man took toward her, he knew that, too.

"How do I know you'll let me live if I tell you where Federica is," Caroline said, just trying to keep him talking. She squelched the urge to turn and run. He'd shoot her. He wouldn't miss. Her options were rapidly closing, but running was suicide for sure.

"You don't," said the hit man. "But you'll negotiate some sort of deal that'll give you hope, and that might be worth taking the chance. Who knows, maybe you'll even get away. You're pretty clever, in my experience." A flicker of a smile crossed his face.

Reflexively, Caroline's mind grasped at the hope he'd offered. Perhaps she could trick him into leaving her unattended long enough to flee. Perhaps she could offer to get Federica but then vanish.

But then she stopped. She'd manipulated enough people to know when she was being manipulated. There was no way the hit man would let her out of his presence. There was no way he'd let her live even if she was willing to tell him where Federica was. And she would never give up someone else's life for the glimmer of hope of saving her own.

Exhaling, she steeled herself, ready to face whatever fate lay at the end of the muzzle.

Across from her, the hit man's smile faded.

"You've made your choice," he said rather than asked.

Before Caroline could answer, a second shadow detached itself from the city-dark alley.

It rose up behind the hit man, bulky and solid, and lunged forward to grasp him.

Surprised, the hit man arched his back, struggling against the thick forearm that held him fast around the neck. With a grunt, he tried to swivel the gun to challenge this new threat, but the newcomer's mass and strength prevented it.

A glint of metal reflected the moonlight.

A knife, Caroline identified the object in the shadow's hand, just before it flashed down hard, slipping across the hit man's neck, slicing hard and deep.

With a gurgling scream, the blond man crumpled to the ground with a look of utter shock frozen on his face.

The dark figure crouched and tilted his head to one side just above the prone shape, as if confirming the absence of any life.

Then he sat back on his heels.

The light from a neighboring building hit his face.

Jake.

Caroline remained frozen as she watched him wipe the knife on the corpse's shirt.

As the Ranger rose back up to standing, he met her eyes.

"I had your back," he said simply.

As if by silent consensus, they left the dead man where he'd fallen in the alley behind the pool hall. If there'd been a time when Caroline would've felt some trace of remorse, it was long past. This was the man who'd killed Hector. This was the man who'd hurt Amy. He could rot beside the decomposing fried chicken for all Caroline cared.

But when they reached the main street, Jake stopped.

"I need your phone," he said.

With a still-shaking hand, Caroline handed the burner phone to her friend.

She watched in silence while he dialed a number and murmured into the receiver.

When Jake returned the phone to Caroline, he shrugged.

"Li'l Ray owes me one," he said by way of explanation.

All at once, Caroline recalled the man she'd seen at the soup kitchen. The one in the heavy denim jacket on a hot day. The one her uncle had described as a fixer.

And she understood: Jake had arranged for the disposal of the corpse. Though her curiosity burned over how that would occur, she didn't ask. She didn't really want to know.

Instead, she kept pace with Jake as he turned in the direction of the Millennium Biltmore.

When he spoke again, his voice was so soft she almost missed it.

"Killing ain't so hard when you know who the enemy is," he said. "But I still don't like it," he added before continuing away from the spot.

CHAPTER 29

From her seat at the back of the gallery, Caroline eyed the front of the John Ferraro Council Chamber.

A panel of people sat on a dais. At the center of the panel, a pale official with sagging jowls and bored eyes watched the audiovisual technician set up his equipment. Beside him, a cadre of younger men and women wearing suits prepared for a long evening. Some had opened laptops on the desks in front of them. Others thumbed through binders.

The podium opposite the dais was empty, as was the long table in front of it where Simon and his staff would sit when they arrived in the vaulted space where the city conducted its most important public business—including presiding over the final stages of the approval process for a multimillion-dollar development project.

Caroline took a breath to center herself. She wished she had her worry beads to distract her until the proceedings on the Bunker Hill project began. She knew her next oral presentation would be the most important she'd ever made. That it would not be in a court was ironic but irrelevant.

Beside Caroline, Federica sat immobile, her eyes downcast.

Meanwhile, Jake guarded the hallway outside the chamber. Though Caroline didn't expect any interruptions or unexpected arrivals, knowing that Jake was out there helped her to focus on the task ahead. She'd spent hours at the pool hall hammering out each of the weapons she'd need to destroy Oasis. Now everything depended on how well she used them.

With a click of the door, Simon entered the council chamber. He was trailed by Conrad Vizzi and another man in a well-tailored black suit. Gregory Parsons, Caroline identified the other man. The sleaze who handled the money for Oasis.

The three men sat down at the long wooden table that occupied the center of the ocean of marble flooring between the dais and the podium.

Moments later, they were joined by Francis Thibodeaux, the lawyer who'd defeated Caroline at the demurrer hearing. Behind him, he pulled the same rolling briefcase he'd brought with him to the demurrer hearing.

"Gang's all here," Caroline murmured, sinking low in her seat so that Thibodeaux wouldn't see her as he passed. She doubted that he'd recognize her any more than he would a fly he'd swatted, but she didn't want to risk it.

Once Thibodeaux had settled into his spot beside Simon, the jowled man at the center of the dais cleared his throat and leaned toward his microphone.

"Let's begin," he said. His voice echoed around the vaulted space, the sound waves ricocheting off the jade-green arches and columns.

The conversations in the room tapered off then ceased, leaving nothing but the occasional cough or shuffle of papers. And an air of anticipation.

"We're here on what's come to be known as the Bunker Hill Project. For those of you who don't know me, I am Martin Barnes, the president of the city council. I'd like to welcome the rest of your city council, as well as the heads of the city agencies involved in the project. Finally, I welcome a representative from the city attorney's office, who is here to advise us on land use matters." President Barnes turned to an African American man seated at the far end of the lower dais. "Hello, Mr. Deputy City Attorney, Preston Jackson."

"Hello, Mr. President Barnes," the deputy said, returning the greeting with a nod.

The president squinted into the lights that a local news station had positioned in front of the dais to better record the proceedings.

"I can see we have a nice turnout from the public. Welcome, everyone. There are many formalities we must comply with in these proceedings. Please bear with me."

He cleared his throat again and lifted a page.

"Notice is hereby given that, pursuant to requirements of the California Environmental Quality Act, the Los Angeles Redevelopment Agency has prepared a final environmental impact report for the proposed Bunker Hill Project. The purpose of this hearing is to consider certification of the EIR and approval of a mitigation plan. To summarize: this project contemplates the city granting Greenleaf Development a ground lease of land on Bunker Hill for a term of ninety-nine years. In exchange, the city will receive the many substantial benefits described in the public filing, a copy of which can be found on our website."

The president let the page tip back down onto the table and made eye contact with the packed gallery of attendees.

"After we hear from Mr. Reed and Gregory Parsons on behalf of Greenleaf, we will hear from Oasis Care's acting director, Conrad Vizzi. We will then take comments from the public. This project involves a significant outlay of public resources, and the mayor has made clear that it is important for the public to have its say." The small sigh that escaped the president's mouth let Caroline know he didn't entirely agree with the charade of letting the public have its say. Perhaps that's why the agenda for the public comment portion of the hearing was so short.

During the president's introductory remarks, Caroline had kept her attention focused on Simon. He looked relaxed, she decided. If she was right, he'd say very little. He'd probably already paid off, provided favors to, or acquired dirt on every person on the city council. Aside from answering a few scripted questions from the council members and addressing a handful of random inquiries from the few members of the public on the agenda, he'd have an easy night.

"We will begin with Mr. Reed and his team," the president said, nodding up toward the large screens. "They will take us through the plans, the environmental impacts, and the proposed mitigations. They'll also describe the financing structure, including the stop-loss provisions protecting the city and the overall public benefits."

Simon stood up. In person, he was taller than Caroline had imagined him. Wearing a well-cut suit that was neither too nice nor too shabby, he eyed the council with warmth.

"I want to thank everyone here for all of their time and attention," he began. "This is going to be a terrific project. One of the best. I build huge, tremendous projects and this will be the most tremendous yet." He threw in a smile for the cameras at the back of the room.

Then with a nod to the audiovisual technician, Simon began his formal presentation.

"When I started Greenleaf Development over a decade ago, I did it to honor my father."

The screen ignited with an image of Duncan Reed.

"My father has always been an old-fashioned kind of guy. My mom died when I was a kid, so it fell on my dad to teach my sister and me what mattered. He taught us that hard work and deep faith would reveal the path to a righteous life."

Knowing what she now knew about the developer, Caroline had to fight to suppress a scoff of disgust.

Simon cued the next slide. The black-and-white image showed a younger Duncan Reed working side by side with a nun, helping the homeless on Skid Row.

"My dad started Oasis when I was eight. Oasis was small back then—just some rooms in a church. I grew up there, really, hanging out and talking to the people we helped. When I was young, I used to think I was one of the founders—I really believed I'd been the one to get Oasis off the ground with my sorting of paper clips and whatnot. Now, with the wisdom of age, I know that Oasis was the embodiment of my father's values. He conceived of it, launched it, and guided it for decades. I know it sounds corny, but my dad's my hero."

Simon paused to let the poignant sentiment hang in the chamber for a while.

Caroline shook her head. She had to give the man credit—he had a natural instinct for showmanship. In the silent eddy of Simon's presentation, she knew everyone on the city council was reminiscing about watching Duncan Reed's TV show and hearing its lessons on kindness and decency. The effect was warming, even for her, she privately conceded.

Simon chuckled. "While I wasn't responsible for launching Oasis, I do know for a fact that I helped bring it into the twenty-first century. This isn't bragging. My dad was full of good intentions, but he had no management systems, and the files were a mess. You should've seen it—everything was written down on these little note cards back then. It was like the card catalogs that people used in old libraries."

For comic relief, Simon brought up a slide showing an archetypical librarian with glasses perched on the end of her nose, wagging a finger at a child holding a teetering pile of books.

The image had the desired effect. A ripple of laughter flowed through the crowd.

Simon joined it, laughing along with the crowd and smiling the same disarming grin that Duncan Reed had used to charm television audiences for forty years.

"When I graduated college, I had a bunch of ideas for redeveloping the inner city. But my idealism ran into some snags. I'd hoped that my dad would provide me with some seed money. But he didn't give me a dime. My dad always said that a man has to do things for himself. That belief extended to his kids. Guess I should've known better after being raised by the guy."

Simon gave a self-deprecating shrug. The effect was endearing.

"I'll be honest. It wasn't easy to start Greenleaf Development. It took me almost two years of going door to door before I found enough investors to finance my first project. But it went all right, and I'm happy to say I've never had to ask the old man for money."

When Simon smiled again, half of the city council and most of the people in the gallery smiled with him. But if the joke lightened the mood for the spectators, it had the opposite effect on Caroline. Simon's affability and charisma were hurdles she'd have to overcome. Convincing this audience that this man they'd supported on numerous projects was a villain was going to be a very tough challenge.

As the chuckles died down, Simon's face grew serious again. "Over the last decade, Greenleaf has benefited from the tradesmen that Oasis has trained, and Oasis has benefited from Greenleaf giving its trainees a chance to build their résumés and gain valuable experience. Along the way, I've gotten to be a part of meaningful partnerships among the private sector, charity, and government. But best of all, I have lived by my father's ideals of community, faith, and service."

In the wake of Simon's gauzy autobiography, one of the council members sniffled and reached for a tissue.

Caroline resisted the urge to roll her eyes.

"Now that you know a little something about me," Simon finished, "I'd like to turn this presentation over to my colleague Gregory Parsons, who will describe the details of our proposal. He'll tell you about the financing structure, as well as the valuable property the city will be receiving in the land-swap component of the deal. After that, Conrad Vizzi will explain how this public-private project will benefit the homeless and other disadvantaged populations at Oasis. I'm sure you're going to love it."

• • •

Two hours later, Simon looked satisfied and the city council looked bored.

As Caroline had suspected, the presentation had been one long puff piece. Someone at Greenleaf Development had created a slideshow of architectural renderings. In each, the Reed Building towered gloriously over Bunker Hill while smiling Oasis workers in green HELPING YOU HELP YOURSELF T-shirts looked on with pride.

The images made Caroline want to throw something at the screen.

Gregory Parsons's description of the land swap had increased the fury brewing in her gut. When he touted the "prime" property the city was going to get as part of its compensation for letting Simon develop Bunker Hill, she knew the city was getting conned.

Not this time, she reminded herself. Not if she could avert it.

Caroline took a breath.

Soon. She'd be doing battle soon.

President Barnes opened the floor to comments from the citizens on the council's short public-input agenda.

The questions that followed were far from hard-hitting. A handful of people asked whether traffic would be adversely impacted by the construction.

Simon easily answered those questions to everyone's satisfaction.

When the fifth member of the public had finished her questions and sat down, Simon caught the president's eye and gave a small nod.

"If there are no other public comments, I'd like to move for a vote," said the president.

"I second that motion," said the councilwoman sitting beside him. As far as Caroline could tell, she'd been doodling on her notebook for the better part of the last hour.

"Um, there appear to be three more names on the agenda for public comment," said the councilman beside the doodler. With his narrow face, big ears, and thick glasses, he reminded Caroline of a mouse. A mouse in a red sweater-vest.

The president exhaled a huff, as if the mouselike councilman was a regular annoyance.

"I thought there were only five," said the president.

"No, there are eight," the councilman confirmed. As if to forestall any further questions, he shrugged at the president.

"Okay, who's next?" the president asked.

"Concerned Citizen Number One."

"I hereby call to the podium for comment Concerned Citizen Number One," the president intoned. It was the same formula with which he'd welcomed the other five citizens up to the podium, all of whom had used their actual names.

Taking one last calming breath, Caroline rose.

She slipped from her pew and headed toward the front of the chamber. On her way, she stopped at the audiovisual technician, who handed her a long cable to connect her laptop to the screens positioned over the dais.

Then she continued up to the wooden podium.

Though she did not look at Simon, Caroline imagined that his face held benign amusement. He'd never seen her before and wasn't likely to recognize her even from pictures, especially with her new haircut.

All of that was about to change.

"Good evening," Caroline said when she reached the podium. "I've heard some great things tonight about this project. I just have a couple concerns that I'd like to bring to the attention of our elected officials charged with serving and protecting our city's interests."

Instead of speaking to the people on the dais, Caroline spoke to the cameras that the news outlets had set up behind the council members. She knew that if Simon had the chance, he'd skew what she was about to say. He'd color it and manipulate it. That everything would be recorded and broadcast would make it harder for him to maneuver.

"My first concern is the value of the land swap," Caroline began. She'd picked the topic because it sounded benign, just the sort of thing a concerned citizen might raise.

Thibodeaux caught the president's eye and raised an eyebrow.

"Mr. Reed has already spoken to that issue," said the president. "The land that Oasis will give to the city as partial consideration for the Bunker Hill ground lease is quite valuable."

"With all due respect, Mr. President, I disagree." Caroline brought up the first slide of her presentation. The image on the screen showed a street lined with rows of trailers surrounded by piles of trash. Power lines crisscrossed the skyline.

"This is Parrino Court," Caroline said. "This is the supposedly valuable land that Mr. Reed is proposing to give to the city as the land-swap part of this deal."

"That property has appraised at a much higher value than its appearance would suggest," said the president. "It's located near the train line and will give the city valuable access."

"Except that your appraisal was provided by Mr. Parsons's company." Caroline looked at Gregory Parsons. "I believe he's run into some trouble in the past with his appraisals?"

She answered her own question by displaying a slide showing the last page of the judgment entered against a Mr. Gregory M. Parsons in the civil fraud action.

The flush of color that painted Parsons's face told Caroline her punch had landed squarely.

"I don't recall seeing a Concerned Citizen Number One on the agenda," Thibodeaux said, rising to his feet. Caroline knew he recognized her now. He was trying to shut her down.

She had prepared for this moment.

With a tap on the keyboard, she brought another slide up on the screen.

"Here's the official agenda. I'm on it. See, I'm number six on the public-input section." She didn't tell him that she'd hacked the agenda. If the council had tried to constrain how many members of the public were allowed to speak, she'd simply remedied their abuse of power by expanding the agenda to accommodate all concerned citizens.

"Concerned Citizen Number One is indeed on the agenda," confirmed the mouselike councilman.

The president shot him a withering look, but Caroline had already moved to the next slide.

"An even bigger problem arises when we look at the money that Oasis used to purchase the Parrino Court property," she said. "As you saw from the official documentation, Mr. Vizzi characterized the money that Oasis used to purchase that land-swap property as coming from charitable donations. But Oasis isn't registered as a charity."

Caroline paused to allow the council members to study the screen shot of the Cumulative List of Organizations. It was the same page she'd provided to her old classmate Wallace Boyd when she'd visited him at the DA's office—a visit that felt like a lifetime ago.

"Oasis operates under the auspices of a fiscal sponsor called Reed Philanthropy," she continued. "What that means is that Oasis provides no tax reporting whatsoever. So, we have no idea what money's coming into Oasis or who's donating to it."

The murmur of conversation behind Caroline told her that the audience, if not the entire city council, was at least mildly disturbed by this revelation.

"Is this true?" asked the councilwoman who'd stopped her doodling to look at Simon Reed's team.

"Technically yes," said Conrad Vizzi, "but Reed Philanthropy makes sure all of our internal operations are proper."

"Except they don't," Caroline said. With a click of the laptop's keyboard, she brought up the tax filings for Reed Philanthropy, fiscal sponsor. "I'd like you to take a look at the identity of the chief administrator of Reed Philanthropy. It's our friend Gregory Parsons."

Caroline paused to let the council members ponder the implications.

"Judging by who's doing the watching, I'd have to bet that Reed Philanthropy isn't watching Oasis too closely. As that lawsuit suggests, when you have Mr. Parsons handling your money and accounting, anything goes."

Again, Caroline waited a moment, knowing that the reporters at the back of the room were wide-awake now. So was Simon, who seethed beneath his affable exterior.

"But I'm not here to complain about Oasis's lack of tax reporting or public oversight," she continued. "That's a problem for the attorney general or the IRS. What I'd like to tell you about now is a scandal of epic and horrifying proportions."

Thibodeaux and Simon huddled together, whispering to each other.

Before they could decide what to do to end her presentation, Caroline brought the PowerPoint image of Parrino Court back onto the screen, split with images of Simon Reed's other development projects. The County Law Library renovation. The affordable housing complexes. The office parks and government buildings and other public-private partnerships.

"Do you know what I see when I look at Simon Reed's buildings?" Caroline asked. She paused to gauge the curiosity shining in the eyes of every member of the city council, including the president, whom she was pretty sure Simon owned.

"I see money laundering," she finished.

A ripple of electric conversation hummed through the chamber hall.

"Everything that Mr. Reed has done has had one goal and one purpose: obscuring the origins of his money," Caroline continued. For weeks, she'd wondered how Simon had hidden the money he'd pilfered from nursing home residents. She'd wondered how he'd gotten his projects funded even in an anemic real estate market. The *Hidalgo* case had planted the seed of an idea, and the research she'd performed at the pool hall had let it blossom.

The scale of Simon's money-laundering scheme was far larger than Rogelio Gonzalez's, but the mechanisms were the same. Turn one thing into another. Take something evil and obscure its origins until it could be sold on the open market.

"Mr. Reed told us that he started Greenleaf Development a decade ago with the help of a group of determined investors. Remember that?" Caroline asked. "He described how hard it was—going door to door, trying to find those early investors. But that's not how he found investors. The truth is, he made them up."

"Made-up investors don't have real money to invest," Simon said from his chair. He smiled and looked around the chamber, as if to make sure everyone was still with him.

Judging from the handful of smiles he received in response, they were.

"Oh, the money was quite real," said Caroline, "but it didn't come from anyone real."

She watched the eyebrows of several council members knit.

"I'm sure you recall that heartwarming story that Simon told about how he grew up seeing his dad's good works and real Christian values," she continued. "That part of the story is true. Duncan Reed was in the seminary as a young man. He believed a rich man had as much chance of going to Heaven as a camel had of passing through the eye of a needle. So he gave his money away to the needy. He didn't even bother to set up Oasis as a charity so he could get the tax deductions. All he cared about was doing good works. Mr. Reed may be severely impaired now, but he spent a lifetime trying to make the world a better place."

The council members nodded their agreement of Caroline's assessment of Duncan Reed.

Caroline was glad to see their response. She needed to separate Simon from his sainted father. Acknowledging Duncan Reed's good works would help her do that.

"Simon's right about another thing, too," Caroline continued. "Duncan Reed believed a man needed to make his own way. And so, when Simon wanted to launch a company, his father didn't provide any money for his son's venture. You remember Simon telling you that, right?"

Again, the heads of several council members nodded up and down.

"So what did Simon to do? How did he raise funds to launch Greenleaf?" Caroline asked. "The answer is identity theft. Coordinated and massive identity theft."

Thibodeaux rose to his feet. "I think we've heard enough crazy theories for one night."

He fixed the president with a pointed look.

"You have the power to end these proceedings once a member of the public has spoken for five minutes, which Concerned Citizen Number One has done," Thibodeaux said to the president. "In addition, Chapter 2, Rule 12(a)(2), bars members of the public from making slanderous remarks about anyone on the council or any matter under consideration by it."

"It's true the president has the power to end my presentation," Caroline said, "but Rule 7 gives this council the power to extend it."

She brought the provision up on the screen.

"As you can see, Rule 7 states, 'The presiding officer may grant or deny speakers additional time, subject to reversal by a majority of the council.' A vote of eight will allow me to continue my presentation, which, I assure you, is not slanderous but absolutely true. If you give me just another five minutes of your time, I promise I will fully document each and every one of my allegations."

A loud murmur of voices reverberated around the council chamber.

Caroline's throat tightened with concern. She'd reached the most dangerous part of the hearing. She'd known when she'd started that after five minutes, her presentation would be at the council's discretion—they could cut her off. She hoped they'd let her continue.

And if they didn't?

She glanced toward the door.

If the council stopped her presentation now, she'd have to run.

She didn't like her chances.

"Fine," said the president. "I call for a vote under the mandates of Rule 15 on the matter of whether Concerned Citizen Number One's presentation shall be ended. Shall the chair be overruled?"

The balding, mouselike councilman was the first to vote.

"Aye," he said in a loud, clear voice.

The councilwoman who'd been doodling gave a second aye.

Caroline eyed the rest of the council, praying that their curiosity overcame their desire to make it home in time for dinner.

Finally, another councilman spoke: "Aye."

Caroline exhaled. She knew she'd get the rest of the votes she needed. Enough council members had expressed a desire to hear her out. The rest would acquiesce out of professional courtesy to their colleagues, if not actual interest in what Caroline had to say.

When the last of the eight ayes had spoken, the president frowned.

"You have five more minutes," he said, "after which we may take another vote."

"Thank you," Caroline said, thinking quickly.

The piercing glare from Simon reminded her of the hearing in the Mateo Hidalgo matter. But this time she wasn't arguing for a little boy's safety. She was arguing for her life. The trail of carnage that Lani had described suggested that Simon had many more tools than the hit man Jake had left in alley. Simon was ruthless and well connected. He'd find ways to destroy her, she knew. If given the chance.

"Simon told us how he worked at Oasis when he was young—he helped by digitizing records and chatting up residents. It all sounded pretty good, right? Except that chatting up residents and digitizing records wasn't all he was doing. He was also opening bank accounts in the residents' names."

"That's not true," Simon protested, half rising from his chair.

Caroline ignored him. "Simon had access to all of Oasis's files in those early years. He's the guy that moved the data from those little note cards to Oasis's first database. In the process, he harvested Social Security numbers and used them to create dozens of fake identities. An army of ghosts. He used that army to get the loans he used to start Greenleaf. That's the original sin of Simon's real estate empire: massive identity theft."

The faces of the city council swiveled toward Simon to hear his answer.

"This is absurd," he said. "And anyway, people whose identities have been stolen always find out about it. It wrecks their credit. There's no way someone who did what she accuses me of doing would be able to get away with it."

Rather than responding directly to Simon, Caroline kept her attention on the council.

"It's true that identity thieves often get caught, but that didn't happen here. Simon has paid off or paid enough interest on his loans to avoid scrutiny from either the banks or the real people whose identities he's stolen. I don't expect you to just take me at my word, though. Instead, I'd like to bring in someone with unimpeachable credibility and no dog in this fight."

Caroline sent a silent prayer to the witness gods that the woman she'd called from the pool hall had decided to show up. She hadn't seen the witness in the gallery when she'd arrived with Federica, and she hadn't wanted to risk standing up to try to find her.

"Concerned Citizen Number Two, please come up to the podium," Caroline said.

At the back of the gallery, a short, dark-haired woman rose to her feet. She pushed her horn-rimmed glasses up the bridge of her nose before gingerly making her way up to the front of the council chamber.

Simon's eyes widened when he caught sight of the bespectacled woman's face.

Caroline knew the reason. When she'd phoned the woman, she'd had only a hunch about how Simon had funded his development projects. But after talking to the woman who now approached the podium, the pieces of the puzzle had slammed together with such resounding force that Caroline had almost cheered aloud.

When the woman stood beside her, Caroline faced the council.

"I'd like to take the unusual step of asking this anonymous citizen what her name is."

"Patricia Amos," replied the woman, tucking her short dark hair behind her ear.

In her periphery, Caroline watched Simon's face go as white as the projection screen.

"Please tell the council what your profession is," Caroline directed the real Patricia Amos.

"I'm a licensed vocational nurse. For the last eight years, I've worked at Meadowlark Convalescent Hospital in Burbank, California."

"And where were you before your current job?" Caroline asked.

"Immediately before? I lived on the streets." Patricia's tone held no shame at the admission.

"Please tell the council how that happened."

"I'm a trained nurse. I graduated fifteen years ago. I worked at various facilities for about seven years. Toward the end of that period, I had some substance abuse issues. I'm lucky I didn't lose my license, but things got pretty grim there for a while, and I ended up on the street. I'm clean now. I've been clean for almost a decade."

"Were you ever a resident of Oasis?"

"I sought refuge there for a time." She looked over at Simon. "I remember Mr. Reed. He was always working in the administrative offices there. He was quite friendly to all of us."

"Did you take part in any of the Oasis job training programs?" Caroline asked.

"No. I didn't need job training. As I said, I was already a nurse. I just needed a roof over my head and a chance to get right. Fortunately, I managed to kick my addiction. I'll always be grateful to Oasis for its substance abuse programs."

"Have you ever run into any credit issues?" Caroline asked.

The council sat forward, listening for Patricia Amos's answer.

"Yes, but not in the way that you'd think. I would get these solicitations for these investment opportunities. I assumed everyone was getting them. I didn't think much of it until about five years ago. Some lender called Great Southern Bank offered me a line of credit based on my past performance with the bank."

"Did you ever look into it?" Caroline asked.

"I did," Patricia confirmed. "I ran a credit report with my Social Security number and discovered that I apparently took out a big loan from Great Southern Bank several years before."

"Did you, in fact, take out that loan?"

"No. It had been repaid, so I guess I'm lucky it didn't wreck my credit, but . . . wow."

"In other words, your identity had been stolen," Caroline concluded.

"Clearly, yes."

"Thank you, Ms. Amos. You may step down."

As Patricia retreated to her seat, Caroline said a silent thank-you. The real Patricia Amos had been surprised by Caroline's phone call. A respected nurse who'd lived clean for many years, she'd been reluctant to discuss her past. But when Caroline had asked if she'd lived at Oasis, everything had changed. And when Caroline had probed about identity theft, Patricia had expressed outrage at what Caroline believed Simon had done.

Even so, Caroline hadn't known whether that outrage would translate into willingness to attend the hearing—and share her story. Caroline was grateful that it had.

Now, she turned back to the council, whose evening plans were long forgotten.

"Patricia Amos is one of many people whose Social Security numbers appeared on those little cards that Simon told you about—the ones he digitized," Caroline continued. "Simon has used the army of ghost identities he created from those Social Security numbers to raise funds to pay for his projects and, when the market goes down, to keep him afloat."

"But this must all show up in Greenleaf's accounting," the president protested.

"Greenleaf's accounting?" Caroline echoed. "You mean the accounting that Gregory Parsons is in charge of? If he's kept any accounting at all, you can bet it's not worth much."

Caroline paused to let the audience consider her words.

"For years, Simon has avoided getting caught. But the economic downturn has made things harder. Selling projects in this market is tough," she said.

"So then why would I be building another project?" Simon asked, looking at the city council, his eyes imploring the members to see the holes in Caroline's indictment.

"Simon needs this project to cover the loans that are coming due on his other projects," Caroline answered. "He's going to use the funds you give him to pay his other debts. He needs this deal, not just so he can stay afloat but so he can avoid falling behind on any of his other projects. He is deathly afraid of triggering the boilerplate terms in the contracts among Oasis, Greenleaf, and the city, allowing an audit if a project falls behind."

Caroline brought up an image of the contract to reconstruct the County Law Library.

"This is a standard contract. Every one of Simon's contracts with the city contains similar default provisions—if Oasis or Greenleaf fails to meet benchmarks, it can be audited. This is the real reason that Simon is so desperate for this project, for new cash flow. When your investors are ghosts or a shell game with public funds, you've got a lot to hide. You cannot let yourself be audited."

"I've hidden nothing," Simon began, but Caroline ignored him again.

Instead, she brought up a screenshot of a recent article quoting DA Donita Johnson about her campaign to prevent government waste and her efforts to ensure that public-private partnerships weren't resulting in overpayment by the cash-strapped city.

"In the current political climate, Simon has had to be extra careful about not falling behind," Caroline said, nodding toward the boiler-plate contract language that the city had recently become interested in enforcing. "But cash has been running low. Ever since the downturn, he's been struggling to stay in the black. So he came up with a new venture. He ramped up the job-training program at Oasis for certi-fied nursing assistants—a program he's figured out how to use to dupe elderly nursing home residents into leaving funds to Oasis."

Vizzi leaned toward Simon and Thibodeaux and whispered some-thing before opening up a laptop and typing furiously.

The dogged expressions on the faces of the three men worried Caroline, but she had no time to worry about what they were planning.

"Here's where it gets personal," Caroline said. She let her eyes linger on Simon for a moment before turning back to the council. "I'd like to tell you the story of what happened to my grandmother. It's a story that's been repeated many times with many other families."

She quickly described her grandmother's handwritten last will, and the bequest of her grandmother's entire estate to Oasis, including the watch. While Simon wasn't wearing it, Caroline noticed some council members looking at his wrist as she finished her story.

"Again, I don't expect you to blindly accept my statements about what happened to my family," Caroline said. "Instead, I'd like to call the last person on your agenda to speak."

Turning back to the gallery, Caroline found the face she sought.

"Concerned Citizen Number Three, please come up here," she said.

With a thick swallow, Federica Muller rose.

A stifled gasp from the long table told Caroline that Vizzi had recognized Federica and knew what she was about to say.

He leaned toward Simon, whose pale-blue eyes blazed with fire.

"The panel appreciates Concerned Citizen Number Three's desire to provide comments," said the president, "but we have strict rules about when our meetings are supposed to end. We are already past the termination time for these proceedings. We must conform to protocol."

Caroline swallowed thickly. She'd hoped to avoid this moment. By inviting Federica up to the podium herself, she'd tried to circumvent what she'd known was coming: a last-ditch effort by Simon and his allies to keep the most torrid part of the scheme from coming to light.

"The council cannot end the hearing until the official agenda is completed," said Deputy City Attorney Jackson from the side of the room. "Public meeting rules govern these proceedings. Those are rather strict, too," he added.

Sending silent thanks to the deputy city attorney, Caroline opened her mouth to speak. But Thibodeaux cut her off.

"I cannot allow my client to be publicly slandered in this manner." Thibodeaux glanced toward the television cameras behind the dais. "These proceedings should not be televised."

As if jolting awake, the president cleared his throat.

But before he could say anything, the mouselike councilman spoke.

"We approved the press credentials and television permits. I don't believe we can revoke them." He looked toward the deputy city attorney and raised his eyebrows.

"That is correct," said Deputy City Attorney Jackson, "you cannot revoke them."

He glanced toward Caroline and gave a ghost of a wink.

Exhaling, Caroline prepared for the end of her presentation. Its success would depend on Federica. She only hoped the skittish caregiver would rally the courage to play her part.

Caroline welcomed Federica to the podium with a hand on her shoulder then stepped back to give the ex-caregiver room to grip the podium like a life raft. It was a technique Caroline had employed to great effect in the past, and she'd counseled Federica to try it, since it was better than passing out from nerves.

In a quavering voice, Federica described her time on the street. Her optimism about Oasis. Her hope that the special CNA program would give her a way to make a better life.

She explained the affidavit-withdrawal scheme and her part in it. She described her disappointment and, ultimately, her horror at what Vizzi asked her to do to ensure that nursing home residents could not change their estate plans once they'd made new wills favoring Oasis.

Though Federica's voice was small, it carried all around the council chamber.

When she stopped, there was no sound. The audience sat shell-shocked.

"Simon Reed has harvested millions by preying on the most vulnerable people in our community," Caroline said, capping Federica's tale with the unavoidable conclusion. "The elderly. The homeless. When the bottom fell out of the market, Simon couldn't flip his completed projects. He couldn't cover his next commitments. Or Oasis's commitments. The whole house of cards was threatening to collapse. The affidavit-withdrawal scheme helped fill some of the shortfall, but even if little old ladies who loved Duncan Reed and fell in love with Oasis wrote the fake charity into their wills, people are living longer these days. It could have been years before Simon saw any of those bequests."

Now Caroline held Simon's eyes.

"So he accelerated things. He used the same ghost identities that he'd used to generate the money for his projects to create cover for a group of special, handpicked caregivers that he and Vizzi induced to do the unthinkable. People who are desperate and powerless can be induced to do craven things. And that's what happened here."

As her damning words reverberated around the chamber, Caroline relaxed slightly. At least the stories from the key witnesses now existed somewhere other than in Federica's mind and Caroline's memory. The television cameras had documented the tales, providing longevity to their damning words and, hopefully, safety to the speakers.

The only motion in the courtroom came at the long table where Simon sat. Vizzi had stopped typing on his computer and was huddled with Thibodeaux and Simon.

Thibodeaux nodded to Vizzi, then stood up.

"These are lies," said Thibodeaux. "These are nothing but paranoid imaginings. Concerned Citizen Number Three has a troubled history. As Mr. Vizzi can attest, this woman was a heroin addict who lived on the streets. She is of dubious credibility to say the least."

Next to Caroline, Federica looked down at her hand and fluttered her eyelids nervously.

"No, this woman was used and abused by Mr. Vizzi, Mr. Reed, and the rest of the con men that make up Oasis," Caroline shot back, leaning into the podium's microphone. "She is another victim of their crimes."

Instead of refuting Caroline's assertions, Thibodeaux smiled a mirthless grin. His dark eyes filled with a cold strain of cruelty.

"As I understand it," he began, "Concerned Citizen Number One has had some troubles, as well. While in high school, she was the subject of an investigation for hacking. Although no charges were brought against her, I believe her father spent some time under the auspices of the government, shall we say. These stories of malfeasance by my client and his business associates are nothing but that—stories."

Caroline's heart squeezed up into her throat. Those records were sealed. That she'd been investigated, that her father had cut a deal to avoid prison—neither piece of information should have been available to anyone.

She wished she could push back against the allegation of fanciful storytelling by putting on the Spreadsheet of Death and the BanCorp data showing the frequency of the affidavit-withdrawal transactions, and the proximity in time between nursing home residents' wills and their deaths. But she couldn't. Not without exposing her father to losing his job, at best, and his freedom, at worst.

Thibodeaux was right: she was stuck relying on anecdotal evidence by two people of dubious credibility to prove her case.

"I would ask the council to disregard Mr. Thibodeaux's attempt to undermine my credibility and the credibility of a caregiver who was trained in the Oasis system and worked for Oasis for years," Caroline said, keeping her voice even. When no one interrupted her, she took a breath. It was time to make the council see the beast that she finally saw in its entirety.

"This scam exists. You've seen the proof of it. Simon Reed has tried to make his crimes invisible. But you can see it all, can't you? Duncan Reed created Oasis to serve the needy, but Simon has used it to serve himself. He's done so at the expense not only of the city, but at the expense of the lives of our most vulnerable citizens."

"But Oasis is Duncan Reed," the president protested. This time, his voice held distress instead of annoyance.

"No," Caroline said. "Oasis is Simon Reed. Simon has preyed on his father's reputation just as he's preyed on the elderly and destitute. Duncan Reed earned his reputation for humility and generosity. Simon has sullied that reputation with greed. Ever since Duncan Reed's stroke,

Simon has been running Oasis. He's hidden behind a veneer of good-ness. But everything that Simon has done has been designed to obscure what's really going on: fraud, theft, and murder."

Caroline scanned the faces in front of her.

The council members looked at one another in open disregard of the rules of decorum. Some leaned toward one another, quite obviously talking about what to do.

Simon scowled at the mutiny taking place before him.

He looked toward Thibodeaux with a pleading expression.

But Thibodeaux stayed mute.

Almost imperceptibly at first, Simon began to pack up his things. Cell phone and wallet both left the long wooden table, slipping unob-trusively into his pocket.

"Everyone has assumed that Simon Reed must be a good guy because his father is a good guy. But Simon has bilked the govern-ment. He's bilked the elderly. He's treated our most vulnerable citizens as expendable resources. He's has been a cancer in this city." Caroline paused and lowered her voice. "No more. This ends right now."

Simon rose from his seat and began moving around the table, aim-ing for the closest exit.

Caroline's heart leaped to full throttle. If he escaped, he'd run. He had the resources to disappear. That some of his money was offshore seemed inevitable.

But then, Simon stopped.

The color drained from his face.

Albert stood in the doorway with three US marshals.

Catching Caroline's eyes, Albert gave a satisfied nod.

Caroline released a long breath and nodded back.

TWO MONTHS LATER

Caroline sat on the steps of the courthouse. The heat wave had broken a week ago. Instead of the winds whipping the heat up to a fever pitch, a cool marine layer sat within the great bowl of Los Angeles like a soothing balm.

In her hands, Caroline held her phone. The security officer had returned the newly purchased device to her after she'd finished testifying and left the courtroom. She'd already picked up the message from her mother, congratulating her on the news that had traveled as far as Portland. The paletería owner had recovered. The police had offered an apology to Caroline for the damage to her reputation. And now she'd been a star witness in a prosecution to bring down a massive criminal enterprise.

The question remained, however, what to do with the e-mail from her father.

Dust has settled, yes? Give a call when you can.

Caroline knew what her dad wanted: a chance at reconciliation. Not between him and her, but between Lily and her. The staunchly stubborn part of Caroline refused to budge. Lily had denied her help when she'd been underground, quite literally. Lily had treated her like a criminal, leaving her to scrape and fight for her survival.

But the more charitable part of Caroline understood.

She'd given Lily and her father so little information. She hadn't told them why she'd left her job at Hale Stern. She hadn't told them about the devastating betrayals that had decimated her plans to enter the legal profession at the highest level. Nor had she told them the reasons why her departure from that firm was not a failure.

Maybe it was time to begin to trust them with her stories.

> **Dust has settled. Will call you and Lily tonight.**

She hit "Send" and then pocketed the phone before she could change her mind.

Her hand brushed the worry beads she'd carried with her since the feds had grabbed clothes for her from her apartment. She didn't need the beads right now. If anything, she felt relaxed. Far more so than she'd been in the last year, in fact.

Footsteps on the stairs caused Caroline to turn.

Albert. He smiled as he approached.

Caroline recognized that smile. It was a smile of victory.

The jury was still in deliberations, but it didn't matter. A guilty verdict was a given. When Caroline had left the witness stand, she'd known that Albert would finish skewering Simon. With help from Simon's sister, Mary Reed, prosecutors had obtained a list of the original residents of Oasis. Law enforcement had tracked each one down, checking to determine whether any had suffered identity theft. Many had. Cross-checking those names with the names of the CNAs at nursing homes across the Southwest had taken time, but they'd gotten the job done—and then matched those names with the untimely deaths of scads of nursing home residents. The scheme was dark and horrifying, and despite law enforcement's efforts, the deplorable details had leaked to the press.

"You're going to start getting calls to become the US attorney, you know," Caroline said, glancing toward the gaggle of reporters waiting to talk to the young prosecutor.

Albert sat down beside Caroline and shrugged. "I'm focusing on one thing at a time. After these convictions, perhaps I'll see about asking for a new chair in my office."

Caroline smiled. She wouldn't have expected anything more bombastic than that.

"Once this is all over, you'll get the watch back," Albert said.

"I know," Caroline said. Her grandmother's will leaving everything to Oasis was a nullity. The entity hadn't been a charity at all; it had been a scam. Though she might take a few months to go through the formalities of tearing up the will, Caroline knew it would happen.

And then the watch would be hers. At last. The old piece of machinery and leather was far more than Exhibit A in a criminal prosecution. It was her grandmother's legacy of kindness. Her own legacy of tenacity. She still needed to find her place in a world without some of her familiar moorings, but she was finally on her way toward doing that.

"Did you see Amy in there?" Albert asked.

Caroline nodded. She'd caught her assistant's eye when she'd left the witness stand. They'd have much to discuss. Far more than the meager contact Caroline had been allowed during the months she'd agreed to stay in protective custody while waiting to testify. She hoped Amy was recovering. She hoped she'd find love again. Though there were no augurs for the future, Caroline decided that the sparkle she'd seen returning to Amy's face after Caroline had finished giving her damning testimony of Simon was a start.

"What are you going to do when this is all over?" Albert asked.

Caroline remained silent. It was a good question. She knew that, like Albert, she'd be courted once the jury delivered its inevitable guilty verdict. Her role in the Oasis prosecution would be publicized by a media always looking for an interesting story. She'd get calls for interviews. She'd almost certainly get job offers, too.

But almost as quickly as the prospect of shuttering her practice to take a job at a big firm occurred to her, she dismissed it. Working with individual clients on cases that mattered to their lives was meaningful. If the news coverage brought more work to her small firm, that was great. But she had no desire to cash in for a big firm job.

"I'm going to keep doing what I'm doing," Caroline said.

She owed a debt to the lawyers on her floor who'd helped to manage her cases during the last two months. She looked forward to repaying those favors and ramping up her practice to such a degree that she'd be giving them her overflow work, not the other way around.

Albert nodded as if she'd given the answer he'd been expecting.

"How's that kid you were working with?" he asked.

"Mateo Hidalgo? He's doing really well. He's still living with his foster parents—the Castillos. They sent me a message just the other day to let me know he's learning how to ice-skate." Caroline smiled. The picture of the little boy was still on her phone. That he'd be okay made her feel like maybe the rest of her life could be okay, too.

Albert glanced toward the reporters waiting on the courthouse steps.

"Guess I'd better get over there," Albert said.

"Don't let me keep you." Caroline knew the unflappable prosecutor would handle the press with cool competence.

But instead of leaving, Albert held her eyes.

"Would you want to get some coffee with me sometime when this is over?"

"You're just asking because I don't smell like a skunk anymore," Caroline said.

"No, I'm asking because I want to know you."

Caroline started to refuse but stopped herself. She'd been an island for a very long time. She'd distrusted everyone, even those who deserved a chance to earn her trust. If she couldn't trust Albert after all they'd been through together, she was hopeless.

"Sure." She smiled.

"My treat this time," Albert said.

"No way," Caroline said.

Albert smiled and held his hands up in surrender. Then the smile faded from his face.

"You did a good thing, you know."

Now it was Caroline's turn to shrug. "I did what I had to do."

"See, we aren't so different, you and I," Albert said with a backward smirk before walking down the steps to talk to the waiting press.

Rising from the steps, Caroline scanned the park in front of the courthouse.

Below a grove of trees, she found what she sought: Uncle Hitch sat on a bench.

When he'd testified the day before to authenticate the watch and describe its history, he'd worn the same suit he had worn to Grandma Kate's funeral. But today he was wearing his usual work boots and oversize flannel.

Caroline made her way to the bench and sat down beside her uncle.

She noted the newspaper neatly folded on top of a messenger bag on Hitch's other side. The headlines were familiar.

Murderous Angel-of-Death Cult
Police and Other Officials Under Investigation for
Corruption
Simon Reed to Face Life Sentence

Caroline didn't have to read the articles. She'd lived them.

"Sorry Jake isn't here," Hitch apologized.

"It's okay," Caroline said, even though she'd hoped to see him. During her time in protective custody, she'd had little contact with the world. Although the media attention from the city council hearing had given her some protection, Albert had thought it safer for her to avoid any possible danger from Simon's minions. Caroline had agreed.

"Jake really wanted to come today," Hitch said. "But he had an appointment at the VA with his new counselor."

Caroline raised an eyebrow.

"He's got a room at a transitional housing facility. It's a small apartment, but it's safe and quiet," Hitch said. "He wants to become a counselor himself. You know, to help people who come back from deployment."

"That's perfect," Caroline said, enjoying the sensation of the sun-warmed bench against her back. "How's everyone else doing?"

"Pretty well," Hitch said. "Lani and Federica are rooming together in the same facility. They got a restraining order against Daryl."

"I'm sure having Jake up the hall is a disincentive to Daryl coming around, too," Caroline noted with a chuckle. She'd relied on his physical presence for her own piece of mind. She knew he'd protect Lani and Federica, too. He was a devoted friend.

"Speaking of Jake, he made something for you." Hitch fished around in his bag until he found what he sought: a newsprint-wrapped gift.

"What is it?" asked Caroline.

"Dunno." Hitch shrugged. "He'd already wrapped it when he gave it to me."

Dipping her fingernails beneath the clear tape, Caroline gently lifted the newsprint off the carved figure of a dove. In elegant swoops and slices, Jake had rendered the bird in repose, its head dipped down in sorrow. Or sleep. At the base of the statuette, an inscription read: "The scars are the places where the light comes in."

Unexpected tears welled in Caroline's eyes.

She'd been cracked open, for sure. First by the betrayals at her big-firm job. And then later by the fallout. The street had been an inconceivable refuge, and one that she'd dreaded in the darkest recesses of her soul. She'd sunk as low as she'd ever feared. And she'd survived. Even more than that, she'd won.

Her chest swelled with an optimism she hadn't felt in years, if ever.

Pulling her emotions to herself, she inhaled her composure and turned back to her uncle.

"What's next for you?" she asked.

"I'm living at that shelter over near Ohio Street. They've got a group over there."

"You could come stay with me," Caroline said.

After a long pause, Hitch exhaled.

"That wouldn't be good for either of us, kiddo," he said.

Where once Caroline might've argued, now she sat silent, listening to the birds chirping in the sycamore trees arching overhead. Somewhere in the wilds of Los Angeles, her uncle had found at least a portion of what he'd lost. She hoped he'd find the rest someday.

As if answering her unspoken question, Hitch cleared his throat and said, "I've been dry for two weeks as of today. Longest I've been dry in years," he added.

Caroline knew it was true. She could tell from the smell of his skin that he hadn't had anything to drink. The lucidity in his brown eyes, too, bespoke sobriety. But he was just at the beginning. And he'd fallen so many times before . . .

"Take this," she said, lifting the Saint Christopher medallion from around her neck and putting it in her uncle's hand.

Hitch looked down at the medallion, then back up at Caroline.

His eyes held a question.

"It was Grandma's," Caroline said. "It's to protect you as you go."

Caroline watched her uncle's eyes tear up as he slipped the silver chain around his neck.

"I've got to get going," he said, rising and turning before she could say anything about his evident emotion. "I guess I'll see you at the soup kitchen at the Ohio Street shelter?"

"You definitely will." Caroline smiled. "Whether you want to see me or not."

Hitch paused, uncertainty etched in his weathered features.

Without hesitation, Caroline closed the gap and hugged him tight.

Then she watched her uncle walk away until she couldn't see him anymore.

ACKNOWLEDGMENTS

First and always, thank you to my family for being the center of my life. Nicole, Eli, Alex, and Ava (and Huxley) are my daily love. I am grateful every day for them.

A special thank-you to my uncle, Hal Heisler. Aside from being my favorite curmudgeon with a heart of gold, Hal is a gifted writer and a brilliant editor. This book is better for all the times he said, "I'm sorry, darlin'. It just doesn't work."

I also need to give special thanks to my dad. Yes, he gets the dedication, too, but he also deserves a separate shout-out for being a wonderful storyteller who enjoys walking and brainstorming. I love doing both with him.

Here are my other thank-yous, in no particular order:

Thank you to Karen Blackfield for Floyd, and thank you to *Los Angeles Times* columnist Steve Lopez for telling the story that inspired Floyd.

Thank you to Ricki Tobisman, Charlene Tobisman-Davis, Barry Tobisman-Davis, and Sue Gordon for reading and copyediting the manuscript again and again. And again.

Thank you to Robin Simons for generously serving as a sounding board on numerous drafts. Her storytelling instincts are a true gift.

Thank you to hacking consultants Zane Lackey, Jake Tullis, and Joel Bremson for patiently teaching me everything Caroline needed to know.

Thank you to the dynamic and incomparable Stephanie Delman, whose dedication and hard work make her not only an excellent agent, but also a joy to share this journey with.

Thank you to editors Jessica Tribble and Charlotte Herscher for their blunt input and great ideas. And thank you to copyeditor Sara Brady for her keen eyes. The whole Thomas & Mercer team is a model of professionalism and grace.

Thank you to freelance editor Sarah Cypher for always making me think.

Thank you to Stefanianna Moore, dear friend and amazing graphic designer. Your input helped make the cover(s) awesome.

Thank you to my excellent and insightful test readers. In addition to the people listed above, they are: Susan Levison, Stephanie Levine, Allison Delman, Michael Delman, Seymour Applebaum, Christine Sherry, Courtney Wolff (and the book club), and Jennifer Michael.

And, finally, thank you to my parents for raising me in a house full of books, ideas, and great conversation. I loved that, and I love you.

ABOUT THE AUTHOR

C.E. Tobisman lives in Los Angeles with her wife, three children, and adorable dog, Huxley. She's an appellate attorney and proud dork. For more about the author and her work, visit www.cetobisman.com or follow her on Twitter @cetobisman_.